# PRAISE FOR THE BLOOD & ANCIENT SCROLLS SERIES

"Blood Ex Libris is a fast-paced, blood-soaked novel of passion, adventure, and vampire politics, as intimate as it is intense."

— Thomas Roche, Stoker Award Finalist

"Pick it up for the sexy, dangerous fun, devour it for the fast-moving storyline, and reflect on it for a long time to come for the genuine scholarship and creativity."

— Lars D. H. Hedbor, author of Tales From A Revolution series

"These books are simply the most fun. Raven Belasco brings much to the table: a lively writing style, a fascinating take on the undead, a great deal of discreetly hidden scholarship, and a sheer joy in creativity which can sweep the reader along pell-mell. Come to these books for the hot sexytimes; stay for the sheer quality; linger for the quiet intelligence that underlies it all."

— Chaz Brenchley, Author of The Books of Outremer, and the Crater School series

## BY RAVEN BELASCO

### THE BLOOD & ANCIENT SCROLLS SERIES

*Blood Ex Libris*

*Blood Demands*

*Blood Eternal*

*Blood Triad: Stories in the Blood & Ancient Scrolls series*

### ALSO

*Adventures in Bodily Autonomy (Editor)*

# BLOOD DEMANDS

## BOOK II
### IN THE
### BLOOD & ANCIENT SCROLLS SERIES

## RAVEN BELASCO

Copyright © 2024 by Immoral Influence Publications. All Rights Reserved.
*Originally published as Blood Sine Qua Non in paperback and ebook in the United States by LMBPN in 2020 & by Immoral Influence Publications in 2023*

Library of Congress Cataloguing-in-Publication Data

Belasco, Raven.

Blood Ex Libris / Raven Belasco

ISBN: 978-1-960942-10-4   |   eISBN: 978-1-960942-11-1

1.   Vampires—Historical Vampires—Vampire folklore—Fiction.   •   2. South American History—Fiction   •   3. Julius Popper—Fiction   •   4. Orélie-Antoine de Tounens—Fiction   •   5. Librarians—Fiction   •   6. Journeys—Journeys of personal growth—Fiction

www.ravenbelas.co & https://www.immoralinfluence.com/

To Cairngorm McWomble the Terrible: my little man, my Dire Terrier, my soul. He deserves co-writer status, really, because when I don't know what to write next he takes me on walkies, and the rest of the time he lies on his cushion by my desk and does all the work by napping vigorously.

**Sine Qua Non** (sine-ay kwaa nohn): "Without which, nothing"; something absolutely indispensable or essential.


Only she who attempts the absurd can achieve the impossible. — Robin Morgan

# CONTENTS

# Author's Note on Language

This book has a bunch of words and phrases that are not in English. Some are in the am'r language, and some are in the languages from around the world, since the am'r get around and often speak the language of the country they grew up in, or the country they are in now.

The am'r words are given definition when they are first used, but if you forget any of them, there is a glossary of the am'r language in the back of the book.

Likewise, there is an index of all the non-English words and phrases you will encounter along the way. If the meaning of those words is vital to the understanding of the story, I've made sure they get explained in the text. However, sometimes our protagonist Noosh doesn't understand what she is hearing. So you have a choice: you can experience the moment as she is experiencing it, or you can go to the index and look up the words if you don't like not knowing.

Whatever you choose, I hope you enjoy the book!

Raven

# PROLOGUE

When I close my eyes now, I can remember how things ended. How things then began.

We were under the desert. Now I am under some mountains. I am always underground these days.

Everyone had left: the bad guys *and* the good guys. Although from the outside, quite what the difference was might seem unclear. It was just me and my patar and his patar.

That is, me and my husband and his father. Or me and my father and his husband. Things that are clear in the world of living humans, or "kee," are not so clear in the am'r world. ("Am'r." You would call them "vampires"...but not to their faces, unless you relish super-strong, exceptionally hard-to-kill creatures feeling cranky about you.) Or, well, things that are clear in the am'r world would not make any sense among the kee.

Not that I could ever go back.

If I ran away, back to the kee world, the irony is that I would seem strong, very strong. Able to bench-press amounts that would shock people. Able to hack through someone's neck without flinching. I would be so self-fucking-reliant. I've survived shit that would make any normal living person melt down permanently.

But I don't fit in that world anymore. What would I do with my strength? Go back to work at the Helen Abigail Winstringham-Fenstermacher Memorial Library? Even a dream job, say, like being Microsoft's Digital Archivist, wouldn't do much for me anymore. Living in a world of grocery shopping, renting an apartment, binge-watching shows on the sofa in the evening—all the mundanities of the kee existence is not something I could go back to. Especially since *daylight* is a bit of an issue now.

But being am'r-nafsh (a "living vampire," who has not yet died the mortal death) is no fucking good. It might seem attractive if you don't know all the details. Who wouldn't want to be irresistible to vampires? To be the most mouth-watering thing they could fantasize about? Having a world of the sexiest creatures all wishing you were theirs? But it turns out that then you can't tell if people want your company for *you* or simply for how delicious you smell—and potentially *taste*, if you'll just hold still long enough. Worse than that, you're neither this nor that, stuck in the middle with the worst of both worlds.

I don't have the strength of a full am'r, nor do I have the experience of having lived in the am'r world for, you know, centuries and stuff. These problems could be ironically re-solved by *dying*—and then living a good long time.

Is everything in am'r world inverted from what I had known in the world I came from? So far, the answer is, "Well, yeah, pretty much."

By dying my mortal death, I could achieve full am'r strength *and* I'd be less sexy to other am'r. Which, trust me, I've learned the hard way would be a Good Thing. Then, by living on as am'r, I could slowly—and undoubt-edly painfully—accrue the knowledge and skills required to be able to effectively rush to the rescue of others instead of sitting around like a princess in a tower, waiting to be rescued.

Which is fucking *exactly* what I'm doing now. The bad guys (the new bad guys, the ones running around in *these* caves, not to be confused with the bad guys we'd gotten rid of back in *those* caves) have captured me. My patar is missing. The patar of my patar (or "gharpatar," in the am'r language) is with me, but trapped in a drugged sleep. And when he wakes up, he is terrifyingly violent—not the kind and gentle lover I've grown to love as much as my patar.

Sometimes I wish we had stayed forever in that little room under the desert.

# CHAPTER ONE

It was a reunion for Sandu and me, and we sorely needed it. Pun intended: we were sore, and boy, we *needed it*. But we had things we needed to do first. We needed to make his patar, Bagamil, undead. Or undeader. Something. As Sandu explained it to me, we needed to wake him up from a particularly death-like (even for a vampire) coma.

"The am'r...*ei bine*, we do not need to breathe the way kee do," he told me in his new I'll-share-all-the-info-you-ever-need-or-even-just-think-you-might-possibly-want mode. This was my reward for not leaving him or defecting to the bad guys—or killing him myself!—after all the shit that had gone down. He continued, "But we do need some oxygen. Before you ask, *draga mea*, I do not understand why, but if we are deprived of all air, we fall into something like a coma. We call it the 'ahstha.' The same will happen if we are completely drained. Or if we are terribly injured and cannot get 'vhoon-vaa,' the blood healing. We do not die. We do not change or heal on our own. We just...maintain."

"And that's why Bagamil is like...*that?*" I pointed to Bagamil's disturbingly dead-looking body.

"Yes. And that's why he," Sandu pointed to another corpselike thing, "is like that."

Oh, right. So, there was this other undead-person-in-a-coma with us. He was a bad guy, but since he currently wasn't much of a threat, he wasn't my highest priority. Sandu paid no attention to him, and I was so exhausted that if Sandu didn't think it was a problem, I certainly wasn't going to worry my pretty little head about it.

"Well, there's air in here now," I tentatively noted. "It came in when we did, and we left the door open. So why don't they wake up?"

"Neither will wake without receiving vhoon," Sandu explained as he grabbed the inert bad guy and pulled him away from Bagamil. It had been quite the tableaux: Bagamil in his sunny golden robes and this villain in his finest tactical gear, both a little singed around the edges but neither burnt to real damage. Both had collapsed on the floor, but Mr. Baddie looked to have been dropped from Bagamil's arms as if he had fallen from a very interesting embrace.

As Mr. Baddie was dragged past me, Sandu stopped to further lecture on the stiff. "Look at how emaciated he is, *dragă* Noosh. He did not get that way from lack of air alone, but also vhoon-lack."

"So, Bagamil, um...?"

"Yes. My patar obviously drained him before the bad air incapacitated him. It was very wise of him, which is unsurprising, of course. He has been am'r for a very long time indeed. I surmise they were fighting, or this one followed Bagamil with the intention to kill him."

"That was one of their goals!" I was hit all too sharply by deeply unpleasant memories. All too recent ones, as well. How strange that I'd been in such a terrible place just a few hours ago. I had not known if Sandu or Bagamil were alive, and I hadn't known if I was going to be horribly tortured and kept as a trophy by one enemy, or horribly tortured and then killed by another. But there had been some serious reversals of the Bad Guys' evil plans, and now here I was in this cave with all the people with whom I'd desperately wanted to be reunited (except Neplach, and—oh, no, I didn't dare think of Neplach, or I'd totally lose control) while everyone else who'd survived was rushing in every possible direction away from us.

It was very quiet now, but it still smelled of explosives and burnt stuff and of stale air.

Sandu's words pulled me from my ruminations. "Yes, of course it was their goal. They would need Bagamil out of their way if Mehmet were to unite first the am'r, and then conquer the kee, and then attempt to rule both worlds. I do not think he and his followers would have encountered the success of which they dreamt. There are vastly more kee than am'r, and they have no lack of weapons that work quite satisfactorily on us."

I shuddered. Yes. I'd seen that first-hand.

"But," he continued, "if they had been very clever and had made into am'r all the world leaders—or killed and replaced them—perhaps they might have had their way."

"'Jinnestan,' Mehmet called it," I told him. "And Bagamil was only his second goal. After killing you."

"*Ei bine*, that was a long time coming. As long as we both walked this earth, one of us was going to have to end the other. That was the only cure for the ages-old infection of our hatred."

I'd wondered about that. Wondered why things had been left for so long, and noted that while Sandu spoke the right sort of words for being the changed man he claimed to be, he did not sound particularly regretful that he had finally gotten a chance to take out his worst enemy in an inferno of death and destruction.

Before I could work up a question, Sandu continued, now speaking of the desiccated am'r at our feet. "If he followed my patar, he would have been very foolish to think himself unnoticed. But this one was very new, barely changed to am'r. Likely he believed all of Mehmet's lies about being 'jinn.'" Here he snorted, more with disbelief than derision. "Young and full of vanity, that he believed he could kill the oldest of us all. *Asteaptă!*"

I didn't have a chance to ask about that "oldest of us all" thing because Sandu stopped and knelt by the withered figure. He sniffed, then leaned in to sniff again.

It was not because the acrid air made it hard to smell stuff, at least not for a full am'r like Sandu. I'd already noticed, without noticing that I'd noticed, that am'r remains did not smell like much. It was like the blood was the only real thing about them, and while there was a solid form, it was basically a shell. It could be reduced to ash with discomforting ease.

*And that's what I'm in the process of becoming. What am I now? If you burned me, would I smell like a pig roast? Or would I just flame up like an oil-soaked piece of wood?*

These are the charming questions you get to ask yourself when you're am'r-nafsh—half-living human, half-vampire—or something like that. Some of the best of both worlds, and some of the worst. Oh, the headaches! And don't talk to me about *buckets!*

Sandu straightened up, obviously having sniffed out what he needed. "This is he." And now Sandu's voice had a dangerous edge. "This is the one who abducted me. Mehmet made him, and then he made many more. The word in our language is 'esteshcinast,' to know by smell. I would know that 'vhoon-anghyaa,' that 'blood-influence' anywhere. And now I get to finish him. 'Tokhmarenc' is the am'r term. It means 'final death.'"

I shuddered. Not because I disliked "finishing" bad guys, and not because I hadn't just gotten some thorough hands-on experience in doing so, but because at that moment, he sounded like Vlad. That is, he sounded like who he was—Vlad Țepeș, Dracula himself.

Or who he'd said he *used* to be. He'd said he had changed, and he was going to prove it to me. But stomping around "finishing" one's enemies seemed pretty Vlad-ish to me.

What else could we do, though? I'd learned pretty quickly in the am'r world, you had to be ready and willing to do unto others before they did unto you.

I hadn't had any time to deal with any of the stuff that had happened to me, nor could I imagine how many decades of therapy that might take. I had no ethical compass anymore. I couldn't even judge Vlad/Sandu, because I had nothing against which to judge him. I was feeling pretty much like a shell, filled with strange new blood and stranger new feelings.

"*Sufleţel*, will you stay by Bagamil? He cannot...sense anything. He will not know you are here. But he is defenseless. *It* would mean a great deal to me if you sat by him for now."

So I went and sat by Bagamil. I even took his hand. It was room temperature, which felt pretty chilly to the still-partially-living human me. I watched Sandu easily haul away the body of one of our enemies.

I smelled new burning in a little while. Tokhmarenc. I rested my forehead on Bagamil's shoulder and didn't think about anything.

When Sandu came back, he sat down beside me and finished his explanation from earlier. This was a new phenomenon in our relationship, and one I deeply appreciated. "So he—"

"Mr. Baddie?"

"Yes, 'Mr. Baddie.' He followed Bagamil to this part of the sanctuary, and then there was another explosion. I believe my patar sensed it in time and pulled his enemy into this room, closing the door. And then, knowing that whatever happened next, he would need the sustenance, he drained your Mr. Baddie before the air was used up or made unbreathable by the fire and smoke."

"Well, that would explain why they were lying like that."

"*Da*, it would. And it explains why they were both in the ahstha for slightly different reasons. But we can find out if we are right simply by waking him and asking."

"Just with...vhoon-vaa? But how will you get him to drink?"

"That, you shall see, *draga mea*, will not be a problem. But I must...I now must tell you some things."

*Hmmmm, not sure I like the sound of that.* But if nothing else, I'd learned I needed every possible scrap and morsel of information I could get about my new world. "Yes. Yes, you must."

"Coming back will be very intense for him. *Ei bine...*" Sandu paused. He seemed more frustrated than he had during any of the really hard things we'd just lived through. "It is difficult to ask things of you when I do not know how you shall respond!"

I laughed. Sandu wasn't sure how to take that, but he was used to me laughing at inappropriate times by now. "My patar. You have changed me. Blood—vhoon—has changed me. Just ask me, and I'll be honest about how I feel. I won't get offended like I would have when you first met me. I—I see things differently, after all that has happened."

"*Draga mea*, your blood would also help Bagamil heal. If you would be an 'izchha' for him...*ei bine*, as you know, vhoon-am'r-nafsh has special properties. I will give him my own, but if you would do vhoon-vaa, it would truly succor him.

"And," at this point, he rushed nervously ahead with his words, "if Bagamil also vhoon-shares with you—becomes your 'bakheb-vhoonho' that is, 'blood-giver'—it would more than benefit you. I want you to be as strong as possible while you are still am'r-nafsh. And after. I thought my enemies would not dare to touch you. I was *wrong*." I could hear it hurt him to admit that. "And I must make provision for the future. I do not want to hide you away. Nor do I think you would let me," he added quickly. By this point, I'd been so thoroughly exhausted for so excruciatingly long that hiding away sounded pretty good, but I knew my feelings would eventually change, so I bit my tongue.

"So," Sandu continued, "if I am not to hide you as most am'r hide their am'r-nafsh, I must make you stronger, safer. I know he would be more than pleased to give you that gift." A pause. "We have spoken of it."

It was time for my own pause as I attempted to sort through what I thought Sandu was saying, what he was possibly half-saying, and how I felt about those things. It also brought up memories I'd been trying very hard to suppress.

"Sandu, I started to tell you before, that I...that I shared blood with Neplach." Damn, this was just as hard to communicate as what Sandu had just faltered through. "You said you *knew*. How did you ... could you smell it?" I looked at my feet, which tapped nervously on the stone floor beside Bagamil's motionless legs.

"Yes, I could smell it. I can smell it now, *dragă* Anushka. But there is no problem, *vă rog! Nu*, had I been there, I would have encouraged you to do just as you did. It is the same with Neplach as with Bagamil. They are 'aojyshtaish'—the elder ones; they are vhoon-strong. You could not ask for a better bakheb-vhoonho. The ties you form with them serve as further protection. Neplach will protect you now as if you were his own frithaputhra."

"He would have. But...but..." I finally lost it the way I had needed to lose it for so long. Too long, and yet all too short a time since I'd lost my uncle-in-blood—my *strýc*, as he had taught me to call him.

Sandu watched me crying for a moment. "I see," he said, voice utterly flat. "I had wondered, when he was not with you and Dragoș. He went to retrieve you before the attack could start, so that you would be with us, protected. You were not meant to battle alone through our enemies to my side. He is ancient, and he has survived more adversity than you can imagine. *Had* survived. I desired to believe it was merely that he had left you safe with Dragoș and gone to deal with other matters." His voice petered out. I looked up at him through my sobs and saw that he looked awful, almost as wizened as if he had been drained of blood. He just sat there and I realized that even Vlad the Impaler could be shocked, could feel a deep loss. I threw my arms out to him, needing to comfort him as much as I needed his comfort.

He crawled into my arms, but he did not cry. He held me tightly, so tightly that I started worrying about my ribs being cracked. I wasn't going to say anything to make him pull away, however, and he could fix any broken ribs with his blood. I assumed. Anyway, I sobbed enough for both of us.

Bloody tears. As I saw the red-tinged drops splash on the floor I was reminded that I now cried blood-tinged tears. And then, of course, I smelled the vhoon—my blood, which supposedly was like some combination of the world's best booze *and* most delicious food to all the am'r who smelled me. To me, it didn't smell like anything special.

However, it was a red flag for the bull that was Sandu. A nice, sexy red flag. I could see that the bull between his legs was suddenly ready to charge.

They say that dealing with death can cause urges to prove that you are still alive: hunger, horniness. A very human thing, a psychologist might say. Since hunger and horniness are basically one and the same for am'r, this was even *more* a vampire thing.

"We will mourn your bakheb-vhoonho properly when Bagamil wakes, *sufleţel.* May we...wake him now?" He said it gently, carefully. *No pressure.*

The way he said it, and the raging erection, made me realize what was on the table was not just blood-healing, but a whole lot more.

"Sandu, you said vhoon-vaa, but...um...do you really mean *that*, or do you mean, uh, 'vhoon-vayon'?"

Did he mean "just healing"...or did he really mean, "Let's do some kinky am'r shit right now!" Because that's how am'r do stuff, right? Feeding involves sex. Healing involves feeding, and sex involves blood. Everything always, always comes down to blood.

Well, I did choose this life—in a hot tub half the world away, and in what felt like another lifetime. It had been my choice, even if I didn't know enough at the time to make an informed decision. Also, I had not been, to be painfully honest, capable in that moment of a *compos mentis* decision, being hopped up on sex-brain-chemicals and vampire blood. But it had been *my choice*, regardless, and I wouldn't—I just wouldn't—try to back out of that, or be half-assed in accepting this choice, this life.

And, if offered a chance to do it all over, I'm not sure I wouldn't make exactly the same choice. So there went any excuse to be squeamish. Ever.

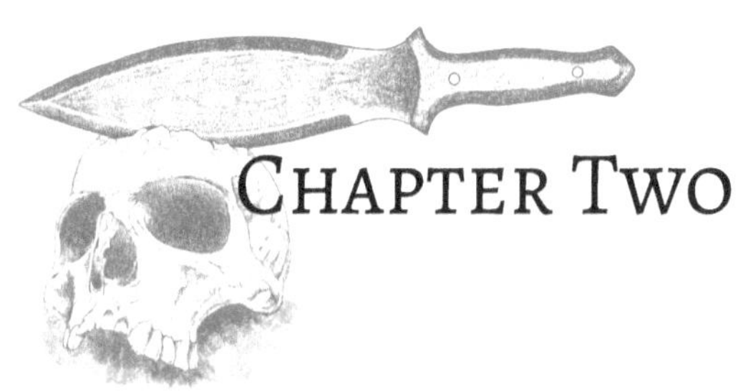

# Chapter Two

Sandu started the waking-up process. He called it 'vhoon-berefteh,' but then explained that was just what the am'r called donating blood. He pressed beside me, alongside Bagamil's body, and ripped open his wrist with his teeth.

And that did not turn me on. Totally did not.

He pressed it to Bagamil's mouth, pushing the lips open with his torn and blood-bubbling wrist. For a moment, nothing happened, and blood poured from the sides of Bagamil's mouth. Then, like someone dramatically coming back to life in a movie, with that huge spasm and indrawn breath, Bagamil full-body-shuddered and began gulping.

He drank like he would never stop. Sandu eventually pulled his wrist away, and Bagamil's arms shot up and grasped for more. Only Sandu's comparable strength allowed him to wrench his wrist out of reach, where the wound could properly close up. Bagamil's eyes opened. He was not looking the healthiest I'd ever seen him, but he was awake and with us.

He looked at Sandu. He looked at me. He looked like a predator.

"The frithaputhra-of-your-frithaputhra would be your izchha, that you may heal. Aojasc' am'ratv!" Sandu told him. Both of them looked at me, waiting. I knew the last phrase, so I did what I could. "I would be your izchha so that you may heal. Aojasc' am'ratv!" I hoped I did not look embarrassingly nervous like a kee, but as cool as an am'r and totally comfortable with such things.

"I see." Bagamil took a longer moment than usual to process the information, and I thought he was trying to access his thinking brain through a more primal one. "Vhoon-vaa or vhoon-vayon, frithaputhra-of-my-fritha-puthra?"

I blushed and the flash of heated embarrassment spread down from my face, seeming to go through my whole body. I could not meet his eyes as I replied, "Vhoon, um, vayon."

He did not just grab me and go to town, thankfully. He smiled at me (lips and teeth still bloody, which made things perhaps a bit less gentlemanly and comforting than he was going for), and then he gently kissed my wrist. This smeared Sandu's blood over it, so the chivalrous kiss became a rather more lascivious lick as he cleaned up after himself, but it went no further. Instead, he sat up, a bit creaky, not back at full am'r grace yet, and he pulled me into his arms and held me, smiling down at me (teeth less bloody this time), his eyes full of love.

Well, love and lust. And bloodlust. But that was the am'r for you.

He asked with his eyes if I was ready. I was not at all sure about *that*, but I was sure that putting things off wouldn't help, so I let my head fall to the side, exposing my neck.

His lips were very gentle, and his Freddie Mercury mustache tickled my skin. His teeth seemed to glide almost painlessly through the skin and the muscle into the vein. I'd thought Sandu was skilled in the arts of vampiric love, but from the way Bagamil bit me, I realized I was in the hands of a master. Well, he was an aojysht—an elder—right? He'd had some time to get his vampiric Casanova skills on.

This was going to be *interesting*.

Bagamil's hands were not...well, very grandfatherly as he drank. That was what he was in am'r terms: my gharpatar, the patar of my patar, my ancestor in blood. They moved gently along my body, exploring, getting to know me. Obviously, this would be more than just a quick platonic vhoon-vaa nip, but still, in the moment, it was super weird getting intimate with Bagamil while Sandu sat close and watched.

*I've never even had a normal threesome before*, I thought plaintively. I mean, I'd once been very intimately *sniffed* in a thermal spring by two female am'r, which was not what you'd call normal, either, but that wasn't the same as what was about to happen.

To be honest, I didn't really know what was about to happen. Or, well, *how* it was going to happen.

But I thought it was going to be one for the record—my record, at any rate. If I had no idea what I was doing, at least the two people I was with were very experienced, so I could be the unsophisticated tyro and it wouldn't bother them or get in the way.

Then I realized I was moaning softly with pleasure. *Maybe I'm a natural*, I thought. Maybe I should just stop thinking and…

Sandu undressed me as Bagamil drank. And by "undressed," I mean he tore the remains of the black sack-dress off me. I was very glad to see it go because I'd been dressed in it by our enemies and had seen some very bad times in it. Also, it didn't smell very nice anymore, what with the sweat and blood and smoke and death. The black trousers that went under it were mostly decorative rags, although part of the decoration was my dried blood, from a sword that just a while ago had gotten stuck, very conveniently, between my legs. They came off quite easily. The pretty lingerie underneath—*Don't think of Obizuth or Bghilt or any of the female jinn right now!*—was gone even faster. None of the disrobing got in the way of Bagamil's mouth or hands.

When Sandu was done, he cuddled up behind me, which meant I got jabbed in the lower back by an impressive erection. I realized he had taken the time to get naked too.

So that's how we're doing this.

I was now perfectly ready to follow along.

Bagamil's long jet-black hair came loose from its braid and spilled down his golden-olive skin, and his eyes were not just shining with love, but glowing with intensity, passion, and fervor. He beamed at me; teeth covered with my blood. And now it was a turn-on.

"Now I become your bakheb-vhoonho." He let his head tilt to the side; my teeth were not sharp enough to pierce the skin, but I felt inspired to lean in and kiss his neck. He sighed happily, and his hands explored me even more urgently. His skin was...a little odd. It felt a bit like vellum, or a butter-soft leather jacket. It was not unpleasant to touch, but you could tell that it was strong and durable and that it had been resiliently protecting him for a long, long time.

I decided I liked it. And the scent of him...well, it was not new; technically. I'd been near him before, of course. But now that my sense of smell was vastly improved, I caught so many more nuances. I could now get a hint that he was Sandu's patar and there was some other commonality that tickled in the back of my throat.

My kisses got fiercer. I wanted to bite him. I wanted to pierce his well-preserved flesh with my teeth and see if his blood was like his scent. I started nipping his neck with my kee-blunt teeth, and he made delighted sounds. His fingers moved around from where they had been kneading my ass and up to my breasts, where they began circling, squeezing, lightly pinching. It was so good it distracted me from my biting.

He got my nipples in his fingers and pinched them hard enough that I gasped and threw my head back involuntarily. Sandu caught me and whispered, "Wait, *draga mea.*" Bagamil used the opportunity to stand and rip off the remains of his singed yellow kaftan. He was stark naked underneath, and his body was long and lean, the muscles wiry and bunched under that tough skin. In some life ages ago, he'd had a darkly tanned gold-olive complexion. The years—who knew how many—of living sun-free had faded it a bit, but that deep gold-olive tone was still there, and it fitted very well on his sinewy body. There was no softness on him, no extraneous padding, as though the years had whittled him into the shape he was—just bone and muscle and skin and the gorgeous hair, and the life force that drove it all.

He was also, well, very complimentarily erect. *That* was sinewy, too, all bulging veins and very defined head flushed a dark red, foreskin stretched tight and smooth.

He sat down again in front of me, and there was a slender glint in his hand. He raised something that looked like nothing so much as a thin shard of smoky black glass to his neck and smiled warmly at me, and then with a flick so fast my eyes could not follow it, there was a cut on his neck, right where I just had been so ineffectually nibbling. There was a pause when the skin didn't even seem to know it had been cut. I stared, fascinated, as a thin line of red finally came up, then my new instincts took over and my lips fastened to the opening, and I felt the first trickle of his blood into my mouth. "Aojasc' am'ratv!" I heard Bagamil say and Sandu echo.

It was like nothing I'd ever tasted before. It was so intense that I more *experienced* it than tasted it. Blood is not something one thinks of as effervescent, but this was. Well, it *wasn't*, of course, but that was the only way to explain it. There was the salt taste, but it tasted bigger and deeper, like drinking the ocean. There was the metallic tang, but that was sharper and stronger, reaching up higher. Somehow, it was like drinking fire.

All this intellectual contemplation did not get in the way of me gulping as the flow of blood, seemingly trying to make up for its late start, started pumping out of Bagamil's neck, pouring hot down my throat.

I felt Sandu arranging his hands on either side of my ass. He bodily lifted me up, moved my hips forward, angled them by twisting his wrists, and then lowered me onto Bagamil's cock, which was angled up quite perfectly to meet me.

Should it be a matter of pride that I did not miss a sip nor spill a drop of blood? Or should it be embarrassing that I'd habituated to this all too easily? Whatever; it was a point to ponder *later*. Now, I had the feeling of that carved adamantine cock sliding slowly into me as Sandu lowered me easily, as if I weighed nothing. I was not fully wet and ready for what was suddenly happening. Nor was I in control of the speed of penetration—that was a combo of gravity and Sandu's patience. I could handle the ache. It only made the pleasure more intense.

The oceanic wave of his blood, the roaring flame of it pouring into me, was a penetration of its own. I drank convulsively, as out of my control as the penetration below. Almost a blessing—before I found out if it might become too much for me—I felt the wound closing. I had a fevered moment of wondering if I dare work it open again with my teeth to keep that incredible blood flowing into me, but I discovered a modicum of common sense and just let my tongue play over the wound as it closed magically together as if that strong skin had never been parted.

With no more technical reason to have my mouth on Bagamil's neck, I let my own neck straighten, and it was at that moment I reached the base of his cock. The surge of sensation went up my straightened spine and seemed to blow the top of my head open to the universe.

I might have been moving in the traditional hip-based dance of sex, but if so, I was unaware of it. I knew only that I was a creature made of sensation. The nerve endings in my body had more to do with constellations of stars in the sky than with a fleshly form that was doing things oh-so-fleshly. Bagamil's blood had entered my bloodstream, mingled with what made me, and begun changing it.

Change could be *good*. Or maybe I just had no idea of what was good and what was bad at that moment because my brain had just exploded. I was raw, like I'd been skinned alive, except that what was skinned off me was Everything I'd Known And Understood Before. I was now a newborn thing, feeling that I and everything around me existed for the first time.

When that is what you are feeling, what are orgasms? Just sensations among the other sensations, and all of it is overpowering, and you cannot tell the good from the bad from the *everything*.

Eventually, I realized that two of the sensations were Sandu's body pressing against my back and Bagamil's arms moving to embrace not just me, but both of us. Then, with the surprise not of a grown woman trying something for the first time, but of a brand-new creature finding *all* new things surprising, I felt Sandu's cock pushing in from behind into an orifice I no longer remembered was for anything other than what it was doing right now.

It just felt right. Maybe it felt intense, but everything felt intense just then. When you are flayed open to the universe, when your every molecule is becoming something other, one intensity is really not discernible from all others.

My eyes had opened at some point in time, and, sometime later, I remembered how to see with them. I was looking into Bagamil's eyes, and they were like his blood: ocean and fire, deep and bright. They would have drowned me or burned me up, except I now had his blood inside me as well. As water cannot drown water, fire cannot burn fire. I was safe in these extremities; I was home.

There was no passage of time in the fire, in the water. We stayed in that particular dance for some while. Then we danced in other ways, found different conjugations and constellations. I was aware at some point that I was on all fours, with Sandu behind me and Bagamil in front. I realized sometime later that Bagamil was no longer in front of me, and when I reached for him with my wide-open mind, I found him behind Sandu, all three of us connected through a current of force and momentum.

I do not think we missed a physical variation, but we came back to the beginning again and again, one in front, one in back, taking turns kissing, and with teeth or the slick little shard of glass (which always seemed to be in someone's hand when they wanted it), pouring our blood into each other. Orgasms came and went and were irrelevant because they never really stopped, only transformed and reformed as the shapes we made transformed and re-formed. As the blood that was *us* moved from one body to another.

I came to lying between them. They were still out in that sleep that is not as scary as the vampiric coma, but which does not look dramatically different from death, at least to someone who is still part kee.

I spent some time sorting out what was individually me, separate from them. It took a while.

The next step was to remember that one of them was Sandu and one was Bagamil. It was harder than it might sound, and I couldn't believe I'd ever thought that Sandu (being Bagamil's frithaputhra) was not just a part of Bagamil. With all vestiges of shock and societally constructed boundaries burned from me, I realized for the first time that *of course* they'd been lovers when Sandu was am'r-nafsh, and who knows how often over the centuries after they were both equally am'r.

I think the girl I'd once been might have been troubled by some jealousy. I'd *like* to think I wouldn't have been bothered by their relationship. I mean, I was bisexual, but I'd never dated a guy who was bisexual. I remembered meeting Eben and Cyrus in the Rave Cave, back in that previous lifetime, and wondering about gayness in am'r.

It was a thought one could only think fresh from the kee world. Queerness couldn't be something *other* among am'r. Once it came down to sharing blood, who had what sort of genitals—and which bits were going where—mattered only in the issue of how it was going to supplement and complement the rapture of drinking blood.

As always, the am'r world was delightfully less complicated than the mortal human one, whether it was digestion, drugs, or sexuality. Maybe another view might be that since one was drinking someone else's blood, it was actually way-fucking-complicated. But it all just struck me as wonderful simplifications. Maybe I'd always been meant to be am'r. I'd have to ask Bagamil what the am'r thought about the concept of fate. Although—and this put the first grin on my face since my brain had exploded—I could guess that the am'r point of view was that fate was something an am'r caused to happen to other people.

I must have shifted microscopically. I was neither uncomfortable on the sandy floor, nor uncomfortably cuddled on one side by the sinewy limbs of Bagamil and the other by the barely more padded form of Sandu. Another am'r improvement: limbs that don't fall asleep, and the ability to find any surface as well-suited for a nap as the softest, comfiest mattress. Maybe simply the movement of the grin on my face woke my beloveds.

Yes. They were my beloveds now. Sandu had been existing in one way or another since, well, 1430-something.

(It was embarrassing that I didn't know off the top of my head what year he was born; I'd have to quietly look that up when I got to somewhere with internet.) And Bagamil was older than I could comprehend, I now realized. Compared to them, I'd only lived for a minute, but now I could call them both *my beloveds*.

Sandu lifted his head and smiled lazily at me. I smiled just as lazily back at him. I felt Bagamil move behind me and turned my head, the smile still on my face. He was already smiling that warm, sunny smile of his that had led me to trust and like him from our first meeting. When he saw my smile, however, a bit of the fire from his blood came into his eyes as well.

I still looked up to him as a grandfather and felt safer with him than I ever had with anyone. However, now there was that intense edge of lust as well—not safe at all, the way the sea will drown you and fire will burn you to nothing but ash. But there they both were, those disparate forms of love, in no conflict, perfectly intertwined in me, reaching to him, connecting with him.

And looking back at Sandu, I loved him just as much as I ever had.

No, I loved him *even more*. I loved him more because he had been one with me just now, when we three were one. I loved him more because he had brought me this whole way from my half-alive kee life and the Helen Abigail Winstringham-Fenstermacher Memorial Library through the changes (for which he'd only barely prepared me) to his home and his am'r life. And he had brought me to Bagamil, and shared with me the love that had bound them for all those centuries. It didn't matter that he'd been a crappy patar at the beginning. He had fallen in love with me—at first sight, he said—and gone after me with passion. He'd fought for me with that same passion. And now, with more of that same, unwavering passion, had given me a gift I was only barely beginning to understand.

While he was admirably consistent on the passion front, he'd also admitted his faults and shown me he was willing to change, to work at being a better patar: both father-in-blood, and life—for the am'r definition of "life"—partner.

I had never been so happy and so loved. There I was, in an empty blown-up cave system under some particularly benighted patch of desert somewhere in the world, and I had never been so happy.

Why can't you just stay in those moments forever?

# Chapter Three

We eventually stopped smiling at each other like idiots and went about our business. And there was business to be gone about. First, there was the cleaning of our filthy selves. I don't mean filthy because of all the sex we'd had. I mean: they'd been covered with dirt and post-blast explosive residues and the blood of their enemies. And I'd been the same, as well as sweaty (that's blood-tinged am'r-nafsh sweat) and tear-stained (also blood-tinged) as well. We smelled terrible (especially me, as I was distressingly aware) and am'r have an all-too-keen sense of smell.

There was a spring, of course. Am'r are as clean as cats, which they resemble in a number of other, less flattering, ways as well, and they tend to choose places to live with excellent bathing facilities. This spring wasn't hot, but it had been widened into a gracious pool, with sconces for the same cool greenish lights as I had seen in Sandu's underground "Castle Dracula" cut into the rock in just the right places. Best of all, it was in a part of the caves that'd had the least damage from the explosions. You could barely smell the acrid stink of burnt chemicals.

It was clean, clean water to start. I have never been so thirsty nor drunk so much. They watched me throw myself down and start lapping it up and they laughed. The water was not too minerally, just right. It tasted so good, so perfectly thirst-quenching.

Of course, there was an inevitable threesome in the spring. After the intensity of the first time, this one was just for fun. A nip-n-sip of blood here and there, but just for the joy of it, not for healing or feeding or any reason other than that we could and it made us happy. We retried all the variations, of course, but we decided we still liked our first position best.

At some point, I was between them, watching them kiss over my shoulder. Sandu's wavy black hair was slicked back and heavy with water. Bagamil's even longer hair was the same. I was surrounded by their arms and their love.

It was worked out that Sandu preferred to drink from the left side of my neck. He insisted the blood tasted better on that side. Bagamil was perfectly happy to sip from the right side. He said he wasn't so finicky and that my blood tasted best from everywhere.

Cleansed and refreshed, we left the spring naked and drip-dried. We just stayed naked for the rest of the time we were there. It's like some Eden in my memory; an ideal time when we were innocent and free and we had the joy of not having eaten any of the fruits of the future.

We had a ceremony to mourn Neplach. To remember he was all-the-way-dead still hurt, but the pain had been transmuted during the time since his horrific death. Bagamil lit a special fire. It was Full Ceremony Time, and Sandu knew all the responses, and I watched with respect as the space was set for us to honor my bakheb-vhoonho.

I told the story of his death. I took it back earlier and started with him sharing his blood with me. Sandu and Bagamil did not have to touch me to be holding me as I spoke; I could feel them supporting me by giving me their full attention.

I spoke about how careful he was with me, behind the cave—a cave that, if I wanted to think about it, was not that far from where we were now. I told them about how, just as Neplach and I were about to escape across the desert,

Mehmet's minions had surprised us. I told them how I was so pathetically incapacitated.

They did not explain to me that I could never have overpowered them all and save him. They did not have to. I knew it, but *still*. I was allowed to be angry at everyone, including myself, for the loss of my *strýc*.

I described of how he'd fought so bravely—like ten am'r, like one hundred am'r, like a dragon, like a force of nature—but still more enemies came on, and eventually they wore him down. In between sobs, I choked out how Mehmet had staked him down and let his enemies feast to the very last drops of his blood before decapitating and burning him. My lips numb with still-living anger, I told them how his head had adorned a spike on Mehmet's vehicle as he drove to attack Bagamil and Sandu.

"It still—it might still be out there!" I realized in horror.

"*Nu, draga mea, taci,*" Sandu soothed me. "I am certain one of ours will have seen it and given it respectful, ah, rites."

"Like we are doing now?"

"*Ei bine, nu.* This is the, ah, memorial service. That would have been more...functional."

"Like?"

"Like respectfully removing it from the pole and then respectfully burning it."

"Burning him just like Mehmet did?" My voice was shrill with distress.

"*Nu*. Very differently indeed: done with the full respect due an aojysht, done to keep his honorable remains out of the hands of any more enemies."

"'Cinyaa'," Bagamil said gently. He said it meant "my beloved" in the language of his people. I had not yet been able to pry from him who those original people, prior to the am'r, had been. "Am'r do not have such burial customs as the kee ones to which you are used. Deaths are both less common and more violent, as is required by our natures. Aojyshtaish often do not have many true loved ones left to mourn them, and their endings occur so infrequently that it is no wonder we do not have many customs attached to those terminations. Most commonly, it is the brand-new am'r who make fatal mistakes in that impetuous time when they first join our world. In those cases, usually there is only the patar to mourn them, as of course they would not have been widely known when they were am'r-nafsh."

It was the middle of a memorial service for Neplach, or I might have glowered at Sandu at that point. When he went against all am'r custom and introduced me, still am'r-nafsh, into am'r society, it'd caused my life to get very interesting very fast, and it had directly led to me being abducted. *That* had directly led to us having this memorial service for Neplach.

But this wasn't the time to get into all that. Bagamil gently directed us away from any potential analysis of that topic, back to memorializing Neplach. I'd gone first, being both the one to have known him for the least amount of time and the one who had been there when he died. Well, died the final time. Sandu went next: "I first heard of Jan…"

His first name was Jan. I had fallen in a strange sort of love with him, but I hadn't known his actual first name while he was alive—or at least undead. He was old before he became a Benedictine abbot (*What?*) and chronicler for Holy Roman Emperor Charles IV. (*Really?*)

Apparently, Neplach had passed for a time as kee in the century before Sandu was born. After Sandu became am'r, he'd spent some time in Italy, pretending to be a Hungarian named Sándor. ("The first time I took the name, *draga mea*, at least a variation of it.") That was when he'd met Neplach, then living under the name Januarius. They'd become friends in a very rare way for the am'r, who are often suspicious of other am'r to whom they're not related by blood. Or even of those who *are* related by blood.

These revelations were followed by a shockingly rowdy story involving Sándor, Januarius, and a secret society that was trying to bring back the Eleusinian mystery cult. The censored and thus very short version: all the cult members woke up the next day to discover that the events of the night before were *very mysterious* in their memories. I wasn't sure if Sandu was practicing the fine art of the tall tale, for which he'd previously shown neither talent nor interest. It was not giving *enough* details that had always been his problem.

"But of course," Sandu said, turning to Bagamil, "this was not news to you, for you were there."

"Ah, but I did not take part in that little, hmmm, adventure. Still, it does admirably illustrate that our Ioannes—which was the name he held when I first met him, cinyaa—remained very devout in his beliefs, but they never kept him from enjoying the am'r life with fresh delight and vigorousness for every night of it."

"His...beliefs?" I asked. I'd been building a very intense curiosity about what the am'r believed. I mean, I had seen what they *could* believe, what with my regrettable experiences with the (jean)ocidal genie, but what did normal (for some value of "normal") am'r society believe?

"Your uncle held to his Christian faith all his days," Bagamil explained.

"But...um...how could being am'r and being Christian work together?"

Sandu started to answer, and I belatedly remembered that he too had previously hinted at an enduring Christian faith. Bagamil got in ahead of him. "You might be surprised, cinyaa. Christianity is a very blood-soaked religion. Ioannes and I had many long and intensely enjoyable discussions about spirituality over the years. He was a man of glorious depths and subtleties. I will miss his company for as long as I exist."

"I—" I choked on the sudden pain rising in me. "I am sorry you lost your old friend in the rescuing of me. It doesn't seem like you got...like it was a very fair trade." I tried to hold back tears as I said this and to keep my voice even. It didn't work.

"That is the wrong way to look at things, my beloved granddaughter. It was your uncle's choice, and he chose it with love. He volunteered to go and help you escape from Mehmet. My frithaputhra," he smiled tenderly at Sandu, "was all set to go, but I needed him to help control our allies. Vlad is a better commander than Januarius, and getting am'r to work together is not...easy."

"Like herding cats, from what I've seen."

"'Herding cats.' Very apt, indeed. Thank you, cinyaa. I will use that phrase."

"*Hei!*" Sandu looked mildly offended. "I have told you that one before. It is a useful American saying."

"A grandchild is always more cherished, my son." Bagamil chuckled. "Get used to it."

# Chapter Four

Bagamil told us more Ioannes/Jan/Januarius/Neplach stories, what he knew from the aojysht's long and varied life. He was almost always with the church in one way or another until modern times when he had told Bagamil that he no longer recognized the religion. I asked how Bagamil had met him, and he got a bit vague and mentioned Macedonia and the 900s. It seems they did something very big and important for many years together, and it didn't end well. I needed to get some quality time with history resources after I got back to someplace with a library and the internet.

We then had another threesome. Because we were still alive, I guess. It felt right at the time.

Afterward, I lay in their arms and thought about the blood running through all of us. We had swapped it so many times that by now it must be entirely commingled. I nudged the sleepy am'r to my right and inquired.

"Being in our various bodies transmogrifies the vhoon, cinyaa. Vhoon as it comes from you is made special by your singular qualities, and while it moves through your patar or me, it is transformed again so that it comes back to your mouth made anew. Sleep now, granddaughter."

"But I'm not tired. And…I'm not hungry, not for *food*. And I don't, um, have to do other kee stuff. Is my blood enough for Sandu and you? Don't you both need to have more blood than I can provide? And does Sandu's am'r blood provide enough nutrition to you? Won't I need to eat at some point?"

"You see?" Sandu muzzily declared to Bagamil. "The questions never stop with this one. They are unceasing. She never sleeps, just wants more answers, more *everything*."

A chuckle from my gharpatar. "I shall look forward to being worn out by an am'r-nafsh." His tone of voice implied "a mere am'r-nafsh," but I decided not to take offense. "And I shall enjoy watching you spend many lifetimes answering all her questions." I was pretty sure that meant Bagamil was aware of how much Sandu had fucked up with me, and what he had promised me, while Bagamil was technically in—what was it?—the ahstha. Of course, by this point in time, it felt like there was no distance between us. There would always be more to learn, at least for me, but we had neither the possibility nor the desire to have anything but complete and total openness.

Sandu pointed out, "It is not my job alone to answer her questions, gharpatar of Noosh!" There may have been some snark in his tone.

Bagamil chuckled again and turned to me. "Yes, cinyaa, we will need more sustenance. Am'r do require 'frangkhi-laat,' that is, 'feeding from a kee.' Eventually. For this brief time, we are sustaining each other, and it is sufficient. It cannot last forever, but for now it is enough."

I snuggled happily into their arms. "And wonderful."

"Yes, it is wonderful."

"The 'vistarascha' is not unlike the 'ahstha,' but it is not quite the same," Bagamil explained. Sandu let him do most of the talking, at least about am'r stuff, I'd noticed. He kind of hero-worshiped Bagamil. So, of course, did I, not only because Sandu did, but because Bagamil had this air of knowing everything and being able to fix anything. Mix with the kindness that oozed from him, add an unnamable quality that made it easy to tell him all your problems—even the stuff you'd never even admitted to yourself—and you'd find yourself listening to him, giving deference to him, hoping you could somehow make him proud of you. After the confusion and chaos of the last few months, this kind of father figure was just what I'd needed most to bring some stability to my world.

"The ahstha is a period of rest. Of unchanging rest, to be precise. The vistarascha is the opposite, a period of change during rest, change from kee to am'r. As am'r-nafsh, you are *not* am'r. It is more the promise of what is to come. You are still kee in many ways. It is impossible to explain what it is to be am'r to one who has not made the vistarascha.

"Once you arrive at your vistarascha, you will rest until the changes are complete. While you transform from your kee life to your am'r life, you sleep, and you sleep deep. The kee word is 'death.' But when you are waking to a new life, how can it be death? If it is death, then you have died many deaths in your life, as you change and grow and become more. In the vistarascha, you *become more*."

"Like a caterpillar magically changing to a butterfly in its chrysalis, huh?" I had to say it.

Sandu jumped in. "She is often this sarcastic, patar. No respect for her elders."

Bagamil chuckled and kissed him, a lingering kiss. "And you are *never* sarcastic, my frithaputhra. She makes a perfect match for you." Then he kissed me, equally drawn-out.

After a while, I pulled away to ask, "How long does the vistarascha last?"

"As long as it needs to. Some am'r have risen in three days. Some have needed the rest of three months. Your patar needed a month; his injuries were terrible. But he had the strength of my vhoon-anghyaa in him, and he has always been an exceptional man."

Sandu looked particularly smug and that reminded me of a nagging question I'd never had the chance to ask. I turned to him. "Hey, history reports that your head was cut off! I read that when they killed Vlad Țepeș, they cut off his head and brought it to Mehmet in a jar of...um...honey, wasn't it? I thought of that when I was waiting around in Mehmet's dungeon."

Sandu chuckled. "Bonfinius believed that was the case, strongly enough to write it down. I wanted to tell him he was very wrong, but of course I could not go back to the court of Cousin Matei at that time. I could not let the world know I had survived in this other form."

"It must have been a real shock when *Dracula* was published, then," I said. "If you thought you'd gotten away with becoming an anonymous am'r, and then suddenly there's a book published that turns into plays and movies and announces to the whole world that *you* became a vampire."

"I did not know about the book or the play at first," Sandu said, his former smug amusement now grim displeasure. "By the time I discovered them, Stoker was dead, so I could not kill him myself."

I think Bagamil and I both frowned at him because his tone changed. "Not that *that* would have changed anything. It was too late. 'Count Dracula' had taken on his own life. A very divergent one from mine, obviously. *Ei bine,* except that we both drink blood, which is irony indeed."

"You're *sure* you were not in England around that time?" I asked, eyes narrowed. "No...*connections* there? What *is* very ironic is how Bram Stoker would use an obscure historical figure like you and get so close to a truth that no kee is supposed to know about. Almost *unbelievable*, really."

"Vlad was not decapitated," Bagamil interrupted. Sandu was looking off into some other, suddenly very fascinating, part of the room. "He was stabbed, what in kee terms would be a 'mortal wound' and that of course led to his becoming am'r at that time.

"I was there with him. He was fighting a huge Turkish incursion and I was assisting him. We had so few men, and there were many, many Turks."

"We were caught between București and Giurgiu," Sandu murmured in a flat voice. "We were dealing with attacks from the front and the rear. I was with the van, and I asked Bagamil to take charge of the rearguard. My men trusted him. He was 'Ignác' at this time, a Bohemian mercenary who had proven himself fighting with us. And then..."

Bagamil gently took over the account. "Vlad was attacked by angry boyars who had passed as loyal Wallachians to get close to him. We needed fighting men so desperately that we had not been overly cautious in the selection process. I, obviously, was not there to protect him. Thankfully, he was am'r-nafsh already. We had planned to keep him in that state while he finished a long and prosperous voivodeship. Not too long, but to give him a chance, with my help, to see his beloved country strengthened and protected from Turkish invasions—"

"*Și de la nenorocitul de clan al Dăneștilor*—"

"Yes, and from the motherfucking Dănești clan, *dragul meu*," Bagamil interrupted, affectionately. "We planned to work together to get Țara Românească into a more stable, lasting shape, and then find a tough, reliable ruler to take over. Then my frithaputhra could have come away with me, and we would have traveled the world, sharing experiences and exploration until the time came for him to take the vistarascha.

"But the treacherous boyars attacked him. It was clear from the extent of his wounds that they had been instructed to kill him very thoroughly, so as to prevent his rising. They were fought off before they could finish their job; of course, it would not have been explained to them just *why* they needed to be so thorough. At any rate, Vlad's vistarascha was still possible, for which I was grateful with all my heart. I let him be buried at the *Mănăstirea Comana*, and I waited. I became a postulant at the monastery and spent many hours kneeling near my sleeping frithaputhra. I had planned to await him as long as it took—his wounds were grievous, and I knew his heart had been broken by the perfidy—but it took him only a month to rise.

"I was doing the office of *Miezonoptica* when he rose. Of course, being a postulant still, I was supervised, by Fratele Petru. He was a kind monk; I liked him. This was unfortunate, since Petru obviously could not be allowed to recognize him. When we heard the scratching and scrabbling under the stone where Vlad was buried, I had no choice but to incapacitate Brother Petru. Well, I must admit I let him help me lift the stones first. They were not beyond my strength, of course, but they were unwieldy, and I was in a hurry. He was very surprised at my strength, but not as surprised as he was that Vlad was rising from the dead after a month.

"As we worked, I wondered aloud to him that perhaps Vlad had only been unconscious, pronounced dead too early. It was very unlikely, for anyone who had seen the wounds would not have believed any life could be left in his body, nor that anyone could be alive after being trapped in the grave for so long. But in those days, many were buried too soon, and indeed, those unfortunates have given more fodder to vampire stories than we am'r ever have. Fratele Petru could not deny that his beloved leader was not-so-dead after all, and I called on his faith to soothe him as we worked the stones out of the way.

"He was rewarded by seeing the hero of Wallachia arise, unscathed and whole, but before he could rush off to wake the whole monastery with the miraculous news, I gently rendered him unconscious."

"And I had my first meal as an am'r," Sandu added. "I shall never forget the hunger I felt upon waking from the vistarascha."

"The 'fraheshteshnesh' is not only a true need, but a ritual, if one that is not given much ceremony," Bagamil explained. "The thirst is so strong that there is little desire in the newly awoken am'r for such things as chants or meditations."

Sandu snorted. Bagamil, who seemed to be one of the main custodians of am'r wisdom and knowledge, did not look bothered.

"Returning to your patar's rising, cinyaa, after he had taken Fratele Petru's unwitting gift, we buried his body. That being the final gift from the monk, since it was not a bad idea to leave a body to be found, if ever anyone was to need certainty that Vlad Drăculea was resting securely in his grave. I had by this time, even in the unworldly community of *Mănăstirea Comana*, heard tales that Vlad's honeyed head had been delivered to Mehmet."

"And he told me!" interrupted Sandu, laughing. " So it delighted me to leave a headless corpse in 'my grave. We never did find out *whose* head was delivered in a jar of honey to Mehmet. I rather imagine that whoever delivered it was impaled—or worse—shortly thereafter, since Mehmet knew my face all too well. And of course, in the years to follow, Mehmet heard that I was am'r, and I found out that, most regrettably, he had become one of us as well."

Bagamil took back the thread of the story, having centuries of practice at being interrupted by his frithaputhra. "I was in the tunic and scapular of the order, and Vlad was in his cerements. After we had buried Brother Petru with as much honor and respect as possible, we went to where I had left a cache of clothing and weapons in the forest."

Sandu took over again. "Then we removed from Wallachia with great celerity. My face was too recognizable to my people, even after he made me shave."

"You are better to kiss without that *mustață*," Bagamil told him and demonstrated that he still felt that way. I never got tired of watching them kiss. And happily, after all those centuries, they had not become tired of kissing each other. I wondered if Sandu and I would still be kissing with such passion centuries in the future.

Bagamil pulled me to them and I stopped thinking for a while.

It seems that time spent in Eden—all times in any Eden—cannot last forever. There must be an ending to such an idyllic time and space that one so desperately wishes would never end. It will be longed for, ached for, the rest of one's life in the cold, hard, not-Eden world.

A cave under the desert may not seem like anyone's idea of paradise, but that was a cave shaped by centuries—I do not know how many—of dwelling, comfort carved into living rock. Bookshelves carved into the walls, and astounding rugs on floors and walls, and cushions for beings who do not feel discomfort but like indolence. And paintings upon the walls. Paintings like I have never seen, paintings that had grown as slowly and naturally as any stalactite over spans of years I could not comprehend. It was art that spoke to me like nothing I'd ever seen in a museum. It was like a beautiful punch to your soul, tapping through the human brain, through the mammal brain, down to the lizard brain—and all your brains knew they loved it, were drawn to it, and felt the power and the truth of it.

Miles of tunnels into the main cave system had been blown to smithereens by Mehmet's pyromaniacal minions, but happily many of the main living areas had avoided the worst damage, and were just a bit shaken up and only smelling slightly of smoke. There were still plenty of chambers for me to explore, books in which to lose myself, paintings to contemplate.

Back in my Eden, sometimes I would wake and find myself alone. And that was fine; a bit of alone time is always good. Always, when my beloveds came looking for me, I could be found in front of one of those paintings, sitting quite still but feeling as if I were spiraling into the art, or perhaps the art was whirling out into me. Once, when I had been there for who knew how long, suddenly I was back in my body, and Bagamil was there, sitting quietly beside me.

"How old is this piece?" I asked him, unsurprised by his until-that-moment-unperceived presence. "Who is the artist? It's incredible. I'd say I cannot understand it, yet I feel I already *know* it, that I grasp it from deep inside me. Or maybe it grasps me. Why does it speak to me like this?"

"The art is older than you can imagine, cinyaa, as is the artist. People have learned many things about how to make art over time, but they have never really learned more than they knew about art from the minute that creative inspiration came into the heads of what we call 'mankind.' There is no need to learn what is already part of you."

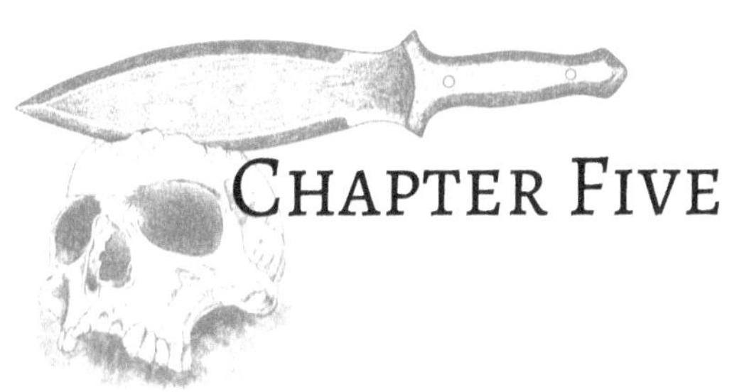

# CHAPTER FIVE

We eventually had to leave that Eden, of course. "A place too perfect to be allowed to stay" is obviously part of the definition of Eden, right?

Before that happened, my gharpatar made me a gift of that thin shard of smoky black glass we'd all been using for me to get blood when neither am'r felt like opening skin with their teeth. It was an amazing little blade, only about three inches long, but so sharp that you had to be very aware of what you were doing when she was in your hand. She would split dermis like a scalpel, almost painlessly. Right at the base, she was wrapped with sinew, or something, to provide a good grip.

"Her name is Sa'mah. It means 'dark,' as she is. I have had her for a very, very long time. She will become part of you, just like you and I have become part of each other."

Dragoș returned after long enough that I'd almost forgotten Sandu had ordered him to come back. He'd brought Apolinar, an am'r I had met what felt like a lifetime ago somewhere under Romania, in a cave full of new friends and certain danger, and with him came Monserrate and Julio.

Apolinar was as Latin as one could be. He had long black hair in a ponytail and thin black mustaches. His skin was a perfect cool tan. He was so perfectly a hidalgo that he seemed at all times to have just ridden up on a magnificent horse out of a historical romance. Monserrate was not unlike Apolinar but managed to look like he was from this time, with short black hair, and his more typically am'r shaved face showing off a richer amber tone, although his eyes were divertingly green. Julio was softer in coloring, with olive-toned skin and brown hair cropped short on his head, and growing in a neatly trimmed beard and mustache. He had almond-shaped brown eyes. He took up less space than Monserrate and Apolinar, who tended to swagger.

They brought jeeps with them, filled with food and other things we'd lived contentedly without this whole time. Amusing luxuries like clothing and shoes. And fake passports and other vital but entirely counterfeit documents. It was time for us to leave Paradise.

Bagamil was now traveling under the name "Ignacio Reyes." With his black hair pulled back, in black cargo pants and a black field shirt, he fit right in with them, no longer wearing the sunshine-gold robes that had always signified him as essentially apart. I mourned the loss.

Dragoș had brought Sandu his own clothing, perfectly fitted black trousers and shirt in a thin fabric suitable for the desert.

Clothing had been bought for me, a long modest black dress in a light, comfortable weave. It had a matching scarf, in case of emergency dealings with kee at border crossings. We were staying low-profile and respecting all local customs while we got the hell out of Dodge.

The clothing was secondary. My first attention was given to food. Food! When Dragoș came in carrying it, I honestly forgot to greet him in my rush upon the comestibles.

There were dried meats, dried fruit, energy bars, a nut mix, protein shakes, yogurt, and chocolate bars. I did not recognize the brand names of anything, nor could I read some of the languages they were labeled in (apparently, they had been gathered in a variety of countries along the way), but at the sight of them, I sat down and started eating, feeling a hunger such as I'd never felt in my life. I was entirely ready to inhale *all* of it, but after I'd eaten without pause for some time, Bagamil (already insisting we call him "Ignacio" for practice) put a gentle hand on my shoulder and suggested I take a break. I was suddenly profoundly embarrassed at my single-minded appetite, and Dragoș did not help by choosing this time to demand his belated greeting and get—start getting—his digs in. The Three Latin Musketeers studiously pretended that nothing indecorous had happened, while offering me flowery greetings. Well,

Monserrate and Apolinar did. Julio simply nodded at me, brown eyes inscrutable.

They all managed not to huff my scent noticeably. Dragoș must have given them a heads-up. However, Sandu's nostrils twitched around Julio.

"What was your kee name?" he asked him, somewhere between polite and demanding.

"Oh, nothing you would have known, señor."

"Who was your patar?"

"I am not of proud lineage such as yours. I doubt you would have met my patar, who, alas, had her tokhmarenc long ago. Unless you spent a great deal of time in South America in the 1890s?"

"No, no. I was elsewhere at that time." Sandu seemed distracted.

Dragoș had been listening to this conversation and eyeing Julio curiously, but when this came up, a grin spread hugely across his face. "Were you not in England at that time? 1893 or so?"

"You remember incorrectly, Dragomir. I was not in England in that decade." Sandu looked annoyed with Dragoș, who was exuding pure mischief. I racked my brain. What the hell was going on in England during that time period?

Oh, yeah. *Dracula* was published then. I gave Sandu serious side-eye as he made himself very busy with packing our swords into special bags made to carry them. Dragoș laughed himself silly. Julio had faded away to discuss travel matters with Monserrate, Apolinar, and Baga—Ignacio.

*Someday, I'm going to get Sandu to tell me what his connection to Bram Stoker and that damn novel really is.*

I didn't know I was leaving Eden. Or, well, I didn't know I'd never get it back. I was eager to return to the world of, well, *the world*, and to the dream archivist job I'd been promised. I didn't realize that Bagamil—no, Ignacio!—wasn't coming back with us. But when we got to Ashgabat International Airport—I will not list the miles and miles of desert, and then roads that were far worse than nice smooth desert sand, nor the times we had to stop just for me to do very kee, very humiliating things behind the funny desert trees—I discovered I was not ready to rejoin the world, after all.

The first shock was being around kee again, with all the odors of the kee world: the clashing scents of myriad sweating kee bodies in various states of cleanliness, food (both good and very bad), and various cleaning and personal grooming products. After the solitude of our underground desert paradise, being around the bustle of humanity was staggering.

I was paying too much attention to traveling for the first time in my life under a false name—Ana Alexandrescu Popa, a citizen of Romania going home, despite not being able to speak her own language—with forged passport and visas, when I suddenly realized Ignacio (and Monserrate and Apolinar and Julio) had melted away, and it was just Sandu and Dragoș and me.

"Where is he?" I hissed at Sandu as we waited in an interminable (and not discernibly essential, or even functional) queue.

"He is *dead*," he replied sotto voce even for an am'r. I had to strain to hear him above the ambient kee noise. "Thus, he cannot be seen by anyone. He is traveling privately from this point on, and until the time seems right, we will maintain that he has met his tokhmarenc."

"You are going to have to explain this all to me very soon," I muttered.

"I shall do so, *draga mea*."

"And I don't know why *we* are not traveling privately," I complained, wrinkling my nose.

"There are many reasons, but one is that it is easier to maintain anonymity if we use normal methods of travel." He smiled at me from behind his sunglasses. We had all gratefully hidden our eyes as soon as we were forced to interact with daylight. Even indoors, under the fluorescent lighting, I was deeply appreciative of my shades. Why did the kee insist on so much light? Being even just an am'r-nafsh in the kee world was like being hungover from the worst bender a person could hope to survive. I hoped that, when it finally happened, the added strength of being full am'r would make it easier to bear light (and scent, and noise, and the ghastly bustle of kee life) but while Sandu and Dragoș managed capably enough in the kee world, they honestly did not look their best. Dragoș was greenish-gray and uncharacteristically snappish, and Sandu had these two frown lines between his eyes, which if he were not am'r would have made some really deep inroads into his face by now. Being an unaging vampire and all, they only showed up when he scowled or was in pain.

I was selfishly a little bit glad that he was also suffering. On the same very mature level, I really loved calling him a vampire in my head, and occasionally (when I felt I could get away with it) with my out-loud voice, because it really irritated him. I wanted to turn and murmur that to Bagamil and watch the sunny smile break out across his face.

*Bagamil.* How could I get by without him? I mean, Sandu had promised to be honest and more helpfully forthcoming with me, but I'd counted on Bagamil to be there as my teacher as well, the one upon whom I could count if (when) Sandu went back to his old habit of utter failure to communicate.

Sandu, having obviously read some of my thoughts—hopefully not all of them—spoke gently in my ear. "You may show you are missing him by publicly mourning him. It is fine for you to display that emotion; it will help keep him safe. I know it is hard for you to be separated from him after all that recently has transpired, but know that you will be with him again as soon as it is safe. The am'r life is longer than you are used to. There will be more and longer absences—and more joyful reunions."

I would have hugged him then, but I did not have to be told that we were somewhere not very PDA-welcoming.

So instead I asked, "How do you just change names for him like that?"

"He has held many names. Bagamil was one he's had for many years, but it was not the name I met him wearing."

"What was that again?"

"Ignác. And Ignacio is a variation, so it is easy for me to think of him this way. He was Egnatius as well a long time before, and many variations over the centuries. It is a name he enjoys, but it was not his first name, and it does not shape who he is."

"What was his first name, then?"

"I think...I will leave it for him to tell you."

Eventually, we got on a plane. Since Sandu could technically not get away from me, I demanded to know what was going on.

"Now—what about your patar?" I hissed, low enough that kee could not make out my words under the roar of the engines, but which I knew Sandu could hear perfectly well.

"My gharpatar. Why did he just take off like that? What are you two *doing?*"

"It is being put about the am'r…" He paused. "We would say *fabrica de bârfe*, and you would say, eh, 'rumor mill,' I think."

"Yeah?"

"Gossip travels fast among the am'r—even before the intranet you shall be building—so there are only eight am'r who know your gharpatar left his defiled sanctuary. All others are being told he met his tokhmarenc there."

"Um, OK. You said before he is 'dead.' Why?"

"This attack by Mehmet was not just to abduct you or gain final vengeance on me. Our late enemy made much of those goals, but his real victory would have been to bring my patar's existence to an end. In his absence, much…mischief could ensue. You do not comprehend how much your gharpatar is admired, almost worshipped. He does not let it affect him on a personal level, but it profoundly affects the world you have joined. It is so incalculable you cannot just look around and see it. It is in the air you breathe, as it were.

"Note that Mehmet did not come after me in *my* home. He drew us out to the safe haven Bagamil has used for ages before I was born a kee. He spoke to his followers of defeating me, but that was an *attainable* goal. It would be easier to get support for *that*. And, under the cover of one killing, achieve another."

I thought back to my time among the deluded "jinn."

"Yes, they never called him by name, and he was mentioned as an afterthought. They called him 'the *Gâvur*,' never by his name. And always as secondary to you, as you said."

"You recognize the reference, of course?"

"Uhhh. No..." A terrible thing for a librarian to have to admit.

"I am certain you know the Byron poem, The Giaour. Byron came across the Turkish word '*gâvur*,' which is an offensive term for unbelievers, like the Arabic '*kāfir*.' What you will undoubtedly find amusing is that Byron specifically uses the word 'vampire' in that same poem, one of its earliest uses in the English language."

I found myself ready to slip down the rabbit hole of am'r history but managed to stop myself in time. "What does this have to do with our Bagamil?"

"Apparently, that term had long been used by Mehmet and the am'r he influenced as a way to diminish Bagamil. Make it seem like one might *survive* attempting to give him the tokhmarenc.

"I am concerned that that effort has paid off, and that your gharpatar will have to deal with an annoying number of challenges and assassination attempts as the unbalanced and the power-hungry reach for a position of leadership they desire—and imagine they understand. If they think that Aojysht-of-aojyshtaish is no longer puissant, they may well reach towards the zenith of the am'r world.

"This would make for regularly irksome encounters for Bagamil—and those of us around him—and be disruptive to your efforts to build my archives. Thus, he has gone off to visit an old ally far away, while we will put about that he no longer exists. This will cause its own issues, of course, but I anticipate that in the chaos surrounding the death of Mehmet, we will have a long while before any am'r attempts to challenge me."

"Why challenge you?"

"Are you not paying attention, *draga mea*? I am the fritha-puthra of Bagamil. I would not be the Aojysht-of-aojyshtaish, I am not the eldest of us all. But I am directly of Bagamil's vhoon-anghyaa and would be considered one of the candidates for his place of preeminence."

I thought about that for a bit.

"You have no…um…older siblings?"

"I had an uncountable amount. Most have met their tokhmarenc, before I entered this world. Being am'r is not a guarantee of eternal life, only of strength enough to try for it."

"Who are the am'r who would contest with you?"

"That is unknown. There are many aojyshtaish, but of them, quite a few have hidden from the world so fully that it is not known for certain that they still exist. It is unlikely they would desire to return to the affairs of the am'r—to 'herding cats,' as you might put it—but there are am'r older than I who might desire that very thing. Or younger am'r who are ambitious beyond their rights and abilities. Those will be dispatched as a matter of course, but it will be irksome to have to deal with them, like an infestation of vermin."

"What if someone with a better right by age comes to you?"

"Then we talk. If they seem reasonable, I inform them of Bagamil's continued existence. If they are unreasonable, I will give them their tokhmarenc."

I stifled a shudder. Sometimes it was easy to forget who Sandu had been. Other times, it was all too easy to remember he'd been The Impaler.

"So, we just pretend Bagamil is dead and see what happens?"

"*Da*. We pretend he is dead. He goes to trusted allies and meditates in a private retreat. He likes that sort of thing, you know. We ourselves enjoy a period of rest while the less stable of the am'r work through how they want to deal with this news. When things start to develop, it will be instructive. If there is too much disruption, Bagamil will again rise from the dead, and that too will be instructive. It is nothing we cannot handle. Just abide by the rules so you do not ruin our experiment. Do not just *pretend* he is dead, convince yourself of it. Cry for him when someone mentions his name, and if an am'r named Ignacio is discussed, do not look overly interested. Do not even ask about him. Come and talk to me privately instead."

"But wait! Won't other am'r recognize him by his, well, his smell?"

"Esteshcinast, you mean, 'to know by smell.' Am'r who have met him, yes. Or who know me or my frithaputhraish. That is why he is going to a very private retreat. The am'r who escorted him away were there to ensure his privacy. He goes to an old friend who understands the situation and will assist Bagamil in choosing the most optimal hideaway. Once he is there, there is no need for any to know where he is, or that he still lives."

"But some of us know. You, me, Dragoș, and your 'old friend,' and the three guys who took him away. That's a lot of people. Isn't there a saying, like, 'Three may keep a secret—if two of them are dead?'"

Sandu frowned at me. "Only Apolinar was supposed to escort Bagamil, but once all three arrived, my only option was either to kill the other two or let them help us. I could have killed them. Once I would have. But I am a different man now. I should not just kill volunteers because I feel like it. They were vouched for. We must trust that if they do not act appropriately, our friend, or Bagamil himself, will resolve the issue."

We were interrupted by our descent. And then we had to deal with yet another kee airport.

There was another flight, and it was daylight, so we hid under our eye-masks and just focused on surviving the experience.

Eventually, we got back to what I liked to think of as "Castle Dracula," but which was really myriad tunnels leading out from...well, to be honest, I'm still not certain exactly *where* it is, but both times I arrived there, it was through a tunnel that began under an unprepossessing building in București.

# CHAPTER SIX

**A**nd there, for a little while, my am'r life as it was supposed to have unfolded actually unfolded.

I was the new collections specialist and digital archivist
for the am'r. It might seem a rather big jump up the
corporate ladder from being the head librarian at the
HAWFML—pronounced "HAW-Fuck-My-Life," a title lov-
ingly bestowed by its employees—who read to the kids at
the children's reading hour. Of course, it was a permanent
exit from the corporate librarianship ladder. I had abscond-
ed from the kee world altogether, and when I had idly inquired about the possibility of going back, there had been
am'r-style hemming and hawing. No one wanted to tell me
I *couldn't*, but it would have been idiotically unrealistic to
pretend I wasn't getting the "No, it's not an option *ever*"
message.

Not that I wanted to go back. What I had now was my
dream job and I was living with someone one could have
described as "the lover of my dreams," if my dreams prior

to meeting Sandu had ever dared reach so high. Or been so weird.

My days (*days*, ha!) looked something like this: wake up sometime in the late afternoon / early evening by myself in a wonderful bedroom in a sweet little rustic cottage that had been set aside for me. My bed was a special place, and waking up there reminded me of the first time I woke up in Romania in Dracula's castle. Sleeping here seemed especially rejuvenating; the slumber like sinking into a welcoming Mother Earth and the waking a gentle rising up from a secure embrace to the simple comfort of being snug under covers.

Sandu inhabited his suite in his underground palace-thing, but it was not *optimized*, shall we call it, for either kee or am'r-nafsh. Getting a hot dinner down there was not trivial, and the less said about the toilet options, the better. So, after we came back from...well, the whole kidnapping and fighting and explosions thing, followed by that sexy idyll, he moved me to the one place (or at least the one place I knew of) where his underground fortress made direct contact with the surface of the earth. It seemed pretty far outside of București, which said something about how extensively he'd tunneled outwards.

I guessed there was a little village or something there, but the kee world was not my world anymore and I'd not gone out to explore it. The world I explored was all underground. To get there, I took a hidden door in the back of a large closet in the bedroom that led into a tunnel within the raw rock wall against which the cottage was built.

I knew why Sandu had this cottage. All around it, on the three sides that were not sheer cliff wall, was a garden, and Sandu loved gardens. With night-blooming flowers, of course, to fit the am'r lifestyle. It was one of his little sybaritic, idiosyncratic indulgences.

I would wake up and take care of my ablutions in the rustic bathroom—which was properly plumbed, so it was rustic only in the adorable sense. When I'd come out to the *seră*, a small conservatory-cum-dining-room, "breakfast" would be waiting for me, dropped off by a kindly but very sturdy old lady who was wrinkled like a dried apple and possibly as old as Sandu while still being a hundred per-cent kee. She spoke no English, so I practiced my beginner Romanian whenever I chanced upon her during drop-off or pickup. She cooked only traditional dishes, which was fine with me. I reveled in learning the tastes of my new home, as well as the language.

Sandu would often join me as I lingered over *pălincă* (a local plum brandy for which I'd acquired a taste, despite alcohol no longer affecting me) and equally strong coffee in the garden, or if the weather were bad, in the *seră*. Since full am'r could not eat or drink, he would sniff the brandy and the coffee and the lingering odors from my meal wistfully. Sometimes this would lead to him telling me stories from his early childhood. To hear the youthful recollections of

Vlad Dracula was fascinating, and for someone who had known such pain and loss in his life to share those intimate remembrances with me was, well, an honor. I was afraid sharing my own small stories would bore him, but he insisted he loved hearing them.

Sometimes, we just went right back to bed. Or didn't make it as far as the bed, but jumped each other there in the *seră*, or in the bathtub, or wherever the mood took us.

Then there was fighting practice. I *loved* that. I'd done tai chi and yoga to keep in shape despite my rather sedentary library job, but those alone would not have instilled the confidence a "mere" am'r-nafsh needs, to think she can learn to fight am'r. No, it was that I *had* fought an am'r, one who was highly motivated to kill me, and I'd been the one to walk away. That made a gal feel *good* and want more.

Yes, of course, I'd had help, and, yes, I'd more *lurched* than *walked* away and, no, I didn't want *more* as in actually getting out there and fighting for my life tomorrow or anything. But, you know, someday in the future. The *far* future. In the meantime, I could love my workouts with Sandu, with Dragoș, and with another am'r friend named Daciana, who was far harder on me than the boys were. They taught me a nasty street hand-to-hand fighting (no Queensbury rules here!) and at the same time, they started teaching me how to use my sword properly. When I say, "my sword," I mean the one I'd killed that evil am'r bitch with. Nothing makes a sword feel so much like it belongs to you as killing any enemy with it. Don't ask *how* they transported it back with us. At the time of travel, I was far too distracted and miserable to notice that the bags of swords—Sandu's and Dragoș's also—were somehow moved through various security checks with no issues. It was undoubtedly some combination of am'r compulsion and bribes.

When not practicing with my sword, they introduced me to other bladed weapons too, and I found that a leaf-shaped short sword called a "smatchet" filled me with pleasure from the first moment I picked it up. I immediately named it Terry Smatchet. Dragoș snorted at that and, since it was on the heavier end of the choices they offered me, muttered something about "overcompensating," but he also seemed delighted by my choice and spent a good deal of time showing me things like a straight stomach thrust, saber cuts across wrists and arms, and how to slice across the right and left of the neck. The matte metal pommel could be used for an uppercut under the chin and also a downward thrust onto the face.

I was not a natural. It was hard work, and all the harder because I was a lowly am'r-nafsh fighting vastly stronger am'r. But my teachers said I was doing well, and I felt good and strong, using my new reflexes and learning things faster and better than I had when I was kee.

Eventually in my "day," I'd get to work. That was just a continuation of pleasure. Throughout the centuries, Sandu had gathered a huge library of kee works now rare or even singular. He'd promised I would get to catalog all of them someday. But first came the even more unrivaled opportunity to catalog and archive private works created over the ages by am'r about their...well...condition? Mutation? Species?

The end goal of all my efforts would simply be to no longer have any questions about what the am'r actually were. The one thing that could effectively herd the cats was *curiosity*, so by gathering enough knowledge in one place, we hoped we could get the am'r to move forward from the old lifestyle of holing up in their various underground strongholds with their frithaputhraish and occasionally going for takeout, as it were, or to kill each other—or kill each other's frithaputhraish. Now, while the am'r were still holed up, they could log-on to an am'r intranet and read about the evolution of their kind and maybe contribute their own thoughts and resources. And over time, possibly even start coalescing as —dare I say it?—a community.

This might seem a little overly optimistic to anyone who'd actually *met* any am'r, but both Bagamil and Sandu were like that. Sandu, in his Vlad days, had very much been an innovator, just not of the sort of entrepreneurship that is socially acceptable these days. And I was such a raw newbie that I could comfortably—or ignorantly—share their exceedingly confident dreams.

So I sorted, then scanned and photographed and otherwise captured documents of all sorts: clay tablets, ostraca, pieces of bark, wax tablets, scrolls of hemp-and-mulberry-bark paper, pieces of papyrus, bamboo slips, miniatures, metal codices, all sorts of parchment (with a possibly satiric preference for human skin), and incunabula, all the way up to the very Gutenberg presses which had printed the myriad screeds against my patar. I must admit I gave a special preferential evening to scanning and preserving and then teasing him about those. Well, teasing him about *certain* bits. The rest of the accusations were so revolting, so stomach-turning, that I shied away from asking about them because I really didn't want to know if any of them were true.

The core of the am'r intranet had been set up before I got there. I had thought it was to be my project, but it turned out that it merely had my name on the label because Sandu was trying to sell me (well, the concept of me) to the other am'r, and he had been perfectly happy to insinuate that the "information specialist" was the person who made all the tech stuff happen. I was just the figurehead of the project. Zoraida was the true tech-goddess, and while I would take credit for the work I *had* done, I would not let even one am'r think the intranet, and the care and feeding of our servers was the work of anyone but her amazing self.

She dressed like a fashion model and listened to EBM and hip-hop. Zoraida tended to beatbox unawares as she worked. Since I also loved EBM, we bonded over music right away, and when she wasn't making her own beats, our underground office-cave throbbed like a nightclub. Her hair was always in some fascinating arrangement of braids, which she got done at a salon in Bucharest that let her make nighttime appointments.

She was deeply proprietary of all tech used in the underground Castle Dracula. My computer-based archiving was arranged through her good offices. I was merely allowed to give her lists of requirements or overly-ambitious desires. Zoraida would upload them into her brain and wander off, beatboxing or humming as she worked through first finishing up the am'r intranet and VPN, then getting stuck into the digital cataloging with me.

It was still early days, and I was in ecstasy setting up my "collections rooms" under perfect conditions I would never be able to experience in the kee world. I could keep the temperature as cool as I wanted, since am'r basically don't notice the temperature. (Although I would be fascinated in the future to explore the real-world limitations on that.) I could keep it as dark as I liked; that whole seeing-in-the-dark thing really came in handy for my purposes. Also, there were not the usual pests one has to deal with in kee libraries.

Part of the cave system Sandu had used in his vampirish burrowing included hot springs, but my library had been set up in a very separate area, which was as dry as I could desire. Still, I wanted proper HVAC controls, not least so I could use a special filtration system after which I had long lusted. Zoraida came upon me one night as I was thinking about how that might be implemented who-knew-how-many-miles below ground where we were, far from the sort of civilization that even *had* specialized filtration systems.

She was always gorgeous—my work lights would catch out amazing carmine highlights in her dark skin where it was raised by high cheek and collarbones—but this evening, she was *radiant*. When I tried to place what was different about her, I realized with distinct discomfort she must have just taken frangkhilaat. *Fed.* It was like being able to tell that a coworker had just gotten laid. Actually, since for am'r those things usually went hand in hand, it was most likely *exactly* that.

To distract from the awkwardness I felt when she asked how I was doing, I gushed about archival science with the thoroughness of the compleat enthusiast. Happily, Zoraida understood that and dove right in, asking her usual deeply intelligent questions. By the time the sun was rising, she was giving expert-level advice on how we might achieve the best-preserved archive in the entire world.

The next evening, after Sandu and I had shared blood and love—by which I mean hot, intense sex—in my very comfortable bed, I curled up in his arms and asked him questions about Zoraida.

"*Draga mea*, most am'r are very protective of their privacy."

"I know, *dragonul meu*. That's why I'm asking *you*, not her."

Sandu sighed and teased out some curls in my hair.

I waited, but he did not seem inclined to give me any answers. "Does she have a patar or frithaputhra she is close to? She just seems so alone. Is she, um, into guys? Or girls? Both?"

Sandu sighed even deeper. "You know am'r are not able to afford the indulgence of choosing one sex over another. There will be times when it is easier to drink from one or the other, and a fussy am'r would not last long. It is so difficult to divorce the act of drinking from the act of love that no matter what preferences you felt in your kee life, once you have passed through the vistarascha, you will in time find yourself able to feel arousal for either gender, if you could not before.

"There are am'r who still tend to choose as frithaputhraish of one sex over another but we cannot know if Zoraida is one of those, because she has never made a frithaputhra. She loved her patar very dearly, but he was given his tokhmarenc all too soon and didn't live to see her go through her vistarascha. Zoraida has never recovered from that and drinks only when she must. She forms no deep emotional connections with any kee. For a long time, she and I had that in common, which is one reason she has spent so much time in my home."

"Oh," I replied, dismayed by what he'd said. I realized I'd just seen Zoraida as basically one-dimensional: super-smart and cooler than me. That was all I'd really thought about her, outside our shared work. I'd never seen her seem the least bit sad or melancholic, which made me feel entirely self-involved and inattentive. Was her high-geekery displacement activity? A wall to keep others out? Well, at any rate, I must learn not to attempt to judge any am'r by their exterior. I was humiliated to discover I'd done so.

"So...um...there's a lot I do not know about...um...am'r feeding." I found myself too shy to ask that particular question, on top of the internal shame of judging Zoraida so shallowly, but it was past time I knew details. "I know that if she made a frithaputhra, they would give her...um...especially good blood. Right?"

"*Da, draga mea.* Just as you vhoon-nourish me so exceptionally." Sandu finished the sentence by moving his lips to the left side of my neck and nuzzling and gently nipping. I let it go on for a while. We might have just finished fucking, but that didn't mean that I wouldn't mind another go. And Sandu was always pleasingly eager. We'd spent more than a few truly glorious nights in the past months, just fucking the whole night long, either coming back to it again and again or else simply not stopping until sunrise. Being am'r-nafsh honestly *did* have one or two things to recommend it, when the fact that I was still mostly-kee wasn't being rubbed in my face. But more sex could always happen after the talking bit, so regretfully I pulled my neck out of nibble range. Sandu sighed, knowing this meant I'd be demanding answers. "So, she just goes and finds a…um…casual partner for…what? Fast food with a happy ending?"

"*Da.*"

"So…if that is inferior…um…food, then how long will that last Zoraida? Or any am'r? How often do am'r need to, um, eat dinner? Dine?"

"*Ei bine*, it depends on the am'r. Some of us need frangkhilaat more often than others, and as we get older, we can survive for longer without, although not by preference. If I did not have you, *sufleţel*, I would need to 'dine' once a month to be comfortable, and would generally do so once a week. Because of Bagamil's strong vhoon-anghyaa, I *can* go far longer, but I would eventually end up dangerously weakened.

"In our—shall I call them our bachelor days?—Zoraida and I often went out and met our needs together. One can be, *ei bine*, distracted when 'dining,' so having a trusted companion along is advantageous."

"You basically went out to score together."

"*Da.*"

"Like bros going to a club. Did you go to clubs?"

"Zoraida is much like a brother to me, but we did not go to *cluburi de noapte.*"

I waited. Waited a bit more. Sandu did not look ready to elucidate on his own. "So, where *did* you go?"

Sandu looked...well, *sheepish* was the closest word, but it was not a natural expression for the face of the man who used to be Vlad Ţepeş, and who still tended to get a bit Impaler-ish in extreme situations. "We visited the *oamenii strǎzii*. We gave moments of happiness to those who endure the most sordid lives and gentle endings to those who wished for death, and we brought them food and money. Medicine, too. And I donate; I endow charities and clinics."

"I don't get it. What's '*oamenii strǎzii*?'"

"You could call them 'street people' or 'homeless.'"

I looked at Sandu and worked through my emotions. He met my eyes openly, vulnerably, and waited.

He had been Vlad Dracula. That man had used not just the helpless lower classes, but anyone he didn't like—which was more than a few people—in any way he chose, mainly brutally and to their death.

I could see that the homeless were the strata of society that probably could be fed upon by am'r with the least risk of the kee world noticing people losing blood or going missing.

Am'r already were using *all* kee as ambulatory meals. Did it really matter if the kee was well-off? Especially if that use came with rewards?

Yes. Yes, it did matter.

I cleared my throat. "I'm glad you are getting enough nourishment from *me* these days."

"*Da, și eu.*" He looked very relieved.

"Still. Um. If and when you need more, maybe you could find less *vulnerable* people to snack upon? Like rich assholes who treat everyone else like dirt and do nothing good for society? And make your charitable donations anyway?"

Sandu smiled. "I have fed on monied assholes many times over the years. I could get used to that rich diet." He paused. "Although obviously there are times when I must take nourishment *in extremis*. Then I will take what sustenance I can get in the moment."

It was my turn to sigh. I had not thought about the philosophical and ethical aspects of being a vampire before I tied myself to one for life. Let's face it, I didn't think about anything very much except the hot sex. But this was the first time the subject had been broached. I could ruminate on it for as long as I needed (I could now say that and mean it!) and work up some more thoroughly thought-out ethical stances on various am'r issues over time.

Honestly, just how much could I drag any amount of am'r society into a world in which there were trigger-warnings and micro-aggressions? I could not force beings who were hundreds, even thousands, of years old to all go to therapy until they politely went through a negotiation checklist with each potential blue-plate special.

Well. That was all for the future. In the now, Sandu seemed willing to embrace change. He should get a reward for that.

So I smiled at him, and when he smiled back with warmth and love and lust, I proceeded to give him the best reward I could think of.

# Chapter Seven

Zoraida and I became the archive-geek dream team. She threw herself into helping me set up the stacks, and together we built a highest-tech museum of the rarest, most important am'r historical items. Only Sandu and Dragoș and Daciana actually visited the museum—but it was early days. Our scanners were ultra-fast. We had an powerful flatbed scanner, the high-end Hasselblad camera I never dreamed I'd get my hands on, and even a vacuum table. Writing that had been illegible for centuries was slowly becoming gloriously decipherable and accessible.

I didn't talk to Zoraida about where she dined. I didn't have the right or enough understanding to invade her business like that. Maybe after I was fully am'r, too? I grew comfortable knowing she had hidden depths I was not invited to see and was able to interact with her on the level she preferred while respecting that it was only a very surface level and I did not "know" her.

One day it occurred to me to ask a very reasonable question. "Hey, I never met you at that big am'r shindig.

You know, the one I was abducted from? Where were you around that time?"

Zoraida smiled at me. She was very skilled at the kind of smile that was warm but completely unyielding. Her speech was softened by a Haitian accent, but her words were always strong. "It seemed like a bad plan. Sandu is very confident, but not always *right*. His people do not see that, since they worship him. *I* do not worship him. I was not needed for my technical skills, so I went home to *Ayiti* to volunteer to rebuild some governmental computer systems."

"But didn't Bagamil ask everyone to meet? Could you turn down Bagamil's...um...request?"

"The Aojysht left it all in Sandu's hands. The other am'r were told they must come, but not given any information. I had more information, having been a companion to Sandu this long while. I made it clear to Sandu that I supported my Aojysht and him, but I wanted no part of their nonsense. I had leave to go from both."

"It really was a huge mess. I'm glad you were not there for it, particularly the fighting that came after."

"Oh, I was there for the fighting. Once you were taken, I left *Ayiti* to fight alongside Sandu and Bagamil. I like a good battle, just not nonsense."

"Oh. I didn't know. I'm glad you...um...enjoyed the fight. And helped defeat Mehmet and save me. Thank you."

"It was my pleasure." Zoraida smiled again, and this baring of teeth reminded me that she was an am'r, not just my geeky co-worker. There was nothing like spending time with am'r to force you to remember that people had many levels.

I didn't just have sex with Sandu and work with Zoraida. Am'r are like cats in their stubborn willfulness, sharp teeth—and their dedicated devotion to personal hygiene. While I had the lovely bathtub up in my cottage, the hot springs in Sandu's warren were a place where am'r would have social time. I not infrequently found myself splashing around with Zoraida and Sandu, or Sandu and various members of his Romanian crew. They had all learned how not to huff my delectable am'r-nafsh scent. Or at least not noticeably.

After that too-intense moment with Dragoș back in the heat of battle, I made sure I was naked around him only in Sandu's company. I'd figured out that Sandu was Dragoș' patar, which meant they had been lovers in the past, and that led to all sorts of thoughts about how Sandu and Dragoș and I could easily have something like Bagamil and Sandu and I'd had in our desert paradise. I knew Dragoș was having thoughts along the same lines. I could *feel* his lust from the other side of the pool when we bathed. I knew that Sandu and Dragoș loved each other from the sheer quantity of teasing between them and how totally and utterly comfortable they were around each other. One thing I had picked up quickly was that am'r were not comfortable in the presence of ninety percent or more of other am'r, possibly because they have an unfortunately consistent tendency to kill each other. But the sexy threesome thing had not happened yet. Well, there was no rush. We had all the time in the world for such explorations.

And then the dreams started.

I didn't say anything at first because it was just too weird, but terrible dreams started invading my daytime rest, destroying the healing sanctuary of my beloved bed. The first involved me looking through another's eyes and being in another's body. I was trapped in that body, and it was No Good At All. It was like when I had been knocked out by the poisoned blood the am'r called 'maadak,' trapped in utter helplessness, passing uncontrollably from unconsciousness to terrifyingly hallucinatory consciousness, with pain rushing like glass through my veins and burning agony into every cell of my being.

Sometimes I saw torturous visions that ripped my heart to shreds, although I did not know the people or the circumstances with which they tormented me. I got all the pain and none of the backstory, but they felt like memories. *Someone's* memories.

Sometimes I just saw cave walls covered in red and black paintings that seemed to capture the essence of madness. I could not tell if those were memories too, or if what I was seeing was "live."

Sometimes I saw people with dazed faces, forced to hold out their wrists to me. When the blood spilled into my mouth, I knew I'd not recovered enough from the last bout of madness to resist my hunger, and after giving in and gorging every drop of blood, the madness would crash over me again.

Sometimes, through the distortion and synesthesia, I saw bodies dragged away from me, torn to shreds—not bodies anymore, just *parts*, and I knew *I* had done it. I did not care. I just wanted more.

I hated myself and I dreaded more.

Next time I would resist, I swore to myself.

The next time, I did not resist.

Another dream was simply a warning—a deep, profound, throbbing warning. Feelings of anger, betrayal, pain, distress, horror, and worst of all, that terrible alarm would reverberate in my mind all night long. If there had been words, they would have been, *"These things are happening to me, and worse things are to come for all of us. You must do something."*

That warning dream started faintly, something I could shake off come twilight. But over time, it grew stronger and was mixed in with the more vivid visions of the other type of dreams. It became harder and harder to shake off my "daymares" as I started my wonderful nights, when I would otherwise have been tempted to say that all my dreams had come true. I didn't want *these* dreams to come true. I wanted them to go away and leave me to enjoy the happiness I had more than earned.

They did not go away. I found my dream-self not just giving in to the poison that would cause my madness and then enduring the terrible results; now I was trying to kill myself. Again, I knew at some level it was not *me* me, but on another level, that did not matter. It hurt just as much.

Demented and despairing, in the dreams, I tried to rip open my wrists so brutally that I could not heal in time to keep from bleeding out.

Another time, I ripped at my carotid with crazed fingers, the slashed skin less painful than the burning in my brain.

When I woke, however, I knew it hadn't worked. My days were haunted by memories of every aspect of this pain.

As if that were not bad enough, the warning dream returned like raw screaming in my brain. The dread and anguish pulsed through my whole being not just while I slept but upon waking, and I knew the nightmare would not let me go. It was part of my reality now.

I was sobbing when Sandu came out of the closet—a moment that normally gave me a daily giggle of amusement. But at this moment, I felt that I would never giggle or even smile again. He moved with that inhuman am'r speed, and I was in his arms before I could start to unwind from my fetal curl.

*"Ce este, draga mea? Cine te-a rănit?"*

That was beyond the "Hello, my name is—" level of Romanian I'd learned so far, but I could understand the concern in his tone and the "We are now at Alert Level Orange. Who do I need to hurt?" underneath his words. All the pent-up emotions from the dreams and my emotional fallout from the weeks of experiencing them came pouring out of me between sobs and gasps for air.

It took a while to get it all out. After I had run out of words, Sandu kissed me. "Why have you not spoken of these dreams sooner?"

"I don't know. They just seemed crazy. Like I was going insane. But they were just dreams, right? I thought maybe part of being am'r was having violent dreams since it's a violent life… At first, I'd forget them after waking up, even though they were so real. When I started *not* forgetting, well, then you'd be there, and we'd fuck, and it wouldn't seem so important." Sandu hadn't made any encouraging noises, so I admitted, "I thought maybe I was *failing* at being am'r-nafsh somehow. I didn't want you to *know*."

"No, *dragă* Noosh, it is I who have failed you. Again. Oh, *scuzele mele sincere!* When I started having the dreams, I should have spoken to you and asked you if you likewise were having them."

"Y-you are having the dreams, too?"

"*Da*. He is in trouble, and is reaching out to us."

That shook me up. I'd thought it was all in my head. No, to be painfully honest, I knew it was *not*, but I couldn't deal with the ramifications of those thoughts and feelings and visions being true and something I needed to act upon.

I *knew* who was sending the dreams. I'd known since the first one troubled my mind. It was Bagamil: He was in trouble.

I took my dismay out on Sandu.

"If you knew this, if you knew these dreams were true and everything, why didn't you talk to me sooner? Why haven't you done anything? Why aren't we on a plane to him *right now?*"

"*Taci, taci.* I had to be sure they were not merely dreams. *Da, draga mea,* many lifetimes of violence can lead to bad dreams for am'r, and there is no shame in that. Since the warnings became stronger, I have been listening to them and studying them to see what details I could discover. It will not help my patar if I run off without any guess as to where he may be in this wide world. And I did not tell you because I had no idea that they would affect you. If I had known you were having the dreams as well, I would have spoken of this to you right away. There may be information you have gathered from the dreams that I have not."

Now I was dismayed. I hadn't known I was supposed to be paying attention to get vital clues. "Oh. I don't think so, Sandu! I mean, I didn't know what I was seeing. I didn't know what to look for!"

"As I said, *dragă* Noosh, that is my fault. But you may have noticed more than you realize. Come, sit across from me. Now, look into my eyes and listen to me."

I looked into those eyes I loved so well, green with flecks of gold. His eyes caught the light like they were somehow multifaceted. Sandu spoke in a low, calm tone, and I felt the slowing of my heartbeat and the calming of my nerves. Then he asked me about the dreams in such detail that I realized his dreams had indeed been much the same as mine. He gently probed for minutiae I'd not been aware of noticing. When revisiting the visions threatened to get me panicky and freaked-out again, he tenderly talked me down.

He was right; I remembered more than I'd supposed. The details of the cave, the terrifying paintings on the walls in dark red and black, even some of the faces I'd seen, distorted and blurry though they'd seemed at the time. I realized Apolinar was in one of the dreams. *Shit*. And the attractive Monserrate. Julio, too, I'd seen in many dreams, the brown eyes I'd once thought soft now seeming hard, even fanatic.

None of this had I *known* I'd seen in those horrific visions.

Sandu kept me calm, and while he did his thing, I relaxed into it. When he was finished, I realized I was more exhausted than I'd been since the end of that awful day, which I preferred to stay well in my past, the day I'd had to fight for my life and watch Sandu and Dragoș fight for theirs, and the horrible cherry on the top had been finding Bagamil looking so terribly, terribly *dead*.

And now...well, Bagamil might still be alive, but for how long, and what kind of life could you call whatever those nightmares exposed? I had a sinking feeling that more terrible days were looming on the horizon.

After all, I was living with the am'r now. Had I really thought I could just stay in my library and have endless hot sex with my lover?

Yeah, I kinda had. *Silly me.*

But, because we were am'r, we did stop to share blood and sex, for the comfort of it, before we did anything else.

And then Sandu started doing his Take Charge And Plan Everything Thing. We went down to the office in Dracula's Medieval Executive Suite, and he got on his computer and the phone, calling airlines and getting treated like a VIP, calling in favors around the world.

I was allowed to listen in, so I knew where we were flying for once, and I had some names of people we'd meet: some bigshot named Lope, and someone named Fausta would pick us up from the airport when we got there. Along the way, I would demand to know the whys and the "How the hell do you think you know where to go from nightmares of a red-painted cave wall?"

Because I was coming along.

Sandu *tried* to leave me behind, safe in my library, protected by Zoraida and Dragoș and the rest of the Romanian crew, but I was not having it.

"I'm not being separated from you. You promised me that. I'm no safer staying here. I was kidnapped from *here*, remember? I might not be much of a warrior at your back, but I did kill the Qarînah, and I've learned a little since then. And if you need sustenance, my blood is the best you could have—you've said so yourself! And don't you dare think you could just slip out while I'm sleeping or something. I would follow you, and *that* would be way more dangerous, don't you think? Me running around out in the world looking for you, smelling all am'r-nafsh-sexy?"

Sandu just looked at me, and I cursed at how much stronger he was than me. Bastard.

"*Da*, I think you must come with me, my stubborn one. This is an unsafe world, as you point out, and I would rather know where you are and what you are getting up to than to be constantly wondering."

It was a very unsatisfactory way to win an argument. *Bastard.*

He had a harder time with Dragoș, who did not see me as an acceptable guard for either Sandu or my own self (an annoyingly rational truth), and after recent events in a certain desert, he was still obviously feeling somewhat protective of us both. But where *argumentum ad passiones* had worked for Sandu, it did not work for Dragoș.

Much of the argument was in Romanian and thus well over my head, although I did catch "patar" and had a feeling Sandu was arguing that he was Dragomir Pricolici's maker—no fond nickname at the moment!—and his frithaputhra had better obey him. Heh, good luck with that! Sandu didn't seem to have much luck in making obedient and docile frithaputhraish. *Must be something in the blood.* Indeed, Dragoș had started using "Voivode" and "*domnul meu Drăculea*" in every reply, which meant he was employing maximum sarcasm.

I strained my ears and brain and came away with the fact that Sandu needed Dragoș to be doing something else, maybe gathering other am'r together to come help us. He couldn't do that *and* start the search for Bagamil at the same time, and he wasn't going to put off the search any longer, so Dragoș would just have to suck it up and deal.

I had a pretty good indication that I'd followed the argument well enough because Dragoș looked wryly at me and back at Sandu and kindly spoke in English. "Ah, so you are giving me the hard job then?" I snickered because, yeah, getting am'r to do anything as a group was far harder than herding cats.

Sandu acknowledged both the joke and that Dragoș was capitulating. *"Da, fiul meu,* you have always been a better people-person, *e adevarat."*

The flight from Aeroportul Internațional Henri Coandă to Flughafen München left at midday, which was the height of am'r hangover time, that headache that comes from the too-bright orb right overhead, shining balefully through your eyeballs into the burning center of your brain. Sunglasses are not really enough; especially when you are also dealing with being back in the kee world for the first time in months, with all the burning nicotine of Kents and Marlboros and a heinous variety of other international cancer-stick brands as well as electronic smoking technology, endless clashing perfumes and colognes, equally clashing food and rubbish scents, booze, cleaning chemicals, and most intense and pervasive of all, kee blood rushing gloriously through kee veins, which was distracting, overwhelming, disturbing.

Well, disturbing for *me.* I wasn't ready to be a realio, trulio vampire just yet. That might sound funny what with all the blood I'd drunk by now, but that was *different*—intimate, private, and always related to sex or love or sex *and* love. To drink from a stranger seemed, well, *disgusting*, and so far, I had taken blood only from beings far more powerful than me, so I knew it was an ethical, consensual thing. But I was a thing that was stronger than a kee, now, and I had seen kee—living human people—drunk from like a bottle of cola. I'd seen them raped and drained and tossed aside like a crushed beer can. That would never be me, *never*. I did not know how, when the day came, I could bring myself to drink from something I used to be, no matter how gently and considerately I did so.

Fluorescent lighting can really cause a headache when you combine it with thinking too much.

Once on the plane, even though the flight was only two hours, eye masks for both of us were in order and we pretended to sleep, trying to block out the waves of kee noise and odor.

After landing at Flughafen München, we had to survive a five-hour layover. Sandu led me, incapable of coping, to a hotel by the airport to wait it out in a darkened hotel room that smelled of stale cigarette smoke and bleached hotel sheets and the last people who'd slept there.

He consoled me with sex. I would have said I wasn't in the mood for it, but as we lay on the bed like two sixes written too close together, I felt him get hard against my ass. Then I felt his lips and breath playing on the back of my neck, and suddenly I was entirely ready. Our clothing was off, and his teeth buried themselves in my neck as I turned my head to expose it just right, the same way I was arching my back to give his cock the easiest angle inside me.

When he'd drunk enough, I straddled his lap and with Sa'mah made a nick in his neck, and then his blood was in my throat, and we rocked together as slow, deep waves of pleasure moved through our bodies. After he came, and after I finally stopped coming, I found I was crying the blood-tinged tears of the am'r-nafsh. He kissed my face, licked the tears away, and murmured sweet nothings to me in Romanian. I'd not yet learned the words, but I understood what he was saying anyway.

It was a rush back through Security, but I felt a bit calmer and stronger and I think I even dozed on the hop to Rhein-Main Flughafen.

It was only a two-hour layover in Frankfurt, so no hotel sex, but it was dinner time, and when Sandu pressed upon me sausages and sauerkraut, I found I could get over the intensity of smells by bringing my taste buds into play. When eating, I felt almost kee again, and it was wonderful.

There was just time for Sandu to do a little shopping for me, an odd fetish of his I did not mind indulging. He found a silky, sexy black jumpsuit, tightly fitted from wrists and ankles to mid-forearm and mid-calf, then loose and drape-y until it gathered in a wide band at my waist. Laced black sandals. New sunglasses, gold with golden-tone mirrored lenses. I felt very posh as we boarded for our longest flight, traveling in the comfortable darkness all through the night. Sandu pretended to sleep while I ate a second dinner, but after all the kee had turned out their lights and fallen asleep in uncomfortable slouches or were plugged into little escapist worlds of headphones and flickering screens, he and I leaned together, and in am'r-level sub-whispers, he told me about the South American am'r, who were as divided and antagonistic as many of the South American countries but who would regard as a leader—if they regarded anyone as their leader—a certain Lope, who lived in Argentina. I could not believe I was flying to that exotic locale, despite the evidence of the words on the screen at the boarding gate and the ticket tucked in my bag.

"You will like Lope, *de fapt*," Sandu murmured in a voice only I could hear, "but remember to always treat *him* with respect and caution. Think before you speak, *draga mea*, because he remembers your words. And treat his women the same way, all of them."

"His...women?"

"*Da, da*, he surrounds himself with only female am'r, both his frithaputhraish and other female am'r who choose to attach themselves to him. They are his, *ei bine*, family, or perhaps clan."

"I'm glad to meet more am'r women. Well, ones who don't intend to kidnap me. I'm also not sure there aren't parts of being a lady am'r you might *not* be able to teach me, if that makes any sense.  You know, like when you forgot

to tell me about suddenly getting my vision back to twen-
ty-twenty, or how you ejaculate blood, or—"

"*Cer iertare, sufleţel!* I shall make apologies to you forever-
more for those past failings whenever you desire to hear
them and perhaps you are right. There are things I might
not remember to tell you or even think of as something that
must be explained."

"I was too shy to ask Zoraida this, but I was working up
to it before the dreams took over. I would like to know why
I have not gotten my period since I became am'r-nafsh...?"

"*Ah. Da. Că.*"

"Yes, *that*. I didn't have time to notice it for a while there,
and while you and I and Bagamil..." I ground to a halt, unable to finish the sentence or even think about that time
without risking breaking down into sobs.

"*Da, micuţo, stiu.*"

"Well, that was kinda *timeless*, you know?" I managed to
say. "And when we came back, I had so much to learn, so
much to *do*, so much to think about—"

"So many other questions to ask," he added, and I could
hear the teasing grin in his voice.

"It's not like a period is something you look forward to,
you know," I continued, ignoring him with injured dignity.
"It's not even something you think about, until, well, suddenly you *do*. And just when I did that, the dreams started
up, and I was so busy worrying about those that it slipped
my mind again."

"And now you remember it in a plane full of kee over the middle of the Atlantic Ocean."

"Well, yes. Maybe it's because I am around kee again, you know?"

"Indeed."

I paused for a second, then rushed forward with the question I was afraid to ask. "I've remembered something the Bat Bitch said to me—that I can't have babies anymore. It has something to do with that, I guess."

Sandu took a breath. Paused. *Long* pause. The thing I'd not asked was: *Is this yet another thing you never mentioned when you were convincing me to join your world?*

"I think perhaps it does, *dragă* Noosh. You are right, you will have to ask a 'lady am'r,' or better yet, a female am'r-nafsh. The am'r cannot have children. Female am'r do not have kee menstruation, and neither do female am'r-nafsh. None of my frithaputhraish ever got pregnant during their time as am'r-nafsh, nor have I heard of such a thing. I know no more than that. Except that it is a good thing, I am very certain. Going around bleeding for a week would make one very...attractive to other am'r. Conspicuous. It would not lend itself to survival. And we am'r, *ei bine*, we make our children in other ways."

As he spoke, the word-picture of walking around bleeding from my vagina while in the company of am'r—with my super delicious am'r-nafsh blood to boot—was all too clear in my mind. I decided to be happy that was apparently not going to be one of my problems. The other emotional ramifications kept me busy for the rest of that long flight. Blaming Sandu for not telling me in advance had never done me any good. If I had *really* cared about having children someday, it probably would have popped into my brain at some point during that fateful night in the hot tub. And hey, from what I understood of kee childbirth, making your children by sharing blood with them as adults was a lot safer and more enjoyable.

It still took me hours to process all the emotions, but they say you're more likely to cry on an airplane anyway. I fell asleep somewhere along the way.

About fourteen hours later, we landed at Aeropuerto Internacional Ministro Pistarini, and I flushed the free eye mask, sodden with bloody tears, down the toilet.

We'd left Romania on the last day of September, and it had definitely been autumn. We arrived in Argentina on the first of October, and it was decidedly spring. We landed after sunset, thank everything, and the evening was still warm, but with a cool breeze that was the nicest thing I'd ever smelled after fourteen hours of recycled kee air.

We were met at the airport by Fausta, a junior am'r who was short and round-faced and friendly like a puppy. A striking am'r puppy—with bark-brown eyes and sable hair and warm tan skin—but a wiggly puppy, nonetheless. It was almost embarrassing how excited she was to meet Sandu, and when Sandu introduced her to me, Fausta would have wagged her tail harder if she'd had one. I couldn't imagine that it was more exciting to meet lil ol' me than Dracula Himself, so it must have been the *eau d'am'r-nafsh* I exuded. Sigh.

Fausta gathered my bags and tried to carry Sandu's too, which he sharply declined, and out we went to her Toyota Etios Liva. It was obviously fresh from the carwash, with a new tree-shaped air freshener dangling from the rearview mirror. (I found the artificial scent vile and opened my window immediately.) Driving it obviously made Fausta inordinately proud. I was just happy it wasn't some kind of sports car. There had been too many of those in my recent past.

It was a sixty-mile drive to the *estancia* where we would be meeting Lope. I got happier and happier as we left the airport. At first, we had miles of blocks of low brick homes and businesses on one side and very flat farmland on the other. Then those blocks came to an abrupt halt, and it was just flat agricultural views with occasional warehouses and abandoned factories. After a while, it was only infrequent farmsteads.

With the windows open, I reveled in the humid air made cool by the speed we moved through it. I could smell grass and soil and rain-to-come.

After a sharp left, the grasslands (which I remembered from school were called the "pampas") changed abruptly to a heavily forested area. Fausta shouted over the wind that this was a *monte*, a mini-forest of old-growth trees: oaks and pines soaring up above acacias and myrtles and laurels. After fifteen more minutes of driving, we pulled up to a sprawling collection of buildings with occasional lights peeking out of windows from buildings hidden amongst the trees. Closest to us was a terra-cotta-colored two-story building with jasmine-covered columns holding forth before large-windowed rooms with old wooden doors flung open between. We climbed a timeworn step onto a lovely old porch decorated in cinnabar-toned tiles.

A tall, slender am'r leaned on a column on the porch, almost lost in jasmine vines. A dark brown cigarillo was held loosely in his fingers, a thin wisp of extremely nasty smoke rising from it. He held it up in greeting and, with a sketch of a bow, said, "Vlad, it has been a long time."

"Abilio, it has." Sandu bowed the exact amount back.

# CHAPTER EIGHT

"L ope says if I *must* smoke these, I *must* do it out here." The am'r shrugged, and the gesture moved down his arm to end in a flicking of ash.

Sandu kept his voice warmly, carefully polite. "I often agree with the Señor, and I am pleased to do so again. How can you bear that smell, old friend?"

"Ah, I have borne many things. These remind me of old pleasures; I still love the smell and the taste of them. My remembrance of things past, one might say, and being out here remembering gives me the pleasure of being the first to welcome you. A welcome back to this house, *¿sí?* You will find the *Señor* in the *sala* with his ladies."

"I will go see him directly. Noosh, meet Abilio. Abilio, Noosh is my frithaputhra and still very new to this world."

Abilio nodded and held the door for us. As I went by, I heard him mutter, "So I smell, so I smell."

Damn, I was tired of that.

The house was lushly decorated in all the rich shades of sunset. Indoor palms and tall spikes of flowering plants competed for space with statuary. An indoor fountain burbled in the otherwise deep quiet. Some rooms were richly tiled, others floored with hardwoods glistening with ages of oil and careful polishing.

Sandu strode unerringly through the rooms with me on his arm. Poor Fausta had lost her voice around the older am'r and was last seen taking my luggage away, hopefully to a room where I could go and have some alone time after the upcoming meeting in the parlor. I crossed my fingers that it wouldn't take too long. The company of lots of am'r was exhausting, even when they were allies.

Sandu pushed open ornately carved, reddish-wood doors, and we were in an even lusher room, if that was possible, decorated in jewel-tone shades.

In the center of the room was an impressive oxblood leather chair that was throne-like in an entirely unsubtle way. Lounging in black leather trousers and a white poet's shirt—that white shirt being quite the dramatic statement for beings who tended to wear all black to hide the bloodstains more easily—was obviously *the* Lope. His women were draped around the room, and indeed upon his person. A petite woman had her arms hanging over his shoulders, her head beside his, but Lope was the one who drew my eyes. Even while he was seated you could see he was short, maybe 5'4. His black hair was shaved into a fade on the sides but lengthened on top to a jumble of short curls. The white shirt was a lovely contrast to his amber skin. His dark eyes flashed with interest as Sandu and I approached him.

Sandu bowed and saluted him with a hearty, "Lope! Aojasc' am'ratv!"

"Aojasc' am'ratv!  *¡Y bienvenido a mi casa!*" Lope smiled. Between the changes to his face as he smiled and the timbre of his voice, I felt a moment of confusion. Lope was suddenly "she" in my perception. My thoughts spun for a moment, but I ended up understanding; at some time, probably very many years ago, Lope had most likely been called "she." He was male now, and the am'r obviously respected that.

Certainly, he had no trouble with the ladies. The ones around him strongly identified as such, at least. The one draped over him knew she was as female as they come, in a very body-conscious black minidress. There was an awful lot of ruching for such a small amount of fabric. Her long black curls cascaded with perfect coiffed-ness down to her waist, her skin was cool ecru perfection, and her eyes were that glorious hazel that seems to shift from brown to gold to green. Her gaze upon me was calm but very watchful.

Lope rose from his chair to greet me, and the draped am'r slunk along beside him with perfect timing and grace. "You must be the Noosh we all have heard so much about." Lope beamed at me. "You are as exquisite as reported." His nostrils flared slightly, and I pretended I didn't see it. The lady on his arm sure did and didn't like it, or me.

"It's a pleasure to meet you, Lope. What a beautiful home you have." I was tempted to comment on how well he had decorated it with attractive women but managed to bite my tongue. Sandu, who could be very prescient with my unspoken thoughts these days, squeezed my arm.

Another woman moved up beside Lope, with the immediate air of second-in-command. She was the most Teutonic ice-maiden-type person I'd ever seen, tall and brutally slender, with skin blueish like skim milk, eyes like ice, and her hair a platinum that was not from a colorist. The hair was cropped in a harsh bob that was ferociously feminine. She glared at both Sandu and me; it was nice not to be singled out for immediate distrust.

"You are Vlad," she said curtly, with an equally sharp nod of her head. Her German accent cut the words even more brusquely.

"Maria," Lope hurried to interject. "He is Sandu now. You would never call me 'Guadalupe'? *Right?*" There was a pause, then Maria jerked her head in a single nod. "Just because you still desire to be 'Maria,' it does not mean the rest of us wish to or can keep our names throughout our existence. Use the names our guests prefer. I will not ask again."

Maria reminded me all too strongly of a certain angry and avaricious am'r I'd had to deal with both literally and figuratively. I hoped Lope was not a would-be Mehmet and Maria not a Qarînah doppelgänger.

"This is Maria," Lope said with a wry grin. He gestured with his left arm, which the first woman had molded herself to, causing a wave of her whole person. "And *this* is Metrizcica." Her smile as she bowed to Sandu and not to me was as beautifully false as anything I had ever seen. It half made me fall in love with her, even as I knew she hated me on spec. I made a mental note to be very careful around Metrizcica. So far, of all the lady am'r I'd met here, only Fausta seemed happy to know me. Not a great start.

"Do you need any refreshment after your travel? No? Then I give you leave to acquaint, or in some cases, reacquaint, yourself with the am'r assembled here. Sandu, I know this is regretfully not a social visit. You have urgent business."

"Indeed, Lope, and well I remember the elegant and opulent nights you hosted in this gracious *estancia*. But we have no time for such pleasure in this situation."

"As you say. Please make yourself comfortable and begin."

Lope resettled himself on his throne, and Sandu moved me to an overstuffed barrel chair. After trying to get comfy there, I gave up on feeling even remotely relaxed when surrounded by strange am'r.

Sandu took center stage, which never bothered him in the slightest. He first addressed his questions to Lope. "As I understand it, an am'r named Ignacio arrived here four months ago in the company of three am'r known to you: Monserrate, Apolinar, and Julio."

Lope nodded. "*Eso es correcto*. The one known as Ignacio was of course also known to me. It was an honor to host the Aojysht-of-aojyshtaish."

"He was not traveling as such."

"No. That was made clear to me and he was treated as just another am'r. Although he was here only for a few days, word got out regardless. You cannot control such news."

Sandu allowed himself to be visibly angry. Since he normally worked very hard to stifle any expression of emotion, this was quite alarming to me.

"I should think that given the details of the circumstances surrounding his visit, which were made *very clear* to you, every effort would have been made."

"Oh, it was, it was! But we are a social people here, not like you cold northern am'r. The Aojysht had not been to this part of the world in many long years. How could my people not desire to meet the am'r famed in our oldest legends?"

The air around Sandu seemed charged with anger. "He was here for protection, which only *anonymity* could confer upon him. That was your task: to keep the secret, discourage gossip, and repel visitors—groupies who merely wanted a lungful of the most famous vhoon-anghyaa."

Lope lounged more insolently. I knew better than to assume he was *not* ready to spring out of his seat with murderous intent. "That distinctive vhoon-anghyaa was esteshcinastii by more than one am'r when the Aojysht touched down in this country. Your plan was never more than an unrealistic pipe dream, made by am'r who have forgotten how to live in the modern world."

It was a tense moment. Lope might be feigning his relaxed pose, and Metrizcica probably always looked like a panther ready to spring, but Maria looked like she was about to invade Poland.

Sandu was very still. He spoke carefully. "It is *curious* that the Aojysht should be so respected, yet his directives so disrespected." He let his words sink into the tense silence before continuing, "Once he is located, we will consider with him the merit of his plans. Until then, all efforts must be made to discover his whereabouts."

Lope nodded. "I agree. We all wish to assist in finding him without delay. He was here only those few days. When guests started arriving in hopes of meeting him, we realized the situation was out of control, and he brought forward plans to remove to somewhere more isolated. I was not part of that. He conferred only with the three who came with him, most especially Monserrate and Julio."

Sandu now directed his words around the room. "Were any here involved with the Aojysht's planning?"

In the pause that followed, I had my excuse to properly look around me. Four female am'r were stationed around the room, and I somehow could tell they were all Lope's people.

Three male am'r were sitting and standing throughout the rest of the room. They looked casual enough, but I did not trust that one bit.

An am'r with olive skin and neatly trimmed wavy black hair was leaning against a wall in the back of the room. His clothing was worn but neat: black jeans and a black work shirt tucked into them. He'd shifted slightly in preparation for speaking and it drew all eyes to him. "It has been a long while since I have seen you, 'Sandu.' It had been a long while since I had seen my other old friend. I am dismayed that my arrival at this abode might have impacted the set of circumstances that concern us now."

Sandu smiled at him with true warmth, I thought. "It has been too long—is it still Augustinus?"

"Agustín, *por favor*, in this new world. I wish I had more to convey to you. I spoke with the am'r now called Ignacio for a brief while the day after he arrived. I happened to arrive that day as well, unaware that I should find him here. We spoke lightly about recent events, and my pleasure at seeing my old friend altered to dismay at what I heard. I have been out of contact for a while now, since I have made a home of which I have become quite fond, which remains private enough even as the kee spread like an infestation, and often many years go past before I feel any need for news and the company of my kind.

"When the 'groupies,' as you term them, started to arrive, Ignacio was troubled and spent much time alone with the three am'r who stayed especially close to him. I had been aware that Monserrate and Julio, both of whom I have met in previous times, were uneasy and even resentful when I was closeted with the Aojysht. I had thought they were merely inflated with their own sense of purpose, serving him so closely, but now I wonder."

Sandu asked in a very calm voice, which I knew meant he was agitated, "Did Ignacio tell you where he was planning to go?"

"He did not. I would have told you from the start if I knew."

There was a pause, and then various of the am'r spoke up. Nobody knew anything, but everyone was belatedly concluding, now that Agustín had pointed it out, that Monserrate and Julio and Apolinar had been acting decidedly fishy. Would've been nice if anyone had noticed that *before* my gharpatar was aojysht-napped.

"I believe I know where Bagamil went." Curt syllables sliced through the ineffectual discussion.

"Maria," Lope's voice was cold, "what have I said about names?"

"Why should we call him 'Ignacio?'" she countered. "We all know of whom we speak, *ja?* The Aojysht-of-aojyshtaish is Bagamil—unless he has met his tokhmarenc. Then, I do not know who the eldest would be."

Sandu was behind her before any of us could do more than blink. Her arm was pulled painfully up behind her back and his other hand wrapped around her throat. I could see from the tension in his forearm that he was poised to rip it open with his fingernails.

She moved as if to try and fight free, but Lope commanded, "*¡Quietos!*" We all froze.

Sandu said, low but clear, "You will use manners with your elders. Or, *Fräulein*, you will not belatedly learn them, but your death will be an object lesson for others. Do you understand?"

"*Jawohl!* Yes, I do."

"Apologize to the nice Impaler," Lope growled at Maria. He was obviously pissed at every aspect of this situation, but mostly, I suspected, that he had to allow Sandu to discipline his people.

"*Ich entschuldige mich, mein Herr.*"

Sandu was beside my chair in another blink; he let his hand rest upon my shoulder. All very relaxed, oh, so *very* relaxed. "Very good, Lope. Now, what did your pet have to say to me?"

Maria glared frosty hate at us, but her words were emotionless. "I overheard them, *Ignacio* and the three speaking. They were in the grove of casuarinas on the southwest portion of Lope's land. They did not know I was there. They spoke of a safe haven that Julio said was his personal refuge. That he knew how to get there by the most private paths.

They assured the Aojysht that there would be satellite communications since he was very insistent on that point. He seemed to trust them completely. By the time I returned to the house, they had gone."

We all considered this. Lope took some long, slow breaths. "Why had you not previously told me about this, Maria?"

If I were Maria, I'd be even more worried *now* than when Sandu was about to claw out my throat. Maria seemed unaware of it.

"I was waiting for the right moment, Lope. You have had so many guests around you and—"

"The right moment was the very minute you left the casuarina grove. You should have been at my side, letting me know you needed to speak to me in private. No. You were sitting on this information, waiting until it would serve you best to share it. That is *not* how a member of this family acts, so scheming and so selfish."

"No, Lope, you do not understand! *Your* interests are my primary concern!"

Lope rose from his throne and stretched languorously before telling her, "That is not what I observe. The interests of this family are not in your heart. Therefore, you are no longer my *familia*."

The arctic eyes began to register some unease. Maria spoke slowly, her accent stronger than ever. "Then will I my leave take." She waited for a second, perhaps to give Lope a chance to call her bluff. Lope met the eyes of Metrizcica and glanced around the room, ignoring Maria.

This small gesture panicked Maria more than anything else. She started to move in that am'r "too fast to follow with the eye" way, but it was too late. Metrizcica and two others of Lope's family surrounded her, left, right, and behind. Metrizcica looked entirely too eager for what was coming.

Lope moved, seemingly casually but with instant translocation, directly in front of Maria. There was no pause. Maria's neck was snapped. Her arms were held, and her twisted head looked over her shoulder. Unwittingly, I met her eyes—because she was am'r she was not dead—and I saw the pain and all-too-belated fear in them. A low whine wheezed out of her mouth.

The three women took Maria's lanky body into an adjoining room. I knew little of am'r culture, but I could guess from unhappily-acquired experience about what might be in store for her. She would not be allowed to heal, and her blood would be drained by Lope's valued family members, stealing Maria's strength. If she was lucky, she would be drained dry, then decapitated and burned. If Lope was *very* cranky about her disloyalty, Maria would be drained only until she was profoundly weakened, and when she had recovered somewhat, she would be drained again, over and over, until the sport stopped being fun.

As if nothing horrific had just occurred, Lope continued to ask around the room, "Does anyone have any further information?"

There was a pause. Just when I decided no one was going to add anything, Abilio spoke up. He'd settled into one of the overstuffed chairs like the one I was sitting in. *He* looked relaxed and comfortable in his.

"Sandu, I assume you recognized Julio?"

My patar did one of those am'r micro-expressions. On a kee, it would have been a full bodily display of startlement. On him, it was just a slight increase in stillness, but I knew how to read it. This was a total shock. However, in the instant after that, he understood how much of a surprise it should *not* have been.

"I…thought I'd esteshcinastii. But I do not recognize his face. Please enlighten me."

"Julio Popper. He's a fellow countryman of yours, an engineer in Europe and Chile and became caught up in the gold fever in '85. 1885, I mean. I remember that time well. What a mess, eh, Lope? *De todos modos*, he became quite infamous in his kee lifetime as an active participant in the genocide of the Selk'nam people of Tierra del Fuego, where he was a petty tyrant who had his own private army, issuing his own coinage and stamps in a colony he held under his personal law."

Sandu nodded slowly. "I know I read of him at the time, but it was the kee world, and I had other concerns."

*1885. Huh. I just bet you did*, I thought, but shelved that issue for another time.

"I believe Julio met Ligeia in Buenos Aires in '93. Do you remember her?"

"Ahhhh, Ligeia! A strong am'r! Yes, I encountered her in Greece, in, oh, the later 1600s. I will not soon forget those memories, even if the years have blurred together. She was in Greece for a long time, was she not?"

"She left after Byron died. She had been unable to convince him to be her frithaputhra, and she mourned him as no am'r has ever mourned a kee. I met her in Baires, where she had gone to get far from Greece and her memories. She was a little unstable, but that did not stand out very much in that time and place. The kee thought her a crazy rich widow, and she scandalized the city by openly taking 'lovers.' There was so much change here, so much disorganization. The rules were not the same as they were back in Europe. We am'r could get away with almost anything, so we did not worry about Ligeia working her way through the pretty boys and girls of the town, looking for distraction from her lost love.

"Julio was in Baires then, on trial for one of his many disputes with the kee government. Ligeia was swept away by him. She did like her men to be more than a little proud, moody, and self-absorbed in their own miseries—no doubt why she loved Byron so—and he was her am'r-nafsh before the trial was concluded.

"I am not clear about what happened after that. I was not paying particular attention to Ligeia and her paramours as I had my own affairs to attend to. The next I heard about it, Popper was 'dead' by mysterious circumstances in the kee news, and the building Ligeia bought when she arrived here had burned to the ground. She was never seen again by kee or am'r, and we have all assumed that she met her tokhmarenc there. A few of us wondered about it, and if I had seen Popper around, I might have put some hard questions to him, but he did not reappear for at least fifty years. By then, I was in Brazil, and the matter had long since ceased to trouble me."

"I did nothing about it either," Lope admitted, seeming as rueful as I'd ever seen an am'r. "Ligeia was fierce and powerful, and I invited her, every time our paths crossed, to come and ease her troubles with my family, but she was very...single-minded. She knew what she wanted, and of course, I had to respect that. When the fire happened and she never reappeared, to be honest, I was not surprised. It happens sometimes; we try to choose frithaputhraish who will be our allies, but sometimes we create our worst ene-my."

"Pat'rkosh..." Sandu breathed. "No wonder I thought I'd esteshcinastii, with the vhoon-anghyaa of Ligeia in him. And that he would take her superior vhoon-anghyaa and end her long life! It may be many years later, but I will ask that hard question of him when I put my *other* questions to him."

"*Bien*." Lope looked around the room again. "Does anyone have any *more* information?"

One of Lope's family called, "*Sí*, patar," then shifted uncomfortably as we all turned to look at her. I realized I recognized her by both looks and scent. She had been at the Rave Cave, and I'd been introduced to her the night before I was abducted by Mehmet. She was tall and sturdily built; the technical term was "like a brick shithouse." She had two-length hair, dark and curly where it was long on top, with blue and purple streaks through some of the curls. She wore motorcycle leathers and boots with the thoughtless comfort of one long accustomed to such clothing. This was a person for whom "cool" was a word used only for indicating temperature. I would have been intimidated by her if she were just kee, but as she was am'r, I was ready to keep a sensible distance from her and do absolutely nothing to piss her off.

Lope seemed surprised to hear from her. "Tecla? What information do you have?"

Tecla spoke in a deep, rich tone. "I do not know if this is relevant, but I know Monserrate. He is the frithaputhra of Orélie."

Every am'r in the room looked startled by this. I didn't think I'd ever seen a group of am'r looking around in surprise. It would have been funny except for how worrisome it was.

Lope looked disgusted. "*¡A la mierda con eso!* I thought he and his ignorant followers—not the Mapuche tribe, but his deluded descendants—had been removed from this part of the world."

"What is this?" asked Sandu. I hoped we'd get more than the usual bullshit am'r answer. We did.

"Ahhhh, this was in the news at the time, right when your countryman was creating havoc further south. A crazy Frenchman named Antoine de Tounens," Lope spat the name, "read a book about Chile and somehow decided he was king of a part of the land he called 'Araucanía.' He came here, renamed himself 'Orélie-Antoine I,' and made hollow promises to the tribes that lived in that region, who thought he offered a way to keep out the rest of us colonists who were snapping up their lands. Well, he only caused them grief—*¡No es de extrañar!*—and brought the might of the Chilean forces down on them all the faster.

"He was expelled. He published his memoirs, suckered some more fools in Europe out of their money, and then snuck back into the country. He caused more trouble. He was expelled again. He came back, *como las enfermedades de transmisión sexual,* and was captured and deported again. Finally, he was too broken—a court back in France declared him both insane *and* having no sovereignty—and he would have died of psychotic frustration, only one of our kind had to go and make an am'r of him."

"*Ce?* Eh, *qué?*" Sandu exclaimed. "He was not am'r already?"

"Why do you think he was deported by kee, not destroyed by us? We would have resolved the situation much more neatly if he had been *our* problem. Instead, his descendants—both kee and am'r—have shown up now and then over the years, making delusional claims to the 'Kingdom of Araucanía and Patagonia.' The kee ones by now know enough to stay away and keep their foolishness in Europe. The am'r for some time would arrive and create a scandal, but we kept an eye open for them, and they all eventually ceased to be a problem. We have not heard his name for years now. The young ones here will not have even heard of him."

Tecla added, "I have hunted down two of his 'heirs.' They both insisted he would return for his crown. Well, until I stopped their foolish mouths. I had esteshcinastii Monserrate, but he assured me that while Orélie was his patar, he had broken away, and wanted no part of his patar's crazy plans. He seemed...*no ser anormal*, just like any other am'r."

Lope was pissed. Again. He was having a bad night with his family. "*¿Por qué no me dijiste esto?*" he growled at Tecla.

Tecla glanced at Sandu and responded in English. "I am very sorry, patar mine. I have let you down."

"Yes, but *why?*" Lope demanded.

"*Pues*... Monserrate had a frithaputhra, still an am'r-naf-sh, very beautiful..." Tecla's voice trailed off as she tried to figure out how to best word things so she didn't end up like Maria.

"I met him first at your summit, Sandu." She turned to him. "You remember I attended as Lope's delegate?"

Sandu nodded, and she continued, "We spoke some at that event, and we returned on the same flights. He knew I had esteshcinastii him, but we did not speak of it.

Looking back to Lope, she continued, "Sometime later, I was upon your business in Baires. That matter with Pedro, you remember?"

"*Sí, sí.* What about Monserrate?" Lope was not interested in distractions.

"He was moving his am'r-nafsh to a new location, and they were attacked. I recognized his scent, and I came to her—to his—aid. I saved them both. She is enchanting, as I said, and I immediately...well, I have not had a frithaputhra in a long while. He said he would soon be very busy, and he needed to put her somewhere safe; that was why they were traveling. He saw how I was taken with her and offered her to me, since I could protect her better while he was so busy..."

Tecla's voice faded under Lope's unyielding anger. There was a pause, and I was terrified we were about to have another Maria situation.

But instead, Lope broke into an understanding grin. "A beautiful girl is best kept a secret, yes? Is she as delicious as this one here?" He gestured at me, and I nearly passed out from the force of the blush combining with the profound desire to become invisible.

I think Tecla would have blushed, if am'r could do that sort of thing. "Even more *deliciosa*—if Sandu will forgive me."

Sandu was playfully formal. "I will forgive your words, *mi dama*, but only because you are so obviously blinded by love."

*Fucking am'r. Is this really the time for this weird old gallantry shit?*

Happily, Lope pulled us back on track. "*Entonces*, you have the girl safe. I have not heard anything about her, so she is obviously not a problem. *Bien*. Now, what information did you get from Monserrate at that time?"

"Only that he had moved to this country some little while ago. When I confronted him about the stink of Orélie's vhoon-anghyaa in him, he told me he was estranged from his patar, not part of the old schemes. He said he did not know if the old crazy was even still alive, or if he had finally gotten a long-past-due tokhmarenc. He seemed candid; I had no reason to doubt him.

"But now, thinking about it, why was he suddenly so busy that he could not care for his am'r-nafsh? That does not make sense. I was thinking only with my hunger. *¡Lo* *lamento mucho!* Lope, I have made a grave error. I should have brought this to you when it happened. I know you are no threat to my girl. *¡Mil disculpas!*"

"No, no! Tecla, old habits die hard, especially with us. I know you did not do this in a treacherous manner. You are my frithaputhra, and I know the longing for a frithaputhra of one's own. *Estás perdonada.*"

Lope turned to us. Well, to Sandu since I was, as always, just the pretty snack at his side. "The question is, why is Orélie's frithaputhra working with Julio? There is nothing good about this. It is not just Ignacio we should be concerned about; something larger is going on here."

Later, as the sky started to lighten, I lay in Sandu's arms in a very comfortable bed, in underground guest quarters on the property. Not too near the main buildings, a comfortable distance for beings who prefer space. The am'r had scattered to similar private little bunkers for the day. Lope was a most considerate am'r host.

After the drama of Maria's death sentence and the revelation of Julio's identity, and then all that weird stuff around this Orélie-Antoine person and whatever *he* could be up to, the party had broken up on a rather subdued note. No am'r had any more useful information—or were going to admit it if they did. Lope left for a while, probably to oversee who got blood from Maria's draining, and by the time he returned, most of the guest am'r had wandered off to do their own thing. I remembered that Sandu had told me that Lope's "family" were all some degree of female, either born that way or presenting that way now, so all the male am'r were visitors paying court or had come for whatever reasons such ornery antisocial creatures devise for spending time in each other's company.

There were no am'r-nafsh, or at least I had not met any. It was deeply discomfiting to be the only one of my kind wherever I went, especially since my "kind" was basically a bacon cheeseburger hot off the grill in a room full of vegans who'd just changed their mind and were really, really hungry for that first juicy bite.

Everyone had shown great restraint in not-so-obviously huffing my mouth-watering unintentional perfume as each stopped by Sandu to say a few words before going about their business. I couldn't imagine ever getting used to being partnered with someone who was essentially *royalty*. The am'r were not fame-seeking creatures, or at least, the ones who were tended to not survive for very long. Sandu had started his celebrity in his kee life, and he assured me the notoriety brought by his fictional counterpart was purely accidental and in no way desired. But the specific distinction the am'r here were responding to was Sandu being the Aojysht's frithaputhra and second-in-command.

I was Sandu's frithaputhra, and I didn't want to contemplate what that meant in terms of power structures. I wasn't even a full am'r yet, but sometime when we were not dealing with a crisis, I needed to have the am'r succession rules explained to me. I had a feeling there was more to it than just, "The most powerful is the king of the hill." Although with am'r, you never knew.

Sandu and I had walked to our underground bungalow through the pre-sunrise monte, the wind blowing off the pampas bringing exotically scented air even before the trees and a variety of novel vegetation added their fascinating perfumes. Frogs and crickets brought the night to vivid life, although the romance of the walk was somewhat disturbed for me when a roar-bark echoed with shocking loudness through the trees. Sandu had squeezed my fingers. "Do not worry; I am the most dangerous predator in these woods," he said with confident laughter in his voice.

It was not as comforting as he probably meant it to be.

Later, after we had fed and pleasured each other, I lay on my side inside his arm as he stretched out on his back. I snuggled my head into the just-right spot under Sandu's shoulder, resting my face on a perfect pectoralis.

"What did Lope say to you," I asked him, "when you two went off alone for forever?" I had been left with two of Lope's family, Tecla and Delfina (who was just about as intimidating as Tecla, but with less leather) and with whom making conversation had been very hard going. I ended up recounting some of the battle I had witnessed in—well, under—the desert recently. I had thought it would be a very safe topic since am'r seemed to fight a lot, but it made them really fidgety and aroused, which was *not* the effect I was going for.

*Note to self: don't discuss anything interesting I've ever done with strange am'r. Just talk about the weather or get into really dry specialist detail about the new am'r archiving and intranet project.*

"So, Julio is really a Romanian?"

"Yes. Well, originally. I spent some of my time digging into his history. 'Iuliu' in my language becomes 'Julio' in Spanish. He was born in Bucureşti at a time when people of Jewish descent were not treated well by my people. He was made stateless due to his ethnicity, so he ended up making his own state, as it were. An autocracy."

"When you met him, you couldn't tell he was Romanian by his accent?"

"*Nu, nu.* He has spent so long here that Spanish seems like his milk tongue. He even has a local accent."

"I remember, you did ask him back then who his patar was."

"I *should* have pushed him more. I am not unaware this whole situation is my fault."

"I wasn't trying to say that! What about Bagamil? He didn't recognize anyone? He is the Aojysht, after all."

"The Aojysht may esteshcinasti to a deep level, knowing the original vhoon-anghyaa of every new am'r he meets—that would not surprise me—but there have been many of us. It obviously did not occur to him to wonder about the vhoon-anghyaa of Ligeia in Julio. Why would it, when there are so many am'r he has not seen in centuries for good and valid reasons?"

"It made *you* suspicious right away."

"*Ei bine*, in all probability it was because I know fewer am'r than he, so her vhoon-anghyaa especially stood out, unexpected as it was. Sometimes having less knowledge can help one focus. Does it matter, *draga mea*?"

"No, no, I guess not." I shifted in his arms, finding another way to be perfectly comfortable. "What about Monserrate being Oreo's frithaputhra?"

"Orélie."

"Whatever. It's still not his real name."

"It's as much his name as 'Sandu' is mine. I do not know what to think of Monserrate being in league with Julio. It could just be a bizarre coincidence."

"Do you really think so?"

"*Ei bine, nu.* It is too bizarre. I cannot guess precisely what they are scheming, but I must believe they are in league, and that together, they tricked my patar into a situation where they could overpower him."

We paused for a bit, considering that, and I pulled his arms tighter around me. "Did Lope have anything else to tell you?"

"He showed me a map of the area where Julio had spent his *kee* years. It is known he has a sanctuary down in that area, but he has not shared its location with any am'r known by Lope. That is not unusual. My patar and I and Lope are the exceptions, opening our homes to am'r who are not our direct kin. We all have more private refuges, of course."

That was interesting. I'd never been to Sandu's "more private refuge." He continued, "There are some mountains that can be identified by their Romanian names, which came from Julio during his *kee* life. Sierra Carmen Sylva is named after she who was queen in Romania during his lifetime. Apparently, he named another peak for the Romanian town of Sinaia, but no one knows now which peak that was. *That* is the one that interests me."

"So Julio has taken Bagamil to some lost mountain?"

"*Ei bine.* It would be in an area known as Tierra del Fuego. It is not the vastest area, all things considered, but there are a number of mountain ranges that will need to be explored."

"Uh. I guess that's better than 'probably somewhere in South America.'"

"Infinitely."

"So, what do we do next?"

"We sleep. And tomorrow, we go down to Tierra del Fuego."

# Chapter Nine

The next night, after enjoying a long shower and changing into another new outfit (soft black joggers with cargo pockets, a knit black mock-neck sweater that clung to me in flattering ways, and tactical boots that were made for walking), we went up to the main house. The evening air held heat and mugginess from the day, but the earth and trees and spring plants smelled very green and fresh.

As soon as we walked in the door, I was whisked off to a very empty-looking kitchen that had not seen an update since sometime in the late 1800s. Perched on an antique wooden chair at a splendid old butcher-block table, I was presented proudly with takeout boxes of pastries they called *medialunas*, which were like a croissant and brioche had hooked up and had delicious offspring. There was also a choice of coffee or yerba mate. I'd never tried the latter, so of course I chose it. Dried leaves were put into a gourd and hot water was poured from a thermos, then a straw they called a *bombilla* was put in at a specific angle, then more water was added. I watched it all in fascination. When it was finally approved for me to drink, it proved to be a strong, bitter tea. The female am'r gathered around me sniffed at it with evident wistfulness and explained that a kee would feel energized and even euphoric drinking it. I, being am'r-nafsh now, could not enjoy that part of the experience. I liked the ceremonial aspect of it, though, and the sharp taste.

What I didn't like was yet again being reminded of my differences, which I was painfully reminded of as Lope's ladies sat around me, watching me drink and eat my breakfast as if it were a show for their amusement. I lived in the am'r world now, with all the strange new customs and the blasé attitude to constant violence, yet I was a thing apart—an eater of food in a world of beings who drank a very different diet, and a user of bathrooms around godlike creatures who never squatted.

Fausta, who was obviously the full-time go-fer, drove Lope and us over to a private landing strip about an hour farther away from Buenos Aires, giving me even more chance to experience spring in the pampas. It was like the prairie of

North America, only with an unnamable difference. Actually, the most nameable difference was not the flora but the fauna. Every animal I saw on the drive looked different from the animals I was used to seeing, some in subtle ways—from things that looked like rabbits but without the ears to a bizarre bird-creature that looked a lot like an emu. I'd been almost dozing when we startled one by driving down the dirt road in the boxy 4x4, which Fausta operated with a deft hand. It made a low booming call, then ran away on its weirdly muscular legs. It felt like we'd gone back in time and awakened a dinosaur.

When we reached the landing strip, a little red airplane waited for us, its door hanging open in welcome. Fausta pulled in near it, and as we climbed out of the vehicle, a short female figure bounced out in a snugly tailored black flight suit. Her blue-black hair was in a pixie cut that framed her wide-eyed, high-cheek-boned face perfectly. Her grin was huge, but not in a little girl way. It was the grin of a comfortable and self-assured woman.

She greeted Lope and Fausta, then turned to us. "*Buenas noches!* I'm Araceli, and I will be your pilot tonight!"

Lope interjected, "There are few things better than the pleasure of flying with Araceli at the stick, but also, this is the very pilot who flew Ignacio and his guides—a term I'm using very advisedly—to their last known destination. Let me make up for the regrettable lack of hospitality I could provide you this trip by sending you exactly where you need to go in the most capable and comely of hands."

"This is perfect, Lope, our thanks," Sandu replied. "And these are trying times. Hospitality reshapes itself to fit the needs of guest and host. I could not ask for more from you, *señor.*"

Lope turned to me. "I have not gotten to know you at all as well as I would have liked, *encantadora dama.* Please say you will return as soon as this business is completed and let us all enjoy your company."

*My delicious aroma, you mean to say.* But I liked Lope as well as you could like an am'r you didn't know very well, and as much as you could like anyone who'd broken someone else's neck in front of you last night. But that was life with the am'r for you, and his old-fashioned charm made me smile. So I replied, *"Gracias, señor."* High school Spanish got me that far. "I hope that on our successful return, we will stop with you for a while."

As Fausta formally bowed Lope into the car and chauffeured him away, Araceli turned to us. "Would Noosh like to sit up with me?" She asked Sandu, but smiled at me to let me know she was just observing formalities that she herself did not take very seriously.

"I do believe she would." Sandu smiled indulgently at me. He tossed our bags into a hole in the side of the aircraft and closed its little door, then climbed in first through a tiny-seeming door right at the back of the wing. He managed to get his body to flow over a folded seat into the back row of two seats in that lithe am'r way. Araceli folded the seat back and climbed into the front left-hand seat. This was also done with catlike fluidity. I climbed in last and felt awkward and still kee-klutzy. I'd never been in so small a plane, and I'd never sat in the cockpit before. I settled in gingerly, terrified of bumping my hand or elbow or knee into some important switch or button. Araceli had to guide me through closing the damn door properly.

She then had to help me figure out the seatbelt. Once it finally clicked into place, she handed me a headset to match her own. Thankfully, I figured that out with more aplomb.

She tossed me her irresistible grin. "Ready for liftoff?" I heard through the headset, her English made more musical by the light accent.

"Um...sure!" I grinned back, trying to seem unfazed. I watched her check displays, flip switches, and press buttons. Then she was holding the...well...the thing pilots hold, and pulling back on it, and we were taking off.

It was pretty damn thrilling.

It took about half an hour to get to our cruising altitude. Along the way, she had radio communications with some radio control place. Once everything was set, she turned to face me. "So, *you* are a surprise. 'Noosh,' yes?"

I sighed. "Yeah, it's Noosh. And you mean, because I'm am'r-nafsh?"

"Of course I mean that. It is not a surprise to see Sandu with a beautiful and capable woman."

The compliment knocked my annoyance right out from under me. I didn't mind being called "beautiful" by someone who so very much was, herself. But for a full am'r woman, and an actual *pilot* at that, to call me "capable" almost made me cry. I hadn't been as full of self-doubt when I was just a kee librarian doing her thing. But being not-fully-am'r in the am'r world had knocked my faith in my competence and general wherewithal down to a nadir I'd not fully realized until this compliment caught me unaware.

"Oh!" I covered the emotional jolt with a gush of words. "Well, I guess the gossip hasn't made its way down here yet. Sandu decided—it seems forever ago—that *he* didn't have to follow the tradition of hiding your am'r-nafsh, so he took me to the big conference thing he held. The one Tecla attended. Then he was *very surprised* when I was am'r-nafsh-napped."

Araceli shook with mirth. Her laughter was magnificent.

"I bet he was! What happened then?"

Remembering the bloodlust that had overtaken Lope's girl-gang back at his *estancia*, I decided to go light on the details. She was fascinated and kept asking more questions, and in the end, I told her as much as I'd told my patar and gharpatar.

It took hours of talking because she shared comparable stories from her life as an am'r in exchange, and our talk flowed back and forth, our anecdotes overtaking each other's, but then curving back to the original topic. I floated delightedly along the river of words with a feeling of sharing and being heard. Zoraida and I had commonalities and a friendship built on mutual geeky respect, but something about her always made me feel uncertain, like I should maintain a level of formality. Araceli and I, however, immediately felt like old friends. In this strange world I'd fallen into, long comfy chats with a gal pal were something I'd sort of given up on. I mean, I loved Sandu and Bagamil, and I was as comfortable around Dragoș as one could be around someone one suspected one would be sleeping with eventually but hadn't yet. But they were *males*. There was something to be said for being a woman in the company of another woman, an ease of mutual understanding, a relaxation.

Although Araceli was an am'r, and one not of my blood.

I must not forget that. I must not *really* relax.

I had assumed before that having power, being powerful, would mean one could slouch untroubled through a world of the less powerful. Maybe that was true for kee, but it most certainly was not true for the am'r. They had so much power, but they spent all their time waiting for the other am'r to inevitably attack them. They had to hide their lovers to protect them from likewise inevitable attack. Well, except for *me*. I didn't get hidden. But even as I demanded to be actively in Sandu's life, I wasn't entirely sure from one day to the next if it was the best idea.

Araceli was a "young" am'r. She had experienced the vistarascha in 1973, as she put it, "a time of real change in many parts of this land we are flying over." She was born in Chile, and her death in the kee world saved her from the terrible rule of General Pinochet. Lope had snuck into the country to be there for her when she rose and had brought her back to Argentina, "Although it was not much safer here for a kee, to be honest."

We talked almost until it was time for us to land after a seven-hour flight down the vast length of Argentina. I looked back now and then at Sandu, but he was always looking out the window, seeming far away in his thoughts. I wished I could see the famous landscapes rushing along below us at one hundred and eighty knots, but most of the way a thick cloud layer blocked everything from view. As we grew closer to our destination, the clouds broke up, and I was fascinated to see moonlight stretching across grasslands or the curving coast, and off in the distance, wrinkles of mountains seeming to rear up out of myriad rivers and lakes. The ocean yawned widely out into the night to our left. I'd never seen such a dynamic landscape. After I lost track of what I was saying at some point, Araceli let me drink in the views uninterrupted, occasionally suggesting I

look in another direction and explaining accordingly what
I was seeing.

The last thing she pointed out to me was a thin, tiny rectangle with glowing lights down each side. Oh, our landing
strip. It didn't look big enough.

The flight got very bumpy during descent, and in the
tiny plane, it was much more intense than anything I'd undergone in the big commercial aircraft that had previously
been my only experience of air travel. Instead of looking out
of the windows, I watched Araceli. She was supremely competent and looked like she was having a blast, so I relaxed
and watched her. I was so enthralled that I was surprised
when the plane's wheels bumped gently—first the two in
the rear, then the one under the nose—onto the ground,
where it felt like we were going even faster than we'd been
flying. We slowed and then stopped before I'd anticipated
we would, although that was a good thing, since the grass
strip we'd landed upon was not overlong.

And then we were climbing out of the plane. I thought
about how good it was that I was *at least* am'r-nafsh,
since otherwise I would have felt horribly cramped after
almost eight hours in that tiny space. More important to my
am'r-nafsh self were the fresh and very vigorous breezes, all
tingly with sea salt.

I belatedly noticed two dark, boxy shapes of vehicles,
both 4x4 types, and a smaller dark shape that detached
itself from one of the cars and went around turning off the

landing lights. Once Araceli had switched off the engine of her plane and flipped a switch to turn off its lights, I watched with a thrill of discomfort as the lights down the strip were doused one by one.

# CHAPTER TEN

Sandu had climbed out of the plane and stood beside me, watching the lights going out up the strip toward us. I heard Araceli moving behind us, getting the bags out of the storage compartment of the plane. She said something low to Sandu that I couldn't make out with the wind whipping around us and I turned to him to ask what was going on.

He was now wearing a well-worn duster of black waxed oilskin. Since I was behind him, I could see that his preferred shorter sword, a curved falcata, was hidden behind the curl of the long skirt of the duster.

We had brought both longer swords and shorter ones with us to South America, but Sandu had suggested last night that we'd likely only want the shorter ones where we were going. We had left the specialized luggage at Lope's, and I'd just tucked Terry Smatchet into my backpack.

I hadn't even *thought* about getting Terry out as we exited the plane, or about traveling with him on me. Now I didn't stand a chance of grabbing him in a subtle enough manner.

In painful truth, by myself I probably couldn't win a fight against a real am'r. I was still in the raw beginner stages of learning. I could slow enemies down, though, and I could defend myself for a little while without being disarmed. That had to count for *something*, but it didn't feel good enough, not right now.

The lights that had been crucial for landing were not needed for am'r eyes in the moon- and starlight, but my am'r-nafsh eyes could not quite make out his features. The direction of the wild breeze changed precipitously, and I realized I had *smelled him* before. Suddenly his face flashed into my mind, and I knew what Araceli had said to Sandu.

"Apolinar." Sandu said it flatly, just as I was thinking it, loud enough to carry over the wind to him.

"*Señor* Solin, *mi amiga* Araceli, and the lovely Noosh. I am here to escort you to shelter and refreshment." This was more than he had said to me back when he was picking up Bagamil, and I realized how heavily his sibilants were lisped.

"Are you?" Sandu wondered. "The same way you *escorted* my patar?"

"*Señor*, let me explain. Monserrate and Julio had plans they did not share with me. I was as surprised as you when the Aojysht went missing. I did not come down with them. Araceli will confirm this."

Sandu looked at her and she nodded, one sharp jerk of her chin. "There was no room for him on the plane."

Apolinar continued. His words were softly confident, but he clearly chose them with care. "I was not part of their plan. I swear this to you. I would never work against you or your patar."

"*Of course* you would not, Apollinaris. How long have we known each other? Since before you left the Old World to help colonize this new one. I remember your lace ruff and paned trunk hose."

Apolinar laughed. Was it forced? "Different times, old friend! Fashion is much less dramatic in this era. I miss such fripperies, but getting dressed is easier at sundown."

"Since you are a *loyal* old friend, perhaps you can answer some questions for me. Why did you not tell me of Julio and Monserrate's plans when you collected my patar from the remains of his home?"

"I told you, I did not know of them. They confided nothing to me." Apolinar's voice was determinedly steady.

"And you know not where they are now? You are not, in fact, going to take us to an ambush?"

"I do not like how you speak to me, *old friend*. If you distrust me, you may find some other method of transportation, one that feels safer to such a *cautious* man as you seem to have become."

"*Cautious?*" Sandu laughed, a sound that surprised me and obviously Apolinar as well. "Are you attempting to anger me by calling me a coward, my old friend? Perhaps you remember the old me too well. Yes, you might have manipulated Vlad that way. Sandu, however, has learned a few things over the years."

"Of course I was not! You misunderstand me!"

Sandu's falcata sung out low and fast. One moment, Apolinar was standing there talking to him, the next, he was missing a leg mid-thigh. He'd managed to pull out a gun in that time, and the clap of his missed shot echoed off the hills that reared up around our strip of land. The loud noise was less shocking than the sudden separation of Apolinar and his leg. He fell over, almost in slow motion. Araceli flashed around behind him. The minute he hit the ground she procured the pistol almost gently.

There had been one great spurt of blood as the leg fell away, then the flow of blood almost magically reduced. I could still see that initial spurt replaying in my mind's eye, however, and the smell of the blood was intoxicating.

Sandu moved around above him, sword tip pointing at him as he spoke. "Anything to add now, old friend? Perhaps the truth?"

"Vlad! This is all a mistake! I truly am your friend, your ally!" Apolinar pressed up on one arm, raising his other to Sandu imploringly. I could almost hear the blood pumping from his leg, and the smell of it was so distracting that I could not focus.

"Then tell me where Julio and Monserrate are holding him."

"I do not know! I swear!"

Sandu's sword sliced out again, and Apolinar's right arm was removed above the bicep. I couldn't take my eyes off of the blood. After this new wound fountained out a powerful spurt, Apolinar gathered the stump tightly in his other hand. Blood oozed through his fingers, and I could smell the heat of it in the cool air.

"That is not good enough, *old friend*. I know how frequently you were in conference with them before they left. I know you are allied with them. You *do* know me of old. Tell me what you know or you can have a taste of my old *skills*."

Apolinar looked to the side angrily. After a moment, he brought up his chin and met Sandu's eyes. "If I tell you what I know, you will heal me and allow me to serve you?"

"No. I would never trust you, but I promise you a clean death. Old friend."

"That is not good enough."

"The other option is for me to remember a few things I learned from the Ottomans. Those wounds will begin closing soon enough, even without the comfort of vhoon-vaa. I *could* remove your other arm and leg, throw what is left of you in the back of this vehicle you have so thoughtfully provided, and take us off to find a private location where you and I can begin our trip down Memory Lane. There are things I have not done to a body in *so* long. How quickly the old urges return." He paused dramatically to contemplate them. "Back then, I could keep a kee alive for an astonishingly extended period of time. Just imagine, with your am'r body, what things I could do over the months, the years. Why, I do not see why it would not be worth trying for *decades*."

This conversation probably should have been upsetting to me, but I was impacted by Apolinar's bleeding as I never had been by blood before. I kept staring at the drips oozing from around the fingers clutching his arm stump. My body very clearly told me that I needed to get over there and get my mouth around it, feel the hot blood gushing into my mouth again and again. Some small kee part of my brain was screaming in horror at this idea, so I stayed frozen. Useless—but at least not doing anything stupid.

"You do not have the time for this!" Apolinar was now speaking in a screechy near-scream. "The Aojysht is imperiled; every minute endangers him further!"

"It has been worth my while so far," Sandu replied coldly. "You have just admitted your complicity with my enemies, and I've only had to remove two of your limbs."

"I-I have not! I only meant, your patar is in danger, yet you waste time attacking your allies. You have not changed, Impaler!"

Sandu smiled. I saw it and it knocked me out of my blood-stupor. It was not an expression I'd seen on his face before, not even when he'd fought his oldest enemy. It was cold—not just heartless but actively cruel. It scared the hell out of me. Had he been lying to me all this time when he said he was a changed man? Had I been lying to myself by believing him?

"Oh, I have changed, Apollinaris. I have learned things from love that make me far more dangerous than the man you thought you knew. But you, little man who fancies himself an avatar of a god, little wannabe godling, *you* are the same stupid, self-involved creature who has stayed alive by running away from any real danger. You have loved none more than yourself, and you have learned none of love's harsh lessons in all this time.

"But this time you did not run away fast enough, old friend. You believed the lies of your confederates and thought I was no longer a true threat, *nu-i aşa*? Did they tell you I was weak, bringing my little am'r-nafsh everywhere with me? Maybe they said—Araceli, how would you say?—it's not a nice way to say a woman is in control of a man?"

Araceli snorted. "*Ella lo tiene con el látigo. O ella lo tiene debajo de su bota.*"

"*Sí, eso, gracias.*" Sandu continued, "So maybe you believed that, or else after the challenge by Mehmet, you felt this was a time when my people and I would be weak, and you could take advantage of that? Go on, old friend, deny that is the case. Use your words to flee."

The blood had stopped dripping out of Apolinar's arm as Sandu taunted him; the crazy am'r healing had begun already. I did not know if am'r were like starfish and could regrow limbs, but even if they could, it wasn't going to happen immediately. Apolinar could probably still kill a weaker creature, but unless he got a big ol' blood donation, he was reasonably helpless in the hands of two am'r. Well, and me.

Apolinar's jaw clenched in rage; Sandu had known just what buttons to press. "You all think you are so much stronger, so much smarter! But after I have the vhoon-anghyaa of the Aojysht-of-aojyshtaish, I will show you *power!* You were lucky to get him as your patar, but it was just *chance!* It could have been me! It *should* have been me! You were just the demented ruler of an insignificant land, grubby savages scratching your fleas in your crude halls.

"Never did such coarseness touch me! I was clad in silks from birth, and drank from gold goblets while you played with wooden spikes. You do not deserve the precious vhoon that rushes through your peasant veins. Our kind has been misruled by you and the besotted fool who keeps you by his side. I will end this centuries-long mistake, and once our vhoon-anghyaa is equal, you will bow to the better man."

Apolinar had started with strident exclamations but ended on a bitter and determined almost-whisper. He wasn't scary. I almost felt bad for him. Well, not really. I was ready for this to be over, though.

"Is that what they told you, old friend?" Dispassionate pity filled Sandu's face and voice. "That you would help drain the vhoon-Aojysht? Old friend, be glad I will give you that honest death I have promised you—for from them you would have received only betrayal and humiliation. Never a drop of the vhoon you've longed to taste."

The light died in Apolinar's eyes. When he replied, I had to strain to hear him. "I have already suffered that humiliation."

"Will you tell me where to go, that I may wreak vengeance upon those who would treat you so—your enemies and mine?"

Apolinar paused, and I could almost see him preparing another argument to join forces with us and fight together. Then he sighed and seemed to shrink in upon himself.

"There is a GPS in the vehicle. It is programmed in there."

"And Monserrate. What do you know of your other companion in this venture?"

"Him? He is a strange one. He did not speak much to me. He swore his help to Julio, as I did, for his right to the vhoon-Aojysht. I tried to get his story, but he would not speak to me. He *spurned* me."

"Tell me about Julio's other allies. How many are there? How many are of strong vhoon-anghyaa? Is Orélie-Antoine de Tounens one of them?"

Apolinar opened his mouth like he was going to pour it all out, then paused. His eyes hardened. "I will give you nothing more. We were never *friends*." He spat the last word.

Sandu sighed. Without turning his head, he addressed Araceli. "Have you vhoon-taken recently?"

"I have. And while I normally do not disdain any chance to strengthen myself, I find I have no taste for that vhoon of his."

*I do!* some primal part of me screamed. The rest of me was disgusted with myself; I kept my mouth shut.

"Your neck, Apollinaris," Sandu said, firmly but not coldly.

The pathetic figure sat up more and hunched over, letting his head fall forward. I could not decide if I was impressed by the courtly ideal from a former age or disgusted by his just giving in. All our enemies before this had fought with every atom of their being to the bitter end. Although it had caused me a great deal of pain and suffering, at the moment I felt respect for it, and commonality with them. *I* would never go out like this. I would scream and struggle until I was all-the-way-dead, even if I looked foolish doing so. It was less contemptible than slouching over and passively awaiting your death.

Sandu judged the awkward angle and used a two-handed blow, full-strength. I knew from experience that chopping off heads was harder than it looked in the movies.

Araceli got a container of gas from the back of her car. I carried our luggage over, finally doing a useful thing. I got out Terry Smatchett belatedly like a blankie of comfort.

Am'r burn quickly. It's like something about them is extra-flammable. As we drove away, the flames were already extinguished, and there was just a smoking charred heap, smaller than you'd expect.

# CHAPTER ELEVEN

Araceli came with us, both because she needed to get fuel for her plane and because I think she was enjoying the adventure. Most of the am'r I'd met were ready to drop everything and go off on a kill-the-enemies-holiday at a moment's notice. Also, there was undoubtedly cachet in going on a kill-the-enemies-holiday with the Am'r Formerly Known as Vlad.

Why couldn't I have hooked up with some anonymous am'r? There was nothing fun about being the equivalent of a rockstar's girl.

Araceli explained that phone service down here could be spotty, so GPS was still a thing. There were a few addresses programmed into the car's GPS system. The landing strip was *"pista de aterrizaje."* There were a few others, which Araceli said were local town centers or places to get supplies. One was simply "nacho."

If it were me, I would have confusedly assumed that am'r, who did not normally consume food, made an understandable exception for a good plate of nachos.

But Araceli saw it go by in the list of saved locations and put out her hand to stop Sandu from scrolling past. It's a big deal when am'r who are not lovers cross the wide barrier of personal space to make physical contact—well, except for killing each other, but that's another sort of intimacy, isn't it?—so I found myself watching with bated breath.

"Nacho. *Nacho! Señor*, I think this is what you are looking for."

"Why is that, Araceli?"

"Well, this will seem very disrespectful, but 'Nacho' is a nickname for Ignacio."

A pause. "You are correct. 'Nacho' may be a common nickname, but to use it for the Aojysht-of-aojyshtaish is clearly disrespectful. However, this is the information we needed. We will deal with the other aspects of it later." He jabbed his finger at the word "nacho." Araceli, who was in the driver's seat, took us off into the navy-gray pre-dawn that was softening the sky, which I'd already learned to see as a warning to get away from the oncoming headache of day.

Am'r are good planners when it comes to getting out of the sun's baleful rays. We did not drive right into a completely unknown situation. There was a battered little farmstead about an hour from the airstrip, the kind of place you wouldn't look at twice. The am'r left such nondescript hidey-holes for themselves wherever they went and thought they might need to go again.

"I keep a stash of avgas here for the plane, and when that gets low, it's not far to the airport from here. I also," she looked shyly at me, "keep supplies of kee food."

I blushed. I needed food less and less since I'd had Bagamil's blood, and could probably go for a week now without eating if Sandu and I were exchanging blood regularly. Still, it was probably best to take in as much fuel as I could before we did...well, whatever the hell we were about to do.

Every breeze brought this amazingly refreshing cocktail of sea air and soft humidity; it was like being able to breathe water. At this remote place, I could smell the scents of earth and plants as well. The house was surrounded by conifers and what looked like beech trees, except not any kind of beech I'd seen before. Smaller trees grew around the house, with leaves like laurel. If I were still kee, I'd have shivered with the cold in the air, but the am'r part of me made it all just deliciously cool. If the sun hadn't been sending the pastel shades of sunrise through the sky, I would have wanted to go for a walk to smell the air. And to try to process the recent...*intensity* with Apolinar.

I'd once had a yoga teacher who told me, "It's not pain you're feeling, it's intensity." It did help my practice to think of it that way. Now, I was applying it to living in the am'r world, where people around me were getting their necks snapped and then being drained to death, or getting chopped into pieces before being flambéed.

*What I'm experiencing is not trauma from all the violence, it's* intensity. *That's it.*

But the sun was coming up, and while I carried my trusty shades everywhere with me these days, they only did so much to resolve the throbbing migraine that was daytime.

So we all went to bed. The ground floor of the house would not have impressed a burglar. Maybe a squatter would have liked it, but it was not furnished or in any other way optimized for kee comfort.

Well, there was a bathroom with a shower, which was nice, and an actual flush toilet.

One day I won't need those, but today, I used it with grateful embarrassment.

Once we went through the hidden door to the base-ment, however, there were a number of small bedrooms, very comfortable and well-appointed, and a main area with table and chairs: a mini-lounge for am'r and their guests as they traveled in rustic but not uncomfortable am'r style.

From a closet, Araceli displayed for me a really unex-citing collection of non-perishable food items—the usual dried-fruit-and-nut mix, some energy bars, and two types of jerky.

"Jerky is from South America, you know," she explained, holding up the leathery strips. "In the Quechua language, it was *ch'arki*. This is cow meat, and this is llama, from a local farmer."

"Oh. Um, thanks."

"There is also Coca-Cola."

"Isn't there, just, water?"

"The faucet in the bathroom works. I am not sure how good the water is. Or there is a small stream behind the house. Most kee here drink Coke, I believe."

"Ah. Thank you, Araceli."

"I am sorry. I do not have an am'r-nafsh right now, so I don't really have a need to think of these matters very often."

"That is...fine. Thank you."

I forced myself to eat trail mix and some jerky—I couldn't tell which was cow and which was llama, honestly—and drink some tap water. I didn't bother to do a search on my phone to see if I could safely drink the water down here. I asked Sandu and he looked at me with an eyebrow raised and asked me if I could get drunk anymore, which was answer enough.

I was relieved that no one was going to suggest a threesome. As much as I admired her, found her attractive, and simply *liked* Araceli, what I really wanted was alone time with my patar.

It was a tiny room with a "double" bed, so close-cuddling was our only option anyway.

Since we hadn't talked on the drive about the million things crowding through my brain, I ignored his erection pressing into my left buttock and rolled to face him.

"So. Mehmet. Apolinar. How many enemies do you have who are jealous of your position with your patar, and who are going to kidnap someone close to you, and then rant at you and plan to kill you? Is this a pattern I should look out for?"

Sandu sighed deeply. I often made him sigh, especially when I wanted to ask questions instead of having sex.

"*Ei bine, dragă* Noosh, when you put it the way you do, *da*, it is a pattern you will see again. Power attracts people in both the kee world and the am'r one. With the am'r, power comes from the vhoon-anghyaa. As with rich and powerful families in the world you are used to, among the am'r, some bloodlines count for more. A strong vhoon-anghyaa bestows more strength, faster healing, or other greater skills of our kind. And the longer we live, the stronger we get, and the more, *ei bine*, *potent* our vhoon becomes.

"The vhoon you receive from me is strong, coming from the lineage of Bagamil, but what you accepted from him was far, far stronger because it came directly from his body, which has survived through more centuries than you can imagine, growing more powerful all the while."

"So, am'r blood is like fine wine?"

"It is not the worst comparison, *prostuțo*. Besides wanting to love you, he wanted to give you a gift that would help keep you safe until you could pass through the vistarascha, and keep being a gift once you were am'r."

I tried blinking away tears, but more came. "It just seemed like, I dunno, joy and love at the time."

"And it was, *sufleţel!* But there was more thought to it than just jumping each other's bums."

"Um...jumping each other's *bones* is the phrase."

"It is a stupid phrase. I like your bum. I like to jump it."

"Not now! I want to know what the stuff Apolinar told you means. And...I don't know, I could really use talking about the things you said to Apolinar when you were being all Vlad-y, but I guess there isn't time for that."

"Not unless we stay up all day. What we should do is give each other strength and then rest."

"It's *convenient* for you that recharging each other's batteries involves sex."

"I will not deny it. I am very happy to be am'r; I have never desired any other life since Bagamil came into mine."

He nuzzled me, but I pulled away again, frustrated. "How can they have tricked him, taken him, when he is so strong? Couldn't he have fought them off? He's hurt—you know he is. They are keeping him scared and helpless! And they are calling him 'Nacho,' for fuck's sake!"

Sandu sobered, and I saw a hint of coldness in his eyes that I flinched from.

*I must always remember that no matter how angry I feel, he has depths of anger I do not want to see.*

"They will not live long enough to regret their lack of respect. You would say it will be the 'old me' who will make them pay for their insolence, but I will not waste the time on drawn-out vengeance. One thing I have learned, it is better to spend time on the good things, such as building our life together, training you to be the strongest am'r-nafsh the world has seen, and helping you create the archive for our kind. To punish them as they deserve would be a waste of my time, so I will just kill them.

"Ages ago, I thought I could show my enemies that they dare not rise against me. The things I did were to prove to the world how strong I was, how brutal. I was not strong. It was—how you say?—a trick of war, an illusion...ah, camouflage! I did not have enough men to protect my country, so I had to pretend my ruthlessness would be enough and hope they 'bought it.'"

"Fake it 'til you make it."

"*Da*. That is the phrase. But I no longer need this. I am strong. I defeated Mehmet and his followers. I will defeat these enemies. My deluded foes can send wave upon wave at me, and *they* will break. I do not need games now. I shall just destroy them all."

This conversation was not going quite as I'd hoped. "But, um, to use your metaphor, the beach the waves break upon gets worn away over time. It's called 'erosion.' It's not a thing you want happening to you. I don't want it happening to us. Will there be endless waves of enemies coming at us forever?"

"*Ei bine*, I have said it wrong. It is easier to say these things in Romanian. When you learn it better, I will be able to share my ideas more easily with you.

"What I mean is, the feats I did as Voivode of Wallachia did not work as I hoped. My reign was too brief, and I did not succeed. Now my strength is real, not an illusion. I will be completely honest with you: there will always be someone who wants to take power from my patar and me.

We have triumphed against them in the past, and the more often we do, it is the building of the strength I wished to display when I was kee—and now, as am'r, I have built *real* strength. You saw how many years it took Mehmet to feel he had a plan that could succeed against me. The stronger we show ourselves to be, the longer we will have between the foolish attacks upon us."

I wished that were comforting. Something felt wrong about his logic, but I was just a librarian from Small Town, USA. What I knew about power struggles came from books and television, and the only things I knew about the am'r world I'd experienced in the last almost-a-year of my life.

So maybe Sandu was right and everything would be fine, and we'd only be putting down rebellions every, what, century? Half-century or so?

He'd said he would make me strong. "The strongest am'r-nafsh the world has seen?" I asked him, focusing on the potentially good.

"With Bagamil's vhoon-anghyaa and mine. With the good vhoon of Neplach as well, and with training and education. You will build half your curriculum as you study our archives. There has never been an am'r-nafsh such as you will become, and once you rise from the vistarascha, there will not be another am'r like you. You shall be glorious to behold."

He tried again to get my mind off talking. "You are already glorious to *hold, draga mea.*"

I pushed his hands off my breasts. "If you can't explain your concepts in English, you're not allowed to do puns in English. It's for skilled practitioners only. And we can stop talking soon, I promise. Just tell me about my gharpatar. How did they *get* him?"

"We will not know for certain until after we have restored him to his rightful place at our head, but the dreams we've had indicate he was drugged with maadak. You remember, that was what was used when Mehmet's people took me. There is no way to know if you drink from a maadakyo; a kee who has been given that drug. It does not show in their behavior or change their scent."

"But how can it be so debilitating for powerful am'r like Bagamil and you?"

"I am hopeful that with your archive of am'r history, the scientifically-minded among us can find solutions for such matters, which have long been of grave concern. *What?*"

"I'm sorry. You can't talk about the am'r and call anything 'grave.' I will giggle every time. Please continue."

"*Ce să fac cu tine?* You do not prioritize the most vital exchange of sustenance, or make time for love—yet when I do as you demand, you laugh at me." He sighed deeply, but the corner of his mouth was twitching, undermining his long-suffering countenance.

"Wait! I think I understood that. '*Ce*' is 'what,' right? '*Să fac*' is 'to do'—I know that! Is '*cu tine*' 'with you'? You said, 'What to do with you?'"

"In English, it would be phrased 'What am I going to do with you?' But *da*, I was wondering that, as you torment me."

"What you are going to do is finish explaining how Bagamil was caught, and then," I said slowly, running a finger down between his pectoralis muscles, "you are going to make love to me with all the skill you have."

Sandu gave me a look that was very much "Challenge accepted." I worried for a moment that I'd overplayed things and he'd jump right to the latter part of my demand.

"Very well. I will finish...and then I will start. Maadak ingested by a kee has no obvious effect on them, but once in the maadakyo, it crosses easily into the vhoon, and that admixture, drunk by an am'r, causes loss of consciousness, and upon return to awareness, severe confusion and hallucination, pain, and a variety of discomforts like vertigo—"

"Wait! I've gone through that! When Bat Bitch kidnapped me. I just thought it was some kind of poison. It's terrible. And...and *that* makes sense. That's why the nightmares were strangely familiar, because I *did* know what he was experiencing. It was just so confusing."

"I have no doubt that she used maadak-infused vhoon on you. I had not heard of it being used on an am'r-nafsh before—"

"Because nobody else brings their precious snacks around with them."

"Would you prefer I left you at home?" Sandu sounded dangerously close to putting me on a plane back to Romania. Well, probably *after* sex.

"I-I don't know. No. Sitting at home and wondering what's happening would be worse than being in danger. And they kidnapped me from *home* last time. I'm not sure I'm safe even there."

"*I* am sure you would be easier to protect there. We do not normally have a significant number of my enemies in my stronghold, as we did when you were 'kidnapped.' *Ei bine*...but you *are* here, and I am content to have you under my protection since Dragoș is not there to protect you, either."

He pulled his head back a little to meet my eyes better. "Do you understand now how Ignacio was taken, despite his strength and wisdom of the ages?"

"Now I've realized *that's* what I was seeing in his own nightmares, his being constantly dosed with maadak, yeah, I get it. I get it all too well."

"Then we can attend to my demonstrating for you 'all the skills I have.'"

# Chapter Twelve

The next evening we got up right at sunset, but Araceli asked if we could hold off on leaving for the "nacho" destination; she needed to get more fuel for the car.

"I want to join you in the search for the Aojysht. I would not miss this for anything. And I checked in with Lope; he feels it would make up for some of the lack of hospitality you have experienced so far. It is a four-hour drive to the location. I must fill the tank. In the meantime, you are welcome to examine the specialized clothes and equipment we have here. That location is at the base of some mountains. I do not doubt there will be further for us to go past the point the car can take us."

She left to run her errands, and we looked through climbing gear stuffed into a large closet in the main basement area.

Araceli and I were thankfully the same size in shoes—in hiking boots, that is—and although she was curvier than I, her hiking clothes fit well enough.

We didn't need the cold-weather gear the way a kee would, but Sandu advised we—and especially me—dress for the cold. "If the vhoon does not have to work so hard, we will not need to renew our sustenance as often."

The hiking clothes that fit him were at least five decades out of date, but I thought he looked adorable in an old plaid flannel shirt under something like quick-drying overalls with a big zipper in the bib that he called "*salopettes.*"

"Will we need, I don't know, rope and carabiners and stuff?"

"Are you an experienced rock climber, *draga mea*?"

"Well, no. I've never done it."

"Then carabiners would not help us much." He pulled a vintage wool military sweater over his head, and I made a face at him while he was blindfolded by it.

"Being am'r doesn't give you the ability to spider up walls, like in the Book That Shall Remain Nameless?"

He stiffened, then sighed—the long-suffering patar.

"I told you, I was not even in the country when Stoker wrote that ridiculous and unfortunate work that references my legend. And as I cannot turn into smoke or a cloud of bats, neither can I slither backward up a wall, ignoring the laws of gravity."

"You seem to ignore lots of other laws. I don't have any proof you *can't* turn into those things. Just your word."

"*Ei bine*, I should think that by now, that would be enough. But you can see me in a mirror, *da*? Sunlight does not burn me up?"

"Well, sunlight makes me want to die, so that's close enough. Sorry, beloved, I think I'm nervous about what comes next. Where are we going?"

"Araceli has shown me a map of the location. You were using the, ah, bathroom." He saw the look of misery on my face and hurried on. "It is in the mountains. After a certain point, the road will become unpassable for a vehicle, and we must walk after that, but this is a place that, while it is not easy to access, is not like climbing Mount Everest. There will be a way to hike to it, although it will be easier for an am'r than a kee, of that I am certain."

"But *I'll* be able to do it? I won't get in the way?"

"You are not a kee, and you are not even a normal am'r-nafsh, *sufleţel*. And Araceli and I will give you any assistance you require."

Finally, we were kitted out for hiking. And armed. Sandu had his falcata. I had Terry Smatchet on my right hip—and my puffer jacket didn't cover it, so I could even reach it easily! We had matches and a lighter each, like a belt-and-suspender thing, and a thin bottle of lighter fluid. I had water in an old metal canteen, and more jerky, and energy bars shoved in a cargo pocket. There was even a small pocket inside my cargo pants, where I had slid Sa'mah, my little obsidian blade, like a good luck charm.

I wasn't used to wearing bulky clothing anymore, but that was less making me antsy than the fact that I knew we would eventually fight our enemies...but only after a four-hour drive and a who-knew-how-long-a-hike into the mountains. Sigh. I was nervous, but also wanted to just get on with it already.

Happily, Araceli returned and kept me from suggesting to Sandu that we take off the too-warm clothing and go back to bed, just to take the edge off. *She* had obviously taken the edge off. Now I understood her errand; she was not just getting fuel for the car. Her skin almost glowed, her eyes glittered, and there was something undefinably arousing about the pure sense of health she exuded. I was suddenly regretful the threesome thing had never been suggested. Maybe after this was all over, Sandu might want to make up for that?

The 4x4 was filled up, with extra fuel containers in the back, and Araceli had brought me a to-go box of something that smelled amazing. "*Pichanga caliente*," she giggled as she handed it to me in the back seat. "Basically, a 'hot mess'!" And it was: a hot delicious mess of fries under chopped spiced meat and fried onions and other veggies, topped with fried eggs. The evening air was cold, but the food was still pretty hot, and at that moment, it seemed like I'd never eaten anything better in my life. Glancing into the rearview mirror, Araceli watched me eat as if she was half-jealous and half-grossed-out. I didn't care if it was the latter since she had brought me this amazing fare. I had to stop myself from licking the aluminum container at the end.

We drove. We drove up, always up. At this time of night, spring wasn't very much in evidence. We seemed to cross lots of water along the way and at first there were lots of trees. Toward the end of the drive, the trees became stubby and wind-gnarled and rare. Even the middle of the desert did not feel as wild and forlorn as this place, with the mountains rearing up darkly around us, blotting out the stars with stark, roughly-hewn peaks.

Despite the am'r blood in me, I found myself glad of the hat and gloves when we got out of the car. The empty *pichanga* container still scented the car, and I found myself tugged toward the comfortable kee world as the doors closed on it. Ahead was desolation and enemies.

We climbed paths the rest of the night. At the base of the mountain, it didn't seem like a mountain or even a real trail, just a long bit of ground without even scrub growing on it, curving upward slowly.

We left the car at midnight. Five hours later, we were still climbing. We'd left our phones in the car since they were useless to us where we were going. Sandu had sent all the information we had to Dragoș and Lope before we left the house. Lope wished us good hunting. Dragoș replied that he was currently in London and would join us soon with some friends to enliven the party.

The GPS came with us in a backpack Araceli carried. She also strapped on an eighteen-inch camp knife, its black powder-coated handle sticking out of a molded sheath with nylon straps.

I wasn't tired or really cold, but five hours of climbing a questionable trail into unfamiliar and daunting mountains had left me in a mood. I wasn't stumbling like a kee would've been, since my am'r-nafsh eyes could see pretty damn well in the starlit darkness. Really, I'd have loved it if we'd been able to lie down, cuddle, and look up at the most amazing array of stars I'd ever seen. Even with mountains rearing up around us, blocking too many glorious points of light, the sky that was left was full of blazing constellations that were completely new to me. Those stars sent down plenty of light for my new eyes. Everything was in grayscale, but I could see fine detail. It wasn't because I was tripping over my own feet that I felt insufferably cranky.

It was the tedium. I'd already figured out that the rockstar life of being the partner of a world-famous jet-setting vampire was filled with unexpected tediousness, whether it was eight-hour flights or sitting around in confinement after being abducted. There are times when your adrenal glands just burn out, and you are left feeling a restless anomie of body and soul. I'd gotten too worked up, and I could feel that Sandu and Araceli were on high alert, and that made me stay semi-jacked up, too. Then hours of trudging uphill with no one to fight had worn me down. Added to that was the tediousness of picking my way through areas of loose rocks, ranging from about the size of my feet (perfect to trip over, or slip away under your step) to boulders (perfect for enemies to be hiding behind).

*The sound of my feet sending scree skittering downhill will give me nightmares for years after this. I'm gonna need so much therapy.*

I dreaded what we would find when we got where we were going, but I needed to get through the getting-there part of things. So I put one foot in front of the other, tried not to break my ankle or make too much noise, grumbled to myself...and panicked at every gust of wind. Of which there were many.

As we went higher, the wind became wilder. A few times, I thought it would blow me right back downhill. I had to force myself to walk against it, lean into it.

And *then* it began to rain. It turned out this moment *could* be more miserable than tedious. The am'r ahead of me didn't care if they were wet and cold; they just kept going, as if being a blood-drinker made them waterproof. Am'r-nafsh? Turns out we're *not* waterproof, and the wind blew the rain almost sideways, right into my face. There was no escape from it. I huddled into my jacket, pulled the cords on the side of the hood as tight as they would go, and trudged on.

And then it began to hail. *Hail!*

About the time I'd decided that I was in some sort of Dantean hell-punishment of eternally climbing a mountain through wind and rain and *actual hail* while being equally worn down from an unceasing freak-out about imagined enemies behind every rock, Sandu signaled silently to Araceli and me. I looked where he indicated and saw nothing.

Sandu slipped *into* the unexceptional rock wall. I realized I was dealing with yet another camouflaged am'r entrance. I thought bitter thoughts about rock-gnawing, endlessly-tunneling am'r and followed Araceli into the unknown.

Except it *was* known. It was another damned cave. I would have happily never gone into another dank cave in some godforsaken part of the world again, but here we were. This was a small example of cavedom; we could have only fit about two more people in with us before needing to move into the even more uninviting tunnel awaiting us at the other end.

Sandu motioned us back outside and gathered us close to him. He subvocalized, "I will take point. Noosh, after me. Then Araceli, please. I doubt we are anticipated, but keep on alert. If we meet anyone, damage them first and ask questions later."

Sandu adjusted his belt and sheath to ensure his falcata was close to his hand. Araceli took her blade out of the sheath; the powder coat made it invisible in the darkness, except for the very edge. Once she took hers out, I decided I'd do the same, since mine were the slowest reflexes of all of us. Sandu would have his blade out of its sheath before I knew we were in trouble. Terry Smatchet was matte too, except for the shine along the one fully sharpened edge and from tip to halfway on the other side. I watched the edges catch the starlight, numb with the panic I was refusing to let myself feel.

In we went, single-file down the tunnel. Why did I have to pick a supernatural group who spends all their time in small, enclosed spaces? Why couldn't it have been were-wolves, fighting in a lovely clearing in the forest under the full moon? Or witches, doing aerial broomstick fighter tactics out in the wide-open night sky? Why must I always be heading with dread into claustrophobic tunnels teeming with bad guys?

We went along with no openings or splitting of the path into more options for a timeless time. I knew from experience that once you entered small tunnels, your sense of time got all messed up, and what felt like five hours could be only fifteen minutes, and vice versa.

At least I was going in with Sandu and Araceli this time, instead of surrounded by enemies who were ready to kill me at the slightest misstep. It was a distinct improvement, and I told myself I should focus on that.

Obviously it was pitch-black, or it would have been for a kee. Sandu and Araceli seemed to get along just fine. I could see enough not to trip too often, although I had to squint if I wanted to make out finer details. Darkness was different with am'r blood in your veins. It didn't feel scary or impenetrable anymore. My rods and cones were obviously mutated forever, but not in a way I understood.

Understanding am'r night vision might come from future studies by am'r optometrists, although it wasn't the highest priority on my "List of things to figure out about the am'r." I *could* make a list of scientists and doctors we needed to bring into the am'r world, though. Or maybe am'r lives were so long that I could just assign various of our allies to become a specialist in this or that branch of science? I focused on this nice distraction. We'd need anthropologists, microbiologists, biochemists, and probably molecular biologists, as well as lots of physiologists and dedicated computational biologists. We'd need hematologists who could see their profession as a whole different field of study. And we definitely needed psychiatrists—a personal one for me, to start.

The rock around us changed; I noticed despite the lack of light and my internal rambles. At the outside of the cave, there had been smooth gray rocks, which we'd been climbing through for hours. This dramatically changed to rough, darker rocks with jagged edges on the top of the tunnel. The outer tunnel was smooth, like it was shaped by water. Or maybe by centuries of am'r traffic. Water must have played some part because we constantly splashed through puddles and occasionally came across gushing underground streams, which could be forded by climbing up footholds on the walls and making a long stretch of leg over to the wall on the other side. In places it dripped on us, and the walls were coated with the mineral artwork of thousands of trickling years. The air ceased smelling of the ocean and offered instead a different wetness in which you could almost name elements from the periodic table: iron, copper, zinc. I was profoundly glad my borrowed hiking boots were waterproof.

We came to what at first seemed to be an underground waterfall but turned out to also be a branching of tunnels. We could go right (wet), or left (wetter). Sandu and Araceli moved into each, sniffed, paused, then sniffed again. I didn't bother because, yet again, my pathetic am'r-nafsh senses wouldn't give them any useful additional information.

Sandu gestured to go left. We reformed our line and went left. The water we waded through was now over the top of my waterproof boots, so my wool socks were soon squelching in freezing misery at each step.

Then the water went away, and slowly the passages we moved through began to seem less damply-cold, although rougher and more jagged-edged. My feet were still miserable, and if I were still kee, I'd have refused to go on until I got a change of socks.

Openings happened more frequently after that, at least without having to wade. We followed Sandu's nose until we reached a sort of junction.

We'd been moving through a passage that was oval with a flat bottom. Abruptly, the walls and floor ahead of us turned into a Dali-esque mess. The floor had obviously liquefied and reformed in a way not conducive to forward travel over it. The walls had partially melted down to meet the floor, and we had to negotiate our way both across the treacherous floor and around inconvenient protuberances.

That took all our attention until an even more dramatic development made Sandu harshly intake his breath. We had come out to intersect a larger tunnel that was roughly triangular, and the floor...stopped. Ceased to be. Was just a rough black chasm down into eternity.

Araceli and Sandu investigated while I, honestly, just held on to a jagged lump of melted half-wall, half-floor and gaped at the hole in front of my feet. I couldn't imagine how we were going to get across what had to be at least thirty feet of abyss.

Araceli made a *hsst* noise, and Sandu moved to see what she'd found. It was a piton driven into the wall on one side of our passage. He examined it and pointed to a matching one, then they both peered across the gap. I followed Sandu's pointing finger to a rope bridge tied up on the far side.

*Visitors Not Welcome*, an imaginary sign read.

"So," I muttered, "we won't need carabiners and rope, huh?"

"We will not, *draga mea*, but give me a moment to plan our advance."

We were not given a moment.

"*Bonjour, mes amis! Désarmez-vous, s'il vous plaît!* If any of you do not speak the glorious French language, I just told you to disarm yourselves. We outnumber you five to one. It's not worth the damage you will take if you resist. Throw your weapons into the pit there. Do it now."

So much for sneaking into the bad guys' lair.

Our heads had spun around. After hours climbing through the stillness of stone with only the dripping or underfoot splashing of water for sound, the resounding command was a real shock.

Sandu and Araceli sniffed. I sniffed too. I could, now that I was looking for it—sniffing for it?—vaguely discern the am'r behind us. I would have felt better that Sandu and Araceli had totally missed picking up on it—not just my inferior am'r-nafsh nose—except that it would've been much better if we *hadn't* been caught by surprise.

"Monserrate!" Sandu growled. "Is that your patar? I would meet him. I have questions for you both."

"*Hola*, Dracula," came another voice, and I recognized Monserrate. "Just toss your arms into that hole there, and we can all have a nice chat."

"That will not happen," Sandu assured him.

"It might change your mind to know that we are wielding guns. Do you have firearms, or does your traditionally hidebound mindset leave you armed only with swords?"

I glanced at Sandu, and for the first time, I wondered why he never carried guns. Right about now, that seemed like a wonderful idea.

"I do not need a gun to deal with the likes of you, stripling. I can slice your hand off before you pull the trigger."

"I think not in this situation. Too many rocks to climb over on the way." Monserrate sounded smug. Sandu's face changed not at all, but I could tell the truth of the statement deeply angered him.

The first voice again, the one with the thick French accent. "*Mon seigneur* Țepeș, you are too experienced in the arts of war to think yourself in a good position to resist us. Merely make a show of good faith, however, and we can discuss collaborating against our common foe."

Startlement crossed Sandu's face before he mastered it again. Since I was thinking, *What the holy hell is this?* I could not blame him.

"You…wish to…join forces?"

"Why not? It would be an honor to fight beside the Dragon of Romania."

Araceli had been what could only be called fidgeting, not something I'd ever seen in an am'r. Sandu turned to her and she subvocalized, "He is lying."

He replied in the softest undertone, "Indeed." They both looked at the gaping chasm. "Can you make it?"

"Lope's vhoon-anghyaa has been good to me. You just worry about your dear frithaputhra, *señor*."

"I will go across with her first." He turned his head back to the unknown number of enemies behind us and spoke loudly. "If we are to be friends, why must we disarm ourselves?"

"We are not *yet* friends," came the reply. "We have plenty of weaponry with us to rearm you. If and when. Just show good faith now, and we can talk. I have much information to share with you, and tools for crossing that obstacle ahead of you. Once we come to an understanding, my men will arm you from their own sides."

Araceli murmured urgently, "With all respect, *señor*, let me go first. You will have your hands full. I am the better choice as scout."

Sandu inclined his head to her. "*Como quieras, chica fuerte.* Lope chose well in you."

"Let me discuss this with my people," Sandu called.

He took my hand and pulled me close to him.

"What's going on?" I hissed.

"The leap is not too great for am'r," he murmured. "But there is the concern of...this is a strange term in English. Is 'booby trap' correct?"

"Oh. Shit. Booby traps?"

"*Shhhh.*" He spoke low in my ear. "When we jump across, we have only a small area on which to land. It is a perfect location for traps. We have both been watching out for them, keeping all our senses alert for such things, but now, we cannot ascertain in advance what traps there may be. It is too far. One must go and find out the hard way."

Well, shit. I didn't like any part of that. Firstly, I hadn't even thought of looking for booby traps. I'd been walking around like an ignorant booby, and only their vigilance had protected me. There was so much I just didn't see coming, didn't know, or even consider. Sure, thinking of this stuff was something I'd get with experience, but until then, I hated being the weakest link all the damn time.

*They could have mentioned to me that we were looking for traps.* That was just silly petulance. It probably didn't occur to them that I wouldn't immediately start looking for them, or they quite rightly assumed their superior senses would pick up any danger long before mine did.

*Of course, I don't think they were expecting* extra *bad guys coming up behind us, either.*

Speaking of extra bad guys, Monserrate chose this moment to call mockingly, "The great Dracula must consult with his underlings before making decisions? Will your little sweet-vhoon am'r-nafsh tell you what to do?"

Sandu did not look as pissed off as I expected. He paused as if to consider Monserrate's words, then slowly replied, "As I am certain you know, I am not here only with my frithaputhra, but with one of Lope's get. While she is my junior, she has the wisdom of strong vhoon-anghyaa in her veins and years of experience that are not invalid."

As Sandu strung out his reply, I stopped listening because Araceli took up all my attention. She walked back and forth a few times from the edge to where we waited, obviously concentrating. She finally stopped, relaxed every muscle, and took some breaths, then momentum overtook her whole body. Her arms and legs pumped twice in a stiff way, and then she took off. It was not the normal *zip* of too-rapid-for-the-eye am'r movement, but it was like watching a sped-up recording of someone running. My heart was in my throat. By the time she reached the edge her limbs were blurred, still running in the air after she took off across the chasm. Her body shifted fluidly in flight, until her legs and arms curved in a graceful arc behind her. In the next moment, she curled her limbs forward so her knees were at her chest, her hands pulled in tight, and she landed perfectly with just the lightest *thump* as her feet hit the rough rock floor on the other side, a good foot and half from the edge. Her arms circled out to counterbalance, and she straightened up and turned to look back to us, a proud grin on her face.

After that, it all went too fast for me to follow. Araceli was there—and then she was not—and many little horizontal blurs followed. There were *schhhh-whoomp* sounds as huge spikes shot out of the wall and landed with heavy quivering impacts deep in the stone of the other wall.

There was perfect silence as Sandu and I looked at the suddenly spiked wall, trying to make out if Araceli was pinned to it. She was not. She waited for a minute, and then carefully raised herself from where she was flat on the floor. Her grin this time was a bit less steady.

She inspected the spikes, more than ten of them, and called softly to us, "They are metal. Very impressive."

"I am sure they are, but you are more impressive, fritha-puthra-of-Lope."

From behind us, the French-accented voice came again, tinged with anger, "What is this? What games are you playing?"

"*Votre Majesté Orélie,*" Sandu replied without obvious mockery in his tone, although I could see it clearly on his face. "I'm afraid we do not need your generous offer of help to cross this precipice. If you will but give us a moment, we will move out of your way, and you may continue unimpeded about your business."

Araceli had been inspecting the area around her. She called back in a low, urgent voice, "I see no obvious mechanisms for this trap. I cannot promise it has not been fully triggered."

"I will deal," Sandu called back to her. "For now, take yourself quickly out of range. Do not cease paying attention."

She laughed lightly. "It's not likely I will be able to *stop* being at high attention for some time to come!" then took off, zero-to-blur, down the tunnel. No more spikes went flying.

We could hear the murmur of whispered arguments behind us. It seemed Orélie the Self-Anointed didn't have a choice; his underlings wanted a say in decisions, too. *Hah.*

Sandu pulled me into his arms and breathed into my ear, "*Sufleţel*, this will not be fun for you. I must do the same as Araceli, only carrying you."

"What? Can you do that?"

"*Hssssh*. Of course I can. Did you think I would leave you behind?"

"No, but that doesn't mean you can do that jumping thing while carrying me."

"I can do far more complex things, *micuţo*. I am more powerful than you perhaps realize. However, the reception we will receive when we land is unknown."

"Oh, I see."

"I will need you not to fight me. You must move with whatever I do without pausing to think, like leaning into the curve on a motorcycle."

"I've never ridden a motorcycle."

"Just trust me, *dragă* Noosh. Trust me with your whole body, like when we make love."

"'Like when we make love.' *Sure.*"

"I will put you over my shoulders now. Please relax."

I wasn't sure how I was expected to relax in this situation, but I forced my muscles to slacken as he pulled my right arm up and around his neck. He bent forward and wrapped his arm around my right knee. Then he squatted and adjusted my body along his shoulders until I was an equally distributed weight.

Only once did I try to help the process. "Relax, please," he told me very patiently, and I forced my body to go limp and my mind not to feel like the worst partner, who definitely should have been left back home so she didn't just get in the way all the time.

"Whatever you are doing, Ţepeş, cease!" Orélie's voice came to us, filled with royal imperative. Sandu ignored it, being used to both ordering and ignoring royal imperatives his whole life as both kee and am'r. "You will drop your weapons and come to me now. Bring your am'r-nafsh. You will both be treated with respect."

"Relax, please," Sandu told me again.

*How the fuck am I supposed to do that?*

We could both hear the Bad Guys moving up through the rocky obstacle course behind us. "Stop! Put her down!" Monserrate barked at us, taking the lead like a good second-in-command.

I then got to experience Sandu preparing for the jump much as Araceli did, but this time I was not viewing but *feeling* his body mechanics as they happened under me. I knew the exact moment he was ready to start running, and I couldn't help but panic as his speed increased. Despite a grip on me that I was sure would leave bruises, I bounced against him in a way I was certain must throw off his rhythm and doom us both.

The sound of the first shot punched into my eardrums. It fragmented the pumice wall where we had been a second before.

Then I felt the powerful lunge as he sprang into the air and my body was forced hard against his shoulders. Sheer terror kept me from getting enough air in my lungs, or I would have screamed the whole way.

Bullets accompanied us as we flew across the chasm. Happily, it's pretty hard to hit moving targets.

He landed and I bounced painfully on him. He didn't even grunt, just raised up his knees all too slowly, and then equally slowly, his fingers lessened their bruising grip as he processed that he was indeed perfectly balanced, and that no horrifying spikes were going to come shooting out of the wall. He waited a bit longer, horribly patient, with bullets still whizzing past us and sending out pumice shrapnel when they struck the walls.

All I could do was try to remember how to breathe.

Centuries later, he bent forward and gently let me down from the carry. I was now appropriately malleable since I was basically in shock. I was quite proud of myself for not having voided my bladder. As my feet touched the ground, I made a concerted effort not to let my knees fold under me. I didn't want to be the only one of us to *not* stick the landing.

I had a moment to be back upright on my pride and my own two feet again. There was a pause in the shooting from behind us, and I could hear voices raised in anger. I was reaching into my brain for something witty to say to Sandu to cover my intense freaking out about this whole situation when his face changed. He grabbed me precipitously and threw me to Araceli.

*Schhhhh...whoomp*
*Schhhhh...whoomp*
*Schhhhh...whoomp*

There were about the same number of spikes as last time, but this time, two had hit home. I found myself pinned to the wall.

I looked down. There was one in the right side of my tummy, and one pinioning my left thigh at a painfully awkward angle against the stone. The spikes were at least three inches across at the wide end, which of course was the end I could see. Blood hadn't even started seeping out around them yet.

I couldn't breathe. *Do my lungs go down that low?* No, of course they didn't; I was probably having a panic attack. I had thought I was in shock a moment ago. *No,* this *is shock. Remember real shock? We've been here before.*

The wonderful thing about real shock is that pain doesn't hurt as much. Yet. I had this faraway idea that I was in terrible pain, agony I didn't even have words for. I did really want to lie down, but obviously that wasn't going to happen for a while.

I couldn't look away from the spikes sticking out of me. I could hear Sandu and Araceli investigating me. "This one is probably in her liver, maybe the...*no sé la palabra, la 'vesícula biliar?'"*

*"Ah, vezica biliara? Ei bine,* I think it is 'gallbladder.'"

I couldn't help them. I didn't know where a gallbladder lived.

"This one is probably a problem. She will need vhoon-vaa the minute it comes out."

"I was thinking *before.* Would you be willing to pull them out when I tell you?"

*"Por supuesto, señor."*

Those words had some impact—impact, hah!—on me. I looked up at Sandu and tried to smile. "So, I guess we've proved that stakes don't dust am'r. At least am'r-nafsh, am-I-right?"

He smiled too warmly at me. "That myth was a wooden stake through the heart, *draga mea*, which I am glad we are not dealing with right now, since even though you would not turn to dust, it would not be fun."

"So what's about to happen is going to be *fun*, huh?"

"Well, there is one part you will enjoy, *micuțul meu însetat de sânge*."

"I know that last word! That one means 'blood.'"

"Indeed, it does, and I will give you some right now."

"OK. That should be a nice distraction."

"I hope so." He was distracted too, though, and started talking with Araceli in Spanish, or Romanian, or a combination of both. I didn't pay attention because I was looking at the spikes again. The blood was seeping out around them now, and it was hard to focus on anything else with that taking up my whole universe.

Sandu brought me back by taking my face in his hand and saying my name urgently. "You need to know that we will take out the point in your torso first, and I will hold you up. Then Araceli will take out the one in your leg, and we will lower you. You must not try to help us. Do not even *think* about it. I will be vhoon-feeding you the whole time, so focus only on that."

"Hey! I got *impaled*, and it wasn't even by *you*! That seems really wrong. So impersonal."

"Anushka! Here, drink!"

I managed to remind him, "Call me Noosh…!" before he ripped open his wrist and shoved it against my mouth. Then his blood was hot and salt-iron in my mouth, and I was swallowing. It was almost enough to distract me from the moment when the spike was pulled from my side. Araceli couldn't be particularly gentle because she had to pull hard to unseat it from the stone in which it was embedded. While it was a very smooth spike, I felt my broken bones and torn muscles catching on it, almost grabbing at it as she pulled it back out.

Whole new levels of pain shot out into every part of my consciousness. Sandu shoved his wrist harder against my lips to remind me to keep swallowing his good blood. Yes, *the blood*. I convulsively guzzled, holding onto the taste of him like a lifeline. I knew this blood; it had flowed into my mouth many times, mingling with pleasure. And pain—but the pain I enjoyed in those moments was not *this* kind of pain, and I could not eroticize these sensations. Once the spike was gone, the place where it had been hurt far, far worse. *Keep drinking. Focus on how the blood feels sliding down your throat. Isn't it wonderful? Don't think about the other things.*

The leg was not as bad, but then it was worse. I mean, even the "not as bad" part wasn't very *good*. I could tell it hadn't hit my femur because I didn't feel her pulling the spike out through bone this time, but in missing the bone, it had hit the femoral artery, and maybe some other important part of my circulatory system. I knew this because once she had tugged the horrible thing loose, I could feel the blood spurting out of my leg with the regularity of my heartbeat.

It's not a nice sensation.

Once the second spike was out, things moved fast. I was lying on the ground before I knew it. Araceli applied pressure to my thigh until Sandu pulled away his wrist, with me reaching pathetically after it...*no, no, don't take my lifeline away*. He reopened the wound with his teeth and then let the blood pour into my thigh wound.

I was still angrily thinking what a waste it was to pour the good blood down *there*, where there was already too much blood, when it could be *soothing me*—when I realized the terrible life-draining throbbing in my thigh had been reduced to mere blinding pain.

*Am'r and their bloody first aid*, I thought giddily but did not protest as Sandu applied his blood to the wound in my side. I was happy to be lying down. Nowhere had ever felt so perfectly comfortable as this tunnel floor. I let my strangely heavy eyelids close and listened to Araceli and Sandu whisper over me.

"They will be across any second."

"No. They will try. You stay with Noosh."

"I would prefer to fight at your side, *señor*."

"There is no room for us both to fight effectively here."

"*Entiendo*," Araceli said, and under her breath, "*Mierda*."

Sandu snorted. "Calm yourself. Still much more fighting for us all."

The first of the Self-Anointed's followers tried the jump. He landed much closer to the edge than Araceli or Sandu had done. Sandu had only to step forward and thrust out his falcata, and when the am'r shifted to avoid the blade—the way he was carrying his gun, he couldn't block it—his balance failed him. He grunted in surprise and fell backwards into the gap. He never even screamed, but we did hear when he eventually found the bottom.

It was a pretty long way down.

Orélie's followers started shooting again, but Araceli and I were far enough around the curve of the tunnel to be safe. Sandu, as far as I could tell, was dancing between the bullets. He mocked them in Spanish, occasionally getting excited enough to switch into Romanian without realizing it. He seemed to be inviting them to put their guns away and come over and fight it out like real am'r.

After a while of this, Orélie apparently got some control over his followers. The gunshots ceased, although we could plainly hear that one am'r had to be pistol-whipped or otherwise beaten, to get him to obey orders.

Sandu stood at the edge after that, straining his ears. After a while, he came back to us. "They know a way around. They are going to go that way and loop back to trap us here."

"She cannot move yet."

"You will remain with her? I must go ahead and scout the way. I want to know what other traps await us while I can respond to them without concern, and I hope to find a good bottleneck to engage them in."

"*Entiendo, señor.*"

"Frithaputhra-of-Lope, you are an exceptional woman, even for one of his vhoon-anghyaa. You will follow when *she* can?"

"We will wait for healing and then come to you in the most careful way."

"I hope to have resolved most things by the time you arrive, but I will try to leave some fun for you, *dragă* Araceli."

"I can ask nothing more, *mi señor.*"

And at that point, I went away for a little while to a place of soft and gentle darkness.

Coming back to my body wasn't an enjoyable experience. Once I was fully conscious and up to date with my most recent memories, I decided it'd been one of my worst ideas ever. I squeezed my eyelids more tightly shut in the hope that I could pass out again.

"*Bueno*, Noosh, you are awake. How do you feel?"

I opened my eyes. Araceli's face was nice to see, despite everything.

"Ugh. I think I'm supposed to say something stoic here."

"It is just you and me. No need to pretend anything."

"Oh, good. I'm too tired to come up with anything. It really hurts."

"That is no surprise. You are healing faster than a kee would. Healing hurts."

I thought about that for a minute. "But not as fast as an am'r, or I'd be healed already. I've seen it."

"*¡Así es!* Your body as it is now has some limitations. It simply cannot repair itself so quickly."

"I hate being am'r-nafsh." I sighed as deeply as the hole in my side would allow.

Araceli looked at me. I could not read the look. "Well, I am not sure I would have made the choices your patar has made. However, many a new am'r has come out of her grave ignorant of the full dangers of our world, knowing only the stories her patar told her. Most am'r do not survive their first year or so. They offend a stronger am'r or make some other stupid mistake. You will not be an ignorant am'r when you rise from the vistarascha."

"Huh. Well, that's nice."

"I made dressings for your wounds while you were passed out."

I looked down. Sandu's plaid shirt had been ripped into strips, which were now wrapped neatly around my thigh and my torso. They were, of course, already saturated at the wound sites, but the bloodstains did not seem to be growing bigger.

"Um, thanks. I'm sorry to be such a nuisance. You probably haven't had to do that kind of thing in years. Um, I hope my blood wasn't, like, a tease or something…"

Araceli's eyes sparkled, but she managed to turn a huge yelp of laughter into a controlled snort. "You know how *exquisito* your vhoon smells to me. I *did* have to clean my hands after I tended your wounds. "

She held up her hands. They were squeaky clean.

"So good you licked the plate clean, huh?"

"*Oh, sí, claro. Eso es bueno.*" She sighed and shuddered a little. "So do not feel you have been a nuisance to me. Your patar will not be sharing your *dulce sangre* with many am'r. Staying with you, he knew I would get your blood on me, that I would taste your blood. He honored me by assuming I could control myself and bring you safely to him with the rest of your blood still pumping through your veins, not filling my belly."

"Ah."

"To that end, if you think you can try it, I would like to catch up with him. But slowly. I think that if we go slowly, you will heal as you go."

Having my bones regrowing and my muscles re-knitting as I walked sounded like such fun. Oh, and my liver re-squidging itself back together—and maybe my gallbladder, too.

"I guess this is the part where I pretend to be stoic."

"*Sí.*"

I sat up. Well, Araceli sort of pushed me up from behind, and I didn't fight it. Since I didn't pass out again at the sitting-up stage, she got behind me and did a mix of pulling me up while at the same time supporting me with her body. If it hadn't been intensely painful, I would have been aroused by her firm curves pressing against me. However, I realized once I was standing that the pain did not spread out through all of time and space, but was localized to the places where the huge spikes had poked their way through my body. That was probably a good sign.

We lurched down the corridor the way Sandu had gone. I caught a faint whiff of his scent, and that filled me with such longing to be by his side that I found new determination for the idea of "healing on the go." Araceli had my left arm draped about her neck. That she was a little bit shorter than me meant it was a nice fit. We stepped in time, starting very slowly as I got used to the concept. We got up to a decent walking speed as the minutes passed.

We didn't talk as we went. I still wanted to ask Araceli so many questions, to simply chat with her as it was so easy to do. But we were wandering around an enemy stronghold, so focusing on potential sounds or scents of enemies was a better idea than casually chatting. Also, my body would have preferred for me to lie still and let it finish healing. Feeling your muscles rebuilding themselves as you walked with them was an excitingly different kind of pain, the kind that screamed, "Why are you being so stupid?"

But Araceli was right. She and I had waited there as long as we could, and longer than we should. It would have been better to never have separated from Sandu, and the best thing I could do was grit my teeth and go as fast as my wounded body would let me.

Or maybe...maybe Sandu was relieved that I was out of the way? Maybe I was such a burden to him that he'd sped off with relief to take care of things before he had to go back to babysitting me?

Well, that *could* be true. I forced myself to allow it to stay in my thoughts objectively while trying not to hold onto the sting of it. If it *was* true, it was a good thing I was injured since it gave him the breathing room to get business taken care of. But we should still hustle to him, because there was one way I knew for certain I could be useful; if he had taken injury, my blood would heal him faster than any other's.

*Once you die, this will all be over.* Unlike kee suicidal ideation, this was merely practical. But it was not less deeply wounding. And speaking as someone who had just been stuck through with huge spikes, I had a new standard for "deeply wounding."

As a kee woman, I could expect to be valued by society for my looks, for my sexual availability, or for my ability to make a home and raise kids. I'd avoided some of that by being a very single librarian who was primarily valued by people who were trying to find the book they wanted, but that did not mean that the larger societal shit didn't impact me.

As an am'r, I had witnessed that women were far more equal. I'd only seen women treated as lesser by one particular am'r who'd been keeping them in a kind of harem, and *he* was batshit-crazy.

And the asshole was dead—all the way dead. So one less misogynist to deal with.

But I wasn't an am'r yet, and as an am'r-nafsh, I was more *chattel* than most kee women ever experienced. Sandu was very good about training me for my future and had given me a job where my intelligence and skill were valued, and for a while, that had distracted me. But everything that happened recently had forced me to see that I was stuck in a place where I was primarily valued for my blood. That was worse than just being valued for my looks.

I wanted to talk about all of this with Araceli. I wanted another woman to give me insight, something that would help me deal with this situation. And if there were no gems of wisdom for me, still, laughing ironically together about how much it sucked would have been good, too.

But all I could do was walk through pain both physical and psychological, stretch my ears and nose for bad guys, and my eyes for booby traps.

As my brain spiraled through these emotions, we'd made our way past various tunnel-branchings, through changes in the composition of rock through which they curved, and varying levels of dampness. Sandu's scent led us on, a rope of connection I could almost *see*.

I was so focused on that scent that when, unexpectedly, there were other odors, I was confused for a moment. We stumbled out into a naturally formed cavern with stalagmites and stalactites—the full underground décor package. A small waterfall washed down to our right, the splashing of the water making me realize how silent my world had been during this unmeasured time.

And how tranquil. It had not felt tranquil, my thoughts being so unquiet, until the outside world rose up to match that trouble.

I had barely begun to take in the new surroundings when six strange am'r encircled us. They seemed to appear out of nowhere, at least to me.

I looked around at them. They were dressed in hiking clothes, as we were. Only a tendency to have bought all-black gear and a certain luminosity of their skin, a certain air of being a predator, made it clear we hadn't just been surrounded by particularly trendy mountain climbers. I could tell by the scent that none of them were kee.

Another detail that caught my eye was the random assorted bladed weapons that were unsheathed and ready in their hands. All lengths of long knife and short sword were represented, from modern tactical knives to vintage daggers, some curved, some serrated, all sharp as hell and ready to slice us up.

Were these Orélie the Self-Anointed's followers? Or the minions of Julio Popper, Señor Super-Colonizer: the man who had set up his own self-aggrandizing colony, killing off the local tribes in the process and putting his name on the stamps and coinage.

Wait. It was in the scent! Some of them had a tang to their skins, to the blood just under that skin. I'd smelled it last when we were leaving the cave under the desert. *Julio*. Some of these am'r had been made by Julio.

The next thing I knew, Araceli had somehow swung me around, so I was behind her, back-to-back. Her knife was naked in her hand. I had no idea how, but Terry Smatchet was ready in my hand, too.

The smatchet is really a *nasty* weapon. When it impacts flesh with any strength behind it, it smashes right down to bone. I had not fully comprehended this, because Sandu and Dragoș did not ever let me, you know, hack *into* them; every attack was parried all too easily. I had seen and felt what it did to the wooden pell in the training room, but not how it sliced so easily through skin and muscle, although pulling it out of bone was *slightly* easier than pulling it out of wood. Or maybe I wasn't going as deep. My wounds slowed me, and it only got worse as the fight continued.

Araceli was amazing. All I had to do was feel where she was going and try to stay at her back. She fought all of them off, while I interacted with one at a time. She covered me from every angle while giving me room to get my occasional attack out there.

Soon enough they were ignoring me, even the ones I'd damaged, and started coordinating their attacks on her. I could guard her back, but that was the limit of my training. I had only fought one-on-one in training, and in the only real fight I'd ever been in, it had been Dragoș and me against the Bat Bitch. At least I wasn't holding Araceli back, but the help I could give her was inadequate for our needs. She began to take injuries. I could hear the blows land, and her grunts of pain, could feel each time as she was hit and recovered, smell her blood as it started flowing.

The latter energized our foes, and they came at her harder than ever. This was where I started to really get some good blows in, but they didn't seem to care anymore. Eventually, one am'r took over keeping me engaged, and after that, my smatchet didn't bite into anyone's flesh, just came up sharp against his heavy blade, which was shaped like a carving knife, but a good twenty inches long.

I felt Araceli stumble and fall backward against me. Our combined weight all went onto my wounded leg, and of course it buckled. I was down, Terry Smatchet useless on the floor under my hand. I tried to get my balance back, but pain throbbed through me, and I couldn't do anything except gasp and try not to pass out. The am'r I'd been fighting put his blade against my throat and kicked Terry Smatchet away, then grabbed a handful of my hair and pulled me away from Araceli. I screamed, but the edge of his blade pressed into my skin. I felt the sharp heat of it slicing into me, so I could only follow where he dragged me, gracelessly and completely out of control.

He had rope, and he bound my wrists cruelly behind me, using that as a handle afterward. My wounds were screaming with pain, so he didn't need more than that. He had turned me to work on the knots, so I was able to see what they were doing to Araceli.

They had finally disarmed her, and all five were on her, ripping her clothes open so they could access veins in legs, arms, and neck. As I watched, she slammed the one on her right arm so hard against the floor that, after a nasty cracking sound, he bounced. But he was back on her so fast she didn't have time to use that free arm to her advantage, and he sliced her arm at the shoulder so it became unusable. They started draining her before she was fully immobilized, and it was like watching wolves around a deer they didn't bother to kill before they started eating. It was as savage as anything I'd seen in the am'r world.

I was screaming, and they just let me. They didn't care, and they were making plenty of noise themselves, feral sounds as they gulped the blood as fast as it pumped from where they had cut her open.

Araceli did not make a sound, however. At first, I think she was trying to pull together her energy to break free, but she never got the chance, and after long minutes of losing blood, she no longer had the strength. Eventually I saw her body slump out of its resisting tension; her eyes glazed over.

I'd stopped screaming and was now crying. I'd seen people I loved killed before, and I didn't want to helplessly watch Araceli—my friend, the proud fritha-puthra-of-Lope—be executed. The am'r who held me seemed to be able to sense whenever my body tensed. He'd noticed my bandages, and whenever I even thought about trying to break out of my ropes and get to Araceli, he'd jab a couple fingers deep into the wound in my side. Each time, I would crumple in his arms until the pain subsided a little. Each time, it subsided less.

They had found the lighter and lighter fluid in her cargo pockets. That made them look through mine and confiscate them, and my pocket of snacks. They missed Sa'mah, thank everything, flat as she was against my upper hip in the inner pocket of my cargo pants. They argued briefly in a language I did not understand. I could guess they were considering bringing her body because she would not die just from being drained, and maybe there was some reason for her not to be given the tokhmarenc? But the one arguing this was overruled, and the one who did the overruling had a longer sword. In three sharp hacks, he took her head from her unresisting body.

They doused her body with the lighter fluid and set it alight. After so long in the pitch-dark of the caves, my eyes were shocked by the brightness and I was blind.

All too soon, my vision recovered.

It had caught first in her clothing. Laughing, they watched until the body seemed to catch from within. Then, as if it were a game, they tossed her head onto the blaze. They cheered as her perfect long black hair flamed up.

They left her there, not even finished burning down to ash.

I was pulled along, surrounded on all sides where the tunnel was wide enough; before and behind where it narrowed. They went too fast for my wounds to handle; the bandages were now slick with an increasing bloodstain that spread into my clothing. I could not see because tears blurred my vision, and they shoved me forward whenever I stumbled.

I was crying not from physical pain, but for Araceli.

# CHAPTER THIRTEEN

If being dragged along to meet my captors wasn't much fun, getting there and meeting them was worse. Along the winding route I was shoved, hauled, and cursed at when I stumbled. At some point, I realized I'd stopped smelling Sandu's scent-trail some time ago and that was even more upsetting.

I was finally allowed to fall to the floor in a space that was like a real room. It had a door that was opened to allow us entrance, and inside was furniture, and people using the furniture.

There was something about the room that struck me as different, but for a moment I couldn't figure out what it was. My nose figured it out first: the gentle scent of burning lamp oil. As the light wavered and settled, I realized there was an oil lamp flickering in the air our bodies had caused to move about the room.

Now, I was sure none of the am'r *needed* that light, and I couldn't imagine it had been put there for my viewing comfort, but I'd noticed that the am'r loved having candles or other lights around the place. I'd asked Sandu about it once, and he'd explained that the play of a flame was a pleasure; that without light, you couldn't enjoy the drama of shadows. I thought it was one of those silly things am'r indulged in because what else were former humans with indefinite lifespans going to do? But as my am'r-nafsh eyes were not quite perfect in the dark yet, it benefited me.

I located Julio by his scent before I saw him, and the intense shock of that recognition made my head spin to find him with my eyes. In the center of the room was a Chair of Obvious Importance for Julio to rest his Colonizer Ass in. He was not seated, but had leaned said Colonizer Ass casually upon the chair's arm. He wore a long olive military-cut wool jacket, with brass buttons, and darker trousers that were tucked into calf-high leather boots. He perched there imperiously, looking down at me with his brown eyes. I wondered how I could have ever missed the dangerous intensity of them.

"Yes, I see you have found her," he said in English, and I wondered why he bothered to include me by speaking a language he knew I could understand. I wasn't going to complain, though.

Mister Pushy Minion, who'd shoved me the whole way here, continued in English. "The other is dead. We are all enriched by the vhoon-anghyaa of Lope, who is descendant of Teófila."

"I esteshcinasti that; it is unmistakable. You have made good use of that resource, and the reward was in the doing." Julio turned to me. "I understand you are here to look for your gharpatar."

I was not prepared for this. This Colonizer Asshole had drugged and abducted the one person I loved as much as Sandu in the whole world, uprooting my true family just as we were finally settling in. He'd ordered the death of Araceli, with whom I could have built an ever-deepening connection for endless years to come. She had been family-in-the-making. I didn't have much to say to him that couldn't be said by Terry Smatchet, wherever he was. I itched to feel him in my hand.

*Think. Be smart. Don't let Sandu's violent blood overwhelm you. Be a fucking* librarian, *dammit!*

"Yes. I'm here for Bagamil, please."

"Oh, aren't we supposed to call him *Ignacio*, now? My people call him *Nacho*. It is an amusing nickname." I glared pure hatred but managed to keep my mouth shut.

"You will be brought to him." He said this so offhandedly that I knew it could not be anything beneficial to me. My thoughts moved to Sandu. Where could he have gone? Was he still at liberty, hiding in their caves? What about Orélie and his followers? What if they had injured or even killed him? If not, could he track my scent to Bagamil and rescue us both?

I should not have even thought of Sandu, because Julio seemed to read my mind. "Your patar—you wonder where he is. He left you quite a while ago."

*Fuck this asshole.*

I didn't want to have to ask. I was already on my knees on the floor in front of him, utterly in his power. How much more groveling could a person need?

Since I had nothing nice to say, I just waited. He'd undoubtedly feel compelled to tell me any more bad news he had for me, no matter what I said. In fact, anything I said right now was probably going to be the wrong thing, so letting Señor Super-Colonizer have his monologue moment was my best bet.

We waited for a while. His minions made no bones about sniffing me like I was a steak fresh off the grill. Indeed, with all my open wounds and soaked bandages that was *exactly* what I was to them. After they'd finally gotten bored with that little game, they settled down into comfortable seating or leaning arrangements. Being am'r, they didn't feel physical discomfort as kee did, so they'd not be shifting in impatience. I was the only one who'd have to work at not doing that, and it *was* work because my wounds had started re-healing again from the latest damage inflicted on them. I just wanted to lie down again.

I was so tired of all of this nonsense. Why must Bad Guys be so damn immature? Would it be inappropriate if I took a nap?

"The one they call Sandu will not be coming to join you," he finally condescended to share with me. There was no gloating in his flat tones, but I knew, regardless, that he was deriving enjoyment from the hurtful information he was imparting. "He neglected to take into account that we have inhabited this sanctuary for a very long time, and we are more than prepared for invaders. Your patar is currently at the bottom of an especially deep hole, in water even I would find chilling. Water still runs down the walls it has washed smooth over many ages of this earth. I am interested in seeing how he manages to get himself out of that difficulty. My eyes are on him and have been on all of you since you parked your car. Assuming he is able to free himself from that situation, he will find himself led into many other such traps. Eventually, he will be weak enough that we will take him easily, despite his powerful vhoon-anghyaa.

"That is his future. Yours, you still have some say in. You cannot escape. There will be no rescue, so do not waste your vhoon upon it. Refusal to cooperate will bring the most severe consequences. You will be given a chance to live with and serve your gharpatar as his izchha and servant. You will be reunited with him. That was what you desired; if you show wisdom, you will have your wish."

I considered that. Everyone else sat back impassively and let me think. It was far more pressure than if they had drummed their fingers and jangled their feet impatiently. There seemed to be one big problem with all of that. Well, one *biggest* problem, above all the rest of its problematic whole.

"So, Bagamil and I will just live here with you from now on?"

Julio looked at me for a bit, then graced me with his words. "Yes. Comply, and it will not be intolerable."

That was it. He didn't explain what the laundry schedule would be, when the weekly shopping was done, what our chores would be, or when curfew was. Absolutely no discussion of allowances. It did not bode well for a happy household. I restrained myself from mentioning this.

What I'd ached for, all this time, was for my eyes to rest upon my beloved in the flesh. It was a nasty sort of irony that it was not Sandu and me on our way right now to rescuing Bagamil, but Señor Super-Colonizer and Mister Pushy Minion escorting me to be his fellow captive. The Minion had roughly hacked off my bonds at Julio's command. They were *not* worried about little ol' me being any sort of threat: not in the state I was in, not when they were taking me to Bagamil.

We seemed to be in the heart of the cave system/stronghold. Oil lamps were spaced out along many of the tunnels to keep the areas between from being completely dark, which was how I noticed the classic prehistoric handprints and paintings of stick figures hunting animals, some obviously guanacos or llamas. I only got quick glimpses as I was shoved along, but I did not need to stop and inspect them.

I'd seen them before. Well, not the llama-hunting ones, but ones that followed: the red and black painted swirls and foreboding, hallucinatory shapes. Those were the images that had haunted my dreams back in Romania. And now I was in the nightmare.

I tried to focus on the fact that soon I'd be reunited with my beloved. After a silent march down a side corridor: twisty, unlit, claustrophobic, we came to another door, this one with two guards lounging outside on benches that were cut from the walls to either side of the door. They stood and looked alert as we came up to them.

"What is his state?"

The am'r on the right replied to Julio, "*Señor*, Nacho was given maadak six hours ago. He has not been making any noise. An hour ago, I checked on him; he was not conscious."

"We will go in. Await further orders."

Mister Pushy was already opening a door with a complicated locking mechanism, which included a metal bar longer than the door. There was an actual key involved, which made the whole thing seem, in a way, even more ancient than the cave paintings.

The door swung effortlessly on its hinges. Considering all the water in these caves, that was either a marvel of engineering or someone had gone crazy with WD40.

*Water. Sandu. No, don't think of him. He will be fine. He's fought more impossible odds, even back when he was kee. He'll be along any moment with that rescue. But for now—Oh, my poor cinyaa!*

Once the door had opened far enough, I could see him in the gloom. Bagamil was stripped of clothes and looking strangely small and helpless, bound to a stone table in the center of the room. I shoved my way past Julio and Mister Pushy. They let me, but honestly I didn't care at that moment that I was a lesser creature and wounded to boot; they weren't stopping me.

For a while, they didn't even exist. Once I was at Bagamil's side, he filled my whole world. The glorious scent of him, his blood calling to mine, and the sight of him—even passed out—made my head spin with happiness and relief. After all those nightmares and all this time, some part of me had worried that I'd never see him alive again. I stroked his hair and his face, then pressed my hand to his chest and felt his heart beating.

"Cinyaa!" I kissed my words onto his ear, knowing and not caring that all the bad guys could easily overhear. "Gharpatar. My darling. My lover. I'm right here. I've got you. I'm not going anywhere."

I would have gone on for a quite a while, but Julio interrupted me. Asshole.

"The Aojysht is not as you have known him. He is not often lucid. He dreams, and the dark things he has done for many, many years do not let him rest easily. Sometimes he is nothing but hunger and you must leave him, or he would rip you apart. He has ripped apart a number of kee since he has been here. And one of my frithaputhraish. Even in this state, he is very strong—the strongest of us all.

"Your vhoon is valuable to him. It might help him rest more easily. It will keep him strong. You may tend him and feed him. We will send kee to you as well. If you need something, call out. Abel and Toño are outside for the time being and will open the door."

The door slammed closed behind them, and I was alone with my cinyaa: the one I'd worried about for so long, shared nightmares with, and come across half the world to find. Here he was and I spent an immeasurable time going over him from head to toe looking for injuries—easy, due to his buck-naked state—and talking to him the whole time. I caught him up with Sandu's and my adventures, poured out my every fear and trauma. I asked him a million questions that hung unanswered in the still, dark air.

One of the first things I noticed about him was a scent of...well, more scent than usual. Am'r are usually exceptionally clean creatures. My cinyaa had not been able to care for himself, nor, obviously, had anyone cared for him in that way. His skin was grimy with dirt and stone dust and the residue of old dried blood. Am'r don't sweat and I didn't think they had sebum or shed used skin cells like kee, but still, there was a smell under all the extraneous dirt that was a stale version of Bagamil's normally wonderful personal scent. It was disconcerting.

Holding his hand, I told him all about Araceli and then put my head down on his lifeless shoulder and cried again. He must have met her on the flight down here, but now he would never get to really know her vivacious beauty.

Eventually, I wound down and looked around me. There was still no light source, but my eyes had had plenty of time to dilate. To distract myself, I focused on the walls. There was cave art in here as well. The designs were done in ocher and charcoal; this area was composed of the lighter, smoother gray stone. Mad swirls spun around the room, and once I started looking at them, I regretted it because they made me feel dizzy, almost sick. The art seemed over-bearing, meant to cow and control people. Of course, once I had seen it, ignoring it was not easy. I kept finding myself looking at it until a wave of queasiness would break over me, then I'd force my head away, back to looking at my beloved.

Bagamil didn't rise to consciousness the whole time. He wasn't in the ahstha: he breathed, and I could hear his heartbeat. His face changed expressions like someone stuck in a bad dream.

But I couldn't reach him. I talked normally, I cajoled, I shouted, I cried, I begged. After finding him physically unscathed, I held his hands, stroked his face and arms, and once I even slapped him. Nothing woke him, and nothing smoothed those vertical lines of pain and worry from between his eyebrows.

At some point, I passed out from exhaustion. Somewhere far above us maybe it was daytime? Or perhaps whole days had passed since we came down into this hell. I had no watch or phone, and I wasn't going to knock politely on the door and ask the guards outside, "Hey, what time is it? What's the date?"

None of my actions, none of my words, none of my thoughts did any good. I curled up in a little ball beside my beloved, and I let go of painful consciousness for a while.

# CHAPTER FOURTEEN

The door being unlocked woke me up. It still somehow moved soundlessly on its hinges, but I could feel the movement of the air where there had been no movement before.

I had cuddled around Bagamil in my sleep, my head resting on his long, unbound hair, my arm across his chest, my leg across his lifeless legs, echoing the stupid ropes that rudely bound him. I sat up and found myself shielding him like a protective mother. I reached for Terry Smatchet's sheath, realized it was empty, and missed the heavy, comforting weight of him in my hand.

But they weren't coming to take him. Instead, the room filled with the scents of Minion Abel and Minion Toño…and a kee. A male kee, who was very excited. I heard his babbling before he came into view, a human shape topped by a headlamp that was shining into my eyes.

"I've always known vampires are real! I've tried to tell people, but everyone just laughs at me. The last place I expected to find you guys was down here! I mean, I'm just on a trip with my Spanish group—*¡Hablo español muy bien, sabes!*—and I always assumed I'd meet my first vampire in, you know, New Orleans or Paris or something. I mean, not that vampires can't speak Spanish, because, duh, obviously you guys do. You just don't see that on TV, right? But I mean, this is real, so obviously you can speak any language or be from *anywhere.* Hey, where's that girl you told me you'd introduce me to? I mean, this has been a cool adventure, but I've been walking for a really long time and—"

Minion Abel cut over him. "Just in here; this is the girl. We will leave you with her. Have fun." The eager guy assumed the latter was directed at him, but it was directed, I thought with more than a little sarcasm, at me too. *Asshole minions.*

Minion Toño handed me a small gourd bottle and said in an undertone, "This is the maadak. If you prefer to drink untainted vhoon before you give it to this izchha, it is acceptable, but Nacho must receive his dose. Beware, he is often violent at waking and during frangkhilaat. If you need help, call for it, and we will come."

Minion Abel added, "Oh, and you can have these back." He contemptuously tossed me a handful of items that I recognized mid-air—the snacks they had confiscated earlier. They landed around me mockingly.

*Thanks, Minion Abel. Snacks will obviously fix all my problems.*

They both turned and walked out, then the door closed and I heard the click of the lock.

So, if I didn't call for help, then what? No matter what noises emanated, they'd just let it play out, and eventually come in and see if anyone survived? What if I couldn't scream for help? I'm just fucked? Great.

The guy in front of me was still blinding me with his headlamp. He just stood there, the light cranked up to eleven, checking me out, while I squinted at him and tried to process what the hell was going on here.

After quite a while of him trying to figure out what he was seeing too, he said, "Hey, what the hell is this? You're, like, injured and shit. You're not a sexy vampire babe who wants to party! And what the fuck is up with that old guy tied to a table? I'm not into that BDSM stuff. I just like vampires—not kinky shit!"

I cleared my throat and tried to sound like a fellow victim. I mean, I *was* currently in a victim-like state, no doubt, but not as much as this poor kid. "I think you've been tricked. Me too! I need your help! So does this poor guy behind me here. The people who brought you here are...um...a gang. Yeah, a gang. We need to figure out how to escape. Hey, could you take that headlamp off and put it somewhere we could both use it? It's going right in my eyes..."

"I don't get it. They told me they were taking me to a vampire party. You know, really off the grid. And they said you were a hot vampire who was looking for a special man to be her lover." He just stood there gormlessly and did not remove the stupid forehead-light.

I tried to look sympathetic while still squinting. "Why don't you come over here and sit down with me? We can hang that light off the corner of the table, and then we don't have to look at the naked guy."

That finally worked, and I took his hand and led him around to the left corner at the head of the stone slab, which conveniently was hewn roughly enough to hold up the light-on-a-headband. It dangled right over our heads as we sat on the floor. Now that I could see the guy, he was in shiny new hiking gear, fresh from the sporting goods store. He himself was fresh too: skin oily with youth, the curls in his dark blond hair so styled that even wearing a headlamp on a long hike had barely impacted them. His dark blue eyes were unhappy and confused, the look of a person who had never previously had to deal with serious issues.

He remembered his manners suddenly. "Hey, I'm Brodie! I go to Cal State Long Beach. I'm doing a tour of South America with my Spanish club. We're down in Tierra del Fuego to do some climbing and go to this crazy nightclub over on the coast. Man, that really pushed my Spanish, trying to yell over the music, but South American girls really know how to dance, and they were so into me! I was taking a break to smoke—the bud they have down here is messed up!—and this guy comes up to me, and at first I think he's gay, so I'm like, 'Bro, it's cool, but I'm not into dudes,' but he had a joint that he shared with me—I mean, he pretty much let me smoke the whole thing! Somehow vampires came up, and he explained I'd been right all along: they *do* exist, and he's a vampire, and he said there was this really hot vampire girl, and I was just her type, but of course, she has to hang out in a safe place away from all the normal people, who totally wouldn't understand." He finished with a petulant whine. "But *you're* not a vampire!"

Sitting beside Brodie, the smell of marijuana seeped off of him, almost blanketing the smell of his blood. Pot didn't smell as enjoyable as when I'd been kee. Brodie was also really sweaty, and it permeated his nice new hiking clothes. He repulsed me and I didn't know what to do.

"Stay there and rest for a minute," I instructed him.

"But I'm hungry!"

"What? Oh, here." I picked up the jerky and granola bars from the floor. The simpleton ripped a bar open and started munching it without any questions.

I went to the side of the door that opened and knocked lightly. A minute later, I heard the key being inserted and turned.

"What?" asked Minion Toño.

"Look," I hissed as low as possible so that Brodie wouldn't hear me, "I know you said I could drink him, but in case you haven't smelled, I'm not full am'r. I eat *food*. So, uh, could you bring him and me some food? He's hungry. I could eat, too."

"Bring...food?" The am'r looked blank.

Minion Abel wandered over. "He *is* the food. He doesn't need food, and you don't either. He will be fine 'food' for you. Drain him before or after you give him the maadak, I don't care. Just take care of the Aojysht. That is your job. Your *only* job."

He started to push the door closed. "Wait! I'm serious! I don't drink kee blood! I *need* kee food. And my gharpatar doesn't just kill kee like that, so we will need to feed Brodie, too, until we let him go."

Minion Toño started making this sound that sounded like nails on a chalkboard. Abel's face twitched in a spasm, then went back to being implacable. It finally dawned on me that Toño was *laughing*.

They closed the door in my face. I heard it lock.

*OK, got it. No plans for Brodie to get out of this alive.*

I slowly made my way back to Brodie. I looked down at him. He was napping, his chin on his chest, snoring lightly. He had devoured my selection of bars and jerky and thrown the plastic wrappers on the ground. *Thanks for checking to see if I wanted any before you gobbled it all down, Brodie, you littering idiot.*

I didn't know how to save this stupid kee boy. He didn't deserve to die, but I was now clear that if Bagamil or I didn't drain him, the minions at the door would gladly finish emptying the bottle.

And what about me? I was starving, and my snacks—which would have barely scratched the surface of my hunger anyway—were a digesting lump of protein and carbs in Brodie's belly.

I could not do frangkhilaat: not drink a kee's blood, a human's blood, a *person's* blood. Every drop of blood that had passed my lips had been offered with eager consensuality by far stronger beings. I could never make a full am'r my victim. But by now I was strong enough that I could force a kee, even a male kee. Mehmet having his way with the kee boat captain was a memory that still haunted me. How could I ever be *that*? I was in the world vampiric, yes, but my guys were the Good Guys and they drank responsibly. They would, in the fullness of time, teach me how to respect my kee "dinners" and use them ethically and renewably.

That was what I'd always assumed—to the extent I'd considered it. Really, I'd just thought about all the sexy good-time blood-drinking I'd have with Sandu and Bagamil...and maybe occasionally other partners. I had always been the izchha, the blood-donor, in my fantasies, always in an actively consensual way; never the one with the power.

But from what everyone had told me, when I first rose from the vistarascha, my first meal, the fraheshteshnesh, would be one of uncontrolled appetite. I wouldn't be able to stop myself from killing that poor person who first crossed my path, so I couldn't even lie to myself and say I thought I was *never* going to kill.

Just...not yet. Not even drink a little bit from a real human. *Not yet.*

I didn't even know if the minions were right. How should I know kee blood was even...digestible? Maybe, as an am'r-nafsh, I couldn't even do frangkhilaat?

As I stood there considering this, a strange thing caught the corner of my eye—a flicker in the dark outside the range of the headlamp. My head swung up after it, eyes straining for whatever it could be.

It was Bagamil's big toe. A somewhat callused, bunioned toe; he had clearly spent much of his life barefoot before he became am'r, and even after, I'd rarely seen him in shoes. I knew and loved that ugly toe. It twitched again, then the next toe did as well.

I raced around to his head, leaving Brodie to enjoy his post-prandial nap. My beloved's eyes were still closed, but they were twitching as if he were in full REM.

"Cinyaa! It's me, your cinyaa! Your *granddaughter*! Wake up! There's so much I need to tell you! Please, wake up!"

He was having full-body twitching now, but wasn't conscious quite yet. I didn't know what to do, how to ease his transition from drugged sleep to not just full-consciousness, but also to an awareness that help was here. That he could wake and find *me*, not enemies encircling him.

He groaned, and despite the hoarse scratchiness, I rejoiced to hear his voice for the first time in too long.

The sound had woken Brodie from his beauty sleep. He jumped up and demanded, "What's wrong with that guy, anyway?"

"Uh, he's been having a...bad trip."

*Well, that's not totally a lie.*

"Oooooh. Why didn't you say so? Hey, bro, it's all right! You'll be fine. Just shake it off. You need some water. Hey, get us some water!" He said this to me without turning around. I wondered if he'd hallucinated me in a French maid outfit, holding a serving tray. He kept right on talking to Bagamil like he was a friend coming off a bender. "I know you must be feeling like shit, my dude, but I'll get you through this. You gotta be freezing! Where did you leave your clothes, my man? I can't wait to hear that story! Here—" Brodie pulled off his parka, then took off one of his sweater layers, awkwardly draping Bagamil's genitals. "That's gotta be better. I mean, I don't gotta see your junk, right?" He laughed. "Maybe we should try and sit you up to—I dunno—open up your airways or something? I saw that on TV. Have you vommed at any point? You gotta talk to me, dude!" He turned to me. "Did he vom or anything? What have you done for him? Why is he tied up? This is no time for kinky shit!"

Brodie didn't bother to wait for explanations that I couldn't give him, anyway. "Let me get you untied, bro. Then we'll sit you up and give you some water. You're probably just really dehydrated." He started tugging on the knots on the bright rock climber's cords holding Bagamil down. One thing about Brodie; he knew how to deal with rope.

Bagamil's head turned. His eyes opened, and I recoiled from the predatory sharpness of his look. There was nothing of my beloved there. Only hunger.

Brodie didn't perceive any danger. "Oh, hey, dude! Welcome back! That was some trip you took! I'm not judging, but maybe cool it a bit next time?" He turned to me. "Where's the water?" I think he was honestly surprised I didn't have a couple of water bottles ready and waiting for him.

That was his last emotion. Bagamil's right arm shot up and grabbed the side of his neck. Brodie's eyes went wide, then he was pulled down to Bagamil's mouth. The ungrabbed part of his neck was torn open with a savagery that froze me.

I watched Bagamil chug Brodie the way Brodie had once chugged beer in red plastic cups. He made animal noises as he drank, a growled *mrrrrrrrrrrr* between gulps.

Brodie couldn't take that for very long. He would bleed out sooner rather than later, especially since it was being helped along by intense suction.

This was not who my beloved was. I unfroze and started screaming, smacking his arms and his face. "No! No! Stop that! Let go! *STOP!*"

I think one of my wild blows smacked right into his eye because it distracted him, and he dropped Brodie. I was close enough to grab the shocked boy and slapped one of Brodie's hands over the gushing wound. He sank to the ground like he'd deflated. I had no more time to attend to him, however, because Bagamil was upon me.

He did not seem to know me. He'd grabbed both my arms and was trying to pull me in so he could rip my throat open. *That* was very clear.

"Cinyaa! Stop! It's me, Noosh! Look at me! Smell me! Bagamil! Wake up!"

I was more powerful than I used to be, but he was ferociously strong. Not just am'r-strong, but the strongest of all the am'r. I felt his fingers crushing deep into my skin and muscle, and as I resisted him, I realized how easily he could break my bones. Always before, he'd touched me so gently that I had not fully understood his strength. The corded muscle of his arms and torso was now given true meaning for me. These were not mortal muscles in a breakable body. I could not harm him with my hands unless I did something like poke his eye out—which was not an attractive option. He, on the other hand, would cause me harm unless he concentrated on treating me like fine china. Right now, he did not know who I was nor did he care.

As I tried to pull away from his cruel grip, unignorable pain started shooting from my side and thigh. How often were those fucking wounds going to be reopened? Tears streamed down my face. "Please! I love you! Cinyaa, you love me! Remember, you love me? Remember you and me and Sandu? Remember Sandu—Vlad! You love him. You love me, your Noosh. Remember your cinyaa. Please!"

His head ducked in so fast I didn't see it coming. I yanked my whole self back fast enough that he didn't get deep enough for a vein, but there was a burning ache along my neck as his teeth frayed the epidermis.

He was worrying the wound, wanting more blood from it, and making that terrible mindless noise again, when I felt him check himself. A very long pause followed, then he pulled back, and the eyes that looked into mine had Bagamil back in them. Most of the face under his eyes was smeared with blood, his mustache was drenched, and when he spoke his teeth were coated in it.

"Cinyaa! Your vhoon, cinyaa! What? What is happening? How are you here? Where is my frithaputhra?"

I was crying harder now. "You were stolen from us. You've been kept drugged. Sandu is trapped somewhere. I don't know how we're getting out of this. I'm so sorry! And that boy—" as he was still pinning my arms, I gestured with my head, "is dying."

He glanced at Brodie and immediately lost interest. "You are injured, cinyaa. You must drink from me." He started trying to pull the bandages off my wounds to see underneath. I batted his hands away.

"I'm not dying. *He's* dying!"

Bagamil sighed, then set me on the table and let himself over the edge to check on the collapsed body. I sat there for a moment, collecting my breath and myself.

"Cinyaa, come here." It hurt to climb off the table and squat next to him. Bagamil had his fingers pressed strongly into Brodie's neck at the site of the wound. "He is unconscious. Too much vhoon-loss. He cannot be saved. The only choice right now is which of us will drain him and end his suffering."

"*What?* No, you can save him!"

"By giving him my vhoon? What would that accomplish, cinyaa? Our captors would just kill him. There is no scenario where this boy leaves here alive. Do we give our enemies a kee enhanced with my vhoon, to strengthen themselves in his draining? Or do we strengthen *you* with the last drops from him and improve our chances? Or does he just bleed out his meaningless death upon the ground?"

"I—I don't drink blood. I mean, I only drink yours and Sandu's blood, not kee blood. And you *can't* just write him off like that!"

"He is already dead; you must accept this. You must come to terms with this situation swiftly, frithaputhra-of-my-frithaputhra. I need you working with me if we are ever to get out of here."

*Fuck. So many long days of being useless, and the* one time *I can be an asset and not a handicap, this* is what I have to do?

"But...I've never drunk kee blood."

He was patient with me. "There is no reason you cannot drink vhoon-kee. What is left in him will not make much difference to me. I am full of his vhoon already, and as well have had some mouthfuls of your superior vhoon. You are injured and in need, thus it will go farther for you. Your vhoon would be the best sustenance for me, but I will not drink from you in the condition you are in now. Feed yourself that you may feed me, so we may each be strongest for what is to come."

*Fucking am'r logic.* That made sense, or at least, the way he said it made sense. If I had longer to consider it, I could probably poke holes in it. What I really wanted was to refute his twisted logic and not drain Brodie of his last drops of blood.

*Not, you know, actually kill an innocent person.*

Bagamil stirred impatiently. I reached inside myself for some resolution, for some strength of purpose. There wasn't much there. I let myself down beside Brodie as he slumped, his lifeblood oozing out between Bagamil's fingers.

I tried to find the scent of his blood as arousing as Bagamil's or Sandu's would have been. It wasn't, but it wasn't...well...*un*appetizing either. Bagamil took his fingers away and, telling myself that I was moving quickly to respect Brodie by not letting his blood spill wasted upon the stony floor, I leaned right in. My lips met the warm blood and the warm skin underneath.

He tasted of booze and pot and junk food, and the sweat on his neck mingled rancidly with the blood, but after the first tentative sip, my body told me that yes, *this* was food to me, and I needed it. After that, I drank and drank, and my throat was still moving convulsively when Bagamil gently pulled me away. Brodie's heart had stopped, and I was sucking harder and harder for whatever final drops I could pull from him.

It should have been humiliating. I knew that, but all I could feel was an awakened hunger that had not been fulfilled.

Bagamil was sitting on the floor beside me, and he pulled me into his arms to rest my head on his chest. The only thing in the world I was aware of was blood. Blood on Bagamil, from Brodie and me. Blood on Brodie's neck and sopping shirt. Blood all over me, from my neck down my side, and down my thigh past my knee. Most of the blood on me was mine, but Brodie's blood was mixed in where he had bled on me while I'd tried to slow his bleeding. While I'd tried to save him—although it was another Noosh who'd done that. I was a new Noosh. I was a murderer.

I was a murderer who looked at the blood soaking Brodie's shirt and wondered if I could squeeze it out of the fabric. I was so *hungry*.

Bagamil was kissing my forehead, my cheeks. He rubbed his lips and nose on my face, his eyes trying to catch mine.

I was in a bad state and we both knew it. He was trying to gently pull me out of it.

"*Hungry*," I told him and started crying again.

"Hush, yes, of course you are, cinyaa. It's only natural. You have been through so much. You need more nourishment to heal. I will give you some vhoon now, and you will feel much better. Yes, yes, *hushhhhh*."

Bagamil's long hair had fallen around me, like a curtain protecting me from all the things I didn't want to deal with. He let go of me with his left arm, brought the wrist up inside the sheltering drape of hair, and precisely opened it for me, then held it to me like a mother holding a bottle for her infant.

I tried to show restraint. I tried to drink delicately, to demonstrate how profoundly I appreciated him giving me his blood when he had so few resources and so much need. I focused really hard on that, and I think I mostly succeeded. It kept me from thinking about other things.

All too soon, Bagamil pulled his wrist away. The flow of blood had already slowed. I managed not to reach after it. I *did* feel better, calmer. Not more like myself—because I would never feel like my old self again. But my new self was more in control.

We didn't need to speak. My cinyaa's hair covered my face. It didn't smell as clean as it always had. It smelled of the stone he had lain upon, musty and somewhat bitter. I didn't care. I was still surrounded by him, held safe by him, reunited with him.

The fact that he'd almost mindlessly ripped me to shreds a little while ago was already fading from my mind.

We had not shared blood in a particularly sexy way, but the act of me drinking from him had excited Bagamil. I couldn't help but feel an echoing excitement, since I'd come to associate blood-drinking with sex—the very best sex. The evidence of it was shoving uncomfortably into my left hip, but hungry as we were for each other, it had to stay there. I regretted it, but really, it was enough, and more than enough, just to be in his arms.

We heard the lock in the door click and felt the rush of air as it opened. He stood instantly. So did I because he'd lifted me at the same time and set me on my feet.

He went right into the attack, broke one minion's neck and dropped him right away, but it was not just Abel and Toño anymore. Minions crowded into the small space.

They immediately grabbed *me*, of course. I was the obvious hostage, and Bagamil couldn't defend me against so many at once. I struggled effectively enough against two of them for a little while, but finally my arm was pulled tightly up behind me. I screamed as a hand poked viciously into my side, into the wound that had only just started to re-knit. Again.

My knees gave out, so all my weight was held up by the arm twisted viciously behind me. Between that and my side, the pain incapacitated me.

"Nacho!" Julio drew the word out with pure mockery. "Will you see your sweet little am'r-nafsh torn apart in front of you? How quickly can you kill us all? Fast enough to save her?"

Bagamil froze. His face was impassive in opposition to Julio's hunger for violence. "Very well. What do you wish?"

"You were feeding from the frithaputhra-of-your-frithaputhra when we arrived." Neither Bagamil nor I corrected his misapprehension. "I suppose you were still thirsty. And no surprise! I wish nothing more than for you to drink your fill." With this, Abel brought in another kee, this time a brunette who seemed more likely to be a local than a traveling student. She was dressed in warm, sensible clothing, not the newest outdoor-store fashions. She did not smell of booze or pot, but she seemed strangely calm for a kee who had just walked into a room filled with the naked and bloody Bagamil, the blood-covered me, the obviously dead Brodie, and the minion with the broken neck—who was technically alive but currently lying rather dead-looking on the ground, waiting to be carried away and eventually be given vhoon-vaa.

It couldn't have been a positive-seeming situation to walk in upon, but this gal, who absolutely smelled kee to me, seemed completely unfazed by it. She didn't look around but focused on Julio. She actually followed him with her eyes. Ah, some vampire glamor thing. He'd been a leader when he was kee, and he obviously was even more so, now that he had am'r powers.

"What I wish is simply that you feed from Maite, here. Since you emptied the boy, you will not need to damage her. Just finish your meal."

"And then I will have a nice sleep, yes?" Bagamil said, irony dripping like acid.

"Yes." Julio said this perfectly flatly and finally.

"Except it's not a nice sleep. Have you ever been poisoned with maadak? Why not leave this girl, a mere am'r-nafsh," here he gestured to me, and I could easily enough look weak and unthreatening since I was mostly trying not to cry from the pain of how I was being held, "and me in this prison, lock your door and guard it? You already have us."

"I am not stupid, Nacho. If you are not kept incapacitated, you will make trouble. I do not wish to deal with your escape efforts."

"Why have you gone through so much trouble already? What do you want from me?"

"There is nothing to gain from discussing this with you. Drink from Maite now, or the frithaputhra-of-your-fritha-puthra dies, your vhoon-anghyaa flowing through her going to strengthen everyone but you."

Bagamil met my eyes. In a movie, this would be where I'd cry, "No! I'm not worth it! Don't give in to their demands!"

But I understood that this Maite was a maadakyo, and that when he drank from her, Bagamil would just go back to his nightmare state for another unpleasant period of time. But he'd survive it, and I'd survive it. Well, unless he ripped me apart upon waking. But that was a problem for the future, and it seemed better than the alternative they were offering.

He pulled Maite to him and fed from her in the least erotic way I'd ever seen. Imagine being served really unappetizing airplane food and pushing it around with your fork, but you didn't eat before you got on the plane, and you're landing so late that every restaurant will be closed, so you end up choking it down. My beloved managed to make that very clear, despite being fangs-deep in her neck. It was a fine piece of improv acting, and I was proud of him.

After a few minutes, he staggered back from her. His eyes became unfocused. The minion holding me—whom I'd memorized the smell of, in hopes of personally killing him at some point soon—let me go. I rushed to Bagamil and caught him before he fell.

"Does he *need* to be tied to this stupid-ass table?" I demanded of Julio.

"It is more convenient, and the ropes slow him down when he is awaking. You have apparently already learned that is best for your continued health."

Bagamil was too heavy for me to keep holding him up, so I let him sit heavily on the table. He sort-of deflated down onto it and a couple of minions retied the ropes. I fumed. Another minion collected the gourd of maadak I'd tossed aside and handed it to Julio, who shook it to ascertain it was still full. He'd obviously expected that.

Julio continued imperturbably, "I am disappointed you did not follow my instructions. As you have not, you will have less self-determination going forward.

"Now, you may care for Bagamil until he starts to awaken again. We will bring to you izchhaish, and you will encourage him to drink before he awakens fully. When *you* require frangkhilaat, if you do not want to drink from a maadakyo, you will be given one more chance to drink before dosing the izchha with maadak—but you will ensure that his feeding comes after that. This is your life now. You choose how comfortable you make it."

I bit my lip because nothing good would come of anything I had to say to him at this point. We would stay on Julio's schedule until I was able to think of a way of getting out of it.

# CHAPTER FIFTEEN

After a few moments of my silence, Julio decided that indicated compliance, and exited without a backwards look. He left the work to his minions. They led away Maite (who seemed even more stupefied after the recent blood loss) and one of them tossed Brodie's corpse over a shoulder. Another two more gently carried their broken compatriot.

I climbed up on the stupid stone table and snuggled at Bagamil's side. He would be out for a while, and it was comforting to press my body to his as I waited. Waited and thought.

It was time for me to step up. Obviously, Bagamil was not himself after over five months of being constantly drugged, and I couldn't just wait around for Sandu to ride in like the cavalry. I had supposedly been given the best am'r blood to be had. It had to do *something* for my brain as well as my body. My brain was the most important part of me; the part that could be made superhuman, if anything could.

We had failed this time because it was clear that Bagamil hadn't taken the maadak. What if next time, I radically decreased the dose? No. Better, as soon as I could get him to perceive the world free of the drug's incapacitating influence, if I could convince him to *act* as if he were drugged. Of course, this would all be contingent upon having privacy to do the deed. Argh! We had wasted this opportunity, but I'd never experienced anything like this before. How the hell was I supposed to understand all the factors and plan around them on the fly?

No, I'd *had* time, and I'd wasted a good part of it by napping. This time, I might cuddle up to my beloved, but there would be no rest until I had come up with a complete plan for his next feeding/poisoning. The plan might not survive first contact with the enemy, but at least I would have *tried*.

As the silence settled back in around us, the warmth that had been generated by the blood I'd drunk and all the activity of dealing with Brodie and Julio and random assorted minions seemed to seep out of me into the stone underneath us. This cave was probably no colder than any other underground space I'd ever been in, but I felt as if it were trying to drain my energy, heat, my thoughts and feelings. I didn't dare open my eyes, because the violently swirling art only made things worse. I held tighter to Bagamil's comatose form, pretended I was not scared and overwhelmed and cold, and turned the force of my mind to finding solutions.

I felt him stir restlessly in my arms, and this time I was ready. I'd undone the ropes. My sweet Sa'mah had stayed hidden in that inner pocket last time; all the blood had been drawn by Bagamil's sharp teeth.

I did not want that level of savagery this time. I honestly didn't know if I could stand to be ripped open and go through the pain of healing again right now. I needed to get at my blood quickly, painlessly, and with as little damage as possible.

My little blade was perfect for that, always so sharp it seemed like she could slice through light or air. I had her out and ready in my hand, and I sat up a bit and opened up my wrist just a little, as a starter until I could get him under control.

I could not have waked him with my voice and my words. I could not have roused him by shaking or slapping. But my blood dripping down onto his lips, then sliding between them as he opened his mouth? That did the trick. His tongue flickered out like a snake's, then his arms came up, captured me, and drew my wrist inescapably to his mouth. He gulped and gulped, and I held still and wished the moment were more like when he made love to me, not this mindless feeding—consummation, not consumption.

His eyes flew open, and after a couple more mouthfuls, he was able to draw his head back and look at me with cognizance in them.

"Husssssssh," I subvocalized to him. I didn't want any minions sitting outside the door to hear us. "Cinyaa, this is what we are going to try…"

He listened. He might have argued a time or two, but I made my points as forcefully as I could, for someone speaking softer than a whisper, and I could see from his eyes that he agreed it was worth a try.

Then he kissed me, deeply and lingeringly, as if he could make up for the previous senseless savagery with the passion that was now in his lips. OK, he kinda could.

Then he took my little blade from me, which had once been his. It fit perfectly in his hand. He opened a cut in my neck and sipped from me slowly and gently, with gratitude and appreciation demonstrated by the way his lips moved like little kisses against the wound and his hands soothingly stroked me as he drank.

It's easier to exist for long periods of time in boring confinement when you have am'r blood in you. This was convenient because ever since entering Sandu's world, I kept finding myself in captivity. Of course, just at this moment, there wasn't much blood in me, am'r or otherwise.

When the key eventually clicked, I came out of a timeless somnolent state. I'd like to say I was instantly at the ready for anything, but really, I just forced myself to try to stand up like I was not feeling mostly-drained-of-blood.

On the stupid-ass stone table, Bagamil lay still in the insulting bondage (I'd redone it as best I could, after he finished drinking) like he was out cold. It had to be even harder on him, than me pretending I was perkily chock-full-o-blood. It was the longest he'd gone without being incapacitated by poison for over five months, so I could imagine how much he wanted to rip off those ropes and dispatch every one of his captors. But it wasn't the time. Not yet.

Another kee was shoved in the door. Immediately after, it was slammed closed and locked again. I looked at the skinny boy, who looked way too young to be in this situation. He seemed as passive and unquestioning as Maite had been. Not another Brodie, at least.

But there was no gourd of maadak with him.

I lurched to the door and gathered enough energy to shout, "What is this?"

A new minion I hadn't previously spoken to called, "*Aquí. Él ya está listo. Asegúrate de que Nacho beba esta vez, o te arrepentirás.*" The Spanish flowed past too quickly for me to make out much of it. I knew "*beba*" was "drink," at least.

"But where is the maadak for him?"

There was a pause outside, and then the response came through the door. "*Ya se tomó la droga. Dije que estaba listo.*"

Something already the drug. Then what? Oh. "I said he was ready."

"Wait! Julio said I would get another chance to give the kee the maadak. What about for me?"

"*Perra, la cagaste. Supongo que no tienes oportunidad esta vez. Bebe lo que tienes, o no bebas, no me importa.*"

Again, it was mostly over my head, but I got the point. The poor boy here was already stuffed to the gills with maadak, and he was the only blood on offer.

My plan was already fucked.

I turned to the boy. I could smell his sweaty but still intox-icating kee-blood perfume. I tried, but you just can't smell maadak in blood. The scent was dangerously distracting.

I tried to remember he was a boy, not just a hu-man-shaped container of blood, but all the cells in my body demanded that I replenish them. It was scary how hard it was to force myself to keep seeing him as a person.

"Do you speak English?"

"A little. *Pero*...no we need speak. *¿Beba?* Drink?"

Thank everything, he really *didn't* speak much English.

I gestured to the farthest wall and tried to think of Span-ish words. I was so tired I could barely stand up, so thinking in another language was like lifting too-heavy weights. "*Por favor, ummm, espere—¿espera?—allá. ¿Sí?*"

He looked dubiously at me, but he wandered over and leaned against the wall. He kept his eyes on us, but not with the look of a nervous captive, just a passive subordinate waiting for their next command. Ick.

I leaned over Bagamil, who was still playing at being stoned to the gills on maadak, waiting for my decision. I subvocalized again, happy that kee ears were so dull and that this particular kee couldn't understand English any-way. "So, my plan's already gone tits-up."

"Yes, cinyaa," he breathed back, warm sympathy reaching from him to me.

I just wanted to lie down along with him, close my eyes just for a minute, and let the problem magically resolve itself.

*So. Tired.*

There were two options I could see. One, I drink the poisoned blood and thus be out of commission for however many hours it would take to recover from the maadak. I didn't like that option very much. Two, we simply kill the poor boy, and I would just not drink. There was nowhere to drain the blood, so we'd have to risk them noticing that the lad had not been drained. It was a bad idea. Not only was it unlikely that they wouldn't notice the boy's ful-ly-sanguinated state, but also, I desperately needed to feed. Lethargy made thinking hard. Would knocking myself out with maadak be worse than suffering from blood depriva-tion? My brain tried to swim upstream through the mo-lasses swamp of impossible deliberations.

I had to admit that not wanting to drink the maadak was partially my ego. The point of this whole exercise was to have Bagamil clear-headed and strong and ready to go, when action was called for. It would be *nice* if I were also clear-headed and strong and ready to go—but if I were not, the amount of help I could provide was not so pivotal that the lack of it would ruin everything. It stung terribly to admit that.

Also, the poor boy had to have *someone* drink his blood, so that someone had to be me. It would not surprise Julio or *los miniones* if they came back and I'd tippled of the poisoned blood as well. More than anyone, an am'r understands the urgent need to feed.

I whispered this into Bagamil's ear. He sighed, a bare hint of breath.

"Yes, that is the right action. It is our only choice. I am proud of you, cinyaa. You are strong, fritha-puthra-of-my-frithaputhra."

"Yeah." I sighed too. "But if I'm out of it, how do I make sure the minions come in?"

"That is not likely to be a problem. They will expect either me or both of us to be incapacitated. The subordinates will most likely enter to remove the body. If you are not yet recovered, I can handle them both easily, now that I am free from maadak and made strong with your vhoon."

"Not 'subordinates.' Minions."

"I'm sorry?"

"I call them 'minions.' It makes me feel a little better."

"I shall call them minions as well, then, cinyaa."

We sat together for a second, looking into each other's eyes and just loving each other. I knew it was time to get the show on the road, so I regretfully pulled away. I didn't know when *los miniones* would barge back in to see what was going on, concerned that things were *too quiet*.

I slid off the table and nearly toppled over from vertigo mingled with supreme fatigue, but I held myself steady with one hand on the stone. I didn't dare close my eyes, just focused them on the boy, who was, thank everything, holding utterly still. I was going to ask his name, and then I decided I didn't need to know. At least this one would not die at *my* hands.

I wondered what I looked like to him: a weird, slow woman covered in bloody bandages and clothing permanently crusted with blood? I couldn't smell very nice, even to his dull kee nose. He was so unresponsive to it all that I guessed he'd seen worse. There was no time to ask him his story, how he'd ended up a milch cow—milch kee!—for Señor Super-Colonizer and his minions.

I used sign language to indicate that we'd sit on the floor, leaning against the table. Once I was safely down, I sighed with my whole soul. Not having to hold my body upright was a great relief to my enervated muscles. The boy sat down and looked to me for how I wanted him. I held my arms open and he calmly climbed between my legs, then rested his head on my shoulder, neck conveniently exposed. I felt sick at the way his will had been stripped from him. I had to admit it did make things easier at this moment, however.

I looked down at his neck and the veins showing a mesmerizing purple through his delicate sandy-brown skin. I couldn't help but be aware of his blood ever since he'd entered the room, but now the scent of it threatened to overwhelm all my other thoughts. My hunger seemed to be part of who I was, as important as my love of books and ever-so-slight OCD. That could not be true. I wouldn't *let* it be.

I held myself in control despite my ravenousness. This was not what I had envisioned as I'd lain there, boldly planning my future as an active participant in defeating the Bad Guys—a "self-rescuing princess." Once I drank this boy's blood, I'd probably just be carried around over someone's shoulder for the rest of our absconding, out of my head on drugs consumed from a helpless young victim. Was this rape, if he'd been glamoured to have no will? Fuck, *probably*. But I wasn't going to have sex with him. The Mongols drank blood from their horses at need. Was this much different from that, in the end?

Fuck. I just thought that.

But I was too exhausted to fight with myself over questions of ethics and the disappointment of how my bold plan had fizzled out.

I slipped out Sa'mah. I would make this painless for the boy, and I would make a cut so small that I couldn't get too much blood from it, not enough to do him true damage.

That had to count for something, right? As much as I need sustenance, I wanted to limit the dose of the drug.

*My first frangkhilaat, I drained an almost-dead boy till he was really dead. For my second, I'm chugging down poison. Not starting a great pattern, here.*

The little obsidian sliver gently nicked his vein. He shuddered lightly but otherwise did not move. My little blade was so sharp that the blood hadn't even started welling up yet. I lowered my head to his neck and echoed his shudder when my lips experienced the intimacy of touching his skin.

As the first blood slipped into my mouth, I was overwhelmed by him: his scent, his taste, his skinny little frame in my arms. His last meal had been highly spiced, and it gave a zing to the smell of his sweat, like the seasoning was coming out of his pores. He'd perspired a fair bit since then, but the stale tang of it didn't bother me at all, with his blood sweet and hot in my mouth.

I loved him. I loved every cell of his blood that flowed between my lips.

I so easily could have loved him to death.

*Open that vein fully; it's just another quick little cut.* The temptation nibbled at my mind and started becoming a fixation. I'd push it away in disgust, but then I'd realize I was considering it again. Each time, it seemed a little less repellant.

Before it could become a true moral quandary, my head began to spin. Hands caught me as I slumped, and I realized

Bagamil was up off the table; he had been watching over me. *Oh, cinyaa!* I wanted to cry out to him, but my mouth wouldn't work right. He lowered me gently on my side and put the delicious boy in my arms as if we had fallen over together. I mindlessly snuggled up to the warm, skinny body. Already the world was spinning, but his solid kee warmth was wonderfully fixed in the increasing whirlwind.

The bottom started to fall out, and down I spun into blackness.

*I'm caught in a black hole. I will have the life and matter crushed right out of me, and there will be nothing left to come out the other side of this.*

*Goodbye.*

# CHAPTER SIXTEEN

These nightmares were familiar. I'd been dosed with maadak before, and I'd also shared Bagamil's poisoned dreams. Familiarity did not make it any easier.

Sometimes it was nauseatingly uncontrolled movement with no spatial orientation to save me. Other times, memories twisted into cruel nightmare. At one point, I was certain I'd ripped the boy to little pieces, then licked every drop of blood from flesh and floor. Later, as I spun in the void, I felt him still safe in my arms, warming my undeserving body.

And the pain. Was it real pain or was it the concept of pain? All the burning, throbbing, shocking agonies the world could supply ripped through my synapses for miniature eternities.

There were periods of blessed unconsciousness, but they did not last long enough. All too soon, I'd be forced miserably back into torment. If there is a hell, it need be nothing more exotic than your soul trapped in an eternal maadak-trip.

And so I missed the first part of the action. Of course I did. Punishment for all my former life's misdeeds was me needing constant humiliating rescue.

The nature of my nightmares changed, although at the time, I'd no notion it was due to external factors. I knew I was flopping around the void in different ways, which involved occasionally slamming into things. *That* was exciting. My nightmares now included loud background noises that didn't relate directly to the plot of the chaos starring me. But that's chaos for you. The new confusion didn't particularly bother me, not any more than the soul-encompassing pain and misery already did.

I rejoined the rest of reality with a woozy sense of desperate urgency. Some deep part of me had sobered up before the rest of my brain. It understood that really serious shit was going down, that I needed to comprehend it and, if at all possible, start being useful.

My first focus was Bagamil—and Sandu! The rush of happiness the first time he moved across my field of vision (and I understood what I was seeing) almost blacked me out again.

I forced myself to get a firmer grip on consciousness, and cautiously moved my head, trying to take in what was happening.

Fighting. Fighting was happening.

We were in a new space. It was still a rock-walled bit of cave, but it differed from the last bit of cave in some very important ways. One, there was no stone table. Two, no scary-ass cave paintings. Three, it was a smaller space, just the dead-end of a corridor. Oh, and four, this meant no door with which to be locked in!

Item four was of possibly dubious value just at the moment, however. Right in front of me, Sandu and Bagamil had taken the place of the door, shoulder to shoulder across the space, fighting a group of … just minions, I thought. I scanned for Julio, but like any Bad-Guy Leader worth his salt, he'd sent his minions to be slaughtered in his place.

The minions were pressing Sandu and Bagamil hard. There were ten of them, and as I watched, they attempted to rush forward and knock my guys back. There was a tense moment as Bagamil parried one short sword with a knife. His parry was blocked, and while his right arm was engaged, another blade came at him. His left arm shot out in super-fast mode and hit the wrist holding the second weapon so hard I heard the bones break. That threat was withdrawn, and Bagamil surprised the one who had blocked him by bringing his knife around so fast that it disemboweled him.

I'd never seen viscera slide, slick with blood, out of a body before. It was...well, it was pretty horrible, even if it *was* a Bad Guy.

With a sick shock, I recognized Bagamil's knife as the one Araceli had carried and used so proficiently right up until the end. Maybe one of the minions who'd killed her had confiscated it?

Well, now it had been reclaimed by us, her friends. Good. I let the anger that was washing through me carry the last of the maadak-disorientation out of my system.

There was another busy period when four minions stepped forward simultaneously to try to overwhelm my patar and gharpatar. Their weapons got tangled, as there simply was no room in such a small space. Falling back to reorganize, they gave us breathing space.

"Sandu! I'm awake!" I called.

"*Sufleţel!* Welcome back! How are you?"

Two more minions came up to try to engage them one-on-one, and I took mental stock of my body. I was sitting on the ground, back to the hard end of the corridor. I didn't feel the need to fall over and curl up in the fetal position, so that was a nice change. I twitched my fingers and toes. They worked. I kicked my legs up and down, then waved my arms a bit—also in working order. I sat forward, rolled my neck, then reached down and poked in gentle exploration at my wounds. They seemed to be mostly healed under the crusty bandages. I wanted to tear the cloth away and look, but I didn't want to find out too late I was *not* healed, so I left them on for the time being. I staggered upright, and in doing so, I found I did not need to stagger. Well-being flowed through me, riding a tide of increasing rage.

I turned my attention to the fighting. Sandu's opponent received a nasty slice in his dominant arm and fell back. Bagamil's challenger fell at his feet, headless and spurting blood. The next minion would have to step over him. And the head. My beloveds stepped back, smiled at each other, and spared glances back to smile at me.

I gave them a huge smile, big enough for all the love I felt for them. "Houston, we have liftoff!"

"*Bravo ție!*" Sandu would have said more, but a minion poked a short sword at him, so he stepped to him to parry the blow.

"How is your mind, cinyaa?" asked Bagamil, practical as always.

"Clear now—except I'm in a very bad mood."

"That is understandable." He laughed. I could tell his un-bothered mirth irked the minion who was forced to fight over his comrade's headless body.

"So that you will not take your anger out on *us, draga mea*, I have something that will improve your mood," Sandu said, laughter in his voice also. He moved his knife to his left hand and fought one-handed as he dug something out of his belt on the far side of his body. He tossed it back to me and then abruptly curved in a deep arch to avoid being sliced through the middle.

I caught the blur that flew at me—happily, by the hilt. The minute it was in my hands, I knew. It was my darling Terry Smatchet!

I felt a strong desire to rush right into the fray but made myself take time to assess the situation. My beloveds were so tightly-packed that unless one became injured, I could not help at their front line. What I *could* do was shortly resolved when Sandu let a minion drop, his neck half-severed. The man fell forward, Sandu having to jump into Bagamil's space to let the injured am'r continue downward, not just collapse onto Sandu himself. The damaged minion hit the floor with a thump and Sandu stepped right over him, above his legs.

"For your anger!" Sandu laughed and was immediately back in the fight.

I dropped to my knees—if my leg still hurt, I didn't notice it at the moment—and raised my arms, holding Terry with both hands. He was not a great blade for these circumstances, with little room between Sandu and the wall for me to work in and even less room between the minion's head and shoulders for me to hack at. Terry sliced best when I could get up some good impetus in a swing—but he had other strengths. I raised him high and brought him down on the middle of the half of the neck that was still attached. I struck so hard that Terry went right through, and I had a moment of panic that I'd chipped him on the rock floor beneath the neck—or what had been a neck. But after I tugged Terry free (which might have been tougher except for the adrenalin spiking my system) he looked just fine. A more thorough examination could occur after I cleaned off the blood. Eventually.

It did take a couple more hacks to get the head fully off. I didn't know if an am'r could, I dunno, somehow reattach their head if it was left too close, so I tossed it to the other side of the corner we were in. Sandu had to kick the body away to get it out from underfoot. He caught one of the front-line minions in his legs with the headless corpse and the am'r stumbled, which was enough for Sandu to bury his blade in the man's shoulder. He lost the sword, but I could see two other long knives on the floor in front of me—one from the minion I'd just chopped up in easy reach, the other from the minion Bagamil had managed to decapitate a while ago. I snagged the closest one and called to Sandu as I held it up. He reached back with exquisite spatial awareness and timing, and was armed again.

We accomplished this just in time for Bagamil to have another treat for me, because Araceli's long knife was not optimal for decapitation, even with his strength. Neither were the close quarters we were all stuffed in, so it was much easier for Sandu and Bagamil to injure the minions just enough for them to collapse, whereupon it was my turn to finish things up while they attended to the not-yet-injured-enough.

Bagamil was using Araceli's knife more as a bludgeon, and this one had come down to me still armed with a short sword and not well-enough injured to be an easy fix. He stabbed wildly at me with one arm, the other being trapped against the wall. He had no room to get a good swing at me, while my Terry's precise forty-two centimeters had plenty of room above him. I rained down blows, building a nice rhythm of stab-and-up, stab-and-up.

Despite being repeatedly stabbed, he was trying to get his sword into play. I narrowly avoided it getting stuck into my good leg and decided *that* was not something I wanted to deal with today. I resolved the matter by the simple expedient of slamming his arm sideways with Terry and then kneeling on the flat of his blade. While he tried to pull it out from under me, I managed to get the neck blow I wanted. After the first good one, his head fell to the side in shock, and I could stab and wiggle Terry again and again until I had removed the head—perhaps not *neatly*, but in a workmanlike manner nonetheless.

I'd missed some of the action above me during this. The sound of gunfire brought me out of the Zen of Hacking-Off Heads.

There was shouting farther down the tunnel. The minions in the back had turned around to engage the Newcomers-With-Guns.

Oh, Orélie the Self-Anointed and his misbegotten followers! I had *forgotten* about them.

Julio's minions near us looked undecided about what their current goal was. Bagamil and Sandu decided to focus their minds, and both lunged forward with a *Yaaaaa!* of attack.

*Boys never do grow up, do they?*

I was now torn between following the action immediately in front of me and what was going on farther down the corridor. There was a lot of noise from the guns and shouting in various languages. I saw a minion take a shotgun blast to the cranium. Even after happily chopping off a head a few moments earlier, the sight was sickening. It was just as effective as decapitation, but more...well, *explosive.* I had to remind myself that Julio's minions were our enemies. The enemies of our enemies were *not* our friends, not here and now.

An am'r with a knife stuck in his neck fell on top of me. I was able to change the angle at which I held Terry Smatchet as we fell, and he ended up buried deep in the am'r's rib cage, close enough to the sternum that I was certain the heart was at least partially damaged. Terry's handle had landed on my own sternum, which was the only thing that provided the counterpressure in that thrust. That *hurt*, but not as much as it damaged the am'r on top of me, who groaned and vomited blood all over me. Bagamil leaned down and removed the blade sticking out of the minion's neck in such a way that the head flopped to the side, more than partially severed. *More* blood spurted over me. Bagamil turned back around, and I had to roll the blood-slicked am'r off the blood-slicked me, then try to work Terry out of his chest. By the time I'd managed it, I felt certain the am'r wasn't going to be getting up and coming at us any time soon. And I was glad, because I was starting to feel worn out, and the idea of finishing chopping off his head or digging out his heart, or whatever, was just too much.

Sandu turned his head to look back at me. "Do you have your, ah…" He turned to Bagamil. "*Ce este ai gaz de brichetă?*"

"'Lighter fluid.' No, she has none, nor her lighter. They were confiscated."

"*Pizda mă-sii!* And mine came out of my pocket in some water."

I remembered what Julio had said about Sandu being trapped in a deep hole full of water and looked closer at him. He was still damp and smelled strongly of minerals. I'd neglected to notice these things until now, which was probably excusable, all things considered. He'd lost his coat, and his plaid shirt which had been provided for my make-shift bandages, so he had only that wool sweater, which had been slowly drying before getting am'r blood all over it, and his salopettes, which were at least quick-drying when not *also* freshly covered in blood.

"I think it is unlikely these will be able to recover," Bagamil said dryly, pointing to the bodies, all missing heads except the half-decapitated one I'd just shoved off me. "I know you like to be meticulous, but even if there is a chance that these enemies could revive to come after us another day, it makes more sense now to leave them and continue our escape."

Sandu growled. Not at Bagamil, but at a cruel fate that did not allow him to leave his enemies in little piles of smoking charcoal. Bagamil gave me a hand up.

The tunnel directly ahead of us was clear of battling bad guys. Well, of active and upright ones. "Where did they all *go*?" I asked desperately, not caught up on the situation.

"Orélie's adherents have been pushed back."

"But they had the *guns*," I exclaimed, and as if to emphasize my words, renewed gunfire sounded, farther down the tunnel and out of direct sight.

"A trapped animal is the most dangerous," Bagamil replied. Apparently, Julio's people had felt *very* trapped between us and the guns.

"They have gone to the right. There is a passage immediately to the left, the one we should have taken before we let ourselves get trapped here."

"May I take the lead, patar?"

"Indeed. And at a run, I suggest."

# Chapter Seventeen

We ran. There was no point in trying to be stealthy; we'd learned that already. I'd missed a certain amount of information that would've been handy to have (When did Sandu get to us? How did we get out of that locked room?), but this was not the moment to get caught up. Sandu led. Bagamil silently ordered me to follow and let him take up the rear. I didn't like taking my eyes off of him, but of course, he was right that he was best suited to be rearguard.

Sandu seemed to have a clue where he was leading us. That was nice. So far, this entire "rescue" had been pure clusterfuck, so I was hoping we were moving to the "competent and victorious" stage. We ran down passageways, squeezed through an unexpected narrow place where the rock changed to that dark pumice-y stuff again, and tried not to slip in the damp places where water leaked down the walls and made unexpected puddles of varying depths.

I was just starting to have some hope of actually escaping from this horrible place when we came to a branching of two ways. Sandu stopped, so we all did. They, of course, were not out of breath. I tried to slow my breathing so the fact that I *was* wouldn't be quite so noticeable. A sense of dread came over me. Everything always seemed to go to shit when we had to stop and choose a way to go.

"We have no good choice, I am afraid," Sandu announced.

"Obviously, we cannot go to the right," Bagamil responded. "Why can we not choose the left—and fast?"

"I know the path to the left. It leads to one of their traps. I have experienced it. I do not suggest we revisit it. We are stuck. *Băga-mi-aş pula!*"

I tried to figure out why the path to the right was a bad choice, but that quickly became clear. The scents of multiple am'r preceded them and hit my am'r-nafsh nose just before they poured through the opening armed with both blades and guns.

Bagamil, Sandu, and I had a moment of gazing comically at each other. It was not clear to me if this was Orélie the Self-Anointed's underlings or Señor Super-Colonizer's minions.

This is a seriously weird problem to have. Which set of ridiculous Bad Guys is it this time?

After they fanned out, one of them resolved our curiosity. "Julio wishes to speak to you. You will come this way."

Well, at least now we knew *which* baddies we were dealing with.

Sandu and Bagamil looked at each other, and I watched them thinking. They—*We, dammit!*—could probably take this group on. I could almost feel them planning who they would go for first, when the scent of more am'r hit us from behind, just before an equally large and well-armed group spread out in the space behind us. Sandu and Bagamil both let all the tension out of their bodies and did not offer any fight in either direction. I understood that meant they were conserving their energies for later, and tried to relax as well. It wasn't easy.

We were of course disarmed. I was very reluctant to be parted from Terry Smatchet *again*, but it did not seem worth being further injured in a useless confrontation.

So we had about thirty am'r as our personal escort to have another nice chat with Julio. Where did he get them all? Did he hoard minions down here or something? It was no wonder they always had kee available to feed guests. With all these am'r around, they needed an all-you-can-drink izchha buffet.

The tunnels we'd moved through had *seemed* so empty. As we were herded to our next confrontation, the thought of even more miles of underground corridors and rooms stuffed with violence-craving minions and mind-controlled kee kept as part dairy cow, part sex-slave filled me with despair.

We ended up either back in the room where I'd seen Julio before, or there was another just like it. By this point in time, the idea that Julio had multiple receiving rooms wouldn't have surprised me.

It seemed this was in the equivalent of the Rave Cave back in the underground Castle Dracula. There was none of the cool bioluminescent lighting that Sandu had, just more oil lamps. Julio and his minions lived in a dreary, cheerless space down here at the bottom of the world. I remembered the exquisitely carved and decorated caves Mehmet had inhabited and felt my choice in abductors had seriously gone downhill.

The minion gang spread out as we entered and filled the room around us, some moving up to stand by Julio, the rest fanning out to have clear shots at Sandu and Bagamil. And me too, no doubt, although, as usual, I was less a threat and more a potential hostage.

But as blades were held unsheathed and guns pointed at us, pride surged up in me. All this for my two beloveds: they were *that* much of a threat. I was honored to stand with them, honored to have their vhoon-anghyaa in me. If we didn't make it out of this alive, I would die fighting by their sides, knowing I couldn't have chosen better companions.

I stood up straighter. Whatever was coming, I'd meet it as a worthy partner to Bagamil and Sandu, a true member of this weird-ass little family.

Julio looked us over in silence. I don't know if he thought we were going to squirm like naughty schoolgirls, but Sandu and Bagamil just stood there in calm stillness and eyed him in the same manner. After a while, I was having a hard time not giggling, despite death seeming reasonably imminent.

Julio perched regally in his Chair Of Importance. Prominent in his hand was what looked very much like an Old West six-gun, and he played with it continuously. I glanced around the room; most of the other firearms were far more modern, including automatic weapons that could clearly cut us in half or otherwise turn our bodies into small pieces of flesh.

Thinking about being ripped in half by gunfire made me a little less thrilled about how much we threatened them in that moment.

Julio was finally ready to speak to us. "You might feel satisfied with what a thorn you have been in my side. You all have been very disruptive to my plans."

*Seriously? Are we just ignoring the completely unrelated bunch of am'r who are running around here, too?*

We just stood there and looked at him.

He didn't seem bothered by our lack of appreciation for his backhanded compliments and continued, "Of course, I expected nothing less from the Aojysht. I had prepared for him to be a test of my powers, and he was everything I expected. But I had not expected you," here he looked burningly at Sandu, "*concetățene*, to find me before I had accomplished my designs."

It was the only time Julio had spoken any Romanian or had hinted in any way of their shared country-of-origin. Sandu gave a short, sharp nod, but it was Bagamil who spoke. "You have never been so kind as to let me know *what* your plans for me are, but then, you have mostly kept me far too intoxicated to pose the question. Now that we are face to face, I ask you for a second time: would you care to tell me what this has all been about?"

"Can you not guess?"

"Oh, I can. Of course I can. But please indulge your un-willing guest."

"*Muy bien*. The vhoon-Aojysht, what else? I could not have had it just by asking you, could I?"

"Obviously not—but then why have you held me here and not already drained me?"

"Oh, we will not drain you *completely*! I understand nat-ural resources, *anciano*, none better. In my life as a kee, no one was better organized, and no one turned empty waste-land into opportunity as well as I. Becoming am'r only sharpened those skills. When I was kee, I could convince others to do my bidding with my words and my superior intellect. Now, I can simply reach out and bend minds to my will.

"Quite simply, with vhoon-Aojysht enriching my already superior vhoon, I will be free to take your place as leader of the am'r, a more worthy successor than the one *you* chose. He is strong-willed, it is true, but he has not the power of compulsion that is my natural gift. To truly guide the am'r—*una pandilla muy rebelde*—you need one of my bent. An artist in coercion and control, not just a headstrong maverick."

"Why did you not bring these ideas to me openly? Perhaps I would have agreed with you."

"Do not offend me, *Nacho*. Your love of your prodigal is well-known—and well-mocked—throughout the am'r world. If I had made an offer to you, would I have walked away from it with my heart still beating? Of course not. And even if you had been so foolish as to let me, you would have known my scent again. Neither I nor my people could ever have gotten close enough to you a second time. There was only one shot, and I was not going to waste it."

"Well, if that is what you believe, why am I not being drained by you or your *minions*," he paused slightly here, and I had to restrain myself from snorting, "at this very moment?"

Julio sighed deeply. *Gosh, poor misunderstood Señor Super-Colonizer. My heart bleeds for you.* "One reason is that *your minions* have invited themselves to my home and made a mess."

Confusion bubbled through me. *Our* minions? Did he think the Self-Anointed and his sycophants were working with us? I felt a strong urge to clear *that* up right away, but Julio was not finished.

"The other reason is that it was not uncomplicated to set up your abduction. Your new policies of trying to make a coalition of am'r are foolish and easy to manipulate. After that, I needed only to keep you docile with frequent maadakyo. However, in your intoxicated state, you are most vicious, and no izchha who is offered to you survives the experience. I have had to set up a whole network to find kee who will not be missed, buying them from their families or from people-smugglers and then housing them, with all their dirty kee needs. I've had to personally put them under compulsion as I rushed to train my most trusted frithaputhraish in the art. Along the way of doing this, I needed confederates, helpers. They have all been promised a share in the bounty of your vhoon as payment for many and varied services rendered.

"It was agreed that not one of us, not even I, would taste a drop of your vhoon until we all gathered together for a primary...decanting. I was awaiting my associates to arrive from their various locations across this world. It was planned for tonight. Indeed, it still will be tonight. We will just have a *show* with our dinner."

That didn't sound good, not at all. If Bagamil was "dinner," undoubtedly Sandu and I were going to somehow be the "show." I knew enough about the am'r that I did not doubt Julio could come up with something that would make even Caligula retch in repugnance.

So, we *weren't* going to die right in this moment. I tried to remember the proud bravado that had been infusing me, but it was one thing to contemplate a last stand that goes out in a blaze of heroic glory, and entirely another to imagine what Señor Super-Colonizer—a man who'd personally wiped out native peoples by the tribe-load—could conceive of as a *fun* way of making Sandu and me recompense him for being such an aggravation and messing up his best-laid evil plans.

"And," Julio continued, "in the meanwhile, my men will warm up for the evening's festivities by killing every one of your allies. I hope none of them were especially dear to you."

I was close enough to Sandu to nudge him, but Bagamil was ahead of us. "I think there may be some confusion on that front. *My* allies are all in this room. The other uninvited am'r roaming your halls with itchy trigger fingers are the followers of Orélie-Antoine de Tounens—a contemporary of yours, I believe. You may recall him?"

Julio looked suspicious. "Why would he be invading my sanctuary, if he is not working with you?"

"Perhaps news of your plans for bartending my vhoon has spread beyond your allies?"

Julio shook his head dismissively. "It matters not if they are your helpers; they have made it clear they are *my* enemies. They will die, and their vhoon will help ensure that all who have arrived to share in your vhoon are so well-fed that they will be content with their measured portion of the vhoon-Aojysht. You will be dessert—an after-dinner port. I hope that gratifies you, Aojysht."

# CHAPTER EIGHTEEN

The horror started with being separated yet again. Julio motioned his command. Although both Bagamil and Sandu tried to respond instantly, they could not be more instant than bullets. Each had their knees shot out—*BAM, BAM*—and shots that were more or less to their shoulders—*BAM, BAM*—so that they were effectively quadriplegic until they healed.

Me, they didn't have to shoot. My poor wounds weren't even deliberately reopened. I was just thrown over a minion's shoulders and carried bodily to a small cell to await being part of the floorshow while those deafening gunshots echoed over and over in my head.

The cell was barely long enough to lie down in, and there was no room for even a bench. It was just me, on the living rock of the floor, alone with all my fears. I curled into the fetal position at the far end and thought about crying, but the tears would not come. I just curled up and let myself, for a little while, sink into tearless despair.

At some point, I felt Sa'mah, overlooked as always, digging into my hipbone. As I had done once before—on a boat full of enemies who had made the violence of the am'r world plain to me—I contemplated suicide as the most obvious solution to my current crisis. I could at least refuse to let Señor Super-Colonizer use me in the floorshow that way. But as true as it had been then, it was still true now; *that* release was not available to me anymore. If I killed myself, I'd just rise from the vistarascha at some point to find myself in a world with Sandu gone and Bagamil kept helpless somewhere as an am'r soda fountain. Fuck—they could just keep my body, and I would rise to find myself still their prisoner.

There was no easy out for me.

Some incalculable period of time later, the door opened, and a figure slid into the sliver of gloom that confined me.

I didn't bother to look up, but my nose was less lethargic than my eyes, and it sent messages of shocked interest up to my brain.

The blood...was completely different than any I'd ever smelled. Not just kee, but not entirely am'r.

*What is both am'r and kee in one body?*

I looked up. *She* was like me. An am'r-nafsh.

The door had closed behind her. She moved slowly, obviously trying not to startle me, and brought her fascinating fragrance to me in my huddle of despair.

She had medium-brown hair, long thick waves of it. It smelled so heart-breakingly *clean*. It also made me jealous of her for having recently bathed. I smelled *terrible*. Her tawny skin smelled even better, spotless of dirt or sweat, with that amazing blood pumping just under it. Her cocoa-colored eyes moved over me inquisitively. As I unfolded from my fetal curl, the extent of my stink (particularly from my old-blood-encrusted clothing and bandages) imposed itself upon her sensitive nose, which wrinkled in a way that would've been adorable if it hadn't been a comment upon my body odor. She sniffed again, though, and I understood *she* was reaching down through layers of scent. I could never have explained *that* to someone who hadn't drunk am'r blood.

"You *are* am'r-nafsh. They said your patar brought you, but I didn't believe them. Why did he bring you?"

"Um…I told him he had to. Who are you?"

"You *told* him…? And he lets you speak to him like that? Your patar *is* Dracula, *¿sí?*"

"Yeah, he is. Who are you?"

"My patar would never let me tell him what to do. And your patar is *famous* for being cruel!"

"He's not as bad as the stories make out. At least not anymore. Look—I won't answer anything else until you tell me who you are."

"Oh! I'm Isidra, frithaputhra of Julio."

I thought I'd smelled his vhoon-anghyaa in her complex fragrance. It smelled better on her.

"Hi, Isidra. I'm Noosh, frithaputhra of Sandu, who once was known as Vlad Dracula. Although you know that already. Um...I don't suppose you want to let me out of here?"

Not that I would know what to do if she *did*, but it seemed worth asking.

"*¡Dios mío, no!* I do not want him angry with me!"

"OK, I get that. But...um...why are you here?"

"When I heard about you, I wanted to meet another am'r-nafsh so much. And then I *smelled* you, and I couldn't help myself. I have so many things I want to ask you!"

"I'm really excited to meet another am'r-nafsh, too, but I...well, I kinda have a lot of other things on my mind right now. I really need to escape and help my patar and my gharpatar."

"You cannot help them. Dracula will die tonight, and the Aojysht will be made...I don't know the word in English, but they will make him so he cannot be a problem for them again."

As I tried to find the words to counter her certainty that this was the only possible outcome, she continued, "They plan to kill you, too, or drain you completely at least. Maybe

I could convince Julio that he should have two am'r-nafsh?" She looked shy. "I would so love a sister."

I shuddered. The thought of living out the rest of my unnatural life in thrall to Señor Super-Colonizer was horrifying, but I had a feeling that Isidra was not optimally emotionally stable, so I tried for a gently-phrased response.

"I would love a sister too, but I don't think I could stay with someone who killed my patar. Does that make sense?"

She looked disappointed. "*Bien. Supongo que sí.*" She thought about it more and added, "I don't think I can save you if you're not willing to be my sister."

"You could save me by just helping me get out of here. Is there someone outside the door?"

"Yes. Julio won't let me move around without an escort, not with all these strange am'r visiting us." She dropped her voice confidingly. "I'm not supposed to leave my suite, actually, but I got Hugo to bring me. I think he wanted to smell you too." She giggled at this. I wasn't sure what to feel. As am'r-nafsh, I'd suffered through enough am'r huffing me to be relieved to find another person who would understand how freaky and disconcerting it was. On the other hand, right now really didn't feel like a time for girlish giggles and gossip. Obviously, Isidra's priorities were not mine. I had, perhaps unfairly, come to the conclusion that Julio had not picked this girl for her brains, but this was not the time to let intellectual snobbery interfere with whatever help I could manage to procure.

"You know..." I said, dropping my voice confidingly as well and trying not to feel guilty about the manipulation I was about to attempt, "we already *are* sisters, really. It's so good to meet another *chica* who understands how hard it is to be an am'r-nafsh around all those strong am'r."

I reached out my grubby, crusty hand and took her clean, soft one. She was charmed and returned the pressure. I almost cried because after everything, the innocent touch of a fellow woman's skin was almost too much for me. Because it made the memory of Araceli flash across my mind, and that was more than I could bear. Because, if I could just come up with the right words, I would shamelessly manipulate this girl who just wanted to be a kind of sister to me. And probably get her in all sorts of trouble.

I thought I knew exactly how I'd do it, too.

"Tell me..." *Crap, what's the word for sister? Think, think! Oh,* "hermano *"is brother, that's right!* "Tell me, *hermana*, is Hugo a special friend? Do you trust him?"

Those soft brown eyes widened. "How did you know? Yes, Hugo is my main guard. I always feel safer with him. He loves me; not just because of how I smell. He is also a frithaputhra of Julio. But he has so many, these days. Hugo is older, and not as afraid of Julio as they all are. He is my special brother."

*Oh, I bet he is.*

How did I know? Am'r nature was not so far from human nature, after all. This was such a relationship trope: the boy, the girl, the boy's trusted friend who is for some reason left to care for the girl, caught in a triangle that eventually spells disaster. It was a very safe bet to find it here, with this pretty, somewhat simple, definitely very young woman.

"Do you know what the plans are for…um…tonight? Does Julio tell you his plans? Or has your 'special brother' told you?"

"Julio…sometimes tells me things. He likes to speak of his great deeds. But Hugo knows about tonight. Do you want to know about it?"

"Yes!" I had to collect myself and lessen my fervor, so I didn't scare her away. "*Sí, por favor.*"

"Hugo," she called softly. Her accent lengthened the name out to "Oooo-goh," said with the intimacy of a lover. I wondered if they had been able to share blood. Since they both had Julio's blood in them, maybe that would cover it? But no, Sandu had Bagamil's blood in his veins, and each had a different…quality. They must just be mooning over each other, with Hugo taking longing sniffs of her while looking into her eyes or something. I really didn't know enough about the am'r to speculate usefully.

While I speculated uselessly, Hugo silently reopened the door of my cell, slipped inside, and pulled it almost shut. There was just enough room left in the cell for me to have a few precious inches of personal space, once I backed tightly against the wall. He moved up by Isidra, and their comfort at the proximity enforced by the narrowness of the cell confirmed their dangerous relationship.

Isidra didn't need to catch Hugo up on what had been discussed. His am'r hearing had followed our discussion without difficulty. He looked a bit uncomfortable when he caught my eye, and I understood. Isidra had given up their secret to me far too easily. I smiled warmly, hoping that and my am'r-nafsh perfume would combine to put him at such ease that he would open up to me as well.

"Hugo," Isidra said, his name a caress, "would you tell us about the plans? Me and, eh, Noosh?" The last part of that was to me. My damn nickname.

"Yes, just 'Noosh.' *Por favor*, Hugo. What exactly is happening?"

Hugo considered. If he was of a similar age to Julio, he probably would have been called a *Morisco*. His skin was a soft brown, his hair made a neat black cloud around his head. His wide eyes were darkly melancholy, and his full lips were framed by a precisely-trimmed circle beard. All the am'r who were running around in these mountains at the bottom of the world were dressed warmly to minimize how much blood they needed to take in, but he made his dark-gray wool turtleneck and military pants work. You could easily see him sitting in a dramatic setting, composing poetry for Isidra. It would be moody love poetry.

"Isidra, do you really wish me to tell the plans of our patar to our enemy's creature?" His rich voice was measured and gentle. His accent was the European flavor of Spanish.

"*Ella no es una criatura, Hugo. ¡Es mi hermana!*" Her reply was so fierce in sisterhood that I felt a rush of shame and my head involuntarily ducked. I looked up to see Hugo watching me with those big eyes. His long years of am'r life had obviously taught him to not be as trusting as sweet Isidra.

"If you wish me to tell her, I shall do so," he replied solemnly. "But I think we will both regret this."

I thought they probably would, too, but I kept my face in the "I'm just a helpless am'r-nafsh, no risk to you" expression.

"Julio has been building to this event for a long time. He did not expect quite so many 'guests.'"

"Orélie's gang has nothing to do with us!" I jumped in to explain.

"That is quite a coincidence," he replied dryly. "However, Julio has accommodated his plans for all of you. Those am'r you disavow are being hunted through our tunnels at this very moment. A large party of them ended up in one of the *calabozos secretos*. Our men wait at the top to finish off the survivors who manage to climb out. The rest will soon succumb to other traps or simply be outnumbered.

"In the end, this suits Julio perfectly. He has bidden all our *invited* guests to join in the hunt with him. They will drain the enemies before giving them the tokhmarenc, so when it comes time to giving sips of the vhoon-Aojysht later, it will be easier to keep everyone to their allotted amount. That has been a concern, but our enemies have kindly given us a way to bring our allies to the table with well-fed bellies."

Now that he was talking, Hugo's concerns about telling me Julio's plans seemed to have been set aside. I had a million questions, but did not want to stop his flow.

"However, since we have you and your patar in our hands now, there will be even more vhoon to fill up on before the great Aojysht is finally *cerveza de barril*. You and Dracula will be offered up to be drained first. His and your vhoon are equally valuable to any am'r." He stopped here and inhaled deeply and obviously. It was not as offensive as many sniffs I'd gotten since entering the am'r world. It just made his point very clearly that my blood was a delicacy. There was probably a note of disapproval as well, wondering why in the hell my patar (or gharpatar, if my patar had no sense) would allow me to be here. An am'r could communicate a lot with their nostrils.

"Do you..." I nervous-gulped. "Do you know the details of that?"

"Details? Oh, *sí, sí*. Your patar will be staked out with broken extremities, so they cannot heal in a good way, you understand? That way, he cannot fight the vhoon-berefteh, the bloodletting."

I understood. I had seen *that* done before with Neplach, my dear uncle-in-blood. I felt sick in a very kee way. I wondered if am'r-nafsh could throw up.

"You, they will not need to do such things to. If you do not fight, your first death will be relatively painless. Well, unless they get *very* excited. That might happen. I do not know what Julio plans for when you rise from the vistarascha. Perhaps he will burn you so you do not rise? I believe that will have much to do with how you behave."

I had heard that whole "your fate will be determined by how well you obey my rules" line from Señor Super-Colonizer—more than could be endured. No one threatened *real* am'r with consequences for naughty behavior; it was understood that *they* understood. Me? No. I was treated like an ignorant child.

Yes, duh, if I kick and scream and have a temper tantrum, I will be punished. I get that. But you know what? Treating me like a child pretty much ensures that I am going to kick and scream for every part of this. I will not fucking make it easy for you.

I shook my head. Hugo was—at the moment at least—not my enemy. If he'd been around Julio for centuries and had been his lover at some point (if not still), then no wonder he spoke like him. Getting mad at Hugo while he was helping me wasn't a constructive use of my limited time.

Ask the right questions. In any quest, it comes down to asking the dangerous beast the right questions.

"So, after Sandu and I are variously dispatched," I asked, keeping the quaver out of my voice, "what will happen to my gharpatar?"

Hugo looked into my eyes and replied bluntly but not without sympathy, "They will remove his extremities and drink from the four fountains until they dry up. After that, he will be placed in a type of coffin, one too small to allow his arms and legs to grow back in any useful way. He will be kept alive and fed just enough that he will produce vhoon-Aojysht for us indefinitely."

He looked away after he finished. Every once in a while, I was made to abruptly remember how cruel and twisted the am'r world could be. Perhaps he was feeling the same?

I had to figure out what to do next, what to say next. In the pause, Isidra's little hand sought Hugo's larger one. He shot me a look again, then shrugged. He was right; what threat was I to them, really? Why would I tell Julio they had laid out his plans for me? And even if I did, who was Julio more likely to believe: his trusted frithaputhra or me?

"Hugo. Firstly, *gracias* for your honesty and trust. This might be the last time anyone treats me kindly before I die. I truly appreciate it. You and my sister Isidra are wonderful, and I wish you both only happiness." I again filled my voice with warmth, still counting on Hugo being susceptible not only to Isidra's am'r-nafsh perfume.

Isidra beamed at me. Hugo nodded, not visibly letting his guard down. Damn. I really respected him—but at this moment, I wished he were as malleable as Isidra.

"Hugo, would you be willing to let me out of this cell? If you would just leave the door ajar, you could take your lady far away before I make my escape."

"*Lo siento, mi dama.* Our scent will linger here for some while. I can explain Isidra's curiosity at meeting another of her kind, *sí*, but I will not endanger her for you."

"I...understand, Hugo. But what if we could mask your scent? If I were bleeding, would that do it? If we cut me and spread my blood around, would that be distracting enough?"

Hugo gave this genuine consideration, which I appreciated.

"I am afraid it would not be enough. Not unless you lost so much vhoon that I doubt you could make an escape."

"Again, *gracias*, Hugo. Can you think of anything else? Any other way to cover your scents? Any other way to get me out of here? Is there...anything I can do for you and your lady that would make the risk worthwhile?"

He smiled sadly at me. "I understand your desperation, *mi dama*, but Julio is a shrewd man. He is also a man who does not tolerate obstructions. Helping you is not worth risking his wrath. And I do not believe that if I helped you, you would be able to get free from this stronghold without being recaptured or dying in a trap. If you wish to survive the death of your patar, I can only suggest finding a way to make yourself valuable to Julio, more valuable alive than dead."

"Yet again I thank you, Hugo, but you misunderstand me. I do not wish to survive the death of my patar or my gharpatar. I wish to free them so we can escape together."

Hugo looked sadly at me. I understood why; my words sounded so ridiculous to him as to be pure fantasy—and they probably *were*—but I was entirely prepared to do the die-trying thing. My options were all bad, so why not go out in that blaze of glory? At least Sandu and Bagamil would know that my love was true—since undoubtedly Señor Super-Colonizer would relish telling them the gory details before implementing their own unpleasant fates.

Isidra dropped Hugo's hand and grabbed mine, empathy leaking out of her eyes with the blood-tinged tears of an am'r-nafsh. "I'm sorry we can't help you, *mi hermana*. We really want to."

I wasn't sure how much Hugo wanted to help me, but I felt pretty sure that to make Isidra happy, he'd allow bad decisions beneath a certain threshold. I decided to count that as close enough, even if not in any way useful, since helping me was a bad decision well past the cutoff point.

All my attempts at maneuvering had yielded only a more detailed knowledge of my doom. I found I was surprisingly relieved by that outcome. Isidra was indeed like a sister, a *younger* sister. But if I could have Daciana, Zoraida—and if only for a little while, Araceli—as big sisters who made the am'r world a more survivable place, then surely it was right to have little sisters to whom I owed something. I couldn't do anything for Isidra right now—and she had Hugo, so how much did she really need me anyway—but I was glad I wasn't going to be presented with the crisis of having to choose myself over her, if there *had* been an opportunity to use her to my ends.

I looked away from Isidra's kind face to find Hugo was gazing unflinchingly at me. He asked, "When they ask you about our visit, will you be willing to say only that the female am'r-nafsh was curious, and you spoke about matters relevant only to that state of being? That I was escort only and spoke not to you?"

"Of course!" I told him. "I'll say that the pretty brown-haired girl," Isidra blushed at this, "stopped by to visit and talk about being am'r-nafsh with me, and there was this cranky, silent am'r who stood by the door. He made her leave before she and I were done talking. I'll make sure they have no reason to think otherwise."

"*Gracias.* I would wish you luck...but I think it better simply to wish you the least painful death possible."

Good at managing expectations was ol' Hugo. "Thank you, Hugo. I can and do wish you and your lady the best of luck in *everything.*"

Hugo was moving Isidra out of the cell as I said this. Isidra was resisting him, obviously yearning to rush back to hug me, but he used his superior strength to gently refuse her the option.

After they left—and did *not* leave the door "accidentally" hanging open; I checked—I felt cold again. Maybe I needed a snack, food-wise or blood-wise? Lately, I didn't think of hunger until there was food or blood right in front of me. I noticed temperature even less. Maybe it was all in my head? I certainly had reason enough to feel chilled at the thought of my immediate future.

I curled back up into a fetal position. What else was there for me to do?

When they came for me, I just let them take me. Indeed, I flopped passively in their arms as they hauled me up from my curled slump against the wall and floor.

It would have been satisfying if my passive resistance were more effective, but it wouldn't have mattered to the minion who came to get me if I'd fought the whole way or obligingly walked on my own two feet. He just threw me over a shoulder and carried me like a sack of grain to the party.

I do not like being carried. Not by a minion. Not even by my beloveds. If I manage to become a full am'r, no one is carrying me anywhere again, ever.

The minion dumped me unceremoniously to the floor in front of Julio, who was of course ensconced in his Chair of Importance. I shook my head; being carried over someone's shoulder and then dropped on the floor is disorienting. Then I got a better look around me. Six Chairs of Lesser Importance winged out to the right and left from Señor Super-Colonizer's Ass-Rest. Most contained the asses of am'r I didn't recognize, at least not by sight, and there were too many conflicting scents of am'r blood for someone as untrained and unpowered as me to be able to separate out each and appreciate their unique fragrance.

There were two scents I did recognize, however. My head spun as the molecules teased up my nose to my brain.

*Sandu. Bagamil. Where?*

More am'r spread out around and behind me, milling about in low-voiced discussions. It made me flash back to the first time I was in Sandu's Rave Cave. Not a happy memory. I really needed to avoid large gatherings of am'r; they were absolutely right that they were solitary beings who should avoid their own kind. I would so honor that if only *they* would stick to it.

I could not see my family. Down on the floor, my view was blocked by legs and torsos kitted out in various cold-weather apparel. I tried to smell which direction they were, but I was so overeager that I ended up confusing myself.

*Where are they?*

As I turned my head like a compass arrow trying to find north, I became aware that Julio was staring down at me, looking as repugnantly self-confident and arrogant as ever. This was the second time I had been in this position before him, and it was two times too many. I picked myself up to stand as assertively as possible, although I didn't like the extra attention this attracted from the am'r around me. I wasn't going to grovel on the floor at Señor Super-Colonizer's feet, however; not right before I died. I had *some* standards.

I hadn't been able to see either Sandu or Bagamil from where I was on the floor. Even standing, I couldn't immediately find them. Julio interrupted my search, making me turn my attention back to him.

"Frithaputhra of Vlad Țepeș, who is frithaputhra of the Aojysht, you have a choice ahead of you."

"*¡Pura mierda!*" I cut in. I'd been listening in to minions from the minute I'd been captured and had stored up as many ripe Spanish curse words as I could figure out from overhearing them. "A choice between what? Serving you, or death? That's not a *choice.*"

All the guests and minions had stopped talking. I was definitely living up to being the floor show, dammit.

Julio's hostile brown eyes flashed with cold, scary anger, but I was too pissed to back down. I stood straighter and pulled my shoulders back.

Julio practically hissed at me, "I think all will agree that you have just clearly made your choice. You can join your patar in the tokhmarenc."

"Better than associating myself with you." I tried to remember a really vile insult in my new Spanish vocabulary and realized that my heart was pounding too fast to allow for such embellishment. I'd be lucky enough not to sound like an idiot in English.

He'd managed to get some control of himself, so he pretended he didn't care that I'd stood up to him and rejected him in front of all his guests and minions. "You *will* make history, Dracula's frithaputhra. I have never heard of an am'r-nafsh who was annihilated so thoroughly that they never rose to become am'r. You will become the first. Such a short time among us, but forever you will be remembered as the am'r-nafsh who raised herself so far above her station that she paid the full am'r price for her impudence.

"I must thank you for adding another unique element to my already extraordinary night. It is not to be missed! I think I will keep your patar alive long enough to spectate it. He is known as a man who keenly enjoys viewing suffering and destruction. Indeed, he made cruel and unusual punishments his specialty, so how could he fail to enjoy this?"

He waved a hand negligently behind him, and I realized why I could not see but only *smell* my beloveds. Behind the Chairs of Importance, black curtains hung from the ceiling to the floor. As a couple of minions followed Julio's nonchalant nonverbal command, it became clear that the fabric concealed the props and actors in Señor Super-Colonizer's Evening of Macabre Terrors.

The fabric to the left was pulled aside to expose Sandu, who was trapped in an insane medieval torture device. Naked. The wrought iron bars twisted in such a way that Sandu's limbs were held out at stomach-turning angles. He had healed, but what twisted healing! Bones were pulled in ways they were never meant to go, and the muscles and sinews had reknit, holding them in those agonizing positions. Even if Sandu could have found the strength and will to rebreak his limbs one at a time and manage to work them back into position with no help from his other arm or legs—and I suspected that given enough time and a handy supply of blood, he *could*, through sheer mulish obstinacy alone—still, the device both caged the limbs and held them pinned through muscle and bone. He had healed over the metal that now acted as bonds *inside* his body. It was an apparatus that could only be contrived by an am'r for the torture of other am'r.

Sandu was awake and aware. As the minions pulled the contraption forward for all to see, I could see him wince once from the jolting of the metal pins through his twisted extremities; then, he composed his face to a perfect blank.

He almost lost that perfect blankness when he saw me. His eyes flashed, but he shut all emotion down. I had to keep myself from crying out.

"Ah, the reunion of lovers," Julio waned poetic in his big moment. "Shall we bring together the whole household?" He did not await input from his audience but gestured to his right. A couple other minions, eagerly anticipating Señor Super-Colonizer's order, were already on their way to pull out the surprise from behind Door Number Two.

My gharpatar was an even more horrific sight. He was not in a special torture device but was cruelly hogtied so that his arms and legs had healed bent unnaturally back behind him at angles that prevented him from using enough force to break the ropes. Again, if he'd had even *one* unbroken, untwisted limb, he was strong enough in will and strength that he might have fought through the pain to set himself free. But even the Aojysht-of-aojyshtaish could not get himself free from *this*. Also naked for maximum exhibition of the cruel torture he was undergoing, he lay on his belly on a wooden rectangle, which I realized with yet another emotional gut-punch, was the special punishment-coffin he would be fitted into after his limbs had been hacked off and he'd been used as the evening's champagne fountain.

His head was resting on its side, his eyes half-open as if he were in a daze. As he was pulled forward, though, I saw energy surge through his body, and he twisted his head around so his chin rested uncomfortably against the wooden coffin lid. His eyes glinted with all their usual intensity when they met mine. I felt like he was telling me he was far from helpless, that this was far from over. I was not sure I believed him. Even if I did, what was I going to do: take out Julio, his guests, and his minions all by myself, then set my beloveds free? I was not opposed to the idea of being the amazing superhero who single-handedly saved the day, but unless a flash of radiation or something came along, I couldn't see how I could access any new superpowers.

Could I *talk* us out of the situation? Be so cunning and calculating as to convince the bad guys to let us all go? No. That would require as much radiation as physical superpowers. I'm smart, sure, but my life before joining the am'r hadn't consisted of me working out my inner Machiavelli, whereas any am'r who had managed to stay alive for even just a few more decades than me had been working on those skills the whole time.

No brawn, no brain, no plan. At least one of those things was called for if I was going to even *try* my single-handed rescue—but what were my other options? Just sit on my underpowered, sub-devious, ill-prepared ass and passively let them drain and kill me to torture my beloveds?

All I was left with was frustration at how my reality was unfolding.

Is pure, undiluted frustration a good enough superpower?

Julio decided to add to my pain by speaking again. I realized with a start that he'd been talking while I had been focused on my thoughts.

Stupid girl! What if he'd said something you could use to your advantage? Let Señor Super-Colonizer mansplain your doom to you. Fucking focus.

He was droning on about the details of everyone's imminent draining and death, about which I already knew far too much, so at least I hadn't fucked up too egregiously this time.

"Tonight will be a letting of the most powerful vhoon the am'r world has ever experienced: not only the Aojysht, but his beloved frithaputhra, infamous in both our world and the kee world as well. As a delicious extra, their lineage runs strong in the veins of Dracula's am'r-nafsh, here. Her sweet, coveted vhoon will be the commencement of this part of your evening's pleasures."

Nope. I couldn't stay focused on this even if he was about to give explicit instructions on how an am'r-nafsh could easily kill him. He sounds like a bad DJ at a corporate function.

"You have trusted me despite vicissitudes, fought beside me in this latest raid upon a sanctuary I had promised you was secure from enemies—although rounding them up and dispatching them has, I think you will grant me, been nothing more than amusing sport to spice up our momentous occasion.

"Honored guests! Here before us is the vhoon-anghyaa of our most noble am'r lineage—in three direct generations! Tonight, we *become* that noble lineage. We will take their strengths and qualities for ourselves. Never before amongst our people has a group of the like-minded united to raise ourselves up together. We have created our own divine right to rule. Now, let it begin!"

Minions appeared to my right and left, and the grips they took upon me were deadly serious. No one was willing to be the one to let me get away with anything.

My arms were pulled hard to either side as I was backed up. I felt a sharp shock against the back of my thighs, then I was pulled over backward. My brain chose that moment to give in to panic and I struggled, although that was roundly ignored by the arms hauling me. My legs kicked and scrabbled against the flat surface I was being stretched out upon, which was a goddamn stone table of my very own. This one, I noticed as I was being dragged across it, had runnels in it like on a meat-carving board. *Fucking stupendous.*

Then more hands were upon me. Some held me down while others reached in and ripped off my clothing. All the clothes I'd been wearing were sturdy cold-weather gear, made to resist tears. Maybe having delicate lingerie ripped off one's body was fun and arousing, but having *these* clothes torn off me twisted and burned the skin underneath—a promise of far worse pain to come.

Speaking of promise, the hands on me were not just tearing off clothing but grabbing my flesh proprietorially, full of threat for the immediate future. Ah. Right. This was going to be a rapey sort of death; *of course* it was. They were not just using me for my delectable am'r-nafsh blood, but they were trying to inflict maximum suffering on those who loved me. It almost wasn't personal—not that that would make it any less terrible for *me*.

So, here we were in the last moments of my life. I would not get to rise as am'r after all. I was going to be raped and drained while Bagamil and Sandu's hearts broke, then burned to a non-reanimate-able pile of ashes. And that was that. My little adventure in the world of vampires was over. Honestly, it was a surprise I'd lasted this long.

I ain't going out like that. I might die the final death today, but I'm not going to just let the bad guys have it all their way. Now's my moment. Choose my death—and make it fast!

The only piece of clothing still on me was my cargo pants, and the left leg was already ripped off at the hip. The right leg was gone from the knee down, and I could feel hands tugging, too roughly to be effective, on the buttons of my fly. Sa'mah was still in my right hip pocket, and I could feel her slicing through the fabric under the pressure, telling me she was ready to go.

I forcibly relaxed my involuntary struggles, then took a deep breath and cleared my mind. Trying to *think* would be my worst strategy right now.

And then. And then.

My body flowed as if each movement was a natural part of the universe. Like the course of stars, each action fated by centuries of accumulated natural forces.

My right arm melted out of the many brutal grips and was down my side and buried in the tiny pocket, finger gliding along Sa'mah's wrapped handle, sliding the beloved blade out into the world, where together we would meet the end as one being.

Our first collective action was to see how deeply we could slice the arms that held me down. The arms holding me were not prepared for it. Sa'mah had become a part of me, and she led me in patterns of movement I could never have planned. Although she was only three inches long, she sliced through tough fabric and am'r flesh like butter. We hardly slowed down on the out-stroke, so on the return, we had the momentum to make forearms unusable, and in one case most-ways sever an offending hand. We danced, and I ended up sitting up on my sacrificial block, maintaining a space around me. The channels in the stone ran with blood that was not mine.

It could not last long. It had not been *meant* to last very long, just long enough to make Sandu and Bagamil proud of me and let them know their blood ran true in my veins. To make them certain they'd chosen right in loving me. Time moved slowly now, so slowly that I could almost count the seconds as they oozed by. In a handful of those seconds, I would turn Sa'mah upon myself, and she would, with her bite so smooth it was almost a kiss, ease my transition toward my final death. All my enemies would be able to do was pour flammable fluids upon me and finish a job I had done very well.

I didn't have time to *think*, but in those creeping century-seconds, I felt a rainbow of emotions rush through my being. Wordlessly, I experienced: pride in myself, joy in the destruction of the enemies of my vhoon-anghyaa, and the most complete contentment in my success, better than any post-coital satisfaction.

Sa'mah swirled around my torso again like poetry, and bodies fell back from our razor flow. Outside the sacred space we'd created were raised voices and a rush of movement as more am'r joined the fight, which meant we'd come right up on our final moment.

Sa'mah raised up, and I trusted that in her complicated descent pattern, I would soon be bleeding out on the floor, not conscious long enough to see the dismay in my enemies' faces nor the pride in my beloveds'.

# CHAPTER NINETEEN

The sounds beating against the self-contained space changed. The attention of the room shifted off me, and I experienced extreme disorientation. My brilliant focus shattered; time sped back up to a confusing chaos. Sa'mah faltered a little in my grip.

There was a general rush toward the disturbance, and I found myself sitting alone on the stone table, wearing nothing but ripped bottoms that were short-shorts on one side and knee-length on the other. At least my blood-crusted clothing and bandages were finally gone, and even though they'd been ripped off me with intent to harm, I was giddy with the freedom of not having them grate against my skin.

I felt...bereft. I'd been ready to die—and still was—but the right moment for death had just brushed past. It could come back at any moment, of course, but until then, the glorious single-mindedness of purpose was gone. In its absence, I realized it was more addicting than any drug, even blood.

*What the hell is going on over there?* I forced my unsteady senses to focus on the commotion.

There was fighting—no big surprise in a room full of am'r. It swelled along the right of the room, past Bagamil in his horrific torture, a mass of bodies giving the strangest impression of being in a mosh pit at a concert. A *particularly* violent mosh pit, because blood was flying, and so were bullets. I was too bespelled to even think about ducking.

And then my brother jumped up to stand on one of the Chairs of Importance.

Dragoș. Dragomir Pricolici, fellow frithaputhra and lover of Sandu. One of the very few am'r in the world around whom I could feel just as safe and loved.

"*¡Hola a todos!*" he shouted with his irrepressible grin. "I'm here to join this fun party! I know the host didn't invite me, but that's never stopped me from enjoying a good *fiesta*, has it, my patar?"

"Not that I've ever known, *nu.*" Sandu called back, smiling. He looked as relaxed as a person in a metal internal-bondage machine could look.

"I found some friends along the way. This guy says he's our ally—" Dragoș waved a hand towards some am'r standing in a protective clump. I strained upward to see over the heads of the minions and the Special Guest Am'r, while trying also trying not to be hit with a bullet or knife or fist meant for someone else. One clump of am'r stood as a group, not mingling (i.e., fighting) with the other partygoers. They were, well, bedraggled and rather damp. One of them stood at their head, as obviously trying to be the leader as a dog standing to quivering attention.

His skin was the whitest white—fish-belly-white. I couldn't imagine him walking through the kee world without people moving away from him in discomfort, assuming something was not quite right with him—and they'd be right. He had shoulder-length hair, still too wet to tell if it was dark brown or black. Its frizzy curls were springing free as they dried around the edges. His eyebrows were huge raggedy caterpillars that sprawled histrionically over each eye. His facial hair was the most impressive thing, however; the wild mustache cascaded down into a full, riotous beard. I was, for the first time, struck by how impractical facial hair was for an am'r. If this guy bit you, he might end up eating his own beard on the first bite and having to smooth it down and try again.

As he stood there, as damp and bedraggled as the rest of the group but quaveringly self-important, I realized I was getting my first glimpse of Orélie the Self-Anointed.

Not the most prepossessing ally to count on one's side, but he was holding a gun, and so were some of his followers. The rest had various types of blades. I just hoped the guns weren't too waterlogged to work properly.

"He was *not* our ally before," Sandu shouted to Dragoș, "but he's welcome to try now!"

"I did pull him and his men out of some kind of oubliette, so he owes us." Dragoș was mid-explanation when Julio finally stopped looking gobsmacked and joined the conversation.

"No, *you* were *not* invited to this party, but making you pay for your interruption will increase our appetites for the feast. *Kill them all!*" he screeched to his disordered minions.

For a while, talking ceased. I figured out pretty quickly that sitting mostly naked on a display table in a room full of berserk am'r with only a three-inch blade to hand was a suboptimal condition. Without any shame, I clambered under the table; just in time for two am'r to crash down upon it. I couldn't tell from the kicking legs who was who, but the one who eventually fell down beside me was a Julio-minion, so that was alright.

Conveniently, the mostly-dead minion had a machete. I pried it from his hands and slid it into the ripped-open pocket on the left side of my makeshift shorts. I slid Sa'mah back into her little pocket. I didn't bother trying to wipe the blood off of either, since what was left of my pants was still encrusted with blood anyway. In my future, there would be a long hot shower, and then *another* shower, followed by a long hot soak—but I pushed that out of my mind. The thought of peacefully floating in clean hot water was too *good* and threatened more than anything to make me break down and cry.

A perfect distraction arrived as a pistol came flying over with a *thunk* that was audible to me even above the shouting and general fighting noise. Just what I needed! It wasn't in reach, but I quickly crawled out, snagged it, and reversed right back to my safe space.

Looking out, I knew I was in exactly the right place for the moment. The cavern around me was nothing but fighting bodies, swinging blades, and regular gunfire that struck friend and foe alike in the pandemonium.

It was hard to tell, but it didn't look like my good guys were wildly outnumbered. Who knew how many am'r Dragoș had brought hiking with him into these caves and how many of Orélie's followers had remained alive to be rescued from Julio's booby traps? However, one side was not yet overwhelming the other. Right now, it pretty much looked like "every am'r for himself."

This pause had been good for me to collect myself, but I was starting to feel antsy. I should be out there fighting with my am'r, not hiding like a coward. But I did also need to ensure I didn't immediately make myself available as a hostage again. I looked down at my shiny new pistol. Well, it was new to me, but the blued metal was scratched and obviously well-used. I was familiar with this specific model. I mentally thanked my friend whose uncle had had a small arsenal and who had barked out gun safety like a drill sergeant. I checked the magazine and was delighted to find twelve rounds. I'd want more all too soon, but in this chaos, it would be easier to find another gun than a new magazine for this one.

What was the most important thing I could do out in the pandemonium? The question barely flitted across my mind before I knew the answer, with no room for self-doubt. There were two people in this room more helpless than I. *For once.* I needed to go protect them.

I poked my head out in the direction of Sandu. He was still stuck in his crazy bondage cage, and for the moment he was alone, watching the action around him with an amused expression. He was idly trying to pull his right arm out of the pin stuck through it. Although it would never work, I knew he'd never stop trying.

I swung around and looked at Bagamil—and then I was out from under that damn table and flinging myself through the thrashing bodies and flying bullets.

I threw myself upon the first asshole who was trying to get an early tap into the Bagamil keg. He had yanked my gharpatar's head up and back by a rough handful of the long black hair and had a long knife against Bagamil's neck. Thank goodness he had that tough old skin, because otherwise, he'd have been a gushing fountain by the time I got to him.

I put the gun to the left of that am'r's head and pulled the trigger. Except for recoil, not much happened from my point of view, but the asshole did stop what he was doing. He staggered, then his knees gave out and he sagged down.

When I saw the exit wound, it was not much bigger, but brain matter had sprayed out with the blood. Maybe an am'r *could* recover from that, but he was out of commission for some time to come.

All this activity had aroused the notice of the am'r around us. I'd barely shoved aside the body of the am'r I'd just dispatched when another came running up, huge Bowie knife swinging. I got him in the knife-hand shoulder and then turned to deal with another am'r. This one had a gun aimed at me, however, and I panicked and fired way too early. He fired as well. Thank goodness it's hard to aim while running; he missed. I fired and missed again, and fear started rising in me, threatening to overwhelm the certainty that had been keeping me going.

Before discovering how epically I could fail, there was a presence at my side. Dragoș was holding a sawed-off shotgun. He fired, and I watched in sick fascination as a two-inch-diameter hole appeared in my assailant's face. He fell forward, leaving a spray of skull fragments and blood and brain matter in the wake of what had been his head.

While I was gaping at that, he grinned down at me. "Did you miss me, *surată mea?*"

"Of course I missed you, big bro!"

"Of course you did. Why would you want to have an adventure without me?"

"*I* didn't want to do this without you. *You're* late."

We'd moved back-to-back in front of Bagamil now, and we had to break off our repartee to fire at onrushing bad guys. The guy I'd hit in the shoulder was back, and it took too many bullets to hit him in the head and stop him. Then there were more am'r to deal with, and I found myself pulling the trigger and hearing the awful *click* of an empty magazine.

I tossed the gun aside and looked around. There were more weapons on the ground, beside bodies that had previously been wielding them, but they were not in easy reach and I wasn't sure which was the best one to try for.

"I need a gun, big bro," I announced over my shoulder. "I have a knife already. What should I do?"

"Use your blade to free our gharpatar. I'll cover you both."

He was as good as his word. But I expected nothing less.

"Are you OK?" I asked Bagamil, even though it was the dumbest question in the world.

"I soon will be, cinyaa," he replied with his usual grandfatherly calm. I was not sure what the ropes they had tied him with were made of, but I could not get the damn machete to slice them. I wasted precious moments on it, then shoved the useless thing back into my makeshift pocket-sheath and dug out my dependable Sa'mah. *She* did the job. Bagamil's limbs flopped in a depressingly useless way as they were released. There was no way he'd be fighting—or even walking on his own—until he'd had a chance to get his limbs set right and give him a whole bunch of vhoon-vaa. Not something we had time for at the moment.

Dragoș was now fighting two am'r, using an iron rod like a spear. He was singing in a loud bellow, so I didn't bother worrying about him. Instead, I looked behind Bagamil at the rest of the room.

Sandu first. He was in the same precarious position, but now he was surrounded by some of our Romanian crew, Răzvan and Atanase—and Daciana! Oh, how happy I was to see her! She was helping Sandu remove his arms and legs from the insane bondage, which I imagined had to be profoundly painful. Regardless, I stopped worrying about him because I knew all three would lay down their lives to protect him.

I scanned the less vital skirmishing and my eyes were drawn to a corner. I knew two of the am'r there. To be precise, I knew one of the am'r—and the am'r-nafsh who was with him. I didn't know what mix-up had led to Isidra being in this hall, but I couldn't imagine Hugo had chosen it. Speaking as an am'r-nafsh, an enclosed space full of battle-roused, bloodthirsty am'r was the single worst place you could be. Isidra obviously hadn't gotten any of the training I had. She stayed behind Hugo as he fought off two am'r, who obviously did not know (or just did not care) that this was their host's beloved tipple and not on tonight's menu.

I stuffed Sa'mah back in her pocket and grabbed the machete from the other side of my former pants. "Dragoș, I gotta go help some people."

"*Bine*. I have good help coming for our patar." He gestured with his head to the left, behind me. I turned for a quick look and felt my heart lighten. One am'r was knocked into another, and while they tried to recover, a nicer machete than mine literally disarmed one (as in, removed the arm that was holding the weapon) and mostly decapitated the other. Zoraida stepped through their falling bodies.

"Zee! It's so good to see you!"

She grinned at me. "Your patar starts so many fights. All I have to do is associate with him, and I am never bored." She wasn't wasting time, however, and was already past me, lifting Bagamil. He turned his head as best he could to look at her, and said half-jokingly, "I do not think we can blame *this* one on Sandu."

"For once!" she said grimly as she cut the ropes that bound him and tried to find the best way to arrange his broken limbs to carry him away from the dead center of the fight.

I was torn, wanting to stay to help. Even as I ran off to fight by Hugo's side, I thought, *This is probably the dumbest thing you can do.* But instinct drove me. I went.

I had to fight to get there, however.

An am'r who had been moving to join in attacking Hugo saw and smelled me and veered off. *Any* delicious am'r-nafsh would do. I thought I recognized him as being one of Julio's special guests. Whatever. He had a gun, but he either didn't want to shoot me (and waste my precious blood) or he assumed I'd be no threat. He was mostly right about the latter, but I had luck on my side because he stepped in a puddle of blood from a decapitated am'r—one of theirs or one of ours, I couldn't tell—slid, and did a ridiculous flailing dance to attempt to keep his balance. I grabbed the moment to swing my machete with every bit of force I had in me.

I didn't cut his gun arm off completely, but he wouldn't be using it to shoot anyone until after he'd had a good long drink of blood, which I wasn't willing to let him have. He was on the ground now and stared up at me in startlement as if a soft furnishing had attacked him. It pissed me off.

"Is it because I'm a girl?" I demanded as I chopped at his arm again, missing the balance of Terry Smatchet as I did. "Or is it because I'm nothing but a walking sippy-cup to you?" I went after his neck. There was a fair amount of arterial spray. "Well, *this* will teach you not to underestimate us girly sippy-cups in the future. Won't. It."

When his head was finally off, I was out of breath, and my body was freshly painted in his blood, Jackson Pollock-style. I moved the machete to my left hand, grabbed his gun and resumed trying to get to Isidra and Hugo.

Hugo now was holding off three am'r. None of them were paying any attention to what was coming up behind them. Even *I* knew better than that.

Am'r Number Three was closest. I brought up the gun, hoping there was still ammo in it. It turned out there were two bullets, which caught him in the chest. He spun to face me, and I dropped the empty gun, moved the machete back to my right hand, then hacked at his head and neck. I didn't get him properly decapitated before Am'r Number Two came at me with a short sword. I jumped back fast and tried to parry that more agile blade with my heavy slab of metal.

That gave Hugo a lovely opportunity to slice open his neck from behind before turning back to Am'r Number One. My opponent was now on the ground, his cervical vertebrae neatly sliced apart at about C3 or C4.

I moved up and stood beside Hugo, protecting Isidra behind us.

"Noosh!" came Isidra's happy cry from behind me. "*¿Estás bien?*"

"I'm fine!" I called over my shoulder. "The blood's not mine."

Hugo glanced at me, then called back at Isidra, "Give her guns!"

This made me look properly behind me. Isidra was doing more than just hiding behind Hugo. They had obviously hit a weapons cache at some earlier point in the evening. Her arms were full of guns, and she had a couple assault rifles slung over her shoulders. My heart swelled with pride in my sister.

She gestured to me with her arms full; I stuck the machete back through the ripped pocket of my blood-washed short-shorts. I grabbed a couple handguns, sticking the first in the other side of my shorts. I'd have liked the sheer power of a semi-automatic rifle, but I'd never shot one and was forced to stick with what I knew.

Hugo was unslinging an assault rifle from his back when I turned around. I'd just started to say something to him, a jokey "Fancy meeting you in a place like this" kind of thing, when there were shots near us, and his body jerked back. A mess of a hole appeared in his stomach, blood making the black fabric glisten in a spreading circle.

"*¡Hijo de puta!*" he growled. Isidra made a sound of distress behind him, and he told her, "*No, estoy bien! ¡Estoy bien!*" He stood up straight again and tracked where the shots had come from. An am'r approached us with his gun extended, calling for us to drop our weapons.

"*¡Vete a la verga!*" Hugo responded, backing up his words with a round that moved across the advancing enemy's body. The sharp retort of the firing echoed too loudly in my ears. The am'r abruptly stopped. His face went slack. He dropped his gun, then his body dropped to the floor as well. The front of him did not look very damaged. Once he fell, what I could see of his back was another matter.

The rapid cracks of the shots had made an impression even over the sounds of fighting and other gunfire. There was a strangely empty pause, and then we heard shouting in a voice I would have been happy never to hear again.

Señor Super-Colonizer was striding over to us, roaring at Hugo. "Why are you shooting our allies, *idiota de mierda?*"

"Your *allies*," Hugo replied with gravity, "wanted your am'r-nafsh for vhoon-berefteh. I thought you would not be pleased by that."

"Pah!" I'd never heard anyone actually say "Pah," before. "You above all others know what these alliances have cost me. If that was all they wanted, give it to them—the most important thing is salvaging this night. Kill our enemies, frithaputhra, not our friends. I should not need to tell you this."

"You commanded me to care for this am'r-nafsh," Hugo said, careful with each syllable. "To do anything else would have been to break my word to you, patar."

"*Sí, sí, bueno.* Now I am telling you, stand with me against our foes, and do not worry about that *perra tonta.*"

I glanced at Isidra. Her face was drained of blood and emotion and set like stone. I moved my eyes to Hugo, and his face was the same. Oh, shit. I nervously adjusted my grip on the gun in my hand.

Even moving that much brought Julio's attention to me. "And *why* are you here shooting our allies with one who has made herself our enemy at every turn? That would make anyone mistrustful of your allegiance."

Hugo looked insulted. And angry. As am'r poker faces went, his wasn't great. "When have I ever given you reason to doubt me, patar? Have I not been fighting by your side all these years? You gave me a task because of your trust in me, and I have been doing everything I could to complete it satisfactorily. If that includes accepting any help that offers itself, well, we have had stranger bed companions over the centuries."

I knew what Hugo meant, but Julio was in a mood and ready to take anything the wrong way. "I do not see why any of those around you have been companions in your bed."

Hugo was obviously counting to ten under his breath. "This is foolishness. We have enough enemies around us. Stand by me, patar, and let us kill them together as we have always done."

"No. No—now I see it clearly. Ever since I gave you the job of caring for my am'r-nafsh, you have been acting above your station. I did not give her *to* you. She is mine still, to dispense with as I will. And *you* are mine, created from my vhoon-anghyaa and thus obligated to me. Obey me now, or I will forget that you are my frithaputhra."

"*¿Obligado?*" Hugo's deep voice soared up and cracked painfully. "I have followed you for love, patar, and again I say I have never given you reason to doubt my loyalty. But a frithaputhra is not the *slave* of the patar. I think it is time I left your side, if you no longer love and trust me."

"*Ah!* You try to turn your betrayal back upon me? *You* are the one who took your love and trust from me! Did I not give you a job for only the most trustworthy? How have you repaid me? On this most vital night of nights, you abet my enemies, kill my allies, and think to steal for yourself the vhoon to which I alone have a right!"

I could feel Isidra seething behind me, but she kept her anger in check. Smart am'r-nafsh. Smarter than I'd have been, since an intense desire to speak up on her behalf was tickling my throat. I was superfluous, however.

"That is all an am'r-nafsh is to you? Just vhoon you own? Was that all *I* was to you, Julio, when I was am'r-nafsh? Just something you *owned?* And I see that I am barely more than that now." Hugo spat the words into Julio's face. "*Muy bien.* If you want *betrayal,* I will give it to you. I am leaving this *maldita fiesta ridícula,* and I will bring Isidra with me if she wishes to go. You will not obstruct us, or you will die trying. *¿Lo entiendes?*"

Julio's face was raw anger. "*Oh, entiendo.*" He spoke with a quiet coldness that was a worrying change from his soap-opera shouting of a moment ago. "That would make you pat'rkosh, *sabes.* For all to see. You would find no allies among the am'r. They will execute you for your sin."

Hugo's face was set. "If I am pat'rkosh, *who* would I have learned that from? Do you think I do not know your secret, *patar?* I have heard whispers about Ligeia, whose vhoon-anghyaa comes down to my veins through yours. If

I killed you, would I not avenge her? Would I not be correcting a sin long unpunished? There are am'r here old enough to remember her, am'r you've tried to destroy tonight. Would my sin cancel yours? I am willing to find out."

Julio paused, then shook his head as if Hugo's words were buzzing pests. "You will not kill me if I kill you first!" He turned his head and waved his gun in the air in the vague direction of his allies, although the opposing sides were so admixed that he included Sandu's Romanian crew and Orélie's followers in his gesture. "*¡Están conmigo!*" he bellowed, clearly expecting a rush of backup.

No one moved. No one had moved this whole time. Julio's and Hugo's little drama had frozen the fighting in the entire cave. We all just watched the train wreck. I'd never seen anything distract an am'r from a fight before. Now I knew: a properly tragicomic spectacle would do it. *Fucking am'r.*

"*Entonces*, you *all* betray me," Sad Señor Super-Colonizer hissed. Honestly, I think it was less betrayal than a simple desire not to get involved in Julio's personal business, but no one was going to convince him of that. I was—I think we all were—waiting for a soliloquy on how Julio had always been alone, had always been left to suffer when it really counted. Hugo mercifully spared us this by shooting him.

It was pretty clear that despite every self-pitying word Julio had spouted so far, he was not expecting anything except Hugo dropping his weapons and facing his infinitely deserved punishment. Julio had actually looked away and waved his gun for emphasis, thus making it useless as a weapon. No matter what he'd said, he still trusted Hugo and didn't see him as a true threat.

Bullets from Hugo's gun slashed through Julio, starting below his sternum and climbing up the center mass of his body, tearing his throat open.

Julio opened his mouth to speak, but nothing came out. His mouth stayed hanging open, and he looked at Hugo. Hugo stared back at him. Everyone else in the room watched in fascination. Then Julio's head fell backward, and the movement ripped those wounds open wider. His dark shirt started glistening with blood that rapidly spread over his shoulders and down his chest, meeting the blood more slowly spreading from the lower entrance wounds across his heart.

He stumbled and moved a leg back to give him balance, but it slipped, and he dropped to his knees. Some vital muscles in his neck had been torn, and he could not lift his head back up to look at us anymore.

He was fighting the damage the bullets had done to him. Given enough time and blood he could heal, but right now we all watched his body give in and finally slump face-first to the floor. At a certain point in the collapse, his head flopped forward obscenely.

As much as I hated him, watching it made me ill. There was more dignity in being honestly decapitated with a blade.

Everyone was still frozen except Orélie the Self-Anointed. With a triumphant scream, he ran up to Julio and emptied out his handgun into his head, maybe four shots. He tossed the weapon away and pulled a straight short sword from a sheath at his waist, the blade tapered like a Roman gladius but obviously not so ancient a weapon.

"You! You have stolen my glory for far too long, Popper! *Enfin, je vais prendre ma place légitime dans ce pays!"* He continued screeching in French as he hacked at the body. At least it wasn't *me* hacking bits off an am'r body for once. But I was just a newbie, and still an am'r-nafsh. It made sense for me to do the grunt work while the more skilled, older am'r did the harder, fancier stuff. Two of Orélie's followers had followed him, and now, so they wouldn't be standing there looking awkward, they were aggressively protecting his back. Since everyone else was still just standing around watching things play out, this failed at making them look less awkward.

I looked at Hugo. He stared at Julio's increasingly mangled corpse, then at Isidra. She was looking with love and concern at Hugo. It was clear Julio was now a nonentity to her; she didn't even care enough about him to revel in his pathetic downfall.

I looked back at Hugo and found him watching me as I watched Isidra. "Um...hey," was the best I could come up with.

"We will leave now."

"Yeah, that sounds like a really great idea. I'd like to leave before it jumps off again too, but I have a feeling that's not going to happen."

"*Mil gracias, hermana,*" Isidra said to me and stroked my arm. I normally would be pretty jumpy about being touched in a situation like this, but her touch didn't bother me.

"Get Hugo out of here," I told her, grinning. "Go start a new life."

She said, "*Hugo, mi amor,*" and I could tell by the way her voice caressed the words that she'd never dared call him that before. Then, arms so full of guns that they couldn't hold hands, they turned and were away out a nearby exit I hadn't noticed, through which they'd obviously been attempting to escape through this whole time.

# CHAPTER TWENTY

Orélie was still shouting at Julio's body, or rather, at the pieces of Julio's body, when I turned back to the room.

"*Du feu, apportez-moi du feu!*" he called to his followers. No one did anything. "Fire! *¡Fuego, cabrones!*" The two doing performative backup just stood there stoically. Obviously, they didn't have an effective method of creating fire on their still-damp persons.

There was an uncomfortable lull in the rest of the cave. Around the room, am'r shifted where they stood or took a moment to check on healing injuries to make sure they were ready to go again. Not only had they been fighting and been interrupted with no satisfying results, but also, so much blood had been spilled in this enclosed space that the air was thick with it. Someone would find an excuse to start letting more blood soon, and this time, there was no unifying force. As ineffectual as Julio had been, he had been an excuse, a reason for fighting on one side or the other. What was brewing now was an insane melee, and with both Sandu and Bagamil so injured, I didn't like my am'r-nafsh chances of surviving it.

To think of them was to look for them. Sandu was now free of the evil contraption and sitting on the ground, getting am'r field medicine. He was currently receiving a blood donation from Răzvan, while members of the Romanian crew formed a protective circle around them. Thank everything, he'd be able to walk again soon.

Bagamil was already standing on his own and looked healed. I could tell because he was still mother-naked. Someone had to get that man some clothing one of these days, although he didn't seem particularly bothered. He stood there stretching and flexing muscles that were bound to at least be a little stiff. He must have used the time while the Hugo-Julio drama was going down to get his joint-resetting and blood healing. I guessed he'd seen enough am'r drama in his long centuries of existence not to find this one particularly compelling. That or he was too smart to stand around gawking when he could be healing.

It suddenly occurred to me that I was alone; Orélie and his followers were between my people and me.

The Self-Anointed was now literally *stomping* on what remained of Julio and cursing in a mix of languages. From what I'd heard about him, sanity had never been one of his strong suits, but the slaying of Julio had clearly put him 'round the final bend.

I really wanted to be far away from his craziness before he realized what a vulnerable, valuable little treat was within his reach.

It was imposed upon my consciousness in this moment, with profound untimeliness, that I was wearing nothing but ripped "shorts" and a thorough coating of blood. In a way, I was more dressed than I would be in some bikinis. And I was armed, which psychologically was all the clothing I really needed. But I had to blink ferociously to not allow myself to consider how my blood-encrusted tits had been bouncing around through all of this. Of all thing things in the universe, this truly was irrelevant: a kee thought which could only slow me down.

I started moving slowly backward, just letting myself drift a little to the right, trying to let my movements be so smooth that they didn't catch anyone's eye.

Of course, Orélie's head jerked right up. His nostrils twitched in that way with which I was all too familiar.

"You are Sandu's am'r-nafsh." I could see on his face that the bloodlust for Julio was changing into a very different sort of bloodlust.

My lip curled. *That means I'm more am'r than you'll ever be,* I wanted to say. What I *did* say was, "And here's his patar now." I also made sure my grip on my gun was firm.

Bagamil had moved with lightning speed up behind Orélie.

"What do you have to say to the frithaputhra-of-my-frithaputhra? Whatever it is, it can be said to me." His voice was exceptionally calm. I wondered if Orélie could figure out that meant danger.

The Self-Anointed spun to confront my gharpatar. He straightened his spine, and in the same movement, used his free hand to toss his unkempt curls back over a shoulder imperiously. "Popper is dead. I killed him. I claim this bastion as mine. I claim his frithaputhraish. I claim his alliances." As he made his claims, his accent thickened and his voice climbed higher, coming close to cracking on the last syllable.

"Do you?" Bagamil asked. A pause. "Do you claim his enemies too?"

Orélie's face scrunched, and his body grew visibly tense. We all tensed too, then watched him force himself to relax. *I* didn't relax.

"I have offered you nothing but friendship. Nothing but assistance in your time of need."

Bagamil's voice was flat. "You offered to take advantage of us in our time of need."

"No! No! You would not even hear me out! You have been nothing but disrespectful to me. *Maintenant*, I am the killer of Julio! You will give me respect!"

Nobody bothered to point out that Hugo had been doing just fine killing his patar before Orélie barged in. I guess no one thought it was worth the effort.

Speaking of people no one thought worth much effort, I wondered if my being a lowly am'r-nafsh might actually come in handy right now. I had a gun in one hand, another in one side of my waistband, and the machete on the other side. Bagamil was taking up the Self-Anointed's attention, and more than that, our people were not slow in arriving for backup. It was more than just the Romanian crew I noted as am'r started sliding casually and *completely coincidentally* into convenient spaces near Bagamil. Am'r I'd not seen since my first introduction into their world were stepping into view, and each brought a little more joy and confidence to my heart.

Wulfhram and his bestie Dubhghall moved up like they were making their way through a crowded dance floor. The intimidating Astryiah was abruptly there, leaning against one of the Chairs Of Importance. And oh, Eben with his old-fashioned muttonchops and his beloved Cyrus were over there, smiling at me. Hisao appeared from behind an unknown am'r, then several am'r dressed equally impeccably (the best-tailored hiking gear I'd ever seen) spread casually away from him.

There was an am'r I remembered as being named Nthanda, tall and bulky with muscle, with dark reddish-brown skin and an infectious smile. Everything else about him was covered by warm layers of clothing and a huge hat with earflaps, which somehow made him more intimidating than ridiculous. He had also brought a few friends with him; I could tell by the way he directed their movements with quick flicks of his eyes.

Orélie's two followers were more than aware of the non-spontaneous nature of these arrivals, and I watched panic move across their faces. They met each other's eyes, looked away. I was not surprised to watch both of them fade away from their Self-Anointed-leader's side with impressive subtlety.

Orélie did not notice. His focus was on Bagamil like no one else mattered in the whole world. Or this whole cave, which was more to the point.

Still, he was an am'r, so no one could approach him without making his natural am'r radar go *ping*. I felt I had a moment, a little bubble of time, in which I—as something he did not perceive as a threat—could do just that.

Should I try to take this asshole out without asking anyone? The Wisest Head I could ask was right past Orélie's shoulder, but I wasn't sure how much I could communicate to him without Orélie noticing something was up. There was a room full of am'r around me, all more knowledgeable and more skilled. What right did *I* have to set myself up as judge, jury, and executioner for a being who was over a century older than me?

On the other hand, as Orélie's whiny voice continued on, I realized I was being pushed past my limits. Or rather, that I had been pushed past my limits some time ago, and now

I was no longer particularly *compos mentis*. I was in just the sort of mood to fuck shit up and damn the consequences.

I never used to do anything *except* consider consequences. I had gotten to this place, right here and right now, by just one time saying "Fuck the consequences" in a hot tub with a guy who'd told me he was Dracula. It felt right to celebrate that dubious choice with another one. Like an anniversary or something.

*Anyway, it's easier to ask forgiveness than permission.*

I let my gun gently drift upward. I would have felt safer using the machete, but the gun was already in my hand, and anyway, it wasn't going to be a very long-distance shot. The Self-Anointed was a mostly static target, his hands waving expressively but his body and head not moving so much. My eyes darted from side to side. I saw allies. I saw some am'r I didn't know, but none of them made any movement beyond their eyes widening with interest.

Bagamil knew exactly what I was doing. As my eyes swept back, he made sure to meet them. He gave a bare smile and very deliberately engaged Orélie with a question.

I never processed that question or Orélie's reply. My brain was entirely taken up with making myself move in this weird kind of smooth-steady-fast motion while time felt like it had essentially stopped.

Finally my gun was at the back of the Self-Anointed's head, and I couldn't control the thought: *This will be schizophrenic regicide!* My hands self-corrected a smidge because he'd moved his head slightly, my finger tightened on the trigger in the same deliberate slow-fast flow. Because I could, I shot again, and a third time, but after the second the gun just clicked. I tossed it aside and pulled my machete out of my shorts.

I couldn't see any blood in the thick mass of his dark curls, but after the second shot he staggered, throwing his arms out. He started twisting around to see me, but Bagamil had brought up a curved blade I hadn't been aware of him holding. He made hyper-fast swinging movements back and forth, and Orélie got a *haircut* that exposed a deeply sliced neck, which immediately started spraying blood.

Orélie staggered backward—onto the machete I was holding out. It didn't go between his ribs as deeply as I'd have liked, but then a hand reached from beside me. It took the machete, pulled it out, and reinserted it; much better. The hand was dark and slim, and I looked up to see Zoraida. She grinned at me in a way that would have been worrying if she'd been my enemy and said, "Here is the good fighting!"

Sandu pulled me to him, and I was stupidly shocked to see how fast he'd healed. He gave me the world's quickest kiss, then moved me back into the center of the Romanian crew, all of whom were armed and bright-eyed with battle thirst.

I peeped out, and Orélie was not to be seen—not standing, at any rate. I thought I could make out a slumped body on the floor and one of Hisao's people doing the boring job of decapitation.

At least I didn't have to finish what I started, and someone else would clean up the mess.

The energy of the room was palpable. Every am'r in it wanted to kill and to drink, then kill more and drink more.

This could go quite badly, I realized, even as I stood inside a mini-fortress of strong am'r bodies. At least half the am'r in this room were not our friends and had been invited here tonight to feast on the blood of Bagamil, with Sandu and me as surprise appetizers. They were keyed up, thirsty for both blood and violence, and stuck here in this enclosed space. My moment of glory taking down the Self-Anointed had added yet more blood to tickle their noses, one more bit of violence to arouse them.

I couldn't see how this *wasn't* going to end as a free-for-all massacre, where alliances that were not centuries-in-the-making were abandoned in the blood-fueled orgy of death. I was pretty sure my side was the strongest and most skilled at killing, but it was going to be a long and unpleasant process—for *me*, at least—to get to the other side of that.

I might not get to the other side as an am'r-nafsh, either—and as much as I'd truly hated being "neither fish nor fowl," I wasn't really quite ready to do the vistarascha thing, where you *actually* die and sometime, maybe months or years later, resurrect as an am'r. *Nope.* I discovered at that moment that I was willing to remain am'r-nafsh as long as Sandu and Bagamil and I could keep it that way.

Bagamil jumped up on a Chair Of Importance. He still patently did not care that he was stark-naked. He did *not* shout, but his voice projected compellingly through the whole room. "Aojasc' am'ratv!" He had unknown centuries of herding am'r, or at least surviving tricky situations, so hope kindled in me that maybe we could skip the killing-floor. Bagamil looked calm and sure, and although I thought he *had* to look calm and sure to pull this off, still, a girl could hope it meant he was drawing on a genuine state of mind.

"I *know* how you are feeling right now. I, the Aojysht, feel it most strongly of all of you. The vhoon-craving does not lessen over the years, as many of you here know all too well at this moment.

"But there is a time for the kind of killing that is in your hearts. Recently, many of you in this room fought at my side and at the side of my frithaputhra, Vlad Țepeș..."

Wow. Bagamil seldom called him by that name, respecting Sandu's insistence that he was a very different man than the one who had lived in the 1400s. This was name-dropping. This was reminding people of the darkest, most violent part of my patar. This was a warning. This was a *threat*.

"And there are even a few of you here who fought *against* us on that day. Which does not have to be a problem. We who are here all walked away from that battle; it is in the past. Creatures like ourselves cannot hold resentment. The years we live are too long, and we would get buried under all the grudges and complaints."

Sandu snorted very, *very* softly. I knew what he meant. So far, I'd not met many am'r who weren't just collections of long-cherished feuds and chips on their shoulders that cracked right on down through their whole selves. But Bagamil was politicking, so his words didn't have to make sense, just sound good and calm people down.

"Julio brought a variety of izchhaish to live in this fortress. The am'r amongst us who have lived here know where they are to be found and how many there are. They also have a system in place for getting izchhaish from local kee communities. It is right that we follow the natural order. Do you feel nothing but vhoon-craving? Yes, so do we all. I call forward those with information on how to get frangkhilaat, our rightful sustenance. Come, display your knowledge to your fellow am'r."

There was a pause while the am'r digested the thought of *not* fighting to the death and swilling each other's blood—and I digested the upsetting realization that I was still too close to the kee world to be comfortable thinking of kee as nothing but walking juice boxes.

*Will it be better when I've been am'r so long that I forget these are real people, with lives and loves that matter as much as my own?*

I pulled out of my thoughts because the pause had gone on too long, and my am'r were doing the minute body adjustments that indicated preparation for fighting. Dammit. Bagamil's speech hadn't worked.

Tension levels shot through the roof. Every am'r was on edge, trying to watch every direction at once. I was still holding the machete, slick with the blood of now dead Am'r-Who-Would-Be-King, and there was still an extra gun sticking into my hipbone. In the end, Sa'mah was waiting in her little pocket, too. We were as ready for this fight as we were going to get.

# Chapter Twenty-One

Bagamil had not let untold centuries of life wear down his natural optimism. I loved that about him, but my gharpatar had also used those ages to hone his battle skills. I loved *that* about him, too.

I think he still had more speech to give on the idiotic futility of the fight we were all about to have and was gearing up for it, but it was like a pause button had been pressed while he was talking. Then, whoever was sitting back on their sofa and watching us all frozen mid-action pressed play.

I think it was a former Julio-minion who started it. He didn't last long, though. He shouted something unintelligible, then started blasting at the massed group of Team Bagamil.

Which included me.

I ducked first and looked around from behind the mass of am'r bodies that surrounded me. Those who had something to get behind had done so as a matter of practicality, but the thing about being am'r is that most bullet wounds are just an annoyance. They sting like hell and will hurt during healing, and a good or lucky shot can seriously impede your goal of killing the other am'r before they kill you first. But most of my am'r were still standing, and either firing in response or responding in another way. That is, running at the asshole who was shooting at them with the full intention of stopping him—not only from shooting, but from ever doing anything else.

Once that started, it was *on*. Everywhere. While I peeked out of my little fortress of am'r, I saw that Nthanda had gotten to the am'r who'd started things first and had thoroughly removed his head from his body. With his people, he was cleaning up anyone in that area who felt inclined to have a go.

Bagamil was no longer standing as a fantastic target on the chair, but was now having a dramatic knife fight with one of Julio's VIPs. I could sense that this was an older am'r, and he demonstrated it by not being dead already.

Sandu was covered in blood-spray and in full Dracula mode. He had a short sword jammed through the am'r's torso so that he was stuck upon it. Sandu was thrusting *another* blade in and out of the chest as if he were playing a game of Operation and trying to find the heart. His knowledge of anatomy could only be called *profound*, though, so he was just having fun. Ugh. At least Dragoș had his back while he was getting his kicks. I looked away, trying not to wonder how many times his frithaputhra had done that for him over the years.

At this point, the fighting came to me. Zoraida carried two gracefully-shaped short swords that she was wielding like they were part of her body. She danced past me as two am'r tried to get under her fluid guard. I could hear her singing to herself, just as if she were deep in a computer system. I considered helping her out with my own machete, but I worried I'd just get in the way of her flow. My conflict was settled by more bad guys incoming in the wake of this battle-dance.

Răzvan, Atanase, Eben, and Cyrus were still standing protectively around me, letting me cower behind them. Now, they felt me move out to join them and kindly made room for me. The next second, a bloody and angry am'r—previous affiliation unconjecturable—was coming at me with a rifle with bayonet attachment.

I hadn't expected that, and the longer reach of his weapon was daunting. He thrust it at me in a really nasty way, grinning disturbingly from a face that was painted wetly red. His short hair was spiky and slick with blood.

I watched his movements with one part of my mind and his eyes with another, desperately catching each bayonet thrust with my blade and knocking it away. He was strong, though, and to be honest, I was exhausted. I could feel myself wearing down, managing to cope, but not being able to figure out how to bash that fucking unfair weapon out of his hands and get a good slice in.

Eben and Cyrus were fighting to my left in a lovely synchronicity, as lovers do, but they sensed my situation. Cyrus stepped forward to solely engage the am'r they were fighting, and Eben said, "Your pardon, Miss Noosh," and brought a steel-hilted smallsword with a wicked pointy tip up in a swirly movement under the arm that was thrusting the bayonet at me yet again. It sliced nicely through the chest muscles, and that damned bayonet dropped hastily. Eben swished his narrow blade around again, and both of the bad guy's arms were useless. My gentlemanly friend then thrust the sword through his chest, and while it was still planted in there, I stepped up and had a whack at his neck with my machete, just so I wouldn't feel useless.

The am'r dropped to the ground, and as I pulled my machete free, his scent registered in my nose and memory. It was that fucking minion who had held me so cruelly for Julio while my cinyaa was forced to poison himself on their maadakyo. I had in that moment promised myself that I would eventually kill this minion with my own hands. Now fate had brought me this generous gift.

It's probably better not to go into details about what I did to him.

When I was done, and panting for air like a kee, Eben gently said, "Miss Noosh, would you be so kind as to dedicate your efforts to just *incapacitating* our opponents? It would be greatly appreciated."

That was his sweet way of saying, "Stop making it harder for us to protect you, you silly little am'r-nafsh." I hated it, but he was right. I'd pushed the limits of what my body could do without rest or sustenance, and I was paying for it now, so I told him, "Sure, Eben, I can do that!" and smiled so he'd understand I appreciated that he'd found something I could do to feel useful.

I went back to squatting (sometimes kneeling) over incapacitated Bad Guys, making sure their injuries were extreme enough that we wouldn't have to worry about dealing with them any time soon. It was gruesome, and I was over it before I started. But I was helping, and that was all that mattered.

That interlude lasted a long and bloody time—until it stopped with the speed of a bullet.

Guns were still being discharged semi-regularly, but I was low to the ground, and I was so focused on hacking off bits that I'd honestly stopped paying attention. I think the am'r who shot *this* bullet was making a dramatic statement rather than with any real hope of effectively using it. Or maybe it was someone who was trying to pick off our guys. Whatever, it flew past everyone else and right into my side, into the part of me that was still not *entirely* healed from being reinjured so many times.

"Fuck!" I sat down in the classic suddenly-go-limp fashion. Since I still did not have a shirt, I got to watch blood pumping out of the entry hole. There was no exit hole since the bullet was still inside me. *Fun!* My ragged shorts were already so saturated that this blood just slid down my side, under the waistband of the shorts, and then oozed out down my outer thigh. I pulled the gun out of the other side of my waistband and set it beside me. I might as well be as comfortable as possible, all things considered.

As I watched the blood, I realized a couple of things. One, I felt very lightheaded, which was silly since I was barely losing any blood, comparatively. Two, people were talking to me, but the sound was very far away and hard to comprehend.

"Miz Noosh." Cyrus's honey-smooth voice penetrated the swirling in my mind. "Can ya get up? We need to move ya someplace mo' secure."

"Southern accents are so pretty. I don't meet many American...ugh, I mean North American am'r. I wonder why that is?"

"Sandu, she is in rather bad shape."

I heard Eben say my beloved's name and looked up. "Sandu! You're looking very Dracula! But I don't really *want* Dracula right now. I want to go to bed. I want a bath! I'm...tired."

"*Futu-i!* Carry her over there, against the wall. Both of you are to guard her. I'll come over as soon as we finish up."

I felt myself being lifted, and cried out as my poor side was stretched. I was carried in strong arms that made me feel safe. They smelled like Cyrus, and that made me think about how I could smell Eben's blood in his; esteshcinast, they called it. It was weird to smell a bloodline, but I'd read somewhere that dogs could smell when people were related to each other. Am'r had even better senses of smell than dogs. Or did they? I didn't really know how good a dog's sense of smell was. I'd never had a dog. Couldn't, with the long hours I put in at the HAW-Fuck-My-Life. But I didn't work there anymore. I was in the am'r world now. Talk about long hours. Now I could never have a dog.

"That's worse than not being able to have a baby," I told Cyrus, but he wasn't holding me anymore. I was leaning against a cold stone wall while sitting on a cold stone floor.

*Oh, but I'm always crashing.*

*In the same car.*

*Am I sitting with Bagamil, who everyone is calling Ignacio, waiting for him to wake up from maadak-sleep? Am I alone in a cell, waiting for Bagamil and Sandu and me to be the chocolate fountains at a stupid am'r murder-party? I hear fighting; am I waking from my drugged state to help Sandu and Bagamil by chopping off am'r heads? No, wait—my side hurts! Araceli is here, and she's keeping me safe while I heal, and then we'll go join Sandu and save Bagamil and go home.*

*Araceli...Oh, no. Araceli!*

*I'm always crashing. In the same car.*

*I've been in these cold underground caves for soooooo long. Don't tell me I don't get cold anymore. I'm cold, dammit. I chose this life, you'll say to me. A life underground. The sunlight makes my brain feel like it will explode and makes me hurt all over, so I have to be away from it. But can't I be somewhere warm? I've sat in hot springs and let the warmth sink deep into my bones. I was there, and Daciana and Astryiah were there, and they were sniffing me, and it was scary but* hot.

*There's been heat. In bed with Sandu. In Bagamil and Sandu's arms, making love for hours, maybe days? I want to be back in those moments, not this horrible looped scene where I'm cold and hurting, and I strain upwards for reality. But when I reach it, it slices my fingers off with the pain of it, so I fall back down again.*

*I'm always crashingIn the same car.*

And then there was blood. Bagamil's blood, the powerful energy of my gharpatar, swirled around in my mouth as consciousness whirled around in my head. I swallowed. I guzzled! It was the ultimate sustenance. It was food and healing, and I tell you, I could *taste* the love.

I was in his arms, those wiry limbs Julio had wanted to hack off and never let grow back. The strength in them always shocked me. Bagamil's Freddie Mercury good looks and easy smile made him seem like he was one of the youngest of the am'r, not the oldest and most powerful. He was covered in yet more fresh blood, and his nakedness made me flash back to our time alone in Julio's waiting-cell. There were too many emotions to unpack, so I focused on letting the blood fill my mouth just enough, then letting it move smoothly down my throat in calm swallows.

Bagamil pulled his wrist away. I brought up my hands and tried to pull it back, but he gently moved me into another lap, the one I knew best of all. Sandu's wrist was at my mouth, and I stopped trying to get back to Bagamil's blood and started suckling the open wound that was in front of me.

Suckling, yes, like a baby drinking precious mother's milk. This would make me stronger, heal me, and grow me in my powers. There could probably be some element that was sexual if I looked deep enough for it, but right now the blood had entered my system and the bullet hole in my side started healing, and the pain of that was enough of a distraction to make me not care about anything except getting more blood into me.

Yet all too soon, I was removed from Sandu's lap. I fought and found a little strength had returned to my body, but fighting made my side hurt badly and I froze in pain. This made it easier for the hands to lower me into another lap. The smell of him was so familiar, like Bagamil, like Sandu...Dragoș! I panicked. There had been sexual tension between us before, and I was not in a place to check in with Sandu. I felt like a just-born puppy with my eyes still closed, not able to do anything but snuggle up to Momma Dog's body heat and instinctively suckle. The stupidity of my worry hit me even as Dragoș offered me his wrist. He was Sandu's frithaputhra, just like me. They were lovers—or at least they had been. Why would Dragoș be off-limits to me? I was thinking like a kee.

I lipped the cut-open wrist eagerly and tasted his blood for the first time. Even more than his smell, there were the notes of our patar and our gharpatar, but they mingled with something uniquely Dragoș and blended perfectly into who he was.

I drank deep, longer than the others, timeless swallows of healing nectar.

I could feel his erection digging into my thigh. I found I didn't care who was around us or what else was going on and I wiggled my hips to let him know that. His other arm came around and took hold of my hip in a way that said, "No, no. Hold still. Not now. Just drink." It was a warm, familiar touch, but very clear in its message.

I stopped thinking about sex and drank deep.

The healing pains stopped me from thinking too much about sex, too. My side was on fire. The old(er) wounds in my thigh ached in a deep, throbbing way. Strangely, muscles in my upper back and chest twisted tight and burned as hot as my side. Pain had long since become an old friend, but this was a *lot* of it at once. I timed my breathing with my drinking in a twisted sort of meditation.

Eventually, the black curtain started to come down again. I fought it, but it was soft and gentle, and as it covered my mind, the pain retreated. Realizing that was enough to make me stop fighting.

# Chapter Twenty-Two

I awoke, and before I opened my eyes and departed the friendly darkness, I stretched my ears. I heard voices, all of which I more or less recognized. They were businesslike and calm, and there was even some low laughter, which I realized was Astryiah and Zoraida together.

That was...nice. Maybe even safe?

I felt brave enough to open my eyes. I was on the floor and not in anybody's lap, about which I felt a momentary pang of sadness.

Silly girl, you'll undoubtedly be in someone's lap soon enough. Focus on important things.

Vision took a moment. I wondered when I'd last used my eyes. Focus slowly sharpened until I could recognize people-like shapes moving around a cave.

Yes, *that* cave. We were still there, only the Bad Guys weren't. Or, well, many still were, but not in one piece. Bodies with various degrees of mutilation were being piled up in the center, with severed heads and other body parts being tossed randomly onto the heap as well.

What a sight! The dubious joys of living in the am'r world.

I spent a few moments wistfully contemplating going back to being a small-town librarian in Nowheresville, USA.

The Romanian crew and our allies were doing this super-fun task. Everyone was covered in blood and moving a bit creakily. As a matter of habit, I looked for my beloveds. Bagamil and Sandu were standing at the far side of the cave from me, talking to Hisao and his am'r. They were blood-soaked as well, and my men were still naked as jaybirds, aside from the blood. Well, am'r were never noticeably modest or shy.

I heard a sound very near me and looked over my shoulder. Oddly, that still felt very stiff and deeply sore. Daciana was there, and with shock, I realized she was missing her right arm below the elbow. The wound was dressed, although not in a way kee medicine would have called "hygienic," since it was strips of bloody fabric ripped from clothing. She smiled at me and said, soothingly, "Do not worry. It will grow back. It will be long and painful, though."

"I'm sorry," I told her, and she laughed. "I will not be stuck like this forever. For what is there to be sorry?"

I realized there were more am'r sitting on the floor on either side of me. We were the triage section. Everyone had lost hands or arms or large chunks of core, either cut off by blades or blown off by bullets. All looked perfectly content to not move, and most had their eyes closed, resting.

"What—what happened?"

"Well, you were shot and collapsed right around the time we were finishing up. You distracted the Aojysht and the Voivode; it took a bit longer because of that."

"Ohmigod! I'm sorry!"

"Stop apologizing. You were starting the vistarascha and they weren't ready for that."

"Neither was I!"

"Well, it would make some things easier, I can tell you. We did all the—how do you say?—the mopping up. They gave you vhoon-vaa there and then. The rest of us along this wall have had a taste of it as well, although none of us were as badly off as you. We all heal, but not as fast as we could with more vhoon. As soon as this is over, there will be *much* healing done." She winked at me, and I could easily guess this was going to be of the sexual healing variety, not the non-sexual field medicine we'd all just experienced.

It sounded good to me, too. Since it also implied getting out of this horrid cave system and back to somewhere with clean beds and hot water and *no* piles of mangled bodies, I was excited about all aspects of the idea.

Daciana fell silent, contemplating her hungers, and although I had a million more questions, I shut up to let her rest. I watched the last few bodies being moved into the pile. Flammable objects were placed around them, including those ludicrous Chairs of Importance. I realized that what I was watching was not some general post-massacre tidying, but preparation to burn all the bodies as efficiently as possible. I decided not to examine how I felt about this because my main feeling was still complete physical exhaustion. Now *that* might be worthy of contemplation, because blood had always perked me right up before. Since Sandu and Bagamil *and* Dragoș had all fed me their potent blood, I should be glowing with vigor and high as a kite. This was potentially quite worrisome. If one had the energy to worry.

My hamster brain tried to scurry around collecting all the things to be concerned about, but I was too enervated; I just watched, emotionless. Bagamil and Sandu chatted with the various groups and solo am'r who'd come along with Dragoș for the fight.

Eben and Cyrus left, pausing to say warm farewells to me before slipping out one of the cave's exits. Other of our allies took themselves off as well, like guests leaving a party. I guessed they were planning to head home—or anywhere but here—this temporary alliance being over because the interesting parts were finished and the rest just looked tedious.

Maybe that was my exhaustion talking? I'd never felt so jaded, but then I'd never lived so long amongst such violence and betrayal and needless, idiotic suffering and death before.

Once the pile was complete, the walking wounded were gathered up from the walls, and we all made our way out of the room. In the end, it was down to the Romanian Crew, Astryiah, and Nthanda and two of his frithaputhraish: Lilani, who had blue-black skin and many thin braids pulled back in a mohawk, and Vivian, who despite his name was a very masculine am'r with russet-brown skin and short dreads and a solemn demeanor. My beloveds, whom I noticed had garbed themselves in clothing that was not too damaged—undoubtedly liberated from the soon-to-be-truly-dead—and Astryiah and Nthanda went back in, and I smelled burning and heard the crackles of fire soon thereafter. They took a long time to come back out, and I guessed they were making sure the fire was raging in such a way that no half-burned am'r would be crawling alive out of it.

When he came out, Sandu put his arms around me. He smelled of burning. I almost pushed him away in revulsion, but I managed to check myself in time and make myself hold him closer. We had *survived*, after all. He'd just done what he had to do to keep us safer. It might be ugly, but I had no right to judge. I was too tired, anyway.

Together, we were a lot of am'r when it came to it. I felt like we were a gang, as we made our way *en masse* down the corridors. To be honest, I had no idea what it was like to be in any kind of gang, but it covered my notions of ganghood. For one, I was going around with people I knew and more or less trusted. Secondly, being in this group made me feel safer since we were more dangerous together than alone. And thirdly, the initiation to be part of this group had been a *bitch*.

At first, I was so glad to be leaving that I didn't question *where* we were going. But as we moved into tunnels I was kind of certain I'd never been in before, and as we seemed to be going farther *in* rather than "out and way the fuck away," I lifted my head and asked Sandu plaintively, "Where are we going?"

"A *humanitarian* mission," he told me with a grin I felt to be untrustworthy.

"Um. Hmmmm. What exactly do you mean?" I was going to add, "And why are *we* the ones doing this?" when we came around a long curving corridor and I realized I could smell kee blood. And kee sweat. And kee food. And the kee results of eating kee food.

"Oh, shit!" I said without thinking.

"*Da*," Sandu confirmed, and then we were in a series of cells like the tiny one I'd been locked in, but with no doors. The smell was even more...intense.

The bad news was that there were at least a hundred cells down here.

The good news was there were only about fifteen kee inhabiting the cells now.

The ugly news was that the other cells had all *been* inhabited.

Each cell had a thin mattress with blankets. They were not washed often enough.

Each cell had a bowl for water and bowls with basic survival foods stocked in them: energy bars, jerky, dried fruit, etc. The usual thing am'r fed their kee because they couldn't be bothered to deal with perishable supplies.

None of these kee were am'r-nafsh, I noticed right away. They were just dirty, brainwashed human beings, sitting on their mattresses, waiting for an am'r to come and use them.

My lethargy flowed away like hot lava was coming up under it.

I wished Julio wasn't dead so I could kill him personally. I had killed his killer, and that felt *wrong*. I couldn't regret being a part of Orélie's death. But I wanted Julio back so I could break all his bones and then set him on fire while he was still alive and conscious.

The kee were all acting stunned. Like the livestock they had been turned into, they let us herd them without a fight, a few protesting out of sheer confusion, insisting on staying in the cell where they'd been told to stay.

The one I chose to collect was one of the stubbornly confused. He sat on the bed, a scrawny thirty-something with a patchy beard and a sweat-stained baggy fleece top and pants. Not my idea of a sex slave, but apparently looks (or scent) didn't matter as much as convenient blood?

I asked his name, and he looked up at me.

"Thiago."

"*Bien*, Thiago," I smiled at him. "Let's go get some food, shall we? Or a shower. Would you like that?"

He just looked at me.

"A hot shower. Doesn't that sound wonderful? Or we'll maybe go outside and smell the fresh air? I'd love that!" I held out my hand. "Come with me, and we'll go get all those things."

He just looked at me.

Damn. My ability to speak another language was at its lowest ebb. I was so tired, but I tried, "*Um, un poco de comida, sí? ¿Un baño?*" I could not even start with "fresh air," so I put every bit of safe-vibed cheerfulness into a hearty, "*¡Vámonos!*"

He just looked at me.

"A bit of help here!" I called, and I failed to keep the panic out of my voice.

"*¿Sí?*" A head popped around the corner of the cell, and I was looking down a little at the unexpected curly head of Lope.

"Lope! *Señor*, I am glad to see you!"

He smiled at me, and I had this lovely feeling that the problem was out of my hands.

"And I am glad to see you alive, Sandu's frithaputhra. It was not something I expected." I imagined it wasn't. "How can I help you, *mi dama?*"

"This one—his name is Thiago—isn't getting up. I don't want to force him." I very specifically wanted no one to force him to do anything ever again. "So, what do we do?"

Thiago looked at Lope, and the dullness in his eyes decreased a little.

"*Ven a mi, mi hombrecito,*" Lope said very gently, and Thiago got up and went to him eagerly.

"*¿Me besarás? ¿Sí?*" he asked, and Lope just smiled at him and handed him to an am'r I couldn't see outside the doorway. I glared down at the thin mattress, needing something to do with my anger. When I looked up, Lope was lounging comfortably against the wall, watching me.

"This is ugly, you are right. We are not all like this down here in *Sudamérica*. Do not return to *Norteamérica* and remember this."

"What am I supposed to remember?" I snapped, forgetting I was talking to a powerful aojysht. "Why didn't you *do* anything about this, if it's not your style?"

"Julio kept it like...*un culto*. We am'r do not pry into each other's business. We nearly forgot he was here for decades. Anyway, it was not my concern."

"Maybe you should *make* it your concern, if you're so damn Society for the Prevention of Cruelty to Kee."

Lope's face had an interesting expression. I was smacked upside the head by the realization that he probably wasn't used to being spoken to like that, even by other powerful am'r—never mind by a pitifully weak am'r-nafsh.

"Sandu's frithaputhra, I regret that you met Sandu before you met me."

I blinked at him. Gods, that was just so am'r of him: all ego and laid-back sexuality, clearly someone who'd not been turned down in centuries. In my mood, it seemed only a few easy steps from that to keeping a hundred people in brainwashed captivity.

Lope seemed to read my mind.

"He was like that as a kee, Julio Popper. Read about him when we get back; there are books on him, I believe. He treated the natives of this country as subhuman, as he did with these kee. Becoming am'r does not make us immoral or depraved. We bring that with us from the kee world. It is at our cores, and it does not change.

"We am'r have not changed as the world has, and perhaps that will not work for us anymore. Julio's habits would have eventually gotten notice from the kee world. Perhaps they already have, but we do not follow kee news. *Es decir*, I know your patar chose you especially to help shake up our world, and I do not see that this is unwarranted. I did not come to his big *reunión* when he asked me. I told him then it was stupid. I did send Tecla to represent me, but nothing she reported impressed me. Now...I do not know, but I will support you both, and we shall see if you are able to shake our world."

Lope winked at me. "And if you ever tire of your patar, you are welcome in my household."

*Sigh.* Up until then, it had been surprisingly positive. And he *had* meant the latter as a compliment, in a really archaic way.

*If you don't like old-fashioned manners, you shouldn't shack up with older men.*

As the thought crossed my mind, Sandu stuck his head through the doorway. His clothing was still crusty with blood, but his hair and skin were clean and still damp. "*Dragă* Noosh, there is a spring here. Cold, I am afraid, but better than wearing dried blood, *nu*? And we found some clothing for you. Should be a good fit, I think."

*Some clothing we found here.* I shuddered. I was still full of rage that wanted to spray outward in every direction, but what was I going to do? Go back to civilization wearing only an unevenly ripped pair of what had once been pants?

I will honor whoever that kee was, I told myself as Sandu led me to the gushing underwater river. The water was freezing. At least that kept me from thinking, as I rinsed myself in liquid that must have been shooting directly up from the Antarctic. Dealing with that exhausted my bodily resources further. I tugged on my new outfit of a flannel shirt and very vintage jeans. Sa'mah was rescued from the bloody rags I'd had to peel off me and stuck in a similar hip pocket. It was better not to think, I realized: Focus on just doing one thing and then doing the next thing.

Lope's am'r were in charge of all the kee, and very happily for me, they'd rounded them all up and were directing them as we all made our final egress from this hellhole. If any of my am'r had snuck in a quick restorative "kiss," I didn't know about it. And I didn't want to know.

And so we left. The "gang" all walked (some of us limped or lurched more than others) through the endless tunnels. Sandu watched me like a hawk. All the Romanian crew did, I noticed. When Sandu got called off to discuss something with Lope or another am'r, I'd find an am'r I knew by my side, ready to talk or just be silent as we walked together.

We walked and walked. We went back the way we came, up through miles of winding passageways, some composed of rough black rock, some of smooth gray rock, some damp and cold, some dry and dusty. Where Sandu and Araceli—*Oh, Araceli!*—and I had done our dramatic jumps, the spiky booby trap had somehow been disabled and the rope bridge now spanned the gap. The experience was also improved by no one shooting at us. Other passageways had been roped off, and Sandu and Dragoș tried to rouse my attention by telling me about the traps they had dealt with on their travels through the cave system. There was an exciting variety of oubliettes: some dropping into water, others onto spikes, and a bunch more pressure-operated ones that launched varied selections of missiles at where you would step next. There was even a proper Indiana Jones-style boulder that had chased Dragoș and his rescue squad for a few kilometers (to hear him tell it) before they ended up in one of the endless oubliettes.

"That was blind luck because we weren't paying attention to anything except not getting run over, ha-ha! But the spikes—this one was spikes—had been ruined by water damage over time, so we ended up in a pile of mushy wood. I've had worse landings!" He grinned his wide Dragoș smile at me, and I did my best to return it with what must have been a feeble grimace. He was very good at rattling on kindly to cover for an inadequate conversationalist.

"We had some broken arms and legs and such to deal with. We know each other a good deal better now, but we can *all* say that about this little trip, eh? In the end, we made a chain and climbed out. Whoever built these traps didn't expect am'r to work together, *nu*?

"It was good we had practice in that when we came across that strange man—Orélie, was it?—and some members of his little cult, all trapped down in another oubliette. We heard them a long way off and thought they were a trap themselves! Next thing you know, we are looking down at a bunch of am'r swimming helplessly. Never laughed so hard in my life! They couldn't figure out how to trust each other enough to get out, or they were too stupid. Or both. Anyway, they said they were allies of our Aojysht, so we figured, more allies are good—even if they are a bit stupid. I mean, always good to have cannon fodder, *aṣa-i?*"

At this point, some jokes were made in Romanian that I didn't follow, and there was much laughter in the group around me. I wondered if I was the only one who felt so worn out, or if every am'r had had a nip of kee blood back in the cells. But no, there was Daciana with her arm not noticeably regrown, and Atanase was still missing his left hand, and Nthanda's Vivian ("Call me Viv") with his whole right arm off at the shoulder. None of them looked upset about their injuries. They were probably focused on all the lovely vhoon-vayon in their future.

"Not that they turned out to be much use as cannon fodder either," Dragoș was saying to me. "But that was fine. Just more for us to give the tokhmarenc, eh? It's been such *fun* since you came around. Not that we didn't have fun before, Sandu and me, but not these great battles. It's like the stories the aojyshtaish sometimes tell, about being in the old days. So hey, don't you feel bad about those of us who are missing some bits. 'Price of admission,' you'd say. *Nu?*"

He turned to Daciana for confirmation. She smiled. "*Așa e!* Not a problem. I told her this."

Atanase waved his wrist stump in the air. "*Da, da*, this will grow right back. *Nici o problemă.*"

Viv was walking nearby, his one arm swinging stiffly since there was not a counterbalance. He was wearing a coat removed from a dead am'r, and the other sleeve was empty and swung in a different way, which messed with me every time I looked at him. He laughed. "I like my Romanian brothers. You'd fit right in at home. *This* is nothing," he added, meeting my eye, and waving his arm in the direction of the missing one. "Just proof we've 'ad some fun."

Beside him, Lilani laughed with a liquid sound. "I have no idea why your patar brings his am'r-nafsh around with him, but if *you're* the one instigating all this fun, thanks, luv. I hope Nthanda wants to do more of these."

*More of these.* I shuddered. *It's not my fault.* Mehmet had started his Evil Plans before I'd been a flirty twinkle in Sandu's eye, even before I'd been born as a kee. And Julio and Orélie had been getting up to their repugnant shenanigans since the 1800s.

*It's not my fault.* Am'r had been killing each other since their beginning, I was quite certain. As long as Sandu and Bagamil don't get killed, what's it to me?

Araceli.

Ouch.

And there were more am'r who, if they met their tokhmarenc, would stab a metaphorical knife into my heart: my brother Dragoș, Daciana and Zoraida and the rest of the Romanian crew, Eben and Cyrus, Wulfhram and Dubhghall, and Astryiah. There was a mounting list of am'r I cared too much about—since they were going to all run straight at danger with their fangs out.

It was also suboptimal that I wasn't sure I could trust most of those "friends" if we were alone and they were peckish. Nthanda's Lilani, I could see and hear, was one of those am'r who just couldn't help themselves. She huffed frequently and deeply in my presence, which I found both unsettling and slightly insulting.

Bagamil came back to my side, took my hand, and kissed it. The am'r around me made room for him with unfussy but automatic veneration. We walked for a bit in silence, then I asked him, "So, what will Lope do with all the poor kee we found?"

"They will be paired with am'r they connect with."

"And become am'r-nafsh?"

The way he looked at me made him seem older, his nose beakier, less like Freddie Mercury with long hair. "Cinyaa, most kee are izchhaish to us. You know this term. We do not give our blood back to them, and they do not ever become am'r. They are not...*partners*. The exchange of blood between am'r and kee makes a bond like marriage, like you and my frithaputhra have. It is unique. It is rare. And," he grinned, "that is good because it is *not good* to have too many am'r running around in this world, as you have seen. The fewer of us, the better. Thus, it is good when an am'r chooses their frithaputhraish wisely."

*Oh, yeah, I can see that. But...*

"Why is my connection with Sandu so special? You and I have shared vhoon-vayon many times. Why is that not the same?"

"The third time you vhoon-shared, that was what made the tie. Once that bond was complete, you can share vhoon-vayon or vhoon-vaa with other am'r, and while there will be an increased connection—'amplified empathy' is perhaps how best to put it—it will not ever be like the bond between patar and frithaputhra."

"Um...why?" I could feel everyone around us listening with interest. By accident of birth—and then second birth within the am'r—I'd skipped centuries of hearing rumors and stories about the Aojysht-of-aojyshtaish and thinking of him as the closest thing to God in the am'r world. I'd skipped right to having him first as a kind of father-in-law, and then as a lover. I was casually comfortable with him in a way everyone else except Sandu was not. I could badger him with what Sandu liked to call my 'incessant questions,' and he had all the loving patience in the world with me. I think the am'r around us were getting a kind of contact high from it.

"Why?" He returned the question with a glint in his black eyes. "You, cinyaa, will help us answer that question. It is a good thing you like asking questions. You will end up being the one who makes finding those answers a part of our world. Very few am'r before you have bothered to ask why. They learned our ways and followed them and survived. Or did not follow them well enough and met their tokhmarenc."

"Ohhhhkay..." It was more than a little frustrating to finally get a chance to ask questions I'd had for a long time, but not getting answers beyond, "You need to figure it out yourself and then tell us."

"Are you saying that since people became am'r, no one has bothered to do anything more than drink blood and fuck for centuries and centuries?" I felt more than heard gasps around me. Apparently, one didn't speak to Bagamil this way. Fuck it—being the ignorant youngest with a North American sense of entitlement had to be good for *something*.

My gharpatar laughed, and it was the happy Mr. Sunshine sound I remembered from what felt like Before Time Began. "Cinyaa, that is mostly what I am saying, but you forgot to add, 'and fight with foe, and turn friend to foe and fight with them, and when they are dead, find more foes with whom to fight.' Most am'r have been content to do nothing but fuck and fight, as you say, down the long centuries. In our defense, I would start by saying that most kee, from whom we am'r derive, have been too content to do this even without the intense drives conferred by becoming am'r. Evolving into am'r does not mean asking more questions of the universe, merely growing stronger, less mortal, developing new powers, and thus existing longer.

"But some kee look at the stars and question them. When those kee become am'r, they do not stop asking questions. I know nothing will stop the frithaputhra-of-my-frithaputhra from such. Over the ages, we have had a handful of scientist and artist am'r who have researched our history, and who have studied our bodies and our ways. However, as well you know, true science needs organization and co-operation, which we have not prioritized until very recently. The result is that those papers—those notes on papyrus or parchment or saved somewhere on obsolete computer technology—are yet for you to find, to gather, and to collate. Your patar started the job. You will complete the collection and then advance the furthering of knowledge about our kind. It gives me more joy than I can express to know you are so eager to carry out this work, and I will help you in every way I can."

At some point, I wondered why Bagamil had switched from answering my questions to telling me what I damned well knew already. I expected such avoidance from Sandu, but my gharpatar had always been the one I could count on to give me tangible facts about my new people and new life.

Then I heard the listening quality of the silence surrounding us and I got it. While Zoraida was already my colleague in this ridiculously enormous task, none of the other am'r had paid much attention to the Exciting Announcement Sandu and Bagamil had made about computering up the am'r world. Once I'd gotten am'r-nafsh-napped in the middle of that summit, everyone was far more excited to go fight a huge battle than to hear about innovative archiving schemes. The Romanian crew could probably be counted on to cooperate, since even the youngest tended to call Sandu "Voivode" and to kind-of kowtow to him. But Nthanda's people hadn't been there for the gathering, and who knew what he had bothered to pass along to them? Lope had sent

Tecla, but had not taken it seriously. No one could guess what Astryiah planned. But what the Aojysht said to me *now* would be heard, remembered, and passed on to other am'r.

Well, Bagamil couldn't have lived all this time and not learned how to play the politics game. And one of these days, I would get him to tell me exactly how long he *had* lived.

"Yes," I said carefully. "I'll need much help with this...duty. Help from all over the am'r world. I certainly wouldn't want to exclude any specific cultural aspects. I need to ensure that voices from all over are given equal space."

Hah. I'd figure out how to play this game, too.

Bagamil beamed at me in a particularly bland way, but I saw the wicked little twinkle in his eye that assured me I'd guessed his intention correctly. I not only felt smug; I felt like I was *allowed* to feel that way.

And then I realized that Bagamil had totally played me. My apathy had vanished, despite how tired and sore I still was. Answering my questions about the am'r and then making me feel like a special part of his agenda had completely sucked me in and made me get over myself.

*Dammit. You might be learning, but never forget he is a goddamn master.*

So, we all had stuff to ponder as we made our way out of the cave system I'd never wanted to visit and desperately hoped I would never find myself in again. Dragoș, being who he was, started singing what could only have been Romanian drinking songs. Sandu joined in right away, which had the Romanians singing along with them by the first chorus. And then they were teaching them to Zoraida and to Nthanda's and Lope's people, and of course Bagamil knew them already and was always ready to do his part for group morale. Astryiah was the sort who would never *not* sing along with a drinking song, and I found myself leaving the caves into the Tierra del Fuegan night with a group of ridiculous singing vampires, observing it all with bemusement...and concern that someone might make *me* join in.

After the singalong was thankfully over, everyone splintered into smaller discussion units. Lope and his family were ahead of us, shepherding the kee. Bagamil was behind them, talking to Nthanda again. Sandu was deep in conversation with Zoraida, and the rest of the Romanians were chatting with Lilani and Viv. Astryiah was at the tail of the group with me, and I could tell she'd been delegated to keep an eye on me. Walking downhill was somehow worse than coming uphill had been, and I'd had to keep myself from pitching ass-over-teakettle several times already.

After an embarrassing misjudging of the slipperiness of a part of the trail featuring far too much scattered scree, which of course had *not* been a problem for any of the am'r ahead of us, I whined aloud, "Aw, fuck! I'm sorry! I don't get why I'm so worn out! Why haven't I healed?"

Astryiah steadied me and kept on holding my arm in hers, like dear old Mrs. Muckenfuss used to do when we walked together, out of affection and connection.

"You do not understand how close you came to the vistarascha, do you?"

"I guess not. I mean, I wasn't aware of much at the time. I guess I had gotten used to being...not unbreakable, but, um, easily healable, if that makes sense?"

"It does, and I assure you the vistarascha always comes as a surprise to an am'r-nafsh, although I do not think many have experienced the kind of injuries you have, nor the amount of vhoon-vaa, either. I can further assure you that the tokhmarenc is an even greater surprise to any am'r."

Astryiah, having found her own words very amusing, chuckled to herself while I contemplated just how close a shave I must have had.

"Why do you think they worked so hard to keep me am'r-nafsh? I mean, I am stuck being so *weak*. Until I become full am'r, I can't become a strong-enough fighter. The limitations of what I am seems like they will always cause trouble."

Astryiah smirked, and I remembered her deeply inhaling my scent in a hot spring back in Sandu's underground castle. That intimacy, and the fact that she'd not given in and drunk my blood illicitly then (nor seemed like she'd lose control and do so now) gave me the feeling I could ask her such questions.

"I think your delicious vhoon that causes so many problems is also *worth* all the problems, in your patar's eyes. It is not just something that is given to you; you give it back to him every time he takes sweet swallows from your pretty, pretty neck."

Astryiah was always this openly lecherous, I reminded myself, but in a deeply feminine way as opposed to Lope, who was a gentleman from an era where casual masculine lechery wasn't a problem in anyone's eyes. It made me uncomfortable, but then, being too comfortable around any am'r was a stupid idea.

"So, all that effort, all that blood, went into making sure I was still just a milch cow." I might have sounded slightly bitter.

"Darling little dairy cow," she replied with a toothy smile, "I do not think you dislike being *milked* so very much? There is a sweetness to feeding your patar that you will never experience again, and an especial intimacy as well. You are married, or something like it, while you are still am'r-nafsh. Once you become full am'r, you will not stay as close, and it will not be so rewarding and so fulfilling."

"But, but...Sandu and Bagamil have stayed close," I protested.

"They are unique among us, it is true. But you have not been around for the centuries where they saw each other but seldom. When I met Sandu, I only knew who his patar was because of the vhoon-anghyaa, not because Bagamil was by his side. They have reunited for this moment, and I do not doubt that it is *you* who keeps the reconnection fresh and vital. But I do not expect it to last very long. Maybe a quarter-century? Maybe even half a century?"

I had started to panic at the idea of losing this wonderful thing between the three of us, but her last words shook me in a different way. The am'r experienced time on such a different scale than kee, and I was still not used to it. Twenty-five, fifty years? That was longer than many kee marriages lasted. I probably didn't need to panic about the brevity of this relationship.

"I have spoken with your patar and your gharpatar," Astryiah said, careful with each syllable, and suddenly I *was* in a panic because this was strangely formal from her, and that felt dangerous. "They have agreed with me that it would be good for you to mingle even more vhoon-anghyaa in your body. It would increase your strengths, especially where mine differ from your patar's, and it would tie me to you as your bakheb-vhoonho, your blood-giver, so that I would have a stake in your continued well-being as both am'r-nafsh and later as am'r."

I almost brought up that she had been a protector to me in the past and had fought in battles on "my" side, so it seemed like she already had assigned herself to that task. Then I considered that she was one of the more terrifyingly mercurial am'r of those who were technically an "ally." Not that she had done me wrong yet, but I could see her getting bored or offended at some trifle and leaving me in the lurch in some future situation, so having her more bonded to me was probably a good thing. A scary thing, though, because I would obviously be more bonded to her in exchange, and I couldn't imagine the full ramifications of that. I nodded and made an encouraging sound in my throat and looked for the most non-committal response.

"So...um...what would we do?"

"It could be as utilitarian as the basic exchange that is emergency vhoon-vaa. I know I would prefer it to be more exciting, more pleasurable, as vhoon-vayon should be."

Astryiah's preference was not what you'd call a *surprise.*

She was a person who allowed others time to think about things, which I appreciated. We walked downhill some more, and I noticed, outside of my racing thoughts, that the world was less starlit blackness and more slate-gray, the precursor to that dreadful time called sunrise. Everyone picked up the pace, which was even harder on me, but I was certain that in my weakened condition, being outside when the sun came up would, if not incinerate me like the stereotypical vampire, make me wish I *could* be that happily unbothered pile of ash. I tried to find a good center of balance for walking downhill and let myself lean a little on Astryiah's arm without feeling any shame.

"And," she continued, as if the pressure of my hand on her arm had told her more than I'd intended it to, "it will make me much more likely to participate in your little library plans. I could tell you stories from my myriad experiences—while we are in bed, which will be much less *tedious* for me."

Any anticipation I was starting to feel at the prospect of having sex and sharing blood with this powerful woman burst like an overblown bubble.

"Tell me there really *aren't* any witches or werewolves, right?" I asked her bitterly.

She paused, and looked at me. Then turned back to watch her footing again. "In my experience, which is not small, witches are kee who just wish for more control over their lives, and who try to wrest it from powers that can never deliver, as they do not exist. Werewolves are kee who long for am'r-like powers, but cannot attract one of us, so they come up with all sorts of silly notions. But I do not understand why you bring this up?"

"Oh, I just was hoping there were not any *more* problematic supernatural creatures for me to have to deal with."

Astryiah paused, and I realized I'd run my mouth without considering the consequences. It felt so good to just let go. Having to spend all my time worrying about what I could say around beings who'd happily rip my throat open and quaff down my blood like I was a cold can of beer had been wearing on me. If I didn't learn more self-control, however, that analogy would happen to me sooner rather than later.

*Dammit, what have I done now?*

"I am happy to be called 'supernatural,'" Astryiah articulated while I tried not to cringe too conspicuously, "but I do not understand 'problematic.'"

*Brazen this out, but try not to dig your hole any deeper. It's the only way.*

"What I meant was, *before* you said that having sex with you was the only way you'd help Sandu and Bagamil's critical plans for transforming the am'r world—" *Yes, good idea, emphasize it's the Aojysht's pet project.* "Before you said *that*, it seemed like the vhoon-vayon you've proposed felt mutually beneficial and organically pleasurable. *After* you said it, it felt to me like you made it transactional. You know, like prostitution in a way. Less about real sharing."

Another long pause, while I tried not to sweat blood. "We come from very different times, *chamuda*. I must remember that about you. I do like your spirit, though. I always have. Do not be afraid to tell me your feelings. I come from a time when prostitution could be a much-honored position, and I am afraid I do not see that term as negative. But I apprehend what you mean; you feel I merely demand to fuck you and drink your delicious blood as payment for my help."

She paused again, then added, "Well, and perhaps I *do* mean that. Tolerating you young ones and your enthusiasms is exhausting. I often feel older than your gharpatar;

*he* never becomes less of an enthusiast, no matter how long he exists.

"So, take it as 'transactional,' which is a very silly word. The world is transactional, *chamuda*, and you must learn that sooner rather than later. So I throw it in as a free lesson, along with the transaction I offer: I will fuck you and drink your blood, you will fuck me and drink my blood, I will be nourished and entertained, and you will be made stronger by my blood and allegiance. And between our fucking, I will pass on knowledge to you that I will most certainly not do otherwise. I have made this offer once, and I will not make it again. You will choose what you choose."

*Well. Shit.*

"May...may I speak to my patar before I give you my answer?"

"Indeed. You *should* make the decision based on his input. I will await your response."

Silence fell between us. It probably wasn't even an uncomfortable silence for her. However, the sky was lightening even further, and now we herd of nocturnal creatures rushed down the last part of the trail, trying to get to the vehicles before the sun was fully up.

As we came around a final hairpin bend, I could see the cars in what seemed like the most glaring sunlight, even though the sun was barely peeking above the mountains that surrounded us. There were six more vehicles than the one I'd left with Sandu and Araceli. *Oh, Araceli!* Would thinking of her ever cease to reawaken the deep ache in my heart?

I wondered with brief panic if anyone had keys to Araceli's 4x4—and if it would even start. How long had I been trapped in those evil tunnels? Would the other cars have jumper cables?

I wanted to be away from there so badly they probably could get a jump off my current of pure desperation.

Lope and his crew managed to clown-car the kee into their three SUVs. I couldn't imagine that in such close proximity, some blood wouldn't be nipped along the way by hungry am'r, although with the sun threatening like it was, maybe they would make for the nearest crashpad first. Since Lope called "*¡Vemos en Baires!*" before their cars left behind a wheel-spray of scree, I guessed they would not be crashing with us.

There was a large SUV for Dragoș and the rest of the Romanian crew. Nthanda and his two frithaputhra were in a jeep. Astryiah had her own high-end SUV and didn't offer anyone a ride.

The first thing everyone did was get their cars open and search inside for sunglasses. Dragoș, my darling brother, had a bagful of sunglasses, apparently having bought the whole rack of them at the last convenience store they passed on their way here. There was a universal sigh of relief as shades settled onto faces. They weren't a perfect cure for sunlight, but oh, were they better than nothing!

We did not have Araceli's keys, but Daciana knew how to hot-wire a car. Perhaps that was a skill that came standard with am'r membership? She drove Sandu and Bagamil and me through the increasing brightness with grim precision, as if she'd spent a lifetime forcing four-wheel-drive vehicles over unpaved roads. Maybe she had; I didn't know enough about her. I had to fix that.

Bagamil sat up front with her. Sandu sat in the back with me and encouraged me to lie down with my head on his lap and close my eyes while he stroked my hair and murmured a nursery song he'd sung for me before. I was out, away from the nasty sunlight, in barely a minute.

# CHAPTER TWENTY-THREE

I woke up enough to stumble out of the car and into the little house we'd left seemingly centuries ago. I wondered if Araceli owned it or if Lope owned it and Araceli had just maintained it for him.

It was, of course, terribly painful to be in a space I associated so strongly with Araceli, but I hadn't woken up fully, so I was somewhat protected from emotional anguish by being too tired to ruminate. Sandu half-carried me, like a sleepy little girl, to the bed he and I'd shared before.

Next time I was awake and groggily aware, I realized that Sandu and Bagamil had squished in on either side of me in the bed and I did not even have enough space to roll over.

"How do you feel, *draga mea*?" Sandu's face was more scrunched with worry than I thought he knew. Around Bagamil and me he could relax, which meant sometimes he didn't keep his usual iron-tight control in place.

"Tired. And still sore." I automatically downplayed just how scary-tired and sore that really was. "Can I just rest

here a little longer? I'm sure that a little sleep's all I need."
Outright lie.

"You are certainly staying in bed, cinyaa," Bagamil said
gently. "But you have a choice to make now. You need
vhoon, vhoon-vaa at the least. You need it very much, but
you have a choice of who you heal with. My fellow aojysht
Astryiah has made us an offer. It is up to you to make the
decision."

I wriggled to make my cramped conditions more optimal, and they accommodated me by also wriggling themselves into new positions. I considered unhurriedly what
my gharpatar had just said. "Made *us* an offer," he had said.
Yes, of course she had spoken to my patar first—and due to
who he was, my gharpatar also—like some guy in the old-
en days asking the parents' permission before requesting
a gal's hand in marriage. I ought to be flattered. But, like
those antiquated nuptials, this was a mutually beneficial
arrangement. It would no doubt be helpful to Bagamil and
Sandu to have the powerful Astryiah more committed to
helping their goals, as well as being someone they could
count on if my am'r-nafsh ass got in trouble again.

"If I say no to Astryiah, what happens?"

"You stay right here, and we three share vhoon-vayon
until you are well, and we are at our peak powers. And full
of happiness and love."

"Would she not take offense to me turning her down?"

Bagamil paused, then said slowly, "She would not...burn things to the ground, but we could not expect anything more than the weakest alliance with her going forward. We would not get any materials from her collection for our archive, nor would we get the store of her great living wisdom added to it. It would be a loss, but not a disaster."

"OK. What happens if I say yes?"

"Roughly: you would spend time with her, and blood, and intimacy. You would both be obligated by a tradition—so old that it has petrified into a kind of law—not to harm each other."

That was nice for me, but how the hell could I have injured Astryiah? Still, I could see how that tradition had come about; you would be vulnerable to another am'r during such an intimate act.

"I know I'm being very kee, here, but I have to ask. You are OK with this?" I looked at Sandu as I said it, looked deep into his eyes, and tried to demand his most sincere truth with my gaze.

"*Sufleţel*, I assure you I would not feel jealousy. I would feel only happiness that Astryiah had become your bakheb-vhoonho, that you were becoming stronger in vhoon-anghyaa. And I would look forward to tasting your enriched blood when you returned to my arms."

I worked at ignoring how that last line made me feel like a milch cow again. *Am'r will be am'r*. I looked at Bagamil.

"You do not need to do this for our sakes, cinyaa. Do it for yourself, or do not do it."

I could always count on Bagamil to tell me the truth. He would be kind, but he would not spare me information that might not be fun to hear. Since he'd just put the whole weight of the decision on me, I had a ridiculous moment of missing Sandu's technique of "don't tell her enough and then just throw her in." Making my own reasoned decision from all the available facts had to be a better option than that. Just not always *easier*.

The beings I was dealing with came from a time of delicately negotiated allegiances, and their world even now was, increasingly obviously, still in some ways better suited to those traditions.

So, stay in bed with my beloveds, where I knew I was safe and loved, and where we would all have the best time in the world while healing and feeding each other? Or go to the bed of a virtual stranger who'd made clear from the start that she was using this situation to get what she wanted from me? I could not imagine what sex with Astryiah might be like. It might be mind-blowingly amazing, or equally likely, it might be alienating and weird and something to be endured with a smile and very good acting skills until it was over.

Neither my patar nor gharpatar would be surprised if I chose the safe option. They understood I came from a different world with vastly altered values, and they did not expect me to be able to handle their reality from the jump.

That's what made up my mind for me, of course—knowing how kind and understanding they would be if I failed to take advantage of this truly beneficial opportunity. Thinking about how carefully their faces would not show any disappointment.

"Alrighty, then. How does a girl go about making an alliance with blood?"

They stopped to kiss me first. Long, deep kisses that promised many more in the future. Such long kisses that they would be walking a bit ungainly until their erections went down. Not *my* problem.

Bagamil got up, threw on a bathrobe he'd found in the room (nice to know he *understood* the concept of there being a time to be naked and a time *not* to be), and went to announce the news to Astryiah. I was happy I didn't have to head right off to her bed, but was also left feeling uncomfortable with what looked way too much like some kind of formal proclamation of upcoming consummation.

It suddenly occurred to me how much I needed to use the bathroom. This cottage barely had proper bed and bathroom facilities, and now, stretched to fit twelve am'r and one am'r-nafsh, the two most important things to am'r—privacy and enough hot water for proper washing—were at desperate premiums. Privacy was less important than being out of the sun, however. No one had claimed the empty rooms upstairs, which had windows. Anyone looking in those windows would have thought the house empty and decrepit, never guessing there were a dozen creatures of the night sacked out in the basement.

The bathroom was upstairs. I would brave the daylight to improve how I smelled, before anything else, dammit. That cold plunge in the caves had been too long ago, and not thorough enough.

I tried to respect everyone's space as I made my way to the stairs. Am'r were seated upon every available chair, most dozing, a few in soft conversation around the main table. Every room with a door down here had the door firmly shut. On my way, I passed Bagamil standing outside one closed door. Astryiah's voice rang too-clearly through the basement, "*Besèder*, Aojysht, I am pleased. But tell her she needs a long bath before she comes to me."

I felt myself blush from the bottom of my feet to the crown of my head, and I worked very hard not to meet anyone's eyes. *Wow, she's really* dedicated *to making the path to her bed as rough as possible for me.*

When I got upstairs, Zoraida was coming out of the bathroom, obviously freshly showered. She saw me headed for it, and a look of concern came over her face. Damn. This was about to be humiliating in one way or another.

"*Bonjou, zanmi mwen* Noosh, I know how these delicate matters trouble you. Two things I will say for your consideration: this is a small house, and we all have powerful senses of smell. Understanding your value on privacy, let me tell you there is a dry toilet behind the house."

Well, fuck. Another day, another squat toilet. But Zoraida was right, and the best kind of friend. I didn't want a houseful of fastidious creatures who'd not had a bowel movement in decades or centuries judging me.

"*Epitou*," she added, "when you shower, there is not much water pressure. There is your choice: you can have more water pressure with cold water, or you can have warm water but a very small trickle of it. Also, do *not* touch the box above the showerhead while the water is running. You will not die—well, *probably* not—but it will not be pleasant."

I muttered some things under my breath.

"Say, '*Fout tonè!*' I cannot translate it perfectly for you, but it's what you mean," Zoraida said with sympathy.

I went outside first and had some time for deep philosophical thought.

I thought about Mica.

For a few amazing months in my second year of my Masters of Library Science degree, I'd dated Mica and had been head-over-heels in love with her. It had ended badly and with so much drama that I'd nearly not completed my degree, and as it was, I'd only graduated Cum Laude. I'd neither dated nor hooked up with a woman since. But then, I hadn't had any men in my life either, until Sandu made his dramatic entrance.

I was not worried about being with a woman again; I was confident I remembered where everything was, having my own set to keep in practice with, as it were. And somewhere along the way I'd figured out that the secret to being a good lover was just to pay attention to how your partner was responding, and give them more of what they liked best. So, I had no need to have performance anxiety. But regardless, I had a swarm of butterflies in my tummy.

When I went back to the shower room, I made the mistake of choosing the "warm trickle of water" option. It took so long to get any part of me even close to clean that I was just as chilled at the end as if I'd turned on the cold water full-blast.

The fact that this kind of cold was bothering me was an unnecessary reminder of how unwell I still was. Pushing through the shower had felt as hard as the fighting had, back in the cave. Trying to figure out the half-rubbed-off Spanish labels on the random assorted bottles in the shower had almost done me in, but I didn't want to end up cleaning my hair with tile scrubber and listening to Astryiah complain about the scent, so I forced myself to figure it out.

I did *not* want to get back into the clothing I'd been wearing, the filthy garb of an abused and murdered kee. I found a happy surprise when I stepped out of the shower, however; Daciana had popped clothing into the room in that silent am'r way while I'd shivered under my inadequate trickle. When I'd opened the shower door, her scent had wafted in, and there was a neatly folded pile of my own clothes. I'd entirely forgotten about the clothing I'd worn to travel down here, the comfy joggers and clingy sweater. It wasn't the sort of outfit I'd wear for a date, but whatever was about to happen with Astryiah wasn't *that*. More like a wedding night, with a bloodstained sheet to display off the balcony the next morning? *Ugh.*

Putting on my own clothing again almost made me cry with happiness, and the fact that Daciana had thought to bring it up to me was simply overwhelming, in my current state. As soon as we got somewhere with shops, I was going to buy her a gift in gratitude—or, well, get Sandu to buy it. I had no money at all.

Very soon Sandu and I would be having a chat about how it was *nice* that he was willing to pay for everything and all, but I was going to be *paid* for my archivist job. And I would be requiring credit cards in my current alias, and access to cash for my own uses.

The fact that I hadn't even bothered to consider this staggered me, but I hadn't been out of My Own Private Castle

Dracula for months, and on the way down here, I'd been with Sandu at all times.

Well, now I knew how easily I could be separated from him—had been painfully reminded of it, *dammit*. It was time to prepare for such future situations.

Well, not *right* now. Instead of standing in a damp bathroom talking to myself in the mirror, what I needed to be doing was tossing my damp but clean-ish hair over my shoulder (I was pretending that the massive system of knots in my curls was going to be salvageable, and I wouldn't just need to shave my head and start from scratch) and sashay proudly to Astryiah's door.

I looked at myself again. Really looked, instead of just using the mirror to detangle the curls around my face.

The girl in the mirror was recognizable as someone I'd seen before. Yes, I'd seen her: the wild black hair, the olive skin with a splattering of freckles across the cheeks, the high cheekbones, the gray almond eyes. I knew all those features.

They had looked better, though. My eyes were dull, and the circles under them were dark and deep—not healthy at all. The olive skin was shading into the pale yellowish-gray range, which was even less healthy. This girl looked like she'd gone through everything I had: loss, heartbreak, injury with not enough time to heal, and spending way too much time deep underground in damp caves. Despite having seen that face for so many years in mirrors, despite it being clear that girl had gone through all the same shit as me, still, as I looked at her, I did not *know* the person I saw. I guess maybe I did not know *me*, not anymore.

About a decade ago I'd nearly drowned. I was swimming in a part of a river where there were powerful currents. I was a strong swimmer, but had underestimated them. As I'd splashed across a seemingly quiet part of the river, I found myself pulled under a rock with inexorable suction.

I had survived, obviously. And it was the only real danger I'd experienced in my life before I met Sandu. But I remembered looking in the mirror after I got back home and not recognizing myself then, either. The girl who'd innocently struck out across a cool river in the hot afternoon sun was not the same girl who looked in the mirror at the scores across her back where the river rocks had slashed her skin. The near-drowning had left much different damage than this...this *bullshit* adventure had done, but it was the same experience. It had changed me so deeply that my new eyes could not recognize the old reflection.

Looking at my dull eyes and gray complexion, I wondered why the hell would Astryiah even want to bed me? My blood must smell pretty goddam *amazing* because "sexy" was not where I was at. I wanted to change my mind and run back to Sandu and Bagamil and hide under the covers, in their arms.

Then I thought about how I'd managed not to drown that day, trapped under a rock in the river. I'd tried twice to claw back out the way I'd been sucked in, using all my core and arm muscles to pull myself along the rock that, where it was not slimy and lacking all grip, was striated razor-sharp. The second time I'd almost reached the surface, just a tantalizing few inches away! After I'd slipped and just managed to catch myself again, I realized I'd not been paying attention to how long I'd been under. I'd no idea how much oxygen was left in my lungs. It was time to decide: expend the last bit of air trying a third time to fight against the current to the surface, or with the air I had left, let go and deal with what came.

I'd let go.

I had whooshed through a just-big-enough hole in the rocks and bobbed up in a little pool with a gentler current, right before where the rapids started in earnest, where I could grab some dry rocks at the edges and climb out onto the far shore.

The memory straightened my spine.

I let go. I tossed my snarl of curls over my shoulders, pulled my shoulders back (thusly thrusting my tits out), and sashayed down to Astryiah's room.

As I knocked, the scents of sandalwood and musk rose from where the door did not meet the floor properly, and they smelled so intensely erotic that they almost knocked the sashay right out of me.

It was of course the same closet-sized space as the other bedrooms, but somehow, with just candles and incense, Astryiah had turned it into a warm and welcoming pleasure chamber.

"Come in," she'd called in a breathy voice I'd have never dared to try.

I managed to keep my sashay on until I got to the bed, but once I sat down, I realized I was entirely out of my depth. All my nerves snapped like overstretched rubber bands, and I found myself perched on the side of the bed pathetically; no idea what to say and beyond that, unsure if I still had the power of speech.

Astryiah was wearing a robe-y thing of sheer bronze cloth a shade darker than her honey-bronze skin and honey-bronze thick waves. The darker fabric managed to drape seductively, while at the same time clinging to her generous, perfectly rounded curves. She had this hypnotic beauty that made it entirely reasonable for me not to be able to form sentences.

"Come over here, *chamuda*. I will help you relax. I've seldom seen a woman so in need of relaxation."

That was true enough. I tried to climb across the bed in a not-ungainly fashion. I achieved mild success.

Astryiah smiled at me, warm and open. "You are used to am'r men. They are fun enough, but this will be very different, so forget what you think you know. First, though, tell me of your bakheb-vhoonho, my old friend Ioannes—*zekher tzadik v'kadosh livrakha!*"

"Neplach, you mean? But what was the rest of that?"

"In my language—or the version of my language they speak nowadays—it means 'may the memory of the righteous and holy be a blessing,' and it is said for a righteous and holy person."

"That honors him well."

"Yes, it does. And I am pleased his vhoon-anghyaa lives on in you. Now tell me about how it happened, for I had not known of his tokhmarenc until your patar told me, and I grieve."

So I told her about standing in the rocks behind a cave in which an unspeakable atrocity was taking place, a woman who'd once loaned me her underwear at our feet, her neck broken and drained of blood. I told her about the rainbow bridge of connection with my uncle-in-blood, and the too-few moments of tender connection before they tore him away from me, despite how hard we'd fought them. I told her I did not want to talk about his subsequent execution, which I'd been forced to endure.

As I talked, Astryiah gradually moved closer to me, like a person trying to catch a frightened animal to rescue it. I was perfectly aware of it and kept myself from pulling away. By the end of my narrative, I was upset enough to appreciate her hand gentling me, even if I did not entirely trust the person to whom that hand belonged.

She started by stroking my arm. The caress moved up to my shoulder, and then one of my frizzy curls was softly twirled around one of her fingers. I started to speak, to apologize for the ragged condition of my hair, but she shushed me. "*Lo, lo,* Noosh. I will not hear that after all you have just been through.

"You are so used to being with men, and they are lovely. But they will not notice the little things, the modest needs that when they pile up, become not so trifling. Your hair needs attention and love. *You* need attention and love; it is the same thing. Come, sit in front of me here. I have an oil I have used on my hair for centuries. Let me give you some attention and love."

I found myself sitting cross-legged in front of Astryiah on her bed with my sweater off—"Let's not get the oils on this pretty shirt, *chamuda*"—and wafts of incense drifting in the air around us. Her knowledgeable fingers worked the oil in, and she patiently finger-combed the knots out, backwards from the ends to my scalp. She spoke in a soft voice as she worked.

"Ah, men. They just want to get their teeth inside you, and their cocks. *Lo, lo*, do not jump to the defense of your men, who I am sure are very skilled lovers in their way. But you and I are making love already, enjoying this growing intimacy, this building of contact.

"It's not the fault of those whose genitals dangle outside their body. This am'r world you have found yourself in is very much about rough penetration, is it not? If it's not teeth, it's something else sharp and deadly. *Lo*, do not tense up! Shhhh, shhhh...I know you've had enough of that recently. There has been enough blood spilled for all of us who were there to sustain our need for violence for some time to come.

"I do not say I do not love it, too. That would be dishonest—and in this space you and I are now in there is only room for truthful words. But *this* right now feeds me too: feeling your body start to unwind, seeing the muscles under your lovely skin relaxing. This quiet. Listening to your breathing, feeling my fingers in your hair. Just because one has violence in one's nature, it does not mean it is impossible to crave tranquility as well."

Her low, smoothly-accented voice was hypnotic, and either the oil she was using was magic, or her skills were incredible. Either way, she was making me melt.

She was still talking, and I knew I should be paying attention since she might already be giving me information I'd want to write down for the archives as quickly as possible. But all I could think about was how good her fingers felt, how they knew exactly how much pressure was *perfect*, how just massaging my scalp and neck was relaxing muscles all over my body, muscles which had not relaxed since I'd started having the nightmares that had prompted this whole disastrous affair.

I must have mumbled something aloud because she told me, "Hush, this was *not* a disaster. You got your much-loved gharpatar back in one piece, did you not? This world is dangerous, and we am'r do not live safe lives. It is not consistent with what we are. A wolf who will not fight for her dinner will not survive in the wild. The kee world has more or less domesticated itself, but the am'r still live in a world of predators and prey. We who become am'r receive many rewards, but we must pay for them. We must fight for our existence thenceforward.

"I am happy for this, for predators must always have their numbers thinned. Too many of us would be a disaster for us and for the kee. As more am'r awaken from the vistarascha, more must end in their tokhmarenc."

"But—" I protested, trying to struggle out of the puddle of relaxed girl-flesh she'd made me, "I've lost friends! Am'r who will now never become aojyshtaish. And Neplach, who was your friend, too!"

"How is this different from the kee world, Noosh? Good ones die too young everywhere. There is no special fairness among the am'r." She laughed at this, a low gurgle of a sound that was arousing to my more relaxed self. I was surprised at my response but didn't fight it.

Her hands had moved now to my shoulders and urged me forward onto my stomach. I let my legs uncurl behind me, and in helping me stretch out, she suavely relieved me of my leggings. Her hands went right back to massaging me: up and down my back, my ass, the backs of my legs. I melted further into the bed.

"You must learn to come out of a battle celebrating your survival, *chamuda*. Rejoicing in the persistence and triumph of those you love. You were up against impossible odds, yet here is your beautiful body, alive and full of vibrancy. Celebrate with passion; do not waste time on regrets."

"I don't feel 'full of vibrancy.' I feel the worst I've felt since before I drank Sandu's blood the first time."

"You simply have not had enough healing. No one knows what to do with you, my unique one. There has never been another am'r-nafsh like you. We must treat you less roughly and with more reverence. I am doing my part in that now. Let me help you heal. Let me help you feel the passion of life and the joy of being am'r. Celebrate survival with me."

Her fingers, as irresistible as her low voice, suggested that I roll over. I would have thought I was barely able to manage to move, but my body turned out to be responsive and eager. I let her tactile urgings spin me to face her.

Astryiah smiled, and that smile finished the process of awakening my body. She stripped off the wispy bronze fabric, leaving a body I'd first seen ages ago in a thermal spring. She was more like a carved statue of an ideal female body than living flesh: her breasts were flawless rounds on her chest, her hips and ass impossibly rounded to perfection. Every part of her was covered in that warm honeyed skin that made you crave not just to touch it, but to lick it. Her face echoed the roundedness: high circles of cheekbones in an oval face, huge deep-set golden-brown eyes, and plump kissable lips, only slightly pinker than her skin.

I did have a moment of wondering what was in the incense that hung around us, that caught in shifting smoke-curtains by the candlelight. But am'r don't need drugs for sex. She was probably fascinating me with her am'r abilities; the musk just an added erotic zing.

The scent of the oil, the clouds of sandalwood and musk were nice and all, but in the next moment, all I could think of was the blood under her skin. It reminded me of going to the ocean when I was a kid and smelling the fresh salty air. Layered under that was the metallic smell that's left on your fingers after you rub them on iron.

I was shocked by how zoned out I was, and felt a rush of angry suspicion: was she was playing mind games with me? But, well, what would fighting her glamor get me? Less enjoyment of this moment, which had to happen anyway. No, no matter *how* she was enhancing my experience, I'd be an idiot to reject it at this point.

Astryiah leaned down, bringing her body slowly past intimate personal boundaries. As her naked body moved closer to mine, I could feel something like surface tension giving way, like an open hand pressing through water. Then her body was against mine, and mine against hers. Her honey-brown eyes were flecked with gold, and getting to look unflinchingly into them at this close range felt like a drug coming on.

I'd never enjoyed looking into another kee person's eyes the way I enjoyed looking into am'r eyes. Someday I'd figure out why. But for now, I reveled in the intensity of our mutual gaze.

I don't know how long I could have gone on just like that, but I knew she was going to lean down that last little bit and kiss me. Her eyes warned me of it, her intention loud and clear in an extra sparkle.

Her lips were so yielding that I forgot how brittle her personality was and fell in love with her. I never wanted to stop kissing her. I was intensely aware that her skin was pressing against mine, and that those curves rubbing along my body felt really good, but the kiss took up my senses. Her breath was scented with fennel, and I prayed to everything that my breath wasn't too terrible.

She didn't act like it was. She acted like the kiss was as good for her as it was for me.

Her hands moved over my body, pulled me to her, slid under me, and held me close while grabbing and squeezing my flesh. The kiss became more about tongues, then even more about teeth as she nipped my tongue and my lips. The little flashes of intensity made me moan, which encouraged her to bite harder. Drops of my blood teased our tongues.

Things went to the next level fast. Her leg had slipped between mine, simultaneously one of mine between hers. I felt how wet she had become as she rubbed against me. It made me feel like I was going crazy with lust.

My hands reached of their own volition to her breasts to feel their supple perfection. Her nipples were already perked up but hardened more under my touch, making it impossible for me not to flick my fingers over them. She had leaned back a little to give me access, and this angled her head just right to start kissing my neck.

An am'r can't just kiss a neck without the full weight of implications making the act vastly more suggestive: menacing or erotic, depending. At this moment, it was her soft lips pressing against a part of my body that had become an erogenous zone. It was the hottest of promises. I pressed my neck up against those lips, unable to stop myself wanting the next step. I felt and heard her laugh in a very satisfied way, but she pulled back. Only the lightest of kisses drifted against my eager skin, down my neck, along my collarbone, then down my chest to my right breast, which was kissed and licked thoroughly before the left one was given equal attention.

I was unable to hold still. Once she got her mouth around one nipple and her fingers around the other, I found myself in the situation of not wanting her to stop...but also having my pussy demanding that attention be paid to it—now, now, now!

She read my mind, or more likely my body, since it was pretty easy to guess what it wanted. Her left hand was on my breast, and the right snaked down my body and slid between my labia to rub my wetness up to my clit, then back down to tantalize the impatient opening.

I was moaning and whimpering, completely lost in the sensations. I was disappointed when hand and mouth were removed from my breast, but what was happening between my legs was good enough that I didn't protest. Astryiah was doing something with her other hand. I started to pay attention to it, but then her finger found just the right pressure and rhythm on my clit and I no longer cared.

Some timeless time later, I resurfaced from the sweetly unremitting orgasm and she smiled at me, an expression full of gratification and yet far more desire. She held up my Sa'mah in her left hand, and I had felt a quick rush of possessive anger—*That's mine!*—before relaxing into the knowledge that she had undoubtedly felt the little blade in the pocket of my leggings when she pulled them off me and had just used it as the nearest sharp thing for blood-sharing, which was the obvious next step.

She teased the sharp obsidian down my body, leaving a red scratch-mark, then leaned down and put her lips to my ear. "*Chamuda*, you will not live long if you let other am'r get their hands on your weapons. I have much to teach you, my too-trusting girl."

I tensed at the mocking tone, but she'd already moved on and was lithely curling upwards onto her knees. She moved forward to where my head rested, giving me a distracting view of her pubic curls and the dark, wet lips between them. The hair was a shade darker than her dark honey-blond on her head, and her labia were a rich umber. Both glistened wetly in the candlelight.

She looked up at me, suddenly solemn. "I would be your bakheb-vhoonho, that you may grow stronger. Aojasc' am'ratv!"

Crap. More am'r ceremonial shit. What the holy hell should I say? "I would do vhoon-vayon with you, so that you may grow stronger. Aojasc' am'ratv!"

Thank goodness, that seemed to do the trick, and we could move on. She spread her knees apart, and then, with a move so practiced she barely looked down before doing it, she nicked the middle of her inner thigh, hitting a superficial vein. Blood immediately started running down her leg, filling the air with the scent previously only been hinted at. It was *invigorating*, that richer saltiness over the ferrous base notes. As she swung her leg over my face, I realized it was more reminiscent of the ocean than any other blood I'd smelled.

My lips were drawn to it, not wanting to waste a drop, wanting it in my mouth and in my body. She stretched back down between my legs just as fast, her tongue right on my clit, showing that she remembered what her fingers had learned about me.

Sensations came hard and fast. I was gulping down waves of blood while waves of orgasm spread upward to meet in my core. I'm not sure how long I drank, but the wound closed too quickly—at least to my greedy point of view. She shifted her hips, and then I had a different fluid to taste.

Having only been with one woman before, I had limited points of comparison between kee vaginal fluids and am'r ones. But there *was* the fact that am'r men ejaculated blood, so I was not surprised to find that the wetness that smeared across my face as I pressed eagerly upwards between Astryiah's legs was mostly blood. But not exactly like the blood direct from her vein; there was a subtle difference in taste. After a while, I noticed that it did not congeal the way blood normally does, so I guessed that difference might be an anticoagulant? It did not in any way detract from the wonderful tang of her.

Astryiah had moved her mouth away from my swollen clitoris, which was now so sensitized that she barely had to move her tongue to make me come, and licked her way down to the same point on my inner thigh where she had cut on hers. I was so high on the mix of her blood and my orgasms that I didn't even brace myself for the bite. The pain of being bitten by an am'r was a complicated thing for me now; too many sense-memories of that sharp twinge being confusingly commingled with profound pleasure.

It was simply a different expression of passion, the feel of her canines piercing my skin and sinking deep to my vein. It made me focus even more into my exploration of her preferences, reading her reactions as she drank from me, wanting the pleasure I gave her in this moment to be perfect.

Astryiah liked hard flicks of the tongue against her clit, which was not a shy, retiring nub of flesh. After an orgasm, she wanted long, slow licks of the whole area, including her outer labia, to get her worked back up to the next. She taught me with hip movements, by pressing herself down onto my tongue until I got the point, and with her cries of pleasure, muffled by my thigh, as my reward. I felt pleased with myself that I was a quick learner.

After she had come enough and had drunk enough, she swung around and wrapped herself around me, laughing with happiness. "This is not so bad, is it, *chamuda?*"

"No, not so terrible," I agreed, feeling more relaxed than I had for a long, long time.

"You look better too, but not better enough. I'm the doctor, and I prescribe more blood and more pleasure."

"OK, Doc! If you insist…"

"Oh, I do insist." She'd set aside Sa'mah on a bedside table and reached her easily. Again with that practiced ease, she nicked a vein in her neck, and I raised my head to meet the blood as it spurted out to me.

As I drank, her long, skillful fingers slid inside me, and I was so primed and ready that I started orgasming from the initial penetration. She didn't let her easy triumph get in her way, however, and proceeded to try every variation of finger-fucking, from just holding her fingers inside me and moving her fingertips against my g-spot, to the canonical in-out-in-out. At that moment, pretty much *everything* was working for me, because at the same time I was swallowing mouthful after mouthful of her invigorating blood, which moved through my body, carrying the pleasure out to every nerve ending.

At some point my greedy guzzling had slowed, and the breakers of orgasm settled into a rhythm with each swallow. The undulations lulled me into a sort of delirium where I was floating in an ocean of blood, my naked body rising and falling on swells of pleasure.

I could have drifted there forever. At that moment I lived in pure sensation. Not one thought troubled my mind, which is the highest compliment a chronic over-thinker can bestow.

I never noticed when it was over. When the cut tissues in Astryiah's neck had self-repaired and left me with nothing to drink, when her fingers had stilled and withdrawn from me. I was zonked out on ecstasy and healing.

I eased back into consciousness gradually. At first it was just sensations of having a body and it *not* hurting, of good-feeling exuding all through me. Of being deliciously comfortable on the mattress. Of the scents of sandalwood and musk and oil and melted candle wax and Astryiah, and under it all, hints of the musty little room that had been turned into paradise for a while.

It was long moments before I was willing to even con-sider opening my eyes. That seemed a sure way to ruin the perfect peace I was experiencing. Eventually, curiosity won out, and I let them crack open. The candles were shorter than they had been but still flickered in the gentle drafts that had moved the incense around so prettily before.

My first real thought was wondering where Astryiah was. I felt a small panic at the loss of contact after such intense intimacy. I looked around and found her sitting cross-legged at the end of the bed, watching me. As she saw me bring her into focus, she smiled, but I felt a pang at how distant she seemed, despite us both still being naked and despite her blood calling out from within her body, to her blood which now was moving in me, a part of me forever.

"Well, *chamuda*, how do you feel?"

"Uhhhh. Much better." I stretched in trial, a little shy about her watching me now. The way my body responded shocked me into an unguarded response, "Oh, wow! My side doesn't hurt!" I reached down to my thigh and grabbed it. "My thigh feels like all that shit never happened to it." I stretched like a cat, reveling in a complete lack of twinges, exhaustion, or any mortal feeling.

"You see now how silly you were to consider turning down my offer."

I decided to ignore her Astryiah-ish tendency to try to ruin my pleasure in her company. I thought I'd distract her by being adorably formal. "My Bakheb-vhoonho—that's the word, right?—I cannot thank you enough for this gift."

"It was not a gift, Sandu's frithaputhra, it was a *trade*. You might feel it was mostly to your advantage, but I assure you that the taste of your scrumptious am'r-nafsh blood has been and will be worth everything I pay."

If she was *trying* to ensure that I didn't fall in love with her in the gentle afterglow of great sex, she was doing a thorough job. I sighed and tried to remember the contentment I'd woken up with.

"Your patar and gharpatar will not want to stay in this location now that my blood has given you further healing, but do not think that Astryiah reneges on her deals! After you return to Sandu's citadel, I will visit you there. I will bring with me my small collection of works on am'r history, and I will donate them to your 'library.' Then I will sit with you and tell you stories from my experience, and when you get tired of listening, when you want to again experience my more discerning loving, we will do vhoon-vayon."

I decided *not* to explain to Astryiah that Sandu and Bagamil were perfectly satisfying lovers. If she needed to think she had the exclusive rights to good sex, well, this was not the moment I would choose to disillusion her.

I sat up, still enjoying how movement felt, and started looking around for my clothing. I saw Sa'mah back on the side table, and out of the corner of my eye caught Astryiah start reaching out for her. I was closer and managed to flatten my hand over the blade before she could reach her. It disconcerted me. My reflexes were so much faster than they'd ever been. I tried not to show it, just slid Sa'mah off the table and reached down for the pile of clothing I recognized as mine.

"You have learned some things already, *chamuda*," Astryiah mocked in a careless voice, and I focused on getting my clothing on and tucking the confusion I was feeling away to process later. So far, blood—either vhoon-vayon or vhoon-vaa—had always brought me closer to the am'r I shared with, a deeper understanding and connection. If my connection to Astryiah was closer now, she was working hard to fracture it—which made no sense since *she* was the one who had proposed this whole damn thing.

*Had she just wanted a sip of my blood that badly?*

It reminded me sharply of how my relationship with Mica had died. I realized that while my body felt better than great, my head and heart were starting to hurt. I needed to get out of this room as fast as possible. I dressed as quickly as my enhanced agility would allow, and slid Sa'mah safely into my pocket.

I had to say *something* as I exited. "It might not have been a *gift*," I told her, trying to keep my voice light and untroubled, "but I still thank you, *aojysht*, for the honor and the pleasure."

I'd managed to say the right thing. She looked marginally less statue-stiff in her naked perfection. "You have done me the honor, *chamuda*. You will make a good student of my life's experiences. I will see you soon."

I had been excused from her company. I tried to sashay out of the room as I had entered it; now restored and even enhanced, it was easier to pull off.

# Chapter Twenty-Four

As I sashayed, I discovered that a number of am'r had already left the little crashpad, collected by Lope's second-string pilot, Fausta, who apparently had been taking lessons from Araceli. She'd flown down commercially to pick up the plane, and was now running the household and guests in batches up to Buenos Aires.

"More and more am'r are becoming excited about our project," Sandu explained to me. "They are now doing what we will call a 'goodwill visit,' and I will ensure there will be talk about that—Zoraida and Dragoș are tasked with that. It will be done subtly, as Lope shows them the pleasures of Buenos Aires."

"What, sight-seeing and stuff like normal tourists?"

"I think it unlikely, but the am'r world has its own experiences."

So, they are going to drink from lots of local kee in nightly orgies and then sit around and gossip, I figured. I didn't say it out loud. I considered how much of the world I'd never see in daylight, because I'd joined the am'r before really *living* a kee life. I had barely taken in any of the joys of South America, and now we were leaving it. Obviously, I couldn't go enjoy a scenic beach...but wait, why not some night swimming? It had been the same with Turkey and the other parts of Central Asia I'd never expected to visit—and honestly, could not be said to have *actually* visited. Even the Romania Sandu loved so much was not a place I'd yet come to know. While I was in the *real* Castle Dracula, it would also have been fun to go see the tourist traps. To walk around Bucharest and get a feel for the city, to snack on street food while shopping, dine out in local restaurants, and hear local music. I'd been so in love with the little world Sandu had built for me that I'd not considered those things until this moment. It hit me hard. I had to do this stuff now—*now*, while I was still able to enjoy food, to be able to pretend that I was a kee, surfing along on the kee surface world, not bothered by the dangerous am'r depths below it. Maybe I *could* have it all. I hadn't even asked yet. Maybe Sandu had been in the am'r world so long that it didn't occur to him to offer such things to me, and all I had to do was *ask*.

I'd ask on the way home, during one of the interminable and deadly dull eternity-moments that comprised international travel. *After* we had the talk about my salary for being Head Archivist for the Entire Fucking Am'r—a kind-of meaningless title, but grand enough that it should pay handsomely, regardless. I might be the only person in the world who'd jumped into a job based solely on the bennies, but I'd only ever cared about having money for my own self-sufficiency. And *this* work was enough reward for me. Hell, I would have *paid* to do it. *But*. But I had found reasons to want some financial independence, now that I'd thought about it.

We traveled in two cars to Aeropuerto Internacional de Ushuaia, because Astryiah did not welcome anyone in her vehicle and drove herself in majestic solitude. I was in the car with Bagamil and Sandu, and I watched them laughing together and thought about the different ways to be an aojysht.

There was not a flight until the next day. The closest hotel to the airport was chosen. The shabby room was non-smoking, thank everything, but still reeked of kee life: of harsh cleaning products, dander in rugs, and the elusive hints of kee bodies in the air put out by the HVAC. The window shades did not keep out enough of the daylight, either.

It had hot water, though, and no limit on it. That made up for everything. I used a plastic shower cap, not trusting the little bottles of hotel shampoo and conditioner not to strip the good oils from my poor hair. It meant my hair still smelled of my time with Astryiah, but a price is always exacted for vanity. My beloveds didn't seem to mind.

We naturally shared a room with one queen-sized bed, not even considering other options. Once we were in there with the doors closed, I felt as close to the comfort of our idyll in Bagamil's broken sanctuary as the kee environment would allow. Well, once the bed was dragged across the room so that no harsh strips of sunlight from the broken slats in the blinds fell upon us.

After enjoying long showers, each climbed into bed until I was back in the right—the rightest—place, with their arms around me. We did not have time for the kind of loving we all wanted: to spend days wrapped up in each other, relearning each other's bodies after the long separation and extreme circumstances we'd just undergone. But there was time enough for each to share blood with me, for our bodies to join together in the current of sensation and love that we so desperately needed.

Afterward, back in our starting position cuddle, I asked them, "Do I taste different?"

They paused, and Bagamil answered first. "Of course, cinyaa, but it is a nice difference. I have known Astryiah for a very long time, but we have never vhoon-shared for any reason during that interval. She has survived all this while by being very...chary...with her trust and her vhoon-anghyaa. I do not even know if she has any surviving frithaputhraish. She is the very model of what we used to be: very solitary, very suspicious."

"She seems more like the Aojysht-of-aojyshtaish than *you* do. Or at least, she acts like it. But the rest of the am'r still give you the...um...greatest respect."

"It was necessary long ago to demand such respect. My...shall we call it 'legend,' has since then grown large enough on its own that I can act as I please. Astryiah does not have that same freedom, and even when she does, she might not choose to embrace it. She is very much who she is."

My "Yeah" turned into a bitter chuckle. "I noticed that." They waited for me to say more. I wasn't ready to talk about my time with Astryiah yet.

Sandu finally decided to offer me something nice to talk about. "Her vhoon-anghyaa will enhance your powers of persuasion, although you must work on them to fully realize the gift. We have already noticed your healing is accelerated. There will be less need for vhoon to be put directly on your wounds to speed the healing."

"Oh. Wow. She said stuff about giving me unique gifts, but I didn't know how much of what she said to take, like, *seriously*."

Sandu smiled. "*That* is a skill one must acquire over time."

"Frithaputhraish, we must start getting ready to go," Bagamil said, sadly but firmly.

"What is our agenda?" I was determined to participate more actively, especially now that Bagamil was back. It could so easily go to being The Bagamil and Sandu Show, and I wasn't having it. "Not just for the flights. I mean, what's next after we get home?"

Sandu responded, "We are not going *home*, not right away. First, we will visit Nthanda. He is a vital ally in and of himself, but he will also help smooth the way with the am'r of his land."

"Oooh! We're going to Africa?"

Sandu looked at me. Bagamil managed not to be looking anywhere in particular. "*England.* Nthanda is the most powerful am'r in London."

"Ah. Oh." I felt my face flame.

"Do not worry. It is because you are not long from the kee world. Such biased assumptions will fall from you, the longer you inhabit the am'r world."

That didn't particularly help. It left me very silent as we performed our final ablutions. They simply enjoyed quick final showers. I showered as well, but also tried to use the bathroom without feeling embarrassed. We had only two small bags. Everything Bagamil had brought with him to South America had been long discarded by Julio. Sandu and I had only a couple changes of clothing, cords for phones, etc. Sandu and I had left some weapons back at Lope's place (to be collected one of these decades) and lost the weapons we'd brought to the "rescue," but at least that meant not having the extra bother of mesmerizing customs agents. I was broken-hearted to leave without Terry Smatchet, but had been assured that another—just as good, they said, but I doubted it—would be procured for me.

In the air, hidden under an eye mask and the roar of the engines, I decided I would *demand* to do some touristy things in London, no matter how many am'r negotiations they wanted to schedule. Big Ben probably looked just as impressive by night, and no doubt our connections would have ways to sneak into museums and cathedrals and stuff after hours, which would be far more fun than sharing them with crowds of kee tourists, anyway. Maybe I could make am'r tourism work for me.

We were on lie-flat beds in first class, on our second flight of the trip, from Ezeiza International Airport to Charles de Gaulle. It was annoying as hell that we had to fly *over* England and then take a third flight *back* to London Heathrow, but such was international travel if you were going to go "low profile" using the kee air travel networks.

Sandu was across from me, Bagamil in the seat ahead. They had snuck me their meals and I'd eaten all three, trying to appreciate the first-class food of Air France but feeling strange about eating. My body was changing, and I was much less kee than I used to be. I was exceedingly aware of every little difference.

We flew over the ocean, and I tried not to think about the one Astryiah had taken me to. I tried not to think about *any* part of the last crazy week.

Of course, I thought about it anyway. As Astryiah had pointed out, I had survived a most unlikely set of circumstances, and it would be very wrong for me not to recognize that.

Under my eye mask, I cried for Araceli for thousands and thousands of miles.

Fuck Astryiah. I could mourn. I *would* mourn. I would not just let my emotions crystallize until my heart was no longer able to make connections.

And then, under the mask damp with bloody tears, I started planning my London tourist itinerary.

# Index of Non-English Phrases

*bebe / beba* • drink • Spanish

*Besèder* • OK/good • Hebrew

*bien* • well • Spanish

*Bien. Supongo que sí.* • All right. I guess so. • Spanish

*Bonjou, zanmi mwen* • Hello, my friend • Haitian Creole

*Bonjour mes amis! Désarmez-vous, s'il vous plaît!* • Hello my friends! Disarm yourselves, please! • French

*Bravo ţie!* • That's my girl! • Romanian

*buenas noches* • good evening • Spanish

*că* • that • Romanian

*casuarina* • type of pine tree • Spanish

*calabozos secretos* • oubliettes • Spanish

*Ce este ai gaz de brichetă?* • What is the word for lighter fluid? • Romanian

*Ce este, draga mea? Cine te-a rănit?* • What's wrong, my dear? Who hurt you? • Romanian

*Ce să fac cu tine?* • What am I going to do with you? • Romanian

*Cer iertare, sufleţel!* • I beg your pardon, my soul! • Romanian

*cerveza de barril* • beer on draft • Spanish

*chamuda* • dear, cutie • Hebrew

*cluburi de noapte* • nightclubs • Romanian

*como las enfermedades de transmisión sexual* • like an STD • Spanish

***Como quieras, chica fuerte.*** • As you like, strong girl. • Spanish

***compos mentis*** • having full control of one's mind; sane • Latin

***concetățene*** • my fellow countryman • Romanian

***da*** • yes • Romanian

***de fapt*** • actually • Romanian

***Da, și eu*** • yes, I am • Romanian

***de todos modos*** • anyway • Spanish

***deliciosa*** • delicious • Spanish

***¡Dios mío, no!*** • My God, no! • Spanish

***domnul meu*** • My lord • Romanian

***draga mea*** • My darling, my sweetheart • Romanian

***dragă Noosh*** • Dear Noosh • Romanian

***dragonul meu*** • My dragon/demon • Romanian

***Du feu, apportez-moi du feu!*** • Fire, bring me fire! • French

***dulce sangre*** • Sweet blood • Spanish

***e adevarat*** • it's true • Romanian

***Ei bine ...*** • Well ... • Romanian

***Ella lo tiene con el látigo. O ella lo tiene debajo de su bota.*** • Literally: She has it with the whip. Or she has it under her boot. (English Slang: She has him pussy-whipped.) • Spanish

***ella no es una criatura, Hugo, ¡es mi hermana!*** • She's not a creature, Hugo, she's my sister! • Spanish

***encantadora dama*** • lovely lady • Spanish

***Enfin, je vais prendre ma place légitime dans ce pays…!*** • Finally, I will take my rightful place in this country…! • French

***entiendo*** • I understand • Spanish

***Entonces…*** • So… • Spanish

***epitou*** • also • Haitian Creole

***es decir*** • that is to say • Spanish

***eso es correcto*** • that is correct • Spanish

***¡Están conmigo!*** • With me! • Spanish

***¿Estás bien?*** • Are you OK? • Spanish

***estás perdonada*** • you are forgiven • Spanish

***fabrica de bârfe*** • gossip factory/rumor mill • Romanian

***fiul meu*** • my son • Romanian

***foarte ciudat*** • complete weirdo • Romanian

***Fout tonè!*** • Closest translation is "Fucking shit!" • Haitian Creole

***Fräulein*** • Miss • German

***¡Fuego, cabrones!*** • Fire, you bastards! • Spanish

***Futu-i!*** • Fuck! • Romanian

***¡Hablo español muy bien, sabes!*** • I speak Spanish very well, you know! • Spanish

***¡Hijo de puta!*** • Son of a bitch! • Spanish

***hola*** • hello • Spanish

*no sé la palabra*  •  I don't know the word  •  Spanish

*no ser anormal*  •  not abnormal  •  Spanish

*no, estoy bien, ¡estoy bien!*  •  No, I'm fine, I'm fine!  •  Spanish

*Norteamérica*  •  North America  •  Spanish

*nu*  •  no  •  Romanian

*oamenii străzii*  •  street people, homeless people  •  Romanian

*¿Obligado?*  •  Obligated?  •  Spanish

*oh, sí, claro, eso es bueno*  •  oh, yeah, sure, that's good  •  Spanish

*pero*  •  a little  •  Spanish

*Perra, la cagaste. Supongo que no tienes oportunidad esta vez. Bebe lo que tienes, o no bebas, no me importa.*  •  Bitch, you screwed it up. I guess you don't have a chance this time. Drink what you have, or don't drink, I don't care.  •  Spanish

*pichanga caliente*  •  hot mess  •  Spanish

*perra tonta*  •  dumb bitch  •  Spanish

*pista de aterrizaje*  •  landing strip  •  Spanish

*Pizda mă-sii!*  •  Fuck me! Literally, "Fuck his mother's cunt." (Romanian swears don't quite work in English....)  •  Romanian

*Por favor, ummm, espere—espera?—allá. Sí?*  •  Please, ummm, wait (formal)—wait? (informal)—over there. Yeah?  •  Spanish *por qué no me dijiste esto* • why didn't you tell me this • Spanish

*por supuesto* • of course • Spanish

*prostuțo* • silly (girl) • Romanian

*pues* • well • Spanish

*¡Pura mierda!* • Bullshit! • Spanish

*¡Quietos!* • Quiet! • Spanish

*reunión* • gathering • Spanish

*sabes* • you know • Spanish

*sala* • parlor / living room • Spanish

*scuzele mele sincere* • my sincere apologies • Romanian

*Señor* • Mister, sir • Spanish

*seră* • dining room • Romanian

*Și de la nenorocitul de clan al Dăneștilor, dragonul meu.* • Yes, and from the motherfucking Dănești clan, my dragon. • Romanian

*Sí, eso, gracias.* • Yes, that, thanks. • Spanish

*sí, sí, bueno* • yeah, yeah well • Spanish

*Sudamérica* • South America • Spanish

*suflețel* • my soul • Romanian

*surată mea* • my sister • Romanian

*taci* • hush • Romanian

*Țara Românească* • the Romanian Country • Romanian

• please (informal) • Romanian

***Um, un poco de comida, sí? ¿Un baño?*** • Um, some food, okay? A bathroom? • Spanish

***una pandilla muy rebelde*** • a very rebellious gang • Spanish

***vă rog*** • please (formal) • Romanian

***¡Vamonos!*** • Let's go! • Spanish

***ven a mi, mi hombrecito*** • come to me, little man • Spanish

***¡Vete a la verga!*** • Go fuck yourself! • Spanish

***Voivode*** • "War Lord"; medieval title used in Wallachia and Transylvania • Old Slavic

***¡y bienvenido a mi casa!*** • and welcome to my house • Spanish

***Ya se tomó la droga. Dije que estaba listo.*** • He's already taken the drug.  I said it was ready. • Spanish

***zekher tzadik v'kadosh livrakha*** • may the memory of the righteous and holy be a blessing • Hebrew

# Glossary of the am'r Language

**AM'R WORD  •  DEFINITION**

**adharmhem**  •  one who endangers am'r as a whole, or the act of endangering the am'r as whole

**ahstha**  •  coma am'r fall into when deprived off too much blood and/or oxygen

**am'r** (sing. & pl.)  •  commonly known as a "vampire" or "strigoi mort"

**am'r-nafsh** (sing. & pl.)  •  In Romanian, a "strigoi viu." A living human being who shared blood with an am'r three times, but not yet died.

**Aojasc' am'ratv!**  •  "Strength and immortality!"

**aojysht** (sing), **aojyshtaish** (pl.)  •  am'r elder

**bakheb-vhoonho**  •  giver of blood, used for am'r who give blood to other am'r or kee. This is a term used for the stronger blood going to the weaker, whether am'r or kee

**cinyaa**  •  my lover

**esteshcinast**  •  verb: to know by smell, specifically to recognize the vhoon-anghyaa of other am'r *(Present tense: "I esteshcinasti", past tense "I have esteshcinastii")*

**fraheshteshnesh** • first blood meal as a newly awoken am'r

**frangkhilaat** • to feed/take nutrition from a kee

**frithaputhra** (sing.), **-ish** (pl.) • "beloved child", title used by a am'r for an am'r / am'r-nafsh made with the former's blood

**gharpatar** • grandfather, maker of my maker

**izchha** (sing.), **-aish** (pl.) • a "sacrifice", a mortal who is selected to donate blood (with or without sex)

**kee** (sing. & pl.) • mortal, non-vampire, living human being

**maadak** • intoxicating drink; poison, gets kee high, effects am'r like strong hallucinogen / tranquilizer

**maadakyo** • corrupted with maadak, a mortal who has drunk maadak

**pat'rkosh** • patar-killer

**patar** • "parent" or "maker"; title used by a am'r or am'r-nafsh for the am'r who made them

**tokhmarenc** • finishing another vampire, dying the final death

**vhoon** • blood

**vhoon-anghyaa** • blood influence, blood-line, the traits that come down from your patar, also the smell of your patar in your blood

**vhoon-berefteh** • to be bled

**vhoon-vaa** • am'r-style healing with blood

**vhoon-vayon** • am'r love making, with other am'r or am'r-nfash

**vistarascha** • dying the mortal death, becoming am'r

# ACKNOWLEGEMENTS

As with Blood Ex Libris, I have had a stunning amount of help in writing this second novel. After having to leave my first publisher and go indie, this has required even more help along the way. Thank you, every one of you who has helped us with this process. I could not have picked everything back up and started over again without your patience and willingness to teach and assist and support throughout this really *not trivially easy* journey.

Tiffany: thank you for being a wonderful friend and even better editor.

Kwasi: thank you for another wonderful cover!

Anne Marie: thank you for making sure that Noosh is the best librarian she can be, and thank you even more for your constant support of me as a writer.

Beatrice: thank you for taking the time from your crazy schedule to make sure that I don't have kee or am'r bodies doing things they really shouldn't.

Adam: thank you for helping me ensure that my descriptions of violence are graphic, not *silly*.

My language peeps: Ligia Buzan, Marie-Pierre Gillette, Mercedes Borrazas Freire, and Tavia Gilbert. You let me have fun with language whilst at the same time making certain my ignorance of those languages is not like me accidentally wearing my underwear outside my clothes. *Merci! Mulțumesc! Gracias!* (And, of course, any mistakes in languages in this novel are *my* fault, not theirs.)

Trent, Bethany, and Krissy: Thank you again for sharing a home with a surly writer who can't be interrupted on pain of profound crankiness and who is practically *useless* when in the throes of creation. Your patience is deeply appreciated.

Thank you to Holy Sepulchre Cemetery in Hayward, CA. I walked Cairngorm there every day while I was writing the first part of the book, and not only did that get me through a lot of plotting as we trotted and sniffed our way in that tree-shaded place of peace, but I'd say a good 80% of the names in this novel can be found on the graves there. I miss the wonderful conversations with the landscaping crew and the other cemetery employees, who always made us feel so welcome.

Thanks as well to all the hikers of caves in Tierra del Fuego who wrote about or took video of their experiences. Without your descriptions, Noosh couldn't have had her adventure in those same caves, since I could not (during that time of pandemic) fly down and spelunk them myself.

Thank you to Lauren for making IIP happen and for every second of believing in us.

Finally, thank you to all the fans of the Blood & Ancient Scrolls series, who have been the most supportive and caring fans an author could ever hope for.

## About Raven Belasco

R aven Belasco has been fascinated by vampires since she was 12 years old. You probably shouldn't let 12-year-olds read Stoker's Dracula, but Raven grew up in a house where, if she could get the book off the shelf, she could read it. Raven also grew up with her backyard mostly comprised of a cemetery filled with graves ranging from the late 1600s through 1800s. If spending your childhood playing on old graves doesn't prepare you for a career writing about the (un)dead, then probably nothing will.

Raven has been writing for magazines and in the publishing field since her twenties. She currently devotes her time to the demands of the am'r, to building Immoral Influence Publications, and to training a terrier to be a Good Boy—none of which are small endeavours!

To keep up with the Blood & Ancient Scrolls series, you can sign up for Raven's Newsletter at https://ancientscroll s.beehiiv.com/subscribe

Or find her online: https://ravenbelas.co/

# About Immoral Influence Publications

*"All influence is immoral."* — *Oscar Wilde*

Immoral Influence Publications: a press dedicated to variety, diversity, quality, and originality.

This press is for readers who are ready to push beyond the limits of genre, find unique characters like themselves, and love beautifully crafted tales.

To see all our authors and their works, visit us at immoralinfluence.com